THE PENGUIN BOOK OF

Contemporary
American Essays

THE PENGUIN BOOK OF

Contemporary
American Essays

MAUREEN HOWARD,
Editor

VIKING

82879

VIKING
Viking Penguin Inc., 40 West 23rd Street,
New York, New York 10010, U.S.A.
Penguin Books Ltd, Harmondsworth,
Middlesex, England
Penguin Books Australia Ltd, Ringwood,
Victoria, Australia
Penguin Books Canada Limited, 2801 John Street,
Markham, Ontario, Canada L3R 1B4
Penguin Books (N.Z.) Ltd, 182–190 Wairau Road,
Auckland 10, New Zealand

First published in 1984 by Viking Penguin Inc.
Published simultaneously in Canada

LIBRARY OF CONGRESS CATALOGING IN PUBLICATION DATA
Main entry under title:
The Penguin book of contemporary American essays.
1. American essays—20th century.   I. Howard, Maureen,
1930–   .
PS688.P44   1984   814'.54'08   84-40265
ISBN 0-670-23983-6

Pages 283–285 constitute an extension of this copyright page.

Printed in the United States of America by
Fairfield Graphics, Fairfield, Pennsylvania
Set in Caslon Old Face No. 2

To Dick Poirier and Bill Pritchard,
love and arguments.

Contents

Introduction

Essays—I can't remember exactly when I first began to love them, with a shy reserve. In grammar school, perhaps, and certainly in the upper grades, when, presumably, we had learned to read and stories were taken away from us. In a daily hour called "English" we were directed to "think," as though we had never thought about the poems and tales that had lured us into the exercise of reading. We were now supposed to admire the fancy in Charles Lamb's "A Dissertation on Roast Pig," to follow the argument in Addison or Steele, to be deeply, adultly moved by the letter of Anne Bradstreet to her children. The new thinking caps passed out with our English anthologies turned out to be cheap affairs, like the pressed-felt beanies we bought in the five-and-dime store that made us all look stamped from the same neighborhood mold.

In those Dark Ages of the American schoolroom we sat in neat rows and prattled back a thin synopsis of each essay. Our responses were to be held within the range from piety to awe, and I suppose it was my firm core of disrespect that made me love the essays we read, in spite of the dreary elevation they were subjected to in school. I had taken to reading, and the dullest of teachers could not ruin my pleasure in Twain's cantankerous twang or Franklin's reasonable wit or the churchy tone that came through in those prescriptive Emersonian sentences with capital letters assigned to Truth, Nature, Soul. I *heard* these writers, though I had no notion of what is called, in literary parlance, a writer's voice, and I suppose that is what I loved about a good essay then and admire it still. An essay, though it takes as many shapes as weather or daylight, always has the immediacy of a real voice, some necessity to the telling that lies close behind the written word.

While I read to assemble this collection, friends would say "Essays" with a dubious air and remind me, quite wrongly, that no one read them anymore. Then I'd suggest John Updike, Norman Mailer, Joan Didion, Lewis Thomas, and inevitably the man or woman who had not touched an essay since required English lit up with a bright recognition, boastful of accomplishment in the essay-reading department.

I started reading with the preconceived notion that the essay had been vital and imaginative, a strong suit in American writing since the Second World War, and came to my final rereading of Stephen Jay Gould and Eudora Welty convinced that it is so. We know there is something about the pace of the last forty years, the amount we have seen, actually beheld with our own eyes, that immediately declares this time as different. Not that events have been richer than, say, the golden period of the High Renaissance (all that Leonardo and Michelangelo in half a century), or history fuller than the mid-nineteenth century (wars and inventions crowded on the time line our children fill in these days in social studies). The difference is technological, of course.

We have watched in a collective of millions: assassination, strafing, moonwalk, courtroom, graveside, triple play, the triumphant candidate with happy family. We have witnessed trivia, lent ourselves to media events, knowing they are nonevents even as we watch and watch. Images with an eerie reality. It has become a flickering backdrop of important and foolish scenes, against which we go about our daily lives. Running time: continual. A wonderful technology. Our adaptation has been clever and quick in finding we have a remote built in, to tune out mayhem or the perilous tilt of Miss America's crown. In seeing so much, hearing so much, it seems inevitable that the essay, that thoughtful form with its way of stopping us with an urgent, particular voice, considering, playing out an idea, would come back with force.

There is no preferred way to read this collection; no sequence or scheme is necessary to the enjoyment of its separate voices or its subject matter, which ranges from high-serious to small revelations of the vacant and absurd. Insofar as I've imposed any arrangement, it is to suggest that a good many essays on matters of public interest—politics, science, culture—take a personal stand, and that first-rate personal essays never remain private business.

I have no position on the contemporary modern essay, as the list of contents clearly shows, for it would be a queer gerrymandered district I would have to set up to bring computers, Boston, and the Irish Elk to work in favor of some forced idea of genre. There is no genre; there is each essay. If I must declare a thesis at all, it is that during a time when the social sciences have dealt us a surfeit of information on our society and ourselves with no solutions, during a time when we have overdosed on visual images accompanied by meager undernourished texts—the news magazines, the nightly roundup—many of our best American writers have been drawn to the imaginative possibilities of short nonfiction.

This book begins with Michael Arlen's "The Tyranny of the Visual." It is an elegant essay that demonstrates how much we have given up by giving ourselves so completely to the visual, how easily we are manipulated and satisfied by stories we are told in pictures. The most ill-conceived gesture in film has a coercive reality that invests it with importance. To Arlen it matters that we are badly trained in a visual language as well as just plain sloppy viewers of nonsense, expecting much less of our entertainment than the Elizabethan rabble in the pit. It matters, too, that our literary classics have been used as fodder for television—sanded and waxed until smooth, uncomplicated, and unmoving, but with a dreadful authority of their own. Arlen's discussion of public television's production of *The Scarlet Letter* will make you laugh and make you cry for the folly and the commercial success of that enterprise. Arlen suggests in sorrow and in anger that there is no choosing sides between the visual and the verbal teams, but that the new team, the visual, should at least be put to the same exacting test we have demanded for so long of words.

After the coverage of large public events, the reruns, the "in-depth" reports, the columns and columns of journalism, the courageous essayist asks what it is that we can sort out and say that we feel or believe. The writer of an essay about our political life brings us news only incidentally. It is his insight, an ingenious or impassioned way of reckoning with the given facts, that arrests us. We could, if we had a mind to, discover for ourselves that the Rosenbergs read "the *National Guardian* (not the frank *Daily Worker*, but the crypto-Communist sheet)" while in prison, but we probably would not draw Leslie Fiedler's conclusion, which is convincing and striking, that Ethel and Julius Rosenberg had melted to personas, lost track of their identities, their particular humanity, in serving the larger cause. In the early profiles of Karol Wojtyla we could learn with some elation that the new pope wrote poems with a liberal bite and a play, *The Goldsmith's Shop*, but we would not know that it smacked of the "poetic drama of Paul Claudel" or be able to make Garry Wills's connection between the pope's creative endeavors and his more prominent religious role: "John Paul is ready for all kinds of technical experiment because his faith is very old-fashioned."

At first it seems that what Fiedler and Wills are up to is simply asking us to think matters through. But the much-publicized espionage case and the display of the modern papacy are highly charged issues, and behind their careful reasoning lies an urgent need to get at the truth, not to let the Rosenbergs or John Paul slip into myth, not to let us fall back on conditioned or distorted responses—for all the harm it will, indeed, do us. There is nothing incidental about the writing of these pieces: Fiedler, as a Jew, in the role of conscientious liberal of the 1950s, tells us: "To disentangle the motives that found a focus in the pro-Rosenberg movement is to write a thumbnail moral history of our time." Wills, a Catholic, writing in the late 1970s, when the stunning curriculum vitae and charisma of John Paul made fresh news, takes a cool, close-up look at this pope, this "media superstar," and sets his personal wariness into a larger view: "Perhaps the modern papacy is innately tragic, a historical freak, trying to combine the eternal Gospel with a passing Renaissance ideal of *The Prince*." Neither of these pieces is a mere editorial. They are demands that we remain bright and vigilant. If we want to argue back, so much the better.

If we say yes, oh yes, we can hear our tone of camaraderie. In either case we have been—in the term we once imported from France, overused, discarded—we've been engagé.

In Lillian Ross's fast and funny "Halloween Party" we are asked in the door not so much to reason with her as to listen and observe. Motherly exasperation turns to outrage as a cynical gang of eighth-graders done up in costumes transform themselves into real demons over the Candy Corn and Cokes. "They are talking about their *careers.* . . . They are talking about Yale and Yale Law School. . . . They are talking about who makes more money, the president of Chase Manhattan or the president of General Motors. Nobody is talking kid talk." It's a short take, all we need to see. These ghosts and monsters are caught up in a cruel parody of our adult lives. Ross's amusing reportage ends in helpless bewilderment, but it tells us more than a sociological update on Larchmont or Shaker Heights, Brooklyn Heights or Hillsborough, more than we can learn about our kids from studies of ETS scores or Ivy League admissions. Russell Baker accomplishes a comparable now-you-see-it-now-you-don't switch in attitudes in "The Flag" while maintaining his gabby, good-humored tone. He's writing about the folderol of flag-and-country patriotism unhinged from reasonable and just cause, turned into a Hollywood version of virile romance. With some useful digression Baker is writing about the misuse of symbols; he's also writing a fine feminist essay and a serious meditation about our society.

Donald Barthelme's madcap performance, "And Now Let's Hear It for the Ed Sullivan Show!" is also serious, a tour-de-force that comes dangerously close to silly. With the energy of first-rate satire, this double-edged essay indicts not only our mindless fascination with being entertained but also the smarties who program the dreamlike routines we applaud. The style is manic, exhausting, an accurate charting of our nervous passivity in front of the set. The last lines of Barthelme's piece—"The Ed Sullivan Show is over. It has stopped"—have a haunting afterglow that suggests we are victims, willing victims. Who has not watched, to a final point of self-loathing, as the light dies on the screen?

I hope that the readers of these essays will come to value highly the accommodations of the form. Tone and style pursued each time out. Essay—from the French *essai*, a trial or to try—an idea cast out dramatically as in James Baldwin's "Fifth Avenue, Uptown," and very skillfully reeled in. Or little tries, like the short jabs of Norman Mailer's "The Ninth Presidential Paper," meant to keep us ducking and darting, wearing us down, an assault. Again, here are two writers concerned with our society; concerned, too, that strength of personality will carry their words.

Baldwin, an American black writing before the 1960s, has every reason to keep his distance, to be meticulous in his argument; nevertheless he charms us into believing that there can be an easy telling of his story. He writes rapturous paragraphs, neat aphoristic sentences: "The determined will is rare—at the moment, in this country, it is unspeakably rare—and the inequalities suffered by the many are in no way justified by the rise of a few." "A ghetto can be improved in one way only: out of existence." "Fifth Avenue, Uptown" is calculated, impressive prose; it echoes the dignity of James Baldwin, the man himself, come back to walk the wretched streets of his childhood with near-impossible containment. There is no place in this essay for false emotion or inflated rhetoric. Baldwin's voice is that of a strong preacher with the Word, and when the Word comes, it is alarming and direct: "It is a terrible, an inexorable, law that one cannot deny the humanity of another without diminishing one's own: in the face of one's victim, one sees oneself. Walk through the streets of Harlem and see what we, this nation, have become."

There is intense anger here—any reader will notice it—but notice more precisely the way in which the fury is kept here at a decidedly civilized pitch while in other passages the argument is built in biblical cadences. No street skirmishes or epithets, just the performance restrained to intelligent, even gentlemanly discourse, and it is a lethal tactic, for it exposes our most uncivilized attitudes. I wish this could be read as a dated piece, but the horrors of Harlem, and the projects of Harlem, specifically, have expanded, then come to rest in a terrible stasis that makes Baldwin's sermon good as new.

Mailer—ah well, he has long begged our indulgence, and received it. I've chosen "The Ninth Presidential Paper" because it seems absolutely characteristic of the way in which this feisty guy has drawn us in over the years. He is talking at us, telling us, lecturing us. He is being Norman Mailer. In an age when political/ theatrical media personalities set blossoms like showy annuals, bloom, and fade, Mailer is still flowering—a hardy perennial. It is part of his talent as a writer that he can pick up the challenge of surviving as a celebrity in an era of passing celebrities. The vitality of Mailer's play for the audience can be daring and magical, but often there is a willed energy in the prose and a desperation in the let-me-entertain-and/or-shock-you line of attack. This column, written in 1963 for *Esquire*, shows Mailer at his best in a portrait of President Kennedy, sharp about the duality of the man: "He is on the one hand possessed of personal bravery, some wit, some style, an aristocratic taste for variety. He is a consummate politician, and has a potentially dictatorial nose for the manipulation of newspapers and television. He is a hero. And yet he is a void."

Mailer's aim is to get at the nature of totalitarianism as he saw it at just that moment in America. How Kennedy's virtues and vices lend themselves to that condition is of interest, but Mailer's more central discussion concerns itself with totalitarianism as reflected in modern architecture. Decrying bland postwar schools and housing developments was old stuff even in 1963, and the essayist puts himself in the unenviable position of dealing with a big bite of no more than received opinion. It is like Mailer to get himself into such fixes and punch his way out. Having said the ordinary—we agree, we all agree like people at a dinner party—he then scandalizes us, nicely ruins the occasion: "Modern buildings tend to look like call girls who came out of it intact except that their faces are a touch blank and the expression in their eyes is as lively as the tip on a filter cigarette." Then, in an old one-two, he switches similes: the proliferation of modern architecture is compared to the process of metastasis in cancer.

There are a dozen places where I take exception to Mailer's faulty arguments (*his* living in a cold-water flat was by choice) and half a dozen where I am just exasperated (that terrible poem of his thrown in, the bit of Yeats out of historical context). But that's Norman Mailer and he is begging for the originality and vigor and ambition and vulgarity that made this country, so I grant him his excesses and his arrogance in dealing with his reader one more time, one more time.

From Mailer to Dwight Macdonald is an about-face, full turn to an informed intelligence so devoted to its purpose there's no posturing. "Trotsky, Orwell, and Socialism" is the only book review in the collection, but it establishes its own terms immediately, uses the Trotsky diaries and the reissue of Orwell's *The Road to Wigan Pier* to lively instructional effect. If we get Macdonald's distinction between the rigidity of Trotsky's mind and the flexibility of Orwell's, we've had a refresher course in early-twentieth-century socialism. Macdonald is an avid, ingenious explicator of texts who makes us feel sharper than our everyday selves as we follow him.

In what at first appears to be a dispassionate legal essay, "How Much Due Process Is Due a President?," Charles Rembar takes as his text the Constitution. In fact, this is a plea that we attend to first principles: "It is as important that an official who has not breached the Constitutional injunction should serve out his term as that one who has committed the trespass should be ousted. Either way, it is the welfare of the Republic that is the subject, not the welfare of Richard Nixon." In the midst of the Watergate orgy this must have been a hard but satisfactory piece to write. Rembar takes the unenviable position of the very good boy on the sidelines, not haggling over replays but interpreting the rules of the game. Not many of the men and women going to law school will find time to write an essay in jurisprudence as fine as Rembar's, but we must hope that they will not forget the strain of practical idealism that he reminds us is written into our Constitution. "How Much Due Process" is strenuous, concerned with how we should have proceeded in a just society at the moment when the majority of Americans were crying for Nixon's head. We cannot rewrite the script for the early 1970s, but I believe we would have been less soiled by Watergate (and the festering legal waters of an undeclared war in Vietnam) if instead of Nixon's resignation we had been allowed due process; that clearer affirmation of constitutional law would have cleansed and cauterized our wounds.

William Gass's "The Artist and Society" is strenuous too, but oh, how lively the prose, wild the images. We are in the presence of a dazzling mind at serious play. Gass demands no less from us than real breathing responses to the events we witness, and from the artist ultimate honesty—"the ability to see precisely what's been done . . . the ability to face up." He is concerned with the freedom of the artist to be judged only on his work and that a work of art exist for its own reality and completeness, an idea we pay lip service to, but heed no more than a programmed have-a-nice-day. There is a restless brilliance to this essay and a fury: society has asked the wrong things of the artist and the tamed artist has performed— Gass uses the startling image of a caged bear. For society to let down the bars, let the bear roam free, is perilous. For the artist set free, the burden is equally hard: "An uncorrupted conscious-ness . . . what a dangerous thing it is."

In an attempt to "see precisely what's been done," Ralph Ellison writes a frank, long story of an essay on Minton's Playhouse up in Harlem, peeling away the nostalgia, the attractive distortions that have grown up about the scene that begot "Dizzy" and "Bird": "this is too much for memory; the dry facts are too easily lost in legend and glamour." "The Golden Age, Time Past" sets the record straight, and in the process Ellison gives us a short, scholarly history of modern jazz, proving that the dry facts are a hell of a lot juicier than dead myth. Like Gass and Arlen he's fighting against hearsay, stale response. What, in fact, went on at Minton's was extraordi-narily professional, an informed musicianship that should not be turned into a movie background—smoke, booze, hip blacks—to delight the fans. This essay of Ellison's does a wonderful job of "placing" jazz, not on a contrived scale of low art/high art/popular art, but telling us what went on at Minton's culturally and at the same time letting the time past just be, giving the music back its own reality.

The anthologist must not play favorites, but I feel a special delight each time I read Guy Davenport's "The Geography of the Imagination," and I'm not through with it yet. What Davenport does is place *us* culturally—Americans—teaches us to see the vast accumulation, the magical hodgepodge that is our American culture. Teaches us, yes, but this is the rare lecture we walk out of on a cloud—a crisp fall day on campus, the library a great hushed temple with Homer, Dante, Racine cut into its brow. Ignorance is not bliss. It's all worthwhile, you see, and I can't tell you why from my class notes because it is in his execution—what Davenport does with an old chestnut of a poem by Poe, his close reading of Grant Wood's *American Gothic*, that man and woman we've all seen reproduced on place mats and fiddled with in advertisements. Why is it exhilarating to know that the farmer's "shirt button is mother-of-pearl, made by James Boepple from Mississippi fresh-water mussel shell, and his jacket button is of South American vegetable ivory passing for horn"? Because it gives us the edge. We are quickened in making these connections: "The imagination; that is, the way we shape and use the world, indeed the way we *see* the world, has geographical boundaries like islands, continents, and countries. These boundaries can be crossed." For all its tedious fame, *American Gothic* cannot tyrannize us into bland admiration or unfounded contempt if we understand the cultural baggage, the vast museum warehouse that Grant Wood imported to Eldon, Iowa, and with an artist's eye selected all that was fitting for that farmer in that place, telling and correct.

Many readers of these essays will remember the great debate over the Two Cultures. We will remember the large, heavy head of C. P. Snow, the British scientist and novelist, his glasses down on his nose with the disapproving look of a headmaster: a man (or woman) cannot consider himself properly educated, properly operative in the modern world unless he understands the Second Law of Thermodynamics. I, for one, was fully shamed and conscientiously got into my head the fact that entropy never decreases. But I spent more time in following the high-minded arguments over the deplorable rift between Science and the Humanities than I did in reading up on information theory or Eddington's "the arrow of time." Lord Snow was right, of course: my ignorance is dangerous.

We will also remember *Sputnik,* or, since events gobble up events, readers over thirty will remember *Sputnik* and the terrible news—it was the Pearl Harbor of technology—that we had slept. That we, smart, savvy Americans, had kids whose knowledge of rockets was limited to prizes in a Cracker Jack box launched with a rubber band, who could not figure their way out of a multiplication table, who could not balance an equation. Suddenly science was in; school, homework, tests were in. My students have laughed at the memory of it—there's something embarrassing about the way in which they were bullied with grainy photographs of a primitive rocket and of rows of little Russian kids combed and pressed, bent over their math in a frenzy of collective get-ahead. One of the most congenial benefits of our race for technological prowess, which is inextricably joined to the arms race (a nightmare spelling bee that must never be won), is that we've produced an energetic strain of science writers who do not speak to us as though from an alien world.

Except for a bit of H. G. Wells and jolly special effects in movies, I find science fiction hopelessly underimagined, fantastic not at all—not compared to the real thing. I offer here an article by Stephen Jay Gould that unfolds with breathtaking grace the mysterious tacks of his paleontological investigations. What Gould delivers in his essays is his joy in process, his pure pleasure in scientific method and an equal pleasure in writing about it, letting us in on the fun. Gould's brightness is akin to Davenport's: both men are made ebullient by their knowledge and are even optimistic in showing us that a lot of learning is a comforting thing. On the whole, science writers tend not to be gloomy. It would seem that for them a lack of solutions is not discouraging, that the problems still to be solved lead to fruitful speculation and to a self-reliance that has to do with a hearty frontier spirit that for most of us is just a memory. In a cheery parable on computers, Lewis Thomas takes on the wonderful machines, spinning out real possibilities— they *can* win at chess—accepting them warmly: "Information is our source of energy; we are driven by it. It has become a tremendous enterprise, a kind of energy system on its own." Dr.

Thomas gives them everything but the capacity to deal with im
probability and ends with a short meditation on the impenetrable
mysteries of the human mind, mysteries that humble us, for we've
not even begun to break the code, a mind so intricate, so powerful,
that, faced with our electronic opponent, it gives us back our self-
respect.

The threat to our kind from computers may be cleverly faced,
but the hardest information since post–World War II is that we
can, without fantasy, consider ourselves an endangered species. The
bomb with its unimaginable consequences, and the more comprehensible data of pollution: there is an emotional connection. Pushed
to the brink, we discovered how careless we had been in our house-
keeping and that we could at least begin the great effort of tidying
up. I have never come across such a fine discussion of ecology—
what might, in fact, be solipsistic and sentimental about that movement—as you will find in Robert Finch's "Very Like a Whale."
But Finch, one of our finest nature writers, has a way of worrying
past surfaces to more worrisome depths. Confronted with a beached
whale on Cape Cod, he wonders what the thousands of spectators
have come for: "The answer may be so obvious that we have ceased
to recognize it. Man, I believe, has a crying need to confront
otherness in the universe. Call it nature, wilderness, the 'great
outdoors,' or what you will—we crave to look out and behold
something other than our own human faces staring back at us,
expectantly and increasingly frustrated. What the human spirit
wants, as Robert Frost said, 'Is not its own love back in copy-
speech, / But counter-love, original response.'" Once again that
image of looking, really looking and taking in what we see. There's
not an essay in this lot that doesn't make a claim for it. Sometimes—
with the scrutiny of Wills, Macdonald, Davenport—we come up
with detailed answers; at other times—Finch, Gass, Thomas, Lillian Ross—inquiry leads to the mystifying, insoluble other.

The title of Edward Hoagland's "Hailing the Elusory Mountain
Lion" indicates the problem: "hailing" and "elusory" (with its echo
of the more ordinary word "illusory") operate against each other.
If Hoagland gets to hail the cat he stalks, he cannot absolutely verify

the experience. The essay proceeds, as his often do, from a vibrant presentation of research (I see the author as a very enthusiastic student come to the door of my office all aglow) to tall stories, homespun myths.

Having gathered fact and fiction on mountain lions, he moves on to a personal account. Hoagland's quest for his lion grows out of his quest for subject matter. We can detect a true engagement of the mind, then of the heart. It is an essay built like a story, for there is a preshadowing of the cat in a lesser confrontation with a bighorn ram: "His horns had made a complete curl and then some; they were thick, massive and bunched together like a high Roman helmet, and he himself was muscly and military, with a grave-looking nose. A squared-off, middle-aged, trophy-type ram, full of imposing professionalism." That's terrific writing, special as the moment it captures, but a memory he can slot, feeling ordinary wonder at the beast, ordinary fear. With the lion, if there was a mountain lion, the encounter is not mystical, but neither is it clear or sure: "I knew my real problem would not be to make myself believed but rather to make myself understood at all, simply in reporting the story, and that I must at least keep the memory straight for myself. I was so happy that I was unerring in distinguishing the deer trails going my way. The forest's night beauty was supreme in its promise, and I didn't hurry." It's a peculiar euphoria that puts the burden on the writer, but it was for that kind of tough encounter, not for tall stories, that Hoagland climbed the mountain.

To be understood, to verify experience in the telling though the experience is almost beyond telling, to make what we have lived through real—John Updike's "Eclipse" does it believably. This short lyric memory turns its back on science, depends on hearsay about a natural occurrence we take to be unnatural. Assuming a common curiosity but everyman's ignorance, Updike, glad that the eclipse has passed, is primitive and profane: "for in my own life I felt a certain assurance evaporate forever under the reality of the sun's disgrace." He's fearful as any aborigine reduced, as we all are, by the black magic of the earth and sun.

Awhile back I slipped into the discussion of somewhat more

personal essays, in which the outer world leads to inner speculation—a sound tradition stretching from the early scientific squibs
of Francis Bacon to weather reports from Thoreau's pond. Though
it is sportswriting, I'd call A. J. Liebling's "Ahab and Nemesis" a
personal essay. It is about a man who loves his job. It is a fascinating
treatise on the fights—a sport I've no use for—a loving, honest
blow-by-blow description of "the Sweet Science of Bruising," a
report from that world, a whole other country. For Liebling,
covering a championship fight was not just another assignment, but
the occasion to strip the event of all its hoopla and imagine what
is special about this drama: thus, stylish, introspective Archie Moore,
the old champ, as Ahab, and Rocky Marciano, the reigning heavyweight, as the thrashing White Whale, the Nemesis, in fateful
confrontation. We watch each round informed by Liebling's long
history with the sport, but the excitement for the reader lies in
watching him test his memory of great fights and great reporting
and pay a final tribute to the intelligence and skill of Moore after
his defeat.

I find that I have chosen several essays that can be read as central
statements of the devotion of a writer to her work. Eudora Welty
is a mostly perfect storyteller, and "A Sweet Devouring" is the
story of how she fell in love with books—all sorts—and gorged
on series in particular, Camp Fire Girls and such, where the story
goes on and on indiscriminately. It's the beginning of her obsession
with stories in their printed form, but told to us so naturally that
we can hear the strong influence of spoken stories that has always
distinguished Welty's fiction. She ends with the discovery of her
first critical insight—that she has been gobbling cheap candy while
on the shelves at home there was Mark Twain, "twenty-four volumes, not a series, and good all the way through."

Strangely enough, so does M. F. K. Fisher in "Once a Tramp,
Always . . ." end with Twain, having found an affinity with that
original man in his longing, while abroad, for American food.
Fisher is our most eloquent writer on food. She brings this essay
with its odd ingredients together like a piquant sauce: it is about
appetites, controlled and insatiable, about sensual satisfactions and

necessary discriminations. It is about secret eating and fairly low desires, but I will not give away the dish that, at Mark Twain's suggestion, she shamelessly consumes. Though Fisher does not force the connection, the puritanical, penny-pinching salad dressing her grandmother dribbled on lettuce was a punishment and the affronted child may have grown up to write deliciously about good food as an act of vengeance. That is our reward.

Joan Didion's "On Keeping a Notebook" would at first seem solely personal, but no. Her point is what do you do with all the personal material—the vignettes, the touching moments, the clever lines. They are a grab bag, cultural detritus, unless, as Guy Davenport has shown us, we give them a meaningful order; that is the work of the artist, the writer. Didion makes it clear that her notes can be shrouded in private meanings: "*'So what's new in the whiskey business?'* What could that possibly mean to you? To me it means a blonde in a Pucci bathing suit sitting with a couple of fat men by the pool at the Beverly Hills Hotel." Then Didion begins to use her notebook in front of our very eyes. It is like watching a child from an observation booth as she takes up a stick, a box, a cylinder—and there's a castle. We find out how the blonde fits into a quick autobiographical scene on aging. I admire Didion's toughness in a society that has exhausted the confessional mode beyond any decent therapeutic end. She's saying, Who cares? Why should anyone care if we cannot make something of our jottings or if a memory remains so fragmented that it cannot inform us? The notebook must become a testing of past experience that leads to some authentic idea of our present self: "It all comes back. Perhaps it is difficult to see the value in having one's self back in that kind of mood, but I do see it; I think we are well advised to keep on nodding terms with the people we used to be, whether we find them attractive company or not." "On Keeping a Notebook" has the feel of reading a notebook, but Didion shapes the random material, controls the passages we see.

This is also true of the method Howard Moss uses in "Jean: Some Fragments." Though he is a narrative presence in this elegiac memoir of the writer Jean Stafford, and there is a simple chronological order—from their first meeting to their last—we are reading scraps built into a collage. This portrait of a difficult, talented woman has the air of meeting her standards of wit and intimacy, of paying a last tribute to the friendship they knew.

The personal essay: "*My* War"—what a presumptuous title. It is meant to offend. How does Paul Fussell claim the Second World War as his own? Well, he does by remarkable inversions bring it down to his particular history and to the outrageous line, "But, thank God, the Bomb was dropped while I was on my way there [Japan], with the result that I can write this." "My War" abrades us with uncomfortable truths. Fussell starts with his ROTC enrollment and career in the infantry, which is amusing and frank— and in the first person. It's not until we know the outcome of that soldier's story that Fussell goes back to tell us who this absurd boy was—an officer at twenty, pompous, tragically innocent—and switches to the third person. The distance between the middle-aged writer and the twirpy American hero is so great he cannot claim that boy as "I": "To become disillusioned you must earlier have been illusioned. Evidence of the illusions suffered by the youth I was is sadly available in the letters he sent, in unbelievable profusion, to his parents. They radiate a terrible naïveté, together with a pathetic disposition to be pleased in the face of boredom and, finally, horror." Lieutenant Fussell is not attractive company but Professor Fussell must spend time with him if he is to reveal the horrors of *his* war and the way it shaped him. I was taught in school never to end a paragraph with a quote, but Paul Fussell, a master of rhetoric, breaks the rules and so will I. "My War" ends with this long view, a final irony taken from Housman:

> Life, to be sure, is nothing much to lose;
> But young men think it is, and we were young.

Elizabeth Hardwick's "Boston: The Lost Ideal" is about *her* Boston. It's written by a smart girl from the South, and it's hard on a city that I presume was hard on her. The bias is purely personal and I'll admit that what I love about this essay, though I have a visitor's fondness for Boston, is that Hardwick is so impassioned, so unfair. Oh, she is hilarious and fierce: Boston is "depleted of nearly all her spiritual and cutaneous oils, provincial, self-esteeming"; has "become a more lowly image, a sort of farce of conservative exclusiveness and snobbish humor." "The merchandise in the Newbury Street shops is designed in a high fashion, elaborate, furred and sequined, but it is never seen anywhere. Perhaps it is for out-of-town use, like a traveling man's mistress." Hardwick's wit, her irreverence, are dramatic, that of a young woman staging a triumphant scene before a dowdy matron. I think of Bette Davis, Katharine Hepburn on a tear. "Boston" will satisfy any reader who has ever lived in a town he disliked or any place that cruelly excluded him as though from a country club he never wanted to join in the first place. But Hardwick has written a serious cultural commentary that defies the dull and codified, the tony authority that forever belittles our drawl, or twang, the fresh sound of a natural voice.

Having declared that I had no thesis in the selection of these essays, I see that in writing about them I all along believed that in a time of too much recorded incidence the writer is more than ever necessary. Someone—and it will not be a face we see on camera stiff with celebrity or an unknown performer caught in the self-conscious moment of his filmed day in the sun—someone must stop the blind drift into armchair viewing. The writers of these American essays can hold us with a harsh or lilting voice, provoke or charm us into hearing them out. As we read, we do hear them, and though we are happy to let them have their say, it's our own voices that thrill us, asking ourselves whether Fiedler might not be a touch cruel or Rembar cool to a fault, our own nay-saying voices saying that Dr. Thomas may be too good to be true. We discover our voices, though we may hear only a bedazzled, inarticulate "Wow" in response to the intelligence of Davenport or Gould. We might actually *hear* ourselves: there are lines in Barthelme, Hardwick, Liebling that can make us laugh out loud. Reading a good essay we are not benched; we feel the concentration of being back in the game.

I come finally to Katherine Anne Porter's "St. Augustine and the Bullfight," in which she tells at least three stories. I have saved this for last like my favorite nougat cream or a glass of *vino santo* with dessert. It is an autobiographical essay, maybe, but it is also the queerest moral tale about the emptiness of adventure. As for its structure, Porter wanders in various directions, like an actress entering, hesitating, coming downstage to us, and we never know how cleverly her scene has been blocked: "Yet I intend to write something about my life, here and now, and so far as I am able without one touch of fiction, and I hope to keep it as shapeless and unforeseen as the events of life itself from day to day. Yet, look! I have already betrayed my occupation, and dropped a clue in what would be the right place if this were fiction, by mentioning St. Augustine when I hadn't meant to until it came in its right place in life, not in art."

We see in those shapely sentences that it's not just St. Augustine she's given away, it's her method. Here's her sly way of showing that she must control the story, find its meaning, treat life with as much respect as art. It is an essay about the unsatisfactory flatness of adventure—adventure that give us "the illusion of being more alive than ordinarily," incidence that strikes a hollow note, and Porter's need to translate it into something better, with careful, often painful observation: "experience is what really happens to you in the long run; the truth that finally overtakes you." This definition of experience is the model for the way in which she shapes and trims the random stuff of life in this essay, and in her fiction for the long run.

I hope that the readers of this collection will find it an experience. There are no prophets among these writers, no visionaries—that seems to me a striking fact. "Times of heroism are generally times of terror, but the day never shines in which this element may not work. The circumstances of man, we say, are historically somewhat better in this country, and at this hour, than perhaps ever before. More freedom exists for culture. It will not now run against an axe at the first step out of the beaten track of opinion." No man or woman of our time could write as Emerson did in "Heroism" in

1841. We do not welcome the shining day that will lend itself to the heroic. We look for thoughtful deeds, not great ones. Though there is a good deal of our history in this volume, it would be hard for any of these contemporary essayists (even with Emerson's "somewhat" and "perhaps") to deliver the word "better" for the circumstances of man. As for our culture—I'd say that all of these writers have had to swing an ax fairly deftly to direct us away from the dreary and often dangerous path of well-worn opinion. To cut your way through the woods seems enough: there does not have to be, there cannot be, the virgin breast of a new land; just a clearing in the overgrowth—the difficult, much-charted landscape of American culture seen close up, acknowledged as our own.

Perhaps we have had just too much to keep track of in this country lately—too much trivia, violence, news from here and there. Perhaps we have finally lost our American innocence, or so it would seem following the strict arguments of the men and women writing here, and we'll not be caught wearing youthful illusions like a party hat on graying hair. I never intended this anthology to be read as a long cautionary tale, though each essay is weighted with its own purpose. These writers should be a pleasure to read: they ask us to attend to our lives, and we may have life still if we take care. Take care.

MAUREEN HOWARD

THE PENGUIN BOOK OF

Contemporary
American Essays

MICHAEL J. ARLEN

The Tyranny of the Visual

I don't think that anyone needs reminding that we are well along in that blessed era when a single picture (sometimes any picture; certainly, any motion picture) is said to be the equal of a thousand words. Of course, words themselves are no longer manufactured or treated with much care, and so the comparison grows more plausible as time goes on. Even so, there have been moments lately when I have had the feeling that—so great has been the spread of visual culture in this century, and so overwhelming its impact on the tender verbal sensibilities of recent generations—what was not so long ago the liberating, sense-expanding dynamic of a new medium of perception now seems in danger of becoming a new kind of aesthetic tyranny: the tyranny of visual storytelling.

In movies, this tyranny commonly takes the superficially modest form of surface or design effects. This is a fashion of presenting a scene or character which relates not so much to the director's feeling for the scene or character as to his feeling for visual technique. For instance, at the beginning of the 1977 movie *Bobby Deerfield* there occurred a typically striking visual sequence, in which the camera first revealed—sparely and carefully framed—the blacktop surface of a road. Then a man (though only his shoes and trousered legs were visible) walked slowly down the road toward the camera. He stopped, turned around, and with equal deliberation retraced a few steps. Then suddenly and dramatically he bent down and picked up an object from the surface of the blacktop: a key. With key in hand, he now walked briskly back up the road to where a sports car was parked; he climbed into it, started the engine, and sped off. Thus, one assumed that Al Pacino (for he was the man on the

1

road) was driving into an adventure story, whose narrative was already underway and whose substance would soon reveal itself. For example, what was all that business with the key? Was it Pacino's car key? Had it been stolen or mislaid? How stolen, why mislaid? More important, what did his having lost or mislaid and then found the key have to do with the next step in the narrative? Was it the missing clue to a burglary, or even the reason for a missed appointment? In other words, what did the visually striking incident of the key on the road actually mean? Alas, the subsequent action of the movie provided no answer to any of these questions. Indeed, from that moment on, the film seemed totally uninterested in the matter of the key, as if it couldn't really remember having posed any questions with it in the first place. The scene had clearly been a kind of game, a visual non sequitur, though one that had been designed quite deliberately to appeal to our traditional literary orientation through the detective-story ballet of the "search," the "clue," and the "getaway." As such, there had been nothing artistic or even playfully inventive about the sequence, as in a director's or a creative cinematographer's happy conceit. What it had been was merely another example of the disconnected visual effect: a scene invested with the look of narrative importance but which related neither to the character nor the story, only to the filmmakers' apparent wish to persuade the audience that it was watching a stylish and important film. Or to put it less kindly: a minor form of visual bullying.

In numerous recent movies, this tendency to exploit visual language has become increasingly pronounced; and, as in the case of verbal language, what one notices are not so much the always abundant examples of cheap, routine visual effects as the increasing instances of "artistic" fakery and commercialism. Consider the Russian-roulette sequences in *The Deer Hunter*. Here the problem is not disconnected gesture, nor is it a simple question of the screenwriter's or director's right to make up detail and incident. The problem in *The Deer Hunter*, it seems to me, has to do with a film that is not so much composed of sequential parts (one part being set in a small town in Pennsylvania, the other in Vietnam) as rendered on two different, and largely unmixable, levels of imagination. Thus, the small-town American scenes are handled with great naturalism and affection; every effort seems to have been made to show us *how things were*. In other words, even if the energy behind these naturalistic and nostalgic details is the energy of dream, it is clearly a dream that was honestly dreamed. In contrast, the Vietman scenes aren't just dreamlike in their unreality and contrivance (in their absence of naturalism) but are the dream, one guesses, of a professional dream-maker—a Vietnam fantasist—who has invested his story neither with honest memory nor honest imagination but with the pseudo-energy of visual effects. Part of the movie, then, is "real" (or is at least the product of a real dream), and this reality attempts unsuccessfully to nourish the "unreal" Vietnam part, with its slick, manipulative Russian-roulette sequences. Of course, we hold our breath and wince when a man takes a partly loaded revolver and puts it to his temple. But what has been gained by these automated responses, save for the further dehumanization of a war that was already bad enough without these glib but "powerful" filmmaker's touches?

"But *The Deer Hunter* didn't have to be true to facts. It showed the poetic truth of the war," a young friend said to me as I was making these complaints the other day.

"How do you know, since you weren't there?" I asked.

"Well, I know because of the movie," he said.

It seems self-evident that visual creativity, be it in fine art or in cinematography, might be expected to follow different laws of technique and dynamics from, say, literary or musical creativity. But it seems strange, though perhaps in keeping with a certain defensive self-consciousness about visual matters, that our new visually-oriented crafts should be assumed to possess a morality of their own: a morality that often seems to speak less to the wider, untidy, unframed, undesigned world of men and women (where most morality is forged) than self-servingly back to the smaller, self-isolated province of visual technique as an end in itself.

Of course, there is nowhere that visual manipulation seems more apparent than in television commercials, but I think the role here of visual technique is deceptive. Superficially (and especially if it has been done well, with no expense spared, and so forth), the television commercial appears to be a kind of game: something playful, a thirty-second play period replete with visual tricks such as cars floating in the air, or knights in armor in the laundry room, or talking cats. The television commercial seems to be a classic example of technique for its own sake; though actually, as should be obvious, the technique serves a very definite and forceful master: the selling of a certain product, or of the emotions that are thought to surround that product. As a member of the audience, one may not much care for the product in question, or may find the sales message distasteful, or the interruption irritating, but the fact is that the visual transaction taking place is a fairly straightforward one. Whatever the intricacy or trickiness of the visual effects, the technique in a television commercial rarely speaks only to itself, unless it is a bad commercial, but follows a very clear, other-directed, even at times humanely logical (if not always ennobling) morality of commerce. On the other hand, without this stern logic to guide it, and without art, or pretensions to art, to whet its ambitions, regular television programming seems to flounder happily in a generally harmless morass of what used to be called B-movie special effects. On entertainment TV, nobody seems to have the time, money, or inclination for lighting or for framing shots. Now and then, an adventurous director will borrow a snappy trick or two from a movie or a commercial, but for the most part television cinematography is too caught up with the day-by-day demands of getting through the shooting script to worry about trying anything fancy. Week after week, detectives stalk criminals along catwalks, bodies float in swimming pools, cars spin around intersections and leap across drawbridges: the visual vocabulary of most television dramas is as skimpy as that of a pulp novel.

All the same, video is perhaps the visual language of the future, even more than film, and there is an area where television has started to abuse not so much its skimpy visual skills as its basic visual power. Ironically, it is public television—that relentless bluestocking of broadcasting—that seems to have been leading the way here, by throwing its weight behind a rather different sort of visual tyranny: what might be described as the reconstituting or transforming or overwhelming of works of literature into sequences of moving images, as, for example, in the recent four-part adaptation of Nathaniel Hawthorne's *The Scarlet Letter*. Now, right away, there is a danger of getting tangled up in one of those ancient arguments having to do with the merits or demerits of transposing books into films, so first let me try to make clear what I am *not* talking about here. I am not, for example, talking about the inviolability of printed matter or suggesting that a story that has been fashioned in one form—be it novel or stage play or Holinshed's *Chronicles*—should always remain in its original form. I am not claiming the inherent or automatic superiority of one form over another: books as "high art" versus film as "low art," as has sometimes been claimed (at least by book people) in the past. After all, the evidence of five or more decades is that some of the most appealing and satisfying movies (perhaps most of the most appealing and satisfying movies) have been adapted from novels or short stories that were often inferior to the filmed version. Indeed, a large proportion of the so-called literary properties that are bought by filmmakers and turned into movies are books of the most routine nature: spy stories or detective stories or the type of popular blockbuster novel that appears to have been written from a movie-oriented perspective, employing "characters" based either on figures in the daily papers or on the personae of movie stars, and, in fact, that is literary only in having made its original appearance as a book.

So what am I talking about? For one thing: *The Scarlet Letter* itself. Worthy Hawthorne! Such a nice-looking writer chap, who married one of those Peabody sisters and worked for years with great effort on his short stories, for which he received a certain regional respect but very little cash. He wrote *The Scarlet Letter* fairly quickly, and as soon as his publisher, Mr. Fields, saw the manuscript he knew that it was going to be a big seller, although, being a publisher, he printed a first edition of only two thousand copies, which sold out in ten days. The second edition, of three thousand copies, sold well too, and subsequent editions and printings have kept on selling. (Perhaps there should be some kind of federal law, however, to prevent schoolchildren from being required to read it—or *The House of the Seven Gables* or Melville's *Moby Dick*—at a stage in life when many of them can barely respond to the literary texture of *Car & Driver*.) For *The Scarlet Letter* is not only a marvelous book, surely one of the very great American novels ever written, but also an extraordinarily, profoundly *literary* work. It is actually quite short, and its brevity imparts a feeling of compression. There is scant incident or action in the narrative. Indeed, the "story" is deliberately unrealistic (almost surreal), for Hawthorne was writing two hundred years after the supposed events, and what he was attempting to portray often has the flow and density of a dream. Fitzgerald's *The Great Gatsby* is a very different kind of book, but it shares with *The Scarlet Letter*, I think, this same dreamlike energy, as well as a marked absence of action and realistic event. At any rate, Hawthorne's novel is not merely a great work of the imagination but one that owes its strength and presence to the "music" of the soul's interior. So rich is this interior music, in fact, that the reader scarcely notices—or, at least, is not unduly troubled by—some of the more conventional aspects of storytelling which Hawthorne has either not much bothered himself with or simply left out. Not only is there a scarcity of realistic event, but a number of the important characters have surprisingly simplistic surfaces. Dreadful Roger Chillingworth, for instance, is a villain without shading, without redeeming feature. Hester Prynne's child, little Pearl, is hardly believable on any remotely realistic terms—this "lovely and immortal flower" who was "worthy to have been brought forth in Eden; worthy to have been left there, to be the plaything of angels." There is also the matter of the author's deliberately contrived employment of natural background and coloring; or, rather, his failure to employ it. For *The Scarlet Letter* is in the main—and, it is clear, purposely—a novel without colors. There are periodic symbolic appearances of the color red, as in a fire and a red rose, and certainly in Hester's scarlet letter, and there are similarly pointed appearances of the color black, as in the prison ironwork and in the mythic "Black Man" of the forest. But with the exception of Hester's own embroidery on little Pearl's dresses, there is an obviously intentional omission by the author of color, the colors of life, certainly the colors of the New England countryside. Indeed, the countryside itself is noticeably absent from the narrative, save for occasional, equally symbolic allusions to the dark and abstract wilderness that exists on the periphery of the story, and which is made vivid only toward the end of the novel in the important scene that finally brings together Hester, Dimmesdale, little Pearl, and Chillingworth in the forest.

Public television's version of *The Scarlet Letter* wasn't altogether terrible. It had a couple of effective moments, especially in the third episode, when Meg Foster seemed to catch for at least a few seconds some of the transfigured bitterness in Hester Prynne. But it certainly wasn't much good. In theatrical terms, both Foster and John Heard, as Dimmesdale, seemed impossibly burdened by a kind of American high-school stage radiance, while Kevin Conway, as Chillingworth, floundered about in a part that probably only a very bad or a very good actor could have made work. And Rick Hauser's ponderous, "classical" direction propelled Hawthorne's brief and compact narrative forward with the stately lethargy of a becalmed galleon. For the most part, it seemed a misbegotten undertaking, perpetrated by people on the creative or producing end who, if they had read the book at all—at least for the purpose of blocking scenes—couldn't have had much feeling for what they'd read. Indeed, as I watched the series trudge its dutiful and cumbersome course through four consecutive evenings, I thought back to some of those foolish Hollywood re-creations of the "classics" and rather missed them—their foolishness as well as their energy: Mickey Rooney in *A Midsummer Night's Dream;* Gregory Peck as Captain Ahab! At least there had been a sort of loopy fun in these portrayals: a Classics Comics approach to serious literature in which serious literature somehow never really got involved; in which the soul of the original work was left where it was, unreached and undabbled with.

But these new, solemn practitioners of visual storytelling are soul devourers. They're *not* foolish or loopy, inviting us to have a good time and to leave our highfalutin literary notions outside in the coatroom. These are serious and dutiful fellows, bound not merely by a responsibility to "art" but also, in the case of public television, by a responsibility to trustees and educators and government committees and so forth. For example, was poor Hawthorne, scribbling at his desk in the eighteen-forties and trying to work out the novel's formal symbolism, so impeded by a lack of proper archives and research materials that he ignorantly costumed most of the characters in *The Scarlet Letter* in dark colors instead of putting them in the generally colorful robes of the era? Well, then, the research facilities and academic consultants of public television were able to correct Hawthorne's deficiency in this regard by costuming the television performers of his novel in the more historically accurate, colored finery of the period. And did poor Hawthorne, lacking a camera and the creative resources of film with which to tell his tale, give his written version of the story a certain closed-in and claustrophobic atmosphere? Well, then, television's cameras "opened up" the narrative by taking us on little scenic excursions outside the town. There are moody glimpses of the sea breaking on the shore, and cheery views of open meadows and fields of wheat. In fact, by the time the significant scene in the forest finally takes place we feel that we have been in the middle of New England's wild landscape all along. Also, even though this adaptation is by television and for television, it must not be forgotten that the original creator of the literary property was Nathaniel Hawthorne, a celebrated writer, and so the television people have found time to pay respects to Hawthorne's prose. Snatches of Hawthorne's exposition are periodically intoned as scene-setting devices by a generally offscreen actor (playing Hawthorne himself!), while additional bits and pieces of the Master's prose pop up now and then as dialogue, often spliced in with the already "adapted" dialogue. Thus, sometimes the dialogue is genuine Hawthorne and sometimes it is genuine television, but more often than not it is a strange composite of the two, which must have struck the twenty-five consultants who worked on the project as a statesmanly way of solving the problem.

"But let it pass! It is of yonder miserable man that I would speak," says Hawthorne's Hester Prynne, whereas television's Hester says, "I'm here not to talk of myself but of him." Does the difference matter? Does it matter that certain details and points of character have been rearranged, or that information provided by the author in a later chapter of the book turns up as dialogue in an early moment of the television version? Does it matter that childish camera tricks are borrowed from old movies to indicate dreamlike effects or the workings of consciousness, most of them as simple-minded as dissolves on logs blazing in a fireplace? In a certain sense, one would be hard put to say—certainly in a dominantly visual society—what great wrong there was in any of this. One mustn't be too linear or too retentive about such things! But it seems to me, in the end, that all these details do matter, though not necessarily detail by detail (as if we were discussing a blueprint that did or did not match the original specifications), but, instead, in that what is at issue—perhaps carelessly rather than intentionally, in the fashion of our time—is a fundamental question of respect. *The Scarlet Letter* is valuable to us and, indeed, to the literate world, for what it is in essence: a work of literature. It may contain a describable "story"; it may contain historical information, right or wrong; it may contain opportunities for costuming and parts for players. But a great novel is not an engineering model, with interchangeable parts, any more than a great painting (say, a Cézanne still-life) is an accumulation of "graphic information" about nineteenth-century French produce (to be improved, perhaps, by the substitution of a pineapple for a plum), or any more than a great film is an accretion of describable film images. Today nobody, I think, tries to rearrange or restructure a great painting (though sometimes great paintings don't get reproduced very well), and nobody, I think, has plans for putting Chaplin's *City Lights* into book form so that a new audience can get a richer feel for the material. But the abuse of the essence of literature occurs with greater and greater frequency, as the new visual forms attempt to feed their commercial or self-serving appetites for new "artistic" material. And always (to hear the adapters tell it) it is *youth* that is being served. Think of how many young people who have never read *The Scarlet Letter* (or who ran away from school when somebody asked them to read it) will now know about Hester Prynne! Know *what?* is one question. Another question, equally unanswerable, might be: How many of those who saw *The Scarlet Letter* on television will now read the book, and read it as Hawthorne wrote it, communing through his language to the soul of the work, and not merely checking off the incidents as they relate to what they saw, perhaps more vividly, on the screen?

The present time is said not to be a happy one for literature. Good poets are largely unnoticed, few serious novels are read, and the audience for the music of words seems to be drifting away, as if mesmerized by painting, prints, photographs, moving pictures, videotape—by the new power of visual imagery. Perhaps the music of words will never reassert its ancient hold on the popular imagination. Perhaps, as some have suggested, the grip of words has become too strong, too tight, thereby unbalancing the ancient, preliterary equilibrium of the human brain. At any rate, for the moment, one has the impression that the mass media, which are largely visual, are in the process of trying to perpetuate an illusion: the illusion being that culture is somehow neutral as to form and can therefore best be communicated and recommunicated by means of the most popular forms of the day. Thus, some of the great literary spirits of our civilization have been made unwitting participants in a curious sort of visual vs. literary Capture the Flag contest, in which the visual team lately appears to have the upper hand, drawing bigger crowds and winning fatter purses. Will the visual team continue to forge ahead, chewing up Homer and Dante and the Oxford English Dictionary and spitting them out in ten-part installments, each verified for historical accuracy by a battery of academics and scripted so as to be easily comprehensible to a ninth-grade audience? One will have to wait for the twenty-first century to find out. Meanwhile, the crucial issue remains in doubt: respect for man and his art. Will the new communication forms advance this respect, as they sometimes seem to be trying to do? Or will they keep on fudging it, waffling, ducking the serious questions, but talking always of freedom—the new freedoms— and of the splendid gifts they bring us?

LESLIE A. FIEDLER

Afterthoughts on the Rosenbergs

Since the execution of the Rosenbergs, it has become possible to see clearly what was for a long time obscured: that there were *two* Rosenberg cases, quite distinct though referred to by a single name; and that this ambiguity make it difficult for the pro- and anti-Rosenberg forces ever to engage in a real dialogue. How often we were talking about quite different things under the same label!

The first Rosenberg case, which reached its climax with their trial in March 1951, involved certain questions of fact about the transmission of secrets to the Soviet Union, culminating in the handing over of sketches for the detonating device of the atom bomb. Implicated in this first case were: the brother of Ethel Rosenberg, David Greenglass, who made a full confession; Morton Sobell; Anatoli Yacovlev, the Russian vice-consul who had got safely out of the United States in December of 1946; and the notorious Communist "drop," Harry Gold. Through Gold, the Rosenberg case was linked with those of the confessed espionage agents, Klaus Fuchs and Allan Nunn May, woven inextricably into a context against which their guilt appeared clear beyond doubt. The denials of the Rosenbergs seemed merely the mendacious pleas of two people fighting for their lives in the face of overwhelming evidence.

In this initial open-and-shut case, scarcely anyone was very interested. In the United States, it did not stir up nearly as much discussion as the Hiss-Chambers affair, or even the trivial business of Judith Coplon. In Europe, it was ignored or meagerly reported, so that the European defenders of the Rosenbergs tended to be happily ignorant of the first or factual case in its real interconnections; and this ignorance in many cases they fought desperately to preserve. The Communists themselves maintained a strange official silence about the Rosenbergs for more than a year after their arraignment, wary, presumably, about identifying themselves with a pair at once so central to their whole espionage effort and so flagrantly guilty; and baffled, no doubt, at how to defend two comrades who had been underground for six years and who refused to admit their party membership in court.

The second, or legendary, Rosenberg case was invented, along with the Committee to Secure Justice in the Rosenberg Case, at the end of October 1951 in Knickerbocker Village, a housing settlement in New York City. The place of the double birth seems almost too apt; the Rosenbergs themselves had once inhabited that melancholy block of identical dwelling units that seem the visible manifestation of the stalinized petty-bourgeois mind: rigid, conventional, hopelessly self-righteous—the mind which dreamed the odd parody of the martyr which was the role of the Rosenbergs in their second case.*

The Rosenbergs stood alone in the new version of their plight—alone except for certain honorable ghosts. Gone were the real accomplices: Yacovlev and Sobell, Harry Gold, Klaus Fuchs and Allan Nunn May, though "Davy" Greenglass, recruited to the Movement at the age of twelve by his nineteen-year-old sister, remained to play the shadowy villain—replaced by the evoked figures of Sacco and Vanzetti, Tom Mooney, the Scottsboro Boys, and, especially, Dreyfus. The cue had been given by the "progressive" *National Guardian*, which had opened the defense campaign with a story headlined: "Is the Rosenberg Case the Dreyfus Case of America's Cold War?" The revised Rosenbergs were no longer spies, but "political prisoners" in the European sense, victims of the class struggle and the Cold War, defenders of the peace, a

---

*The Rosenbergs of the second case possess a certain kind of immortality; that is, they will continue to live in the official history and art of the Communist Movement, until, for one reason or another, their particular segment of history is forgotten or refalsified. But not yet! In 1954, the hit of the season on the Warsaw stage was a play called *Ethel and Julius*.

persecuted minority—these very people, it must be remembered, who would not confess their political allegiance in court, and who for six years had been under instructions not even to appear "progressive."

The long-drawn-out process of appeal in the American courts had made it possible to set up the symbolic Rosenbergs in place of the real ones; between the first exposure of two spies and the appeal of the "framed up victims before the bar of world opinion" came the year (soon two, and three) of separation and imprisonment and real suffering. The Communists banked on this stretch of time to screen their sleight-of-hand; and it worked. Even those who had followed the first trial carefully found it difficult to keep it in mind; and the maintenance of the anti-Rosenberg position soon fell largely into the hands of those who countered liberaloid sentimentality and rancor not with facts but with their own even more wretched "Down with the Communist Rats—God Bless America" sentimentality and rancor. The second, the legendary, Rosenberg case possessed the imagination of the world.

It is the second case which I wish to discuss. There is no point in rehearsing the first; as far as I am concerned, the legal guilt of the Rosenbergs was clearly established at their trial, and it is from an assumption of that guilt that I begin. What I want to examine (and this, after all, is the enduring point of the matter) is why the Rosenbergs, for all their palpable guilt, won their second case before the world; why there arose such a universal condemnation of their sentence; and why so many, in the teeth of the evidence, even believed in their innocence.

One can say in a general way that in the second case the Rosenbergs were not tried at all, but that by a bit of prestidigitation they, too, disappeared along with Gold, Yacovlev, and the rest; and that we were called up to judge in their places Sacco and Vanzetti or Dreyfus. And how did they get in? Through the evocation of these almost traditional victims, a kind of moral blackmail was practiced on us; the flags of the gallant old causes were unfurled, and we were expected to respond by revivifying the battered belief that the political dissident (but in what sense is the present-day flag-waving

Communist a dissident?), the proud rebel (but in what sense were the Rosenbergs, peering slyly out from behind the Fifth Amendment, rebellious or proud?), the Jew (but in what sense were the Rosenbergs Jews?) is always framed, that the guilt is always on the other side.

What a relief to be able to reassert that simple-minded article of faith after Fuchs and Nunn May and Hiss, and after the thousand betrayals of the Soviet Union. The fact that the Rosenbergs were remarkable chiefly for their difference from the older martyrs, that the whole point of their affair lay in that difference, was hardly remarked; scarcely anyone wanted to see them as they were, but merely to *use* them for self-exculpation—for joining together once more the ranks that had marched unbroken for Vanzetti, but had since fallen hopelessly apart.

And yet the question remains. Why this occasion rather than another; why this improbable pair; and why (outside of the United States itself) so nearly unanimous a response to their plight? To disentangle the motives that found a focus in the pro-Rosenberg movement is to write a thumbnail moral history of our time.

One must begin, I suppose, by separating out the absolute cynics, the Communist bureaucrats who used the case coldly when it was convenient to use it, as they had ignored it calmly when it was convenient to ignore it; and who knew that they could not lose in any event. For if the freeing of the Rosenbergs would have been for them a minor victory, their death was a major one in the struggle against the United States. After a certain point, the energies of such functionaries were patently directed at insuring that clemency would not be granted. I do not want to seem to make master-minds out of shabby Communist bureaucrats, but surely a certain elementary cunning rather than mere stupidity led them to do everything that would infuriate official American opinion, make any revision of the death sentence seem an admission of a judicial error.

It is no accident, I think, that the only plea which came near saving the Rosenbergs was prompted by an outsider who had been expelled from both the Communist party and the Communist-controlled defense committee. The suffering and death of the Rosenbergs were *willed* by the makers of Communist opinion and relished by them, as every new lynching in America, every bit of violence against the Jews, is willed and relished as further evidence that they are right! These are the professional accomplices of calamity; and if they cried "innocent," it was because they thought that the greatest possibility of disaster lay in such an assertion.

These conscious exploiters of the case were a tiny minority, yet one which had ready to hand a mass of naïve communicants already trained to believe, sincerely and even fervently, what that minority decided they should believe. In this sense, one can think of the bacterial-warfare campaign and the various "peace" petitions as preparations for the Rosenberg case, as the Rosenberg case in turn is no end in itself but a rehearsal for the next real or manufactured issue on the Communist agenda. This prefabricated public is made up not only of the naïver party members, activists to whom ideas are unknown and the mute attenders of meetings, but also of fellow-travelers and the "innocents" who read nothing but the Communist press, or even only the Communist posters (knowing, of course, that all other sources of information are "bought"). For such believers an event does not even *exist*, much less have a significance, until it is recognized by their journals; and so for them there had simply been *no* Rosenberg case until the party had given the go-ahead signal after months of discreet silence. For them, only the legendary case was real.

The Communists have long controlled in Europe large numbers of "advanced" workers, peasants, and petty bourgeois by manipulating a mythology inherited from a hundred years of political struggle: the belief that the state and its courts are always wrong; that the bourgeoisie is always wrong; and especially that the United States, the bastion of capitalism, is always wrong*—with the corollaries that no Negro, Jew, or "progressive" (i.e., Communist or sympathizer) can ever be anything but innocent. This group was

---

*Only the notion that priests are always wrong could not be exploited in the Rosenberg case; otherwise it was a perfect ritual expression of the sub-Marxist catechism.

joined by an even larger periphery, stalinized to the extent of not believing its own press and of accepting in critical instances the opinions screamed in the piazzas by those whom they consider more "devoted" and "unselfish" than themselves, because they are louder and more assured. Together these formed a sizable public which appears really to have believed that the Rosenbergs were innocent in the basic sense of the word, guiltless of the crime with which they were charged. This they knew, not from scrutinizing the record, but from consulting the opinions of those who had always defined for them the truth. They would have believed it quite as firmly if there had been no such people as the Rosenbergs—as, in a sense, there were not.

Such a rank and file, stalinized at second and third remove, did not exist in the United States, which possesses in their place a mass of people politically innocent and merely indifferent to such affairs in a way no European can understand. To this oppositely corresponding American group, the *second* Rosenberg case had no existence; so that between them and their European opposite numbers there was not even ground enough for real disagreement.

In both Europe and America, however, a substantial minority of intellectuals shared a third position which asserted the innocence of the Rosenbergs, or at least maintained the final irrelevance of their guilt. This position combined in varying proportions two complementary attitudes: the *wish* that the Rosenbergs might actually be innocent; and the conviction that they were *symbolically* guiltless whatever action they may have committed. The first feeling led to an incantatory declaration of the Rosenbergs' guiltlessness, based on the belief that what these intellectuals repeated with truly unselfish fervor could not help but prove true; and, in any event, the Rosenbergs *couldn't* have done it, couldn't have committed treason—or these intellectuals, too, might have been guilty of as sordid a crime when in their own heedless youth they also had been Communists or had at least defended in perfect self-righteousness their Communist friends against the "Red-baiters."

But, even if the Rosenbergs *had* performed the act, this line of argument continues, treason was not what they had meant; they had been acting for a better world, for all Humanity (i.e., for the Soviet Union, whose interests all the more enlightened had once known were identical with those of mankind); and, anyhow, Russia had been our ally when the Rosenbergs gave them a helping hand, standing with us side by side against the Nazis; and, after all, Russia had not yet used the Bomb, will never use it, never, never, *never* (to stop believing this would mean having to rethink their whole lives), so that sharing the atomic secret in this somewhat unorthodox fashion was really a blow for world peace: just look at the present *détente*, etc., etc. In light of all which, isn't it better simply to declare that the Rosenbergs were "innocent," as a kind of shorthand for an analysis too complicated to explain to the uninitiated without re-educating them completely.

How near the conscious surface such reasoning was carried on must have varied from case to case; but in almost every instance it led to the by-now-customary double bookkeeping of the Communists' friends, the exploitation of a vocabulary which makes it possible to say, at one and the same time, "They didn't do it at all; it's a frame-up!" and, "After all, they had a right; their hearts were pure!" This is a fantastic enough position in any event, but when held by the accused themselves (and it *was* held by the Rosenbergs, as I shall show), it becomes utterly fantastic, the obverse of those equally absurd "symbolic" declarations of guilt in the rigged Russian trials.

Finally,* one is left with those who cried only for mercy, for the conversion of the death sentence, "even if they were guilty as charged." It is difficult to disentangle the position itself from those who maintained it; to redeem it from the scandalous way it was used by the Communists, who sought to confuse hopelessly the two kinds of protest, to make every cry for grace seem an assertion of

---

*I am relegating to this footnote the "diplomatic" advocates of mercy— those who urged a revision of the sentence in order to "placate world opinion" or in order "not to give the Communists a martyr." This was not an important group, and the point of the whole case is precisely that the Rosenbergs were *incapable* of becoming martyrs.

innocence, and more: a condemnation of the United States, the Atlantic Pact, the European Army, and God knows what else. One is so appalled at the cynicism of many of the exploiters of "mercy," with their own record of political executions without appeal, without trials—and after the most ignominious of self-degradations—that he is tempted to discount the whole movement.

Even where the Communists played only a secondary role, there was evident in the shrillness of the cries of horror (rising from countries where only a little while before the lynching of political enemies was considered an act of virtue) a desire to celebrate the fall of America from innocence, to indulge in an orgy of self-righteousness at our expense. There is no political act (and the simplest cry for clemency was inevitably a political act) that is not marred these days by the obsessive envy and anguish of the Europeans in our regard. If the Europeans could only have believed as firmly as they pretended that we had utterly yielded to hysteria and persecution, the balance of guilt that tilts so annoyingly in their direction would have been righted; and they might have loved us more, not less. But they could only *want* to believe this, not really credit it—any more than they have been able to really accept the stories of germ warfare in Korea. In a Europe that tends to admire where it is horrified, and to be overwhelmed by the fascination of ruthlessness, even our approximate innocence, or the mere inefficiency at terror that is its equivalent, is a reproach.

Yet, allowing for all that was stage-managed or disingenuous in the pleas for clemency; discounting the rather professional nature of some of the ecclesiastical protests; allowing for the sob sisters who are ready to howl bitterly at the sentencing of the most sadistic wretch; setting aside the pleading based on a general condemnation of the death penalty, which does not bear precisely on this case; and discounting the almost mechanical reflex of those to whom since Hitler any threat to any Jew seems a recrudescence of the old horror, one comes to a residual protest that cannot be explained away, and in the face of which we must as Americans admit a real, a perhaps tragic, failure of the moral imagination.

The final protest that existed behind all the others based on stupidity or malice or official dogma was the humane one. Under their legendary role, there were, after all, *real* Rosenbergs, unattractive and vindictive but human; fond of each other and of their two children; concerned with operations for tonsillitis and family wrangles; isolated from each other during three years of not-quite-hope and deferred despair; at the end, prepared scientifically for the electrocution: Julius' mustache shaved off and the patch of hair from Ethel's dowdy head (and all this painfully documented by the morning papers in an America that can keep no secrets); finally capable of dying. This we had forgotten, thinking of the Rosenbergs as merely typical, seeing them in the context of a thousand other petty-bourgeois Stalinists we had known, each repeating the same shabby standard phrases. That they were individuals and would die they themselves had denied in every gesture—and we foolishly believed them. In the face of their own death, the Rosenbergs became, despite themselves and their official defenders, symbols of the conflict between the human and the political, the individual and the state, justice and mercy; and this symbolic conflict only those who knew they were guilty could fully appreciate.

It is, in the end, no mere matter of protesting an excessive sentence, but of realizing that they *count*, these people moved always like puppets from above, that they count as *human*, though they committed treason in disregard of all real human considerations in the name of an intolerably abstract "Humanity." It is wonderful in a way that two individuals did still count to so many people in a world as accustomed as ours to mass slaughter and injustice become mere routine.

There is no sense in becoming enraged at the fact that these two, our *only* two victims, should have stirred up the response that could not be brought to focus for the millions of victims of Soviet firing squads; that most of the world should have been crying out for the lives of two American spies, convicted by due process, at the very moment when Willy Goettling and a score of nameless others were being summarily shot in Soviet Berlin. We should rather be flattered that as a nation we continue to act on a plane where moral judgment is still possible; elsewhere assertions of human value seem merely pointless, and the only possible protest is silence, the resolve at least not to hail institutionalized murder as social justice.

Some Americans have, indeed, felt flattered at being among the last peoples to whom real protest is still conceivable, not merely permitted by law, but possible to the uncorrupted moral sense; and they have been willing to stop there, arguing that this very fact sanctions the execution of the Rosenbergs, by proving it the sort of exceptional act we can still morally afford when political considerations demand it. But the point is surely that clemency to the Rosenbergs was what we could *not* afford to deny. The world had turned to us (that part at least still not hopelessly stalinized) for a symbolic demonstration that somewhere a government existed willing to risk the loss of political face for the sake of establishing an unequivocal moral position. A minority at least understood that the Communists were doing everything in their power to make any concession on our part seem a cowardly retreat; but they hoped we would have the courage to seem in that sense cowardly. I cannot help feeling that even among the rank-and-file Stalinists there existed on some deeply buried level the shadowy desire for someone somewhere to assert that the political man was not all of man, that our humanity is neither fictional nor irrelevant.

This opportunity we let slip away from us, in part because of our political innocence, in part through a lack of moral imagination, but also through a certain incapacity to really believe in Communists as people. In the official declarations of Eisenhower, one senses behind the cold reasoning from cause to effect, and the shaky conclusion that the secrets transmitted by the Rosenbergs unleashed the Korean War, the failure of the military mind to see beyond a justice defined in codes. In the justifications of Judge Kaufman, on the other hand, one feels a personal hysteria—a fear of Communism magnified by the sense that in the United States, where so many Stalinists have been Jews, the acts of the Rosenbergs were an attainder of the whole Jewish population. But the Rosenbergs were not, after all, excessively punished merely because their fates happened to rest in the hands of a military man and a Jew, but because mass opinion in America, in so far as it took notice of them at all, *wanted* their deaths, as an example and token.

When counter-pickets to the Rosenberg defenders carried placards demanding "Death to the Communist Rats!" there was involved, beyond an old American metaphor for spies, a wish to believe that the enemy is subhuman, an animal to exterminate rather than a man to confront. Needless to say, the Communists themselves need no lessons in this sort of maneuver; we have only to remember the words of the Rosenbergs' lawyer before the White House on the eve of their death: "I don't know what animals I am dealing with, but I know that I am dealing with animals." Yet we have no right to let ourselves be provoked into answering the Communists with equivalent strategies; differently from them, we still have much to lose; and in trying to dehumanize our opponents we may end by dehumanizing ourselves.

When the news of the Rosenbergs' long-delayed execution was announced before the White House, the counter-pickets cheered. A critical episode in the moral and political coming of age of America had reached its climax; the hopes for a world of equity and peace that had moved the more sensitive and intelligent in the 1920's and 1930's, had been used as camouflage by a brutally imperialistic power and had ended by leading two undistinguished people into a trap of lies and espionage and death; and the counter-pickets *cheered*! One is tempted to echo the words of Irwin Edelman* just before he was chased out of Pershing Square by an irate crowd:

*Edelman is one of the most extraordinary figures in the whole affair. Thrown out of the Communist party in Los Angeles in 1947 for advocating more inner party democracy, and expelled from the official Rosenberg defense committee as a heretic, he nonetheless provided the nearest thing to a legal out for the Rosenbergs. His pamphlet, *Freedom's Electrocution*, inspired two rather eccentric lawyers to make the plea which brought into special session the Supreme Court, which had recently reviewed a case against Edelman himself on a charge of vagrancy. He enters and exits from the affair in a style that provides a real contrast to the Rosenbergs' sly, maddeningly mendacious conduct. He seems a survival of the old-fashioned American radical, refreshingly honest beside the new "underground" models. One would bid those who think the Rosenbergs were killed for being radicals to notice that in a presumably hysterical America it was the real radical who was free to come to their aid.

"If you are happy about the execution of the Rosenbergs, you are rotten to the core!" But, if this reaction seems the final indignity, there is much worse to come.

Our failure placed in the hands of the Communists the advantage of being able to exploit the very human considerations that they were least capable of feeling. And there was an additional advantage in their cynicism itself, which left them able to *use* the Rosenberg children, the coincidence of the electrocution date with the fourteenth wedding anniversary of Ethel and Julius, their frustrated love, and the shocking physical details of their death with a complete lack of squeamishness. On the hoardings of the whole world, the embraces of the Rosenbergs and their approach to the Chair were turned into clichés, occasions for public orgies of sentiment. The Judaism of the condemned pair was played on tearfully by the same activists who had screamed for the death of the Russian Jewish doctors until the line was changed; and the believers that religion is the opium of the people cried out against executing the Rosenbergs on the Sabbath.

But all this, it must never be forgot, was not until the leaders of the party had decided it was *safe* to be sorry—safe for the party, of course, and not for the Rosenbergs. The disregard of the Stalinists for the individuals whose causes they support, their willingness to compromise their very lives for the sake of making propitious propaganda, has been known to everyone since the days of the Scottsboro Boys. But unlike those boys, or Tom Mooney, or the other classic cases, the Rosenbergs were actual comrades. This did not mean, however, that there was any more real desire to save them; indeed, as enlightened and disciplined members they would be expected to approve the tactics that assured their deaths in order to blacken the United States in the eyes of the world. Their actual affiliation was, in fact, an embarrassment, something not to be played upon but concealed. The Manchester *Guardian* and other liberal journals might talk of "making martyrs for the Communists," but the Communists, victims of the frantic game of hide-and-seek they had been playing with themselves ever since the dawning of the Popular Front, expended a good deal of energy to hide the fact that these martyrs were "theirs."

"Death for the Rosenbergs Is a Victory for McCarthy!" the posters read, and who, in Europe, at least, remembered that McCarthy had never had anything to do with the affair? Surely the chief evil of McCarthyism consists in branding honest men as Communists out of malice and stupidity. But how does this concern calling a Communist a Communist, or with deciding by legal process that a spy is a spy? These creatures of Soviet foreign policy were labeled the defenders of all "freedom-loving peoples," sacrificed to nothing less than their love for "American Democracy."

There were no limits to the absurd masquerade. A hundred marching Communists in London put flowers at the foot of a statue of Franklin Roosevelt, with an attached card reading: "That Roosevelt's Ideas May Live the Rosenbergs Must Not Die!" Not Marx or Lenin's ideas, please note, but Roosevelt's. It is all of a piece. Julius draped after his death not with a red flag but with the ritual prayer shawl of the Jews; not "The Internationale" sung but "Go Down, Moses" and the Psalms; the American flags flying brazenly over the cortege and the rabbi to intone unbelieved-in prayers at the grave. But the hoax would not quite hold to the end, for the crowd at the funeral parlor booed when a rabbi, invited for the sake of camouflage, reminded them that the Jewish religion teaches forgiveness of enemies. In an instant, the fake piety and humanity had disappeared from the carefully prepared faces, and those who had cried for mercy a little while before hooted down the mention of its name.

But there was worse yet. I was in Rome when the news of the Rosenbergs' death came through, and I can speak only of what I actually witnessed; but there, at least on the faces of the Communist crowds surging and screaming before the American Embassy, I saw evidence of *joy*. They were glad, these young activists, that the Rosenbergs were safely dead; for a little while they had been afraid that some last-minute reprieve might cheat them out of their victory celebration, that they would be unable to go through the streets in their Sunday best chalking up "Death to the Killers of the Rosenbergs!" and to sit afterwards over a bottle of wine content with a good day's work. But even this is not the utterest obscenity.

That the American public should deny the humanity of their enemies is terrible enough; that the Communists should deny the humanity of their comrades much worse; but that two people should deny their *own* humanity in the face of death is the ultimate horror, the final revelation of a universal moral calamity. For even at the end the Rosenbergs were not able to think of themselves as real people, only as "cases," very like the others for which they had helped fight, Scottsboro and Harry Bridges and the Trenton Ten, replaceable puppets in a manifestation that never ends. There is something touching in their own accounts of reading each issue of the *National Guardian* (not the frank *Daily Worker*, but the crypto-Communist sheet) to share in the ritualistic exploitation of themselves. But even before the "progressive" journal had begun to spread their story, they themselves had written to each other the foreseeable platitudes of the propaganda on their behalf. From the start, they had not been able to find any selves realer than those official clichés. If there is a tragedy of the Rosenbergs, this is it.

The persistently evoked image of Sacco and Vanzetti had led many to expect in the correspondence of the Rosenbergs some evidence of an underlying honesty, some frank and simple declaration of faith; but they could not hit upon any note that rang true. Reading the "death-house letters" of the Rosenbergs, one has the sense that not only the Marxist dream of social justice but the very possibilities of any heroism and martyrdom are being blasphemed. It is a parody of martyrdom they give us, too absurd to be truly tragic, too grim to be the joke it is always threatening to become.

Ethel's last appeal to President Eisenhower was the first of their letters I read; and it is surely among the most embarrassing, combining with Ethel's customary attempts at a "literary" style, and the constitutional inability to be frank which she shared with her husband, a deliberate and transparent craftiness. She, who had already been writing about Eisenhower in private as "our gnaedige Gauleiter," refers in a painfully adulatory beginning to that embarrassment "which the ordinary person feels in the presence of the great and famous" and which has kept her from writing to the

President before. Only the example of Mrs. Oatis,* who "bared her heart to the head of a foreign state," has led Ethel, she explains, to look for "as much consideration from the head of her own." She has been unable to avoid the note of reproach in this comparison of mercy on either side of the Iron Curtain, but to take off the curse she hastens to protest her ignorance, in the typical gesture of the Communist who has felt obliged to praise, however mildly, something publicly identified with his real allegiance. "Of Czechoslovakia I know very little, of her President even less than that. . . ." This unconvincing avowal, however, does not satisfy even her, so she tries the alternative gambit of gratuitous flag-waving, announcing quite inconsequently that for America she "would be homesick anywhere in the world."

She then reminds Eisenhower that before he became President he was a "Liberator," but it is not really a congenial memory to her who has still ringing in her ear her own cry of "Gauleiter" and the conventional Communist characterization of the American general staff as "heirs of the Nazis." The transition to this note is easy: her execution will be, she charges, "an act of vengeance," and not the first, she reminds Eisenhower, identifying herself and her husband with the 6,000,000 hounded Jews of Europe, and the President with the masters of Buchenwald—those "ghastly mass butchers, the obscene fascists," who are presently "graciously receiving the benefits of mercy," while "the great democratic United States is proposing the savage destruction of a small unoffending Jewish family. . . ."

At last she is at home. The hatred, the obvious irony, the ready-made epithets of the Communist press are released like a dog's

---

*The evocation of the Oatis case raises problems which demand another article: the prefabricated stalinoid public's celebration of Oatis' release as an unparalleled act of generosity; his own attitude toward himself and his sentence; etc. Here I would like to note merely how neatly this reference joins together two problems that are really one. Why do the guiltless confess on the other side of the Curtain, while the guilty protest their innocence here? In both cases, "symbolic" truth-telling, a shorthand for the uninitiate, is at stake.

saliva at the *ting* of a bell. How happily she forgets that she has been defending the concept of mercy, and using the word "democratic" of her own country without sarcasm. But "a small unoffending Jewish family"—it seems incredible that anyone could speak so about herself, her own children.

At last she is ready for the final series of elegantly unctuous appeals: in the name of "fealty to religious and democratic ideals," as "an offering to God," in the name of the President's wife who will "plead my cause with grace and felicity," or of "the province of the affectionate grandfather, the sensitive artist, the devoutly religious man." And the rhetoric reaches its high point with the reminder that "truly the stories of Christ, Moses and Gandhi hold more sheer wonderment and spiritual treasure than all the conquests of Napoleon." Against the shadow of these names the alternating venom and flattery seem especially evident; and we are left astonished at the self-righteousness that dared evoke them.

The letters which the Rosenbergs wrote to each other from their cells in Sing Sing seem at first glance superior at least to this. Ethel, to be sure, is still hopelessly the victim not only of her politics but of the painfully pretentious style that is its literary equivalent; but Julius, more the scientist in his view of himself, manages from time to time to seem sincere and touching. One is moved by his feeling for his wife, which is more than love—an almost frantic dependence and adulation; and by the tears that stand in his eyes after the visits of his children. But even these scenes, we remember, were, if not staged, at least edited for publication; published in a context of the most banal thumbnail editorials ("I was horrified to read . . . that our government is planning an accord with Spain . . . to ally ourselves with the most reactionary, feudal, and Fascist elements in order to defend democracy . . . something is very rotten in Denmark . . ."*) at the wish of the Rosenbergs themselves.

*The reader checking these quotations against the English text of the letters will find certain discrepancies, for I am translating them back from the French text of the *Figaro Littéraire*, the only one available to me. There is, however, a certain justice in this procedure; for the documents of the legendary Rosenberg case were intended primarily for Europe, and should be seen backward through Europe to be truly appreciated.

In part, their self-exposure was aimed, as they declared, at raising money for their children; but, in part, it must have been intended to make political capital out of their own misery and frustrated passion. Finally, the letters are incomprehensible either as genuine expressions of feeling or as partisan manifestoes, since they consist almost equally of intimacies which should never have been published, and lay sermons which should never have been written to each other by a husband and wife confronting their deaths. The line between the person and the case, between private and public, had been broken down for them long before and could not be redrawn even in the extremest of situations. A single logic connects the Communist hating on order the person he has never seen; the activist ignoring on the street yesterday's best friend who has become a deviationist; the wife leaving her husband the day after he is expelled from the party; the son informing on the father; the accused in Russia slavishly vilifying themselves in court—and the Rosenbergs exploiting their final intimacies to strike a blow in the Cold War.

It is in light of this failure to distinguish the person from the cause, the fact from its "dialectical" significance, that we must understand the lies (what are for us, at least, lies) of the letters. The most flagrant, of course, is the maintenance by the Rosenbergs of the pose of innocence to the very end and *to each other*! We have grown used to Communist spies lying in court with all the conviction and fervor of true victims; there was the recent example of Alger Hiss, to name only one; but we had always hoped that to their wives at least, in darkness and whispers, they spoke the truth. Yet the Rosenbergs played out their comedy to the end; and this we should have foreknown.

Some, I recall, advocated a conversion of their sentences on the tactical grounds that they might in the long run confess; and some have even been shaken by their consequent persistence in the cry, "We are innocent!" An occasional less-convinced Stalinist, bullied into complicity like David Greenglass, can be bullied out again into a frank admission; but the true believer believes above all in his own unimpeachable innocence. Precisely because the Rosenbergs could have committed espionage as they did, they could not ever confess it. A confession would, in a certain sense, have shed doubt on their complicity.

They were able to commit their kind of treason because they were incapable of telling treason from devotion, deceit from honesty. It was not even, though this would be easier to accept, that they chose deliberately between rival allegiances: the Soviet Union versus the United States. They did not know that such a choice existed; but believed in their own way what they continued to assert, that they had always loved and served " American Democracy." It is misleading to think of them as liars, though their relationship to everything, including themselves, was false. When Julius, who had stuck up in his cell a copy of the Declaration of Independence clipped out of the New York *Times*, refers to it as if in passing so that all the world will know he is really a misunderstood patriot, one is tempted to call him a poseur and a hypocrite; but he is something much more devious.

When he and his wife carefully observe the coming of each Jewish holiday and sentimentalize over their double heritage as Americans and Jews, they are not deliberately falsifying, though they neither know nor care what Judaism actually is about; they will use as much of it as they need, defining it as they go. "In two days," Julius writes, "it will be Passover, which recalls the search of our people for liberty. This cultural heritage has for us a special significance, because we are imprisoned . . . by the Pharaohs of today. . . ." And in another place he remarks that "the culture of my people, its fight to liberate itself from slavery in Egypt" is astonishingly like "the great traditions in the history of America"—and, one understands though it is left unsaid, like those of the Communist party.

Ethel, typically, insists on defining her enlightened position more clearly. Thrilled by the sound of the shofar, she thinks of the Jews everywhere hastening to the synagogues to pray for a Happy New Year, but hastens to remind them via her husband that "we must not use prayer to the Almighty as an excuse for avoiding our responsibilities to our neighbors . . . the daily struggle for social justice." And she concludes, astonishingly, with the appeal: "Jews and non-Jews, Black and White, we must all stand together, firm, solid, and strong." It is like the curtain line of an *agit-prop* choral production at the combined celebration of *Rosh Hashanah* and the anniversary of the Russian Revolution.

Judaism happens to lie closest to hand because of the accident of the Rosenbergs' birth, but any other tradition would have done as well—and does. Not only the Christ, Moses and Gandhi of Ethel's letter to the President, but Roosevelt and "Butch" LaGuardia in their letters to each other—the list might be extended indefinitely. For they have been told, and are prepared to believe a priori, that they are the heirs of all the ages: Lincoln, Washington, Jefferson, Isaiah, Confucius, Leonardo da Vinci, Ivan the Terrible, Charlie Chaplin, and Christopher Columbus have all contributed to their patrimony.

They even like to think of themselves as sharing in the peculiarly American mana of the Brooklyn Dodgers. "The victory of the Dodgers," Ethel writes, "over the Phillies quickly restored me to my customary good spirits," and one takes it for a relatively harmless example of the pursuit of the popular and folksy that led Ethel to sing folk songs in the death house. But she cannot leave it at that; the editorial follows the next day, between declarations of love: "It is the Dodgers' unconquerable spirit which makes people love them. But where they have especially covered themselves with glory is in making an important contribution to the rooting out of racial prejudice." We have moved from melodrama to comedy, but the point is always the same. What is involved is the system of moral double bookkeeping invented to fool the Examiners, but so successful that it has ended by bamboozling the bookkeeper himself.

Nothing is what it seems: the Communist parties advocate revolution, and they do not; the Communist International has been dissolved, but it exists; one commits crimes, but he is innocent. Anyone can call war peace, or lies the truth; but to believe such assertions so that one will face death for them requires a trained will and imagination. For such belief, the Rosenbergs had been in training ever since they had combined wooing with the study of Communist literature; and they had finally reached a degree of perfection which enabled them to attain the final stage of subterfuge, to go "underground."

To me, even more extraordinary (for it seems on the face of it *pointless*) than the assertion of their innocence is the Rosenbergs' stubborn silence about their political affiliations. In court, they had refused to speak on constitutional grounds; in their letters to each other, these "martyrs of the Communist cause" never mention the word "Communism," unless in quotation marks as an example of the slander of their enemies; while the name of the Soviet Union is, needless to say, avoided like a dirty word.

The expurgation goes sometimes to fantastic lengths, of which the most amusing example occurs in a letter of Ethel's written on June 21, 1951. "My beloved husband," she begins, "I feel so discouraged by this unjustifiable attack on a legally constituted American party! The specter of Fascism looms up, enormous and menacing..." But she does not identify the party beyond labeling it "American"; and the explanatory note attached by the defense committee in the published volume is equally coy. "Seventeen men and women had been arrested and convicted in New York under the recently passed Smith Act." If one already knows that those otherwise unqualified "men and women" were the leaders of the Communist party, all well and good. If not, it is apparently better to persist in one's ignorance.

The upshot of the whole business is that the Rosenbergs were quite incapable of saying in their last letters just what it was for which they thought they were dying. Not only had they excluded themselves from the traditional procedure of the old-style radical, who rises up in court to declare that he has acted in the teeth of accepted morality and law for the sake of certain higher principles; they could not even tell the world for what beliefs they were being framed. Beyond the cry of frame-up, they could only speak in hints and evasions; so that they finished by seeming martyrs only to their own double talk, to a handful of banalities: "democracy and human dignity," "liberty and peace," "the greatest good of our own children, our family, and all families," and finally "the interests of American Democracy, of justice and fraternity, of peace and bread and roses and the laughter of children."

To believe that two innocents had been falsely condemned for favoring "roses and the laughter of children," one would have to believe the judges and public officials of the United States to be not merely the Fascists the Rosenbergs called them, but monsters, insensate beasts; and perhaps this was partly their point. But one must look deeper, realize that a code is involved, a substitution of equivalents whose true meaning can be read off immediately by the insider. "Peace, democracy, and liberty," like "roses and the laughter of children," are only conventional ciphers for the barely whispered word "Communism," and Communism itself only a secondary encoding of the completely unmentioned "Defense of the Soviet Union." The Defense of the Soviet Union—here is the sole principle and criterion of all value—and to this principle the Rosenbergs felt that they had been true; in this sense, they genuinely believed themselves innocent, more innocent than if they had never committed espionage.

The final pity was that they could not say even so much aloud—except in certain symbolic outcries of frame-up and persecution, and only through the most palpable lies. It is for this reason that they failed in the end to become martyrs or heroes, or even men. What was there left to die?

Yet despite all this, *because* of it, we should have granted them grace. The betrayal of their essential humanity by their comrades and themselves left the burden of its defense with us. This obligation we failed, and our failure must be faced up to. Before the eyes of the world we lost an opportunity concretely to assert what all our abstract declarations can never prove: that for us at least the suffering person is realer than the political moment that produces him or the political philosophy for which he stands. Surely it is not even a paradox to assert that it is our special duty to treat as persons, as real human beings, those who most blasphemously deny their own humanity.

GARRY WILLS

Pope John Paul II

Novelists have toyed with the scandal of a Marxist on the throne of Peter. But has fact already outrun fiction? We might think so when reading Karol Wojtyla on the alienating effect of industrial labor:

The Car Factory Worker

> Smart new models from under my fingers
> whirring already in distant streets.
> I am not with them at the controls
> on sleek motorways; the policeman's in charge.
> They stole my voice; it's the cars that speak.

During the conclave that elected him Pope John Paul II, Wojtyla was seen reading a Marxist journal, and he is the first pope to give the *abbraccio* to Communist mayors of Italian cities. Then why do the anti-Communists love him so?

It would be an odd man in any circle who could write this:

While the somatic dynamism and indirectly the psycho-emotive dynamism have their source in the body-matter, this source is neither sufficient nor adequate for the action in its essential feature of transcendence.

And then write this:

> The moon became a tambourine
> thrumming deep in their eyes
> in their hearts, deep.

Odder still for that man to become pope.

. . .

Athlete, linguist, theologian, musician, poet—this Wojtyla pope seems too good to be true, and probably is. He is, for one thing, ominously likable. His Wednesday audiences in Rome had to be moved out of the new audience hall into St. Peter's itself, to handle the crowds, and then into the piazza of Bernini. The crowds grew, early last summer, to 100,000, tying up Roman traffic even after the hour was moved back to placate city officials. The pope outdraws rock stars, and his name sells disco records. *Time* magazine, in a cover story on the dearth of leadership, found him the only natural leader of obvious stature on the world scene. A writer in the Jesuit magazine *America* thinks he may fulfill Plato's dream of the philosopher-king. There has been no such elation around a new pope since the election of Pius IX in 1846. Nightly torchlight processions turned out all Rome for the first days of that reign, and the world press rejoiced that an enlightened ruler had arrived to reconcile Rome with progress. Yet *Pio Nono* came, in fact, to make that reconciliation impossible for the next century and more. His liberal political views fell victim to his theological conservatism.

Now John Paul is cheered by the ecclesiastical right and left, by cold-warriors and peaceful coexisters, by the Communist mayor of Rome and a Ukrainian dissident from Russia. He cannot, one would think, please all these antithetical types, yet he seems to. Most of the world thinks of him as open and flexible, but the most intransigent bureaucrats of the Vatican Curia think he is really on their side. Who is wrong? Or can this miracle worker square the circle, make dogmatist lions lie down with ecumenical lambs?

One solution to the mystery is to see in Wojtyla a consummate diplomat and compromiser, one who distributes his favors so even-handedly, left and right, that he does not get trapped in a sterile one-sidedness. That reading would make the pope succeed at what Jerry Brown calls "canoe politics"—paddle a bit on this side, then on that. But such flexibility in a Brown looks wishy-washy, and that is the last thing one would say of Wojtyla, this chunkily handsome man with the blunt stare and the John Wayne lumbering walk.

Still, his record is curiously ambiguous for one who seems to
radiate decisiveness. During the Nazi occupation of Poland, he
neither collaborated nor defied—he withdrew to a seminary in
Cardinal Sapieha's house. (Some romanticizers of his youth claim
he went into hiding there because he was on a Nazi "wanted" list
for helping Jews, but the pope's own friend Mieczyslaw Malinski
makes it clear that all seminarians had to live indoors because they
could not get the German work permit that gave access to the
streets.) At the time when Cardinal Wyszynski was imprisoned,
Wojtyla managed to avoid his superior's fate, yet went farther than
he in stressing freedom of religion. In Poland he championed
liturgical reform and ecumenism, but in Rome he stressed un-
changing doctrine, like his rigidly Thomist mentor, Father Re-
ginald Garrigou-Lagrange. On the tenth anniversary of *Humanae
Vitae*, Paul VI's encyclical condemning contraceptives, Cardinal
Wojtyla was the principal speaker at a Milan conference celebrating
the encyclical.

Since becoming pope he has emitted contrary signals. Two of
his early acts were a moratorium on the laicization of priests (which
lets the discontented leave their ministry without forcing them out
of the Church) and a strengthening of an "apostolic constitution"
on doctrinal uniformity in papal seminaries. He went to the Puebla
conference in Mexico, where the "hot" issue was liberation theology,
and avoided using the term all the time he was on Mexican soil.
He has, apparently, given the cardinal's hat to a Lithuanian, Ste-
ponavicius of Vilna, encouraging one of the most resistant ethnic
groups in the Soviet Union, yet he did it *in petto*, secretly, so as
not to offend the Russians. In the same way, he granted a private
audience to the Ukrainian dissident Valentyn Moroz but removed
his name from the official list of those received. Unlike his part-
namesake, Paul VI, John Paul stayed out of the Italian elections
last June—which only helped the Christian Democrats (papal in-
tervention in electoral politics regularly backfires in Italy). One
leftist member of Parliament I talked to in Rome said she feared
John Paul will make reaction respectable, while most people say he
is making liberal attitudes blossom in that oddest of settings, the
pope's great Renaissance palace.

How can John Paul send so many signals in so many directions without getting tangled in his own footwork? Far from looking dithery, his every gesture comes off as magisterial. He combines an easy friendliness with an equally easy certitude. As people plop all kinds of silly hats on his head, he never looks silly. A journalist who went with him to both Mexico and Poland told me John Paul never seemed, like most visiting officials, to be puzzled by his surroundings. Entering a strange room, he knows where all the doors and obstacles and people to be greeted are. His authority is accepted because he does not have to assert it—he, like everyone else, just assumes it is there.

I was thinking of this as I waited in the rain for one of his Wednesday audiences last June. I stood, by the rail he would pass, with a tiny Italian nun who shared her umbrella with me and a tall Chilean priest who had shrewd and disillusioned things to say about governments and the Church. When the pope came along the rail, they both lunged and grappled like any groupie at a rock concert. I tried to lean back and watch, despite the frenzy, with some journalistic detachment. I certainly felt no emanation of excitement from the pope. He keeps a distance of his own, dipping in but moving on, his eyes taking in the whole scene while his hand is seized and released. I had heard he brought an American style of politics to the Vatican—"working the fence" as deftly as Lyndon Johnson ever did. But American pols try to summon a quick effusiveness, feign momentary intimacy, as they shake each hand. A President, asking for votes, is a suitor. Leading a democracy, he must be ostentatiously egalitarian despite the trappings of Air Force One gleaming behind him. John Paul, with Bernini's columns swirled around him, feels no such need. When his sweeping eyes meet those of another person leaning back, their expression is just short of a wink. His calibrated friendliness is paternal, not democratic. A favorer of the *abbraccio* (especially with children, as Amy Carter learned), he welcomes the world to his arms—but to give warmth, not take it. And though he encourages directness, one sees at a glance that he would not tolerate "liberties" with his person. He is even less a Mick Jagger than a Lyndon Johnson.

The pope's principal scholarly work, *The Acting Person*, is an

attempt to reconcile the anthropology of Max Scheler with Aristotle
and Aquinas—a tricky maneuver, since Scheler tried to reconcile
Plato and phenomenology. The doctrine of Scheler that Wojtyla
stresses, even in his poetry, is the way man's grasp of particulars
is both an a priori knowledge of essences *and* a renewed act of self-
possession:

> Only the one who has possession of himself and is simultaneously
> his own sole and exclusive possession can be a person.

> Love and move inwards, discover your will.

The strong will of this self-possessed man, all of whose moves
are so controlled and sure, creates a mystery: Why, with his sure
grasp of himself, has he remained so elusive to others? Even his
appearance fluctuates oddly: He manages to look both lean and
lumpy, handsome and feral, refined and vulgar. In the Vatican,
no one knows the first thing Roman gossips want to know about
any pope: Who has his ear? He is everywhere and nowhere—the
first pope to visit all the agencies of the modern Vatican, to begin
the systematic journey to every parish in Rome. He likes people
around him—at his daily mass in the Vatican gardens, at meals,
in the planes he takes to far places. It is as if his years of travel
through the Iron Curtain have given him a Frostian dislike of
walls. He has not defied the Curia, just gone around it, ignored
it, been off on his travels.

All this energy is free to play because the pope shows no doubt
about his goals and beliefs—as Chesterton said, the hands are free
because the heart is fixed. Wojtyla seems to have escaped the soul-
searching that other Christians have gone through in recent decades.
A symbol of that is the way his play, *The Goldsmith's Shop*, reflects
the poetic drama of Paul Claudel. Like the early Maritain—or,
for that matter, Pound and Eliot in the same period—John Paul
is ready for all kinds of technical experiment because his faith is
very old-fashioned. This shows up in his sophisticated use of folk
piety, especially to the Virgin. In Poland, a Catholicism familiar
in the thirties and forties has been preserved as in a time capsule—

and not surprisingly. Persecution tends to call up heroism, will-power, determination, the fixed heart—and tends, as well, to put doctrinal questioning aside "for the duration." The noble folly of defiance is thrown, as a halo, around the mere caution of old dogmas. In a persecution men die for beliefs they have not time, in the crush of heroic events, to discuss. Even accidental symbols of the faith became banners of resistance—the pope told priests in Rome to resume their clerical dress as a proud uniform. John Paul's words have the noble simplicity of a voice from the catacombs.

But that voice, bracing and almost swashbuckling when it sounds from the catacombs, can be disturbing when it issues from a throne. John Paul said, in Mexico, that priests should administer the sac-raments and let the laity deal with politics. That division reflects a subtle and old-fashioned clericalism, separating (and ranking) spheres of the natural and the supernatural, but it also reflects, no doubt, John Paul's experience in Poland, where simply adminis-tering sacraments *is* a political statement, a defiance of official atheism. John Paul's attitude toward the state is tinctured with theocratic traditions from Poland's past—which makes him well disposed toward the "integralism" of Spain's right-wing lay order, Opus Dei. (A collection of John Paul's addresses to Opus Dei members in Rome has been published in Italian as *The Church's Faith*.)

In theology, John Paul is even more doggedly "orthodox" than Paul VI was. Asked to preach a series of sermons to the papal household in 1978, he devoted one discourse to praise of Paul's reassertion of the reality of the devil, brought Mariology into every discussion, and attacked the ideal of scientific progress that has given us nuclear weapons—and the means of contraception. Some have accused John Paul, in this period, of politicking among Italians for the pope's chair (he said he sat with Italian-speaking bishops at synod conferences because they were having a problem with the Communists), but there can be no doubt that his faith is sincere and unquestioning.

Well, what's the matter with that? Perhaps the Church needs a return to certitude about its own doctrines; that may make it deal more confidently with the world's problems. Besides, what does the world at large care about internal theological disputes of the Catholic church, so long as the pope uses his moral authority for such causes as peace and human rights? The trouble with this analysis is that Pope Paul VI (like *Pio Nono*) demonstrated how sterile can be the combination of political liberalism and theological conservatism. No one could have been more sincere or eloquent than Paul in arguing the cause of the poor and the oppressed. But he shot down his own troops before they could carry his enlightened social program into action—driving priests and nuns and laity away from the Church with his views on contraception, on the role of women in the Church, on the celibate priesthood. The flow of missionaries, money, priests, and nuns to implement the pope's humane programs dried up. And this new pope is even less ardent on social programs than Paul was and more rigid on doctrine.

To understand the crisis of the Catholic church, one must recognize that the Church's distrust of the modern world was effectively challenged by John XXIII and the Second Vatican Council. But the distrust once reserved for "outsiders" has now been transferred *inside* the Church, from such niceties of doctrine as the pope's infallibility (defended against Protestants) to questions of internal morale and manners. I was shocked, while at dinner with an urbane monsignor high in a Vatican agency, to see him turn ferocious with glee over John Paul's moratorium on the laicizing of priests. Many in the Curia hated Paul VI's comparative leniency on that count. (Paul thought that if celibacy was to be maintained, it must be a free choice.) "Now," said the monsignor, "we don't have to pretend that we believe Father So-and-So when he tells us he found Christ by screwing Sister Mary Sue." I asked what possible good could come of forcing those soured by the priesthood to stay on—or, more likely, to leave both the priesthood and the Church. "It is the morale of those who stay that we have to consider." Apparently, those who freely choose celibacy can enjoy their choice only if others are made to suffer for disagreeing with it.

John Paul is the pope least likely to change those self-defeating attitudes in the Church. That is why we should take very seriously the confidence that Curial conservatives have in their new man. They have been there a long time and know what works to their advantage in the long run. The stronger-willed the new pope, the more will he impose his Polish church's views on the role of priests and nuns, on women and the Virgin, on celibacy and discipline. In fact, there may be something anachronistic in the wish for a "strong" pope. What does that mean? The larger the man, the smaller looks the toy castle in which he has to stand, so that his best efforts undermine his own work. That was true even of John XXIII, who asserted his will by creating the commission on contraception that has largely emptied Catholic churches. It was especially true of Paul VI, who went forward with reforms while seeing how they backfired. A Marxist politician in Rome said, "Paul at least had some doubts about his own role in the world—. a tragic sense that I found appealing. This new man has no doubts at all. That's what's scary."

Perhaps the modern papacy is innately tragic, a historical freak, trying to combine the eternal Gospel with a passing Renaissance ideal of *The Prince*. What would St. Peter make of its modern trappings—he who came to Rome as a missionary to the Jewish community that had embraced Christianity, undoubtedly unable to speak Latin, probably accompanied by his wife, and who was killed before he ever had a chance to become "bishop of Rome"? He was not a man self-possessed, but "carried where he did not wish to go." What would he make of the media superstar who rides as high in the world's opinion now as Pius IX did in 1846? Would he find in him an apostle or The Prince? That question might give pause even to the formidable John Paul II, if he were given much to pausing or to doubts.

LILLIAN ROSS

Halloween Party

A letter has arrived from a woman we know:

My thirteen-year-old son gave a Halloween costume party for a bunch of boys and girls. I became his financier as he talked endlessly about his Count Dracula costume. Count Dracula seems to have been the most popular Halloween costume for the past ten years— a black satin Count Dracula cape ($18.95), Count Dracula fangs ($1.25), clown whiteface makeup ($2), and Zauders stage blood ($2). The menu for the party included fried chicken, spaghetti, Cokes, salad, and cupcakes with orange or chocolate icing (cost per guest: $7). The candy, for visiting trick-or-treaters as well as for the guests, was orange and black jelly beans, sugar pumpkins, Candy Corn, Tootsie Rolls, Raisinets, Almond Joys, Nestlé Crunch, Baby Ruths, Milky Ways, Heide Jujyfruits, Peanut Chews, and Cracker Jacks (total: $38.65). My son also had eight cookies, six inches in diameter and decorated with black cats ($1.25 each); eight little plastic pumpkins full of hard candies, each with a trembly plastic spider on top ($2.50 each); eight orange-colored balloons that blew up to resemble cats (eighty-five cents each); eight orange-colored lollipops with jack-o'-lantern faces (seventy cents each); a large paper tablecloth showing a black witch standing over a black caldron with spiders popping out of the caldron ($2.25); matching napkins ($1.10); matching paper cups ($2); matching paper plates ($1.75); a "HAPPY HALLOWEEN" sign ($1.25); a dancing skeleton ($3.99); something called a Happy Spider ($4); a classic jack-o'-lantern, made of a real pumpkin ($4, plus labor). Total investment in props: $181.59. Total investment of labor in jack-o'-lantern, kitchen cleanup, and laundry: $35. Total investment in emotion and puzzlement: indeterminable.

I watch the guests arrive. The first one, A, comes as Darth Vader, of "Star Wars." B comes as Luke Skywalker, of "Star Wars." C comes as The Incredible Hulk. D comes as a tramp. E comes as a ghost. F comes as a ballerina. G comes, in one of her mother's old evening gowns, as Bette Midler. All are in an advanced stage of hysteria. A pulls at C's costume. G immediately starts throwing sugar pumpkins at E. They've given themselves an hour before they move the party out to ring doorbells and see what they get. They tear into the fried chicken, most of them eating three bites and wasting the rest. They sprinkle jelly beans on the chicken and on the spaghetti. They pick at the spaghetti, which is on the menu because my son said everybody likes spaghetti. They eat it one strand at a time, dropping a strand on the floor for each strand they consume. They gulp down the Cokes, another "must"—their appetite for the caffeine insatiable. And what are they talking about, these eighth graders who are eying each other fishily? They are talking about their *careers*. They are talking about getting into Exeter. They are talking about Yale and Yale Law School. They are talking about how to get in here and how to get in there. They are talking about who makes more money, the president of Chase Manhattan or the president of General Motors. Nobody is talking kid talk. Nobody is talking about the present time and what to do with it. Nobody is talking about learning. Nobody sounds *young*. A, a pudgy boy who tries to find out the marks of every other child in his class, wants to be "a successful corporation lawyer." He doesn't say just "corporation lawyer." It's success that he's bent on. He informs my son that he intends to have more money than his uncle, who is a corporation lawyer in Philadelphia. Next, A tells my son that he wants to go to Exeter. Why? "Because Exeter is a stepping-stone to Harvard," he says. Not Exeter for the wonders of Exeter but Exeter because it will be useful *after* he leaves it.

B, with his mouth full of Almond Joy, is asking the others a question: "Do you want to be a little fish in a big pond or a big fish in a little pond?"

What has that got to do with getting an education? How about the excitement of learning algebra? How about that wonderful grammar teacher who showed you how to recognize the participle absolute? Why aren't you talking about your French teacher's getting you to speak French with an accent that would wow them in Paris? I want to butt in with my questions, but I keep my mouth shut.

Now A is talking. His mother, he is saying, has taken him rock climbing, because rock climbing is an impressive activity to put down as his "interest" on the application to Exeter.

"But you *hate* rock climbing!" says D, who is a mischief-maker with the face of an angel under his tramp makeup. "You hate to move your *ass*," D adds.

All right, who else is here? C, who is wearing a mask of The Incredible Hulk. C is the jock of the group. He has been in training since the age of two in the craft of giving nothing away. He's wary and tight and already immunized to the teeth against charity for its own sake. He, too, wants to be a corporation lawyer; so do B and D. The girls, though—the ballerina and Bette Midler—both want to be big-corporation presidents. They are both relaxed, being well aware of what women's lib has done for them. E, the ghost, is the only one with a simple costume, made of a sheet. A, talking to B, points out that E doesn't have to bother about a costume, because he's rich, very rich. His grandfather lives in Texas and owns real oil wells—not new ones but very old and very productive oil wells. E wants to be a movie director and has promised to give my son, who at the moment wants to be an actor, a starring part in his first movie. They are pals. Both of them are regarded with suspicion by the ones who want to be corporation lawyers.

What else are they saying? They're still talking about Exeter. Apparently, A is obsessed by Exeter—it is he who keeps bringing the conversation back to it.

"They ask you to write a 'personal letter' to them," this little busybody says. "They say, 'This letter should represent you as accurately as possible.' But then they tell you in the catalogue what they want, so all you have to do is tell it back to them."

C finally talks. "The way *you* always figure out what the teacher wants and give it right back to *him*," he says.

D squirts a little Coke at A, and the future lawyers get up and make for the door. They cram their loot bags with the orange and black jelly beans, the Candy Corn, the cookies, the trembly spiders, the balloons, the jack-o'-lantern lollipops, and the rest. They make a big point of thanking me loudly. The girls amble out, smiling knowledgeably at each other. E and my son run to catch up to them. They, too, thank me extravagantly. And they all go off, in their disguises, to do their tricks and get their treats. I am left wondering what it's all about.

RUSSELL BAKER

The Flag

At various times when young, I was prepared to crack skulls, kill and die for Old Glory. I never wholly agreed with the LOVE IT OR LEAVE IT bumper stickers, which held that everybody who didn't love the flag ought to be thrown out of the country, but I wouldn't have minded seeing them beaten up. In fact, I saw a man come very close to being beaten up at a baseball park one day because he didn't stand when they raised the flag in the opening ceremonies, and I joined the mob screaming for him to get to his feet like an American if he didn't want lumps all over his noodle. He stood up, all right. I was then thirteen, and a Boy Scout, and I knew you never let the flag touch the ground, or threw it out with the trash when it got dirty (you burned it), or put up with disrespect for it at the baseball park.

At eighteen, I longed to die for it. When World War II ended in 1945 before I could reach the combat zone, I moped for months about being deprived of the chance to go down in flames under the guns of a Mitsubishi Zero. There was never much doubt that I would go down in flames if given the opportunity, for my competence as a pilot was such that I could barely remember to lower the plane's landing gear before trying to set it down on a runway.

I had even visualized my death. It was splendid. Dead, I would be standing perhaps 4,000 feet up in the sky. (Everybody knew that heroes floated in those days.) Erect and dashing, surrounded by beautiful cumulus clouds, I would look just as good as ever, except for being slightly transparent. And I would smile, devil-may-care, at the camera—oh, there would be cameras there—and the American flag would unfurl behind me across 500 miles of glorious American sky, and back behind the cumulus clouds the Marine Band would be playing "The Stars and Stripes Forever," but not too fast.

Then I would look down at June Allyson and the kids, who had a gold star in the window and brave smiles shining through their tears, and I would give them a salute and one of those brave, wistful Errol Flynn grins, then turn and mount to Paradise, becoming more transparent with each step so the audience could get a great view of the flag waving over the heavenly pastures.

Okay, so it owes a lot to Louis B. Mayer in his rococo period. I couldn't help that. At eighteen, a man's imagination is too busy with sex to have much energy left for fancy embellishments of patriotic ecstasy. In the words of a popular song of the period, there was a star-spangled banner waving somewhere in The Great Beyond, and only Uncle Sam's brave heroes got to go there. I was ready to make the trip.

All this was a long time ago, and, asinine though it now may seem, I confess it here to illustrate the singularly masculine pleasures to be enjoyed in devoted service to the Stars and Stripes. Not long ago I felt a twinge of the old fire when I saw an unkempt lout on a ferryboat with a flag sewed in the crotch of his jeans. Something in me wanted to throw him overboard, but I didn't since he was a big muscular devil and the flag had already suffered so many worse indignities anyhow, having been pinned in politicians' lapels, pasted on cars to promote gasoline sales and used to sanctify the professional sports industry as the soul of patriotism even while the team owners were instructing their athletes in how to dodge the draft.

For a moment, though, I felt some of the old masculine excitement kicked up by the flag in the adrenal glands. It's a man's flag, all right. No doubt about that. Oh, it may be a scoundrel's flag, too, and a drummer's flag, and a fraud's flag, and a thief's flag. But first and foremost, it is a man's flag.

Except for decorating purposes—it looks marvelous on old New England houses—I cannot see much in it to appeal to women. Its pleasures, in fact, seem so exclusively masculine and its sanctity so unassailable by feminist iconoclasts that it may prove to be America's only enduring, uncrushable male sex symbol.

Observe that in my patriotic death fantasy, the starring role is not June Allyson's, but mine. As defender of the flag, I am able to leave a humdrum job, put June and the kids with all their humdrum problems behind me, travel the world with a great bunch of guys, do exciting things with powerful flying machines, and, fetchingly uniformed, strut exotic saloons on my nights off.

In the end, I walk off with all the glory and the big scene.

And what does June get? Poor June. She gets to sit home with the kids the rest of her life dusting my photograph and trying to pay the bills, with occasional days off to visit the grave.

No wonder the male pulse pounds with pleasure when the Stars and Stripes comes fluttering down the avenue with the band smashing out those great noises. Where was Mrs. Teddy Roosevelt when Teddy was carrying it up San Juan Hill? What was Mrs. Lincoln doing when Abe was holding it aloft for the Union? What was Martha up to while George Washington was carrying it across the Delaware? Nothing, you may be sure, that was one-tenth as absorbing as what their husbands were doing.

Consider some of the typical masculine activities associated with Old Glory: Dressing up in medals. Whipping cowards, slackers and traitors within an inch of their miserable lives. Conquering Mount Suribachi. Walking on the moon. Rescuing the wagon train. Being surrounded by the whole German Army and being asked to surrender and saying, "You can tell Schicklgruber my answer is 'Nuts.'" In brief, having a wonderful time. With the boys.

Yes, surely the American flag is the ultimate male sex symbol. Men flaunt it, wave it, punch noses for it, strut with it, fight for it, kill for it, die for it.

And women—? Well, when do you see a woman with the flag? Most commonly when she is wearing black and has just received it, neatly folded, from coffin of husband or son. Later, she may wear it to march in the Veterans Day parade, widows' division.

Male pleasures and woman's sorrow—it sounds like the old definition of sex. Yet these are the immemorial connotations of the flag, and women, having shed the whalebone girdle and stamped out the stag bar, nevertheless accept it, ostensibly at least, with the same emotional devotion that men accord it.

There are good reasons, of course, why they may be reluctant to pursue logic to its final step and say, "To hell with the flag, too." In the first place, it would almost certainly do them no good. Men hold all the political trumps in this matter. When little girls first toddle off to school, does anyone tell them the facts of life when they stand to salute the flag? Does anyone say, "You are now saluting the proud standard of the greatest men's club on earth?" You bet your chewing gum nobody tells them that. If anyone did, there would be a joint session of Congress presided over by the President of the United States to investigate the entire school system of the United States of America.

What little girls have drilled into them is that the flag stands for one nation indivisible, with liberty and justice for all. A few years ago, the men of the Congress, responding to pressure from the American Legion (all men) and parsons (mostly all men), all of whom sensed perhaps that women were not as gullible as they used to be, revised the Pledge of Allegiance with words intimating that it would be ungodly not to respect the flag. The "one nation indivisible" became "one nation *under God*, indivisible," and another loophole for skeptics was sealed off. The women's movement may be brave, but it will not go far taking on national indivisibility, liberty, justice and God, all in one fight. If they tried it, a lot of us men would feel perfectly justified in raising lumps on their lovely noodles.

Philosophically speaking, the masculinity of the American flag is entirely appropriate. America, after all, is not a motherland—many places still are—but a fatherland, which is to say a vast nation-state of disparate people scattered over great distances, but held together by a belligerent, loyalty-to-the-death devotion to some highly abstract political ideas. Since these ideas are too complex to be easily grasped, statesmen have given us the flag and told us it sums up all these noble ideas that make us a country.

Fatherland being an aggressive kind of state, the ideas it embodies must be defended, protected and propagated, often in blood. Since the flag is understood to represent these ideas, in a kind of tricolor shorthand, we emote, fight, bleed and rejoice in the name of the flag.

Before fatherland there was something that might be called motherland. It still exists here and there. In the fifties, when Washington was looking for undiscovered Asiatic terrain to save from un-American ideologies, somebody stumbled into an area called Laos, a place so remote from American consciousness that few had ever heard its name pronounced. (For the longest time, Lyndon Johnson, then Democratic leader of the Senate, referred to it as "Low Ass.") Federal inspectors sent to Laos returned with astounding information. Most of the people living there were utterly unaware that they were living in a country. Almost none of them knew the country they were living in was called Laos. All they knew was that they lived where they had been born and where their ancestors were buried.

What Washington had discovered, of course, was an old-fashioned motherland, a society where people's loyalties ran to the place of their birth. It was a Pentagon nightmare. Here were these people, perfectly happy with their home turf and their ancestors' graves, and they had to be put into shape to die for their country, and they didn't even know they had a country to die for. They didn't even have a flag to die for. And yet, they were content!

The point is that a country is only an idea and a fairly modern one at that. Life would still be going on if nobody had ever thought of it, and would probably be a good deal more restful. No flags. Not much in the way of armies. No sharing of exciting group emotions with millions of other people ready to do or die for national honor. And so forth. Very restful, and possibly very primitive, and almost surely very nasty on occasion, although possibly not as nasty as occasions often become when countries disagree.

I hear my colleagues in masculinity protesting, "What? No country? No flag? But there would be nothing noble to defend, to fight for, to die for, in the meantime having a hell of a good time doing all those fun male things in the name of!"

Women may protest, too. I imagine some feminists may object to the suggestion that fatherland's need for prideful, warlike and aggressive citizens to keep the flag flying leaves women pretty much out of things. Those who hold that sexual roles are a simple matter of social conditioning may contend that the flag can offer the same rollicking pleasures to both sexes once baby girls are trained as thoroughly as baby boys in being prideful, warlike and aggressive.

I think there may be something in this, having seen those harridans who gather outside freshly desegregated schools to wave the American flag and terrify children. The question is whether women really want to start conditioning girl babies for this hitherto largely masculine sort of behavior, or spend their energies trying to decondition it out of the American man.

In any case, I have no quarrel with these women. Living in a fatherland, they have tough problems, and if they want to join the boys in the flag sports, it's okay with me. The only thing is, if they are going to get a chance, too, to go up to Paradise with the Marine Band playing "The Stars and Stripes Forever" back behind the cumulus clouds, I don't want to be stuck with the role of sitting home dusting their photographs the rest of my life after the big scene is ended.

DONALD BARTHELME

And Now Let's Hear It for
the Ed Sullivan Show!

The Ed Sullivan Show. Sunday night. Church of the unchurched. Ed stands there. He looks great. Not unlike an older, heavier Paul Newman. Sways a little from side to side. Gary Lewis and the Playboys have just got off. Very strong act. Ed clasps hands together. He's introducing somebody in the audience. Who is it? Ed points with his left arm. "Broken every house record at the Copa," Ed says of the man he's introducing. Who is it? It's . . . Don Rickles! Rickles stands up. Eyes glint. Applause. "I'm gonna make a big man outa you!" Ed says. Rickles hunches a shoulder combatively. Eyes glint. Applause. Jerry Vale introduced. Wives introduced. Applause. "When Mrs. Sullivan and I were in Monte Carlo" (pause, neatly suppressed belch), "we saw them" (pause, he's talking about the next act), "for the first time and signed them instantly! The Kuban Cossacks! Named after the River Kuban!"

Three dancers appear in white fur hats, fur boots, what appear to be velvet jump suits. They're great. Terrific Cossack stuff in front of onion-dome flats. Kuban not the U.S.S.R.'s most imposing river (512 miles, shorter than the Ob, shorter than the Bug) but the dancers are remarkable. Sword dance of some sort with the band playing galops. Front dancer balancing on one hand and doing things with his feet. Great, terrific. Dancers support selves with one hand, don and doff hats with other hand. XOPOWÓ! (Non-Cyrillic approximation of Russian for "neat.") Double-XOPOWÓ! Ed enters from left. Makes enthusiastic gesture with hand. Triple-XOPOWÓ! Applause dies. Camera on Ed who has hands knit before him. "Highlighting this past week in New York . . ." Something at the Garden. Can't make it out, a fight probably. Ed introduces somebody in audience. Can't see who, he's standing up behind a fat lady who's also standing up for purposes of her own. Applause. Pigmeat Markham comes on with cap and gown and gavel. His tag line, "Here come de jedge," is pronounced and the crowd roars but not so great a roar as you might expect. The line's wearing out. Still, Pigmeat looks good, working with two or three stooges. Stooge asks Pigmeat why, if he's honest, he's acquired two Cadillacs, etc. Pigmeat says: "Because I'm very *frugal*," and whacks stooge on head with bladder. Lots of bladder work in sketch, old-timey comedy. Stooge says: "Jedge, you got to know me." Pigmeat: "Who are you?" Stooge: "I'm the man that introduced you to your wife." Pigmeat shouts, *"Life!"* and whacks the stooge on the head with the bladder. Very funny stuff, audience roars. Then a fast commercial with Jo Anne Worley from Rowan and Martin singing about Bold. Funny girl. Good commercial.

Ed brings on Doodletown Pipers, singing group. Great-looking girls in tiny skirts. Great-looking legs on girls. They sing something about "I hear the laughter" and "the sound of the future." Phrasing is excellent, attack excellent. Camera goes to atmospheric shots of a park, kids playing, mothers and fathers lounging about, a Sunday feeling. Shot of boys throwing the ball around. Shot of black baby in swing. Shot of young mother's ass, very nice. Shot of blonde mother cuddling kid. Shot of black father swinging kid. Shot of a guy who looks like Rod McKuen lounging against a . . . a what?? A play sculpture. But it's not Rod McKuen. The Doodletown Pipers segue into another song. Something about hate and fear, "You've got to be taught . . . hate and fear." They sound great. Shot of integrated group sitting on play equipment. Shot of young be-spectacled father. Shot of young black man with young white child. He looks into camera. Thoughtful gaze. Young mother with daughter, absorbed. Nice-looking mother. Camera in tight on mother and daughter. One more mother, a medium shot. Out on shot of the tiny black child asleep in swing. Wow!

Sullivan enters from left applauding. Makes gesture toward Pipers, toward audience, toward Pipers. Applause. Everybody's having a good time! "I want you to welcome . . . George Carlin!" Carlin is a comic. Carlin says he hates to look at the news. News is depressing. Sample headlines: "Welcome Wagon Runs Over Newcomer." Audience roars. "Pediatrician Dies of Childhood Disease." Audience roars but a weaker roar. Carlin is wearing a white turtleneck, dark sideburns. Joke about youth asking father if he can use the car. Youth says he's got a heavy date. Pa says, then why don't you take the pickup? Joke about the difference between organized crime and unorganized crime. Unorganized crime is when a guy holds you up on the street. Organized crime is when two guys hold you up on the street. Carlin is great, terrific, but his material is not so funny. A Central Park joke. Cops going into the park dressed as women to provoke molesters. Three hundred molesters arrested and two cops got engaged. More cop jokes. Carlin holds hands clasped together at waist. Says people wonder why the cops don't catch the Mafia. Says have you ever tried to catch a guy in a silk suit? Weak roar from audience. Carlin says do you suffer from nagging crime? Try the Police Department with new improved GL-70. No roar at all. A whicker, rather. Ed facing camera. "Coming up next . . . right after this important word." Commercial for Royal Electric Jetstar Typewriter. "She's typing faster and neater now." Capable-looking woman says to camera, "I have a Jetstar now that helps me at home where I have a business raising St. Bernards." Behind her a St. Bernard looks admiringly at Jetstar.

Ed's back. "England's famous Beatles" (pause, neatly capped belch) "first appeared on our shew . . . Mary Hopkin . . . Paul McCartney told her she must appear on our shew . . . the world-famous . . . Mary Hopkin!" Mary enters holding guitar. Sings something about "the morning of my life . . . ceiling of my room. . . ." Camera in tight on Mary. Pretty blonde, slightly plump face. Heavy applause for Mary. Camera goes to black, then Mary walking away in very short skirt, fine legs, a little heavy maybe. Mary in some sort of nightclub set for her big song, "Those Were the Days." Song is ersatz Kurt Weill but nevertheless a very nice song, very nostalgic, days gone by, tears rush into eyes (mine). In the background, period stills. Shot of some sort of Edwardian group activity, possible lawn party, possible egg roll. Shot of biplane.

Shot of racecourse. Camera on Mary's face. "Those were the days, my friends. . . ." Shot of fox hunting, shot of tea dance. Mary is bouncing a little with the song, just barely bouncing. Shot of what appears to be a French 75 firing. Shot of lady kissing dog on nose. Shot of horse. Camera in tight on Mary's mouth. Looks like huge wad of chewing gum in her mouth but that can't be right, must be her tongue. Still of balloon ascension in background. Live girl sitting in left foreground gazing up at Mary, rapt. Mary in chaste high-collar dress with that short skirt. Effective. Mary finishes song. A real roar. Ed appears in three-quarter view turned toward the right, toward Mary. "Terrific!" Ed says. "Terrific!" Mary adjusts her breasts. "Terrific. And now, sitting out in the audience is the famous . . . Perle Mesta!" Perle stands, a contented-looking middle-aged lady. Perle bows. Applause.

Ed stares (enthralled) into camera. "Before we introduce singing Ed Ames and the first lady of the American theatre, Helen Hayes . . ." A Pizza Spins commercial fades into a Tareyton Charcoal Filter commercial. Then Ed comes back to plug Helen Hayes's new book, *On Reflection*. Miss Hayes is the first lady of the American theatre, he says. "We're very honored to . . ." Miss Hayes sitting at a desk. Louis-something. She looks marvelous. Begins reading from the book. Great voice. Tons of dignity. "My dear Grandchildren. At this writing, it is no longer fashionable to have Faith; but your grandmother has never been famous for her chic, so she isn't bothered by the intellectual hemlines. I have always been concerned with the whole, not the fragments; the positive, not the negative; the words, not the spaces between them. . . ." Miss Hayes pauses. Hand on what appears to be a small silver teapot. "What can a grandmother offer. . . ." *She speaks very well!* "With the feast of millennia set before you, the saga of all mankind on your bookshelf . . . what could I give you? And then I knew. Of course. My own small footnote. The homemade bread at the banquet. The private joke in the divine comedy. Your roots." Head and shoulders shot of Miss Hayes. She looks up into the lighting grid. Music up softly on, "So my grandchildren . . . in highlights and shadows . . . bits and pieces . . . in recalled moments, mad scenes and acts of folly. . . ." Miss Hayes removes glasses, looks misty. "What are little grandchildren made of . . . some good and some bad from Mother and Dad . . . and laughs and wails from Grandmother's tales . . . I love you." She gazes down at book. Holds it. Camera pulls back. Music up. Applause.

Ed puts arm around Miss Hayes. Squeezes Miss Hayes. Applause. *Heavy* applause. Ed pats hands together joining applause. Waves hands toward Miss Hayes. More applause. It's a triumph! Ed seizes Miss Hayes's hands in his hands. Applause dies, reluctantly. Ed says ". . . but first, listen to this." Shot of building, cathedral of some kind. Organ music. Camera pans down facade past stained-glass windows, etc. Down a winding staircase. Music changes to rock. Shot of organ keyboard. Close shot of maker's nameplate, HAMMOND. Shot of grinning organist. Shot of hands on keyboard. "The sound of Hammond starts at $599.95." Ed introduces singer Ed Ames. Ames is wearing a long-skirted coat, holding hand mike. Good eyes, good eyebrows, muttonchop sideburns. Lace at his cuffs. Real riverboat-looking. He strolls about the set singing a Tom Jones–Harvey Schmidt number, something about the morning, sometimes in the morning, something. Then another song, "it takes my breath away," "how long have I waited," something something. Chorus comes in under him. Good song. Ames blinks in a sincere way. Introduces a song from the upcoming show *Dear World*. "A lovely new song," he says. "Kiss her now, while she's young. Kiss her now, while she's yours." Set behind him looks like one-by-two's nailed vertically four inches on centers. The song is sub-lovely but Ames's delivery is very comfortable, easy. Chorus comes in. Ah, ah ah ah ah. Ames closes his eyes, sings something something something something; the song is sub-memorable. (Something memorable: early on Sunday morning a pornographic exhibition appeared mysteriously for eight minutes on television-station KPLM, Palm Springs, California. A naked man and woman did vile and imaginative things to each other for that length of time, then disappeared into the history of electricity. Unfortunately, the exhibition wasn't on a network. What we really want in this world, we can't have.)

Ed enters from left (what's over there? a bar? a Barcalounger? a book? stock ticker? model railroad?), shakes hands with Ames. Ames is much taller, but amiable. Both back out of shot, in different directions. Camera straight ahead on Ed. "Before I tell you about next week's . . . show . . . please listen to this." Commercial for Silva Thins. Then a shot of old man with ship model, commercial for Total, the vitamin cereal. Then Ed. "Next week . . . a segment from . . . the new Beatles film. . . . The Beatles were brought over here by us . . . in the beginning. . . . Good night!" Chopping gesture with hands to the left, to the right.

Music comes up. The crawl containing the credits is rolled over shot of Russian dancers dancing (ХОРОШО́!). Produced by Bob Precht. Directed by Tim Kiley. Music by Ray Bloch. Associate Producer Jack McGeehan. Settings Designed by Bill Bohnert. Production Manager Tony Jordan. Associate Director Bob Schwarz. Assistant to the Producer Ken Campbell. Program Coordinator Russ Petranto. Technical Director Charles Grenier. Audio Art Shine. Lighting Director Bill Greenfield. Production Supervisor Herb Benton. Stage Managers Ed Brinkman, Don Mayo. Set Director Ed Pasternak. Costumes Leslie Renfield. Graphic Arts Sam Cecere. Talent Coordinator Vince Calandra. Music Coordinator Bob Arthur. The Ed Sullivan Show is over. It has stopped.

JAMES BALDWIN

Fifth Avenue, Uptown:
A Letter from Harlem

There is a housing project standing now where the house in which we grew up once stood, and one of those stunted city trees is snarling where our doorway used to be. This is on the rehabilitated side of the avenue. The other side of the avenue—for progress takes time— has not been rehabilitated yet and it looks exactly as it looked in the days when we sat with our noses pressed against the windowpane, longing to be allowed to go "across the street." The grocery store which gave us credit is still there, and there can be no doubt that it is still giving credit. The people in the project certainly need it—far more, indeed, than they ever needed the project. The last time I passed by, the Jewish proprietor was still standing among his shelves, looking sadder and heavier but scarcely any older. Farther down the block stands the shoe-repair store in which our shoes were repaired until reparation became impossible and in which, then, we bought all our "new" ones. The Negro proprietor is still in the window, head down, working at the leather.

These two, I imagine, could tell a long tale if they would (perhaps they would be glad to if they could), having watched so many, for so long, struggling in the fishhooks, the barbed wire, of this avenue.

The avenue is elsewhere the renowned and elegant Fifth. The area I am describing, which, in today's gang parlance, would be called "the turf," is bounded by Lenox Avenue on the west, the Harlem River on the east, 135th Street on the north, and 130th Street on the south. We never lived beyond these boundaries; this is where we grew up. Walking along 145th Street—for example— familiar as it is, and similar, does not have the same impact because I do not know any of the people on the block. But when I turn

east on 131st Street and Lenox Avenue, there is first a soda-pop
joint, then a shoeshine "parlor," then a grocery store, then a dry
cleaners', then the houses. All along the street there are people who
watched me grow up, people who grew up with me, people I
watched grow up along with my brothers and sisters; and, sometimes
in my arms, sometimes underfoot, sometimes at my shoulder—or
on it—their children, a riot, a forest of children, who include my
nieces and nephews.

When we reach the end of this long block, we find ourselves on
wide, filthy, hostile Fifth Avenue, facing that project which hangs
over the avenue like a monument to the folly, and the cowardice,
of good intentions. All along the block, for anyone who knows it,
are immense human gaps, like craters. These gaps are not created
merely by those who have moved away, inevitably into some other
ghetto; or by those who have risen, almost always into a greater
capacity for self-loathing and self-delusion; or yet by those who,
by whatever means—World War II, the Korean war, a policeman's
gun or billy, a gang war, a brawl, madness, an overdose of heroin,
or, simply, unnatural exhaustion—are dead. I am talking about
those who are left, and I am talking principally about the young.
What are they doing? Well, some, a minority, are fanatical church-
goers, members of the more extreme of the Holy Roller sects.
Many, many more are "moslems," by affiliation or sympathy, that
is to say that they are united by nothing more—and nothing less—
than a hatred of the white world and all its works. They are present,
for example, at every Buy Black street-corner meeting—meetings
in which the speaker urges his hearers to cease trading with white
men and establish a separate economy. Neither the speaker nor his
hearers can possibly do this, of course, since Negroes do not own
General Motors or RCA or the A & P, nor, indeed, do they own
more than a wholly insufficient fraction of anything else in Harlem
(those who *do* own anything are more interested in their profits
than in their fellows). But these meetings nevertheless keep alive
in the participators a certain pride of bitterness without which,
however futile this bitterness may be, they could scarcely remain
alive at all. Many have given up. They stay home and watch the

TV screen, living on the earnings of their parents, cousins, brothers, or uncles, and only leave the house to go to the movies or to the nearest bar. "How're you making it?" one may ask, running into them along the block, or in the bar. "Oh, I'm TV-ing it"; with the saddest, sweetest, most shamefaced of smiles, and from a great distance. This distance one is compelled to respect; anyone who has traveled so far will not easily be dragged again into the world. There are further retreats, of course, than the TV screen or the bar. There are those who are simply sitting on their stoops, "stoned," animated for a moment only, and hideously, by the approach of someone who may lend them the money for a "fix." Or by the approach of someone from whom they can purchase it, one of the shrewd ones, on the way to prison or just coming out.

And the others, who have avoided all of these deaths, get up in the morning and go downtown to meet "the man." They work in the white man's world all day and come home in the evening to this fetid block. They struggle to instill in their children some private sense of honor or dignity which will help the child to survive. This means, of course, that they must struggle, stolidly, incessantly, to keep this sense alive in themselves, in spite of the insults, the indifference, and the cruelty they are certain to encounter in their working day. They patiently browbeat the landlord into fixing the heat, the plaster, the plumbing; this demands prodigious patience; nor is patience usually enough. In trying to make their hovels habitable, they are perpetually throwing good money after bad. Such frustration, so long endured, is driving many strong, admirable men and women whose only crime is color to the very gates of paranoia.

One remembers them from another time—playing handball in the playground, going to church, wondering if they were going to be promoted at school. One remembers them going off to war— gladly, to escape this block. One remembers their return. Perhaps one remembers their wedding day. And one sees where the girl is now—vainly looking for salvation from some other embittered, trussed, and struggling boy—and sees the all-but-abandoned children in the streets.

Now I am perfectly aware that there are other slums in which white men are fighting for their lives, and mainly losing. I know that blood is also flowing through those streets and that the human damage there is incalculable. People are continually pointing out to me the wretchedness of white people in order to console me for the wretchedness of blacks. But an itemized account of the American failure does not console me and it should not console anyone else. That hundreds of thousands of white people are living, in effect, no better than the "niggers" is not a fact to be regarded with complacency. The social and moral bankruptcy suggested by this fact is of the bitterest, most terrifying kind.

The people, however, who believe that this democratic anguish has some consoling value are always pointing out that So-and-So, white, and So-and-So, black, rose from the slums into the big time. The existence—the public existence—of, say, Frank Sinatra and Sammy Davis, Jr. proves to them that America is still the land of opportunity and that inequalities vanish before the determined will. It proves nothing of the sort. The determined will is rare—at the moment, in this country, it is unspeakably rare—and the inequalities suffered by the many are in no way justified by the rise of a few. A few have always risen—in every country, every era, and in the teeth of regimes which can by no stretch of the imagination be thought of as free. Not all of these people, it is worth remembering, left the world better than they found it. The determined will is rare, but it is not invariably benevolent. Furthermore, the American equation of success with the big time reveals an awful disrespect for human life and human achievement. This equation has placed our cities among the most dangerous in the world and has placed our youth among the most empty and most bewildered. The situation of our youth is not mysterious. Children have never been very good at listening to their elders, but they have never failed to imitate them. They must, they have no other models. That is exactly what our children are doing. They are imitating our immorality, our disrespect for the pain of others.

All other slum dwellers, when the bank account permits it, can move out of the slum and vanish altogether from the eye of persecution. No Negro in this country has ever made that much money and it will be a long time before any Negro does. The Negroes in Harlem, who have no money, spend what they have on such gimcracks as they are sold. These include "wider" TV screens, more "faithful" hi-fi sets, more "powerful" cars, all of which, of course, are obsolete long before they are paid for. Anyone who has ever struggled with poverty knows how extremely expensive it is to be poor; and if one is a member of a captive population, economically speaking, one's feet have simply been placed on the treadmill forever. One is victimized, economically, in a thousand ways—rent, for example, or car insurance. Go shopping one day in Harlem—for anything—and compare Harlem prices and quality with those downtown.

The people who have managed to get off this block have only got as far as a more respectable ghetto. This respectable ghetto does not even have the advantages of the disreputable one—friends, neighbors, a familiar church, and friendly tradesmen; and it is not, moreover, in the nature of any ghetto to remain respectable long. Every Sunday, people who have left the block take the lonely ride back, dragging their increasingly discontented children with them. They spend the day talking, not always with words, about the trouble they've seen and the trouble—one must watch their eyes as they watch their children—they are only too likely to see. For children do not like ghettos. It takes them nearly no time to discover exactly why they are there.

The projects in Harlem are hated. They are hated almost as much as policemen, and this is saying a great deal. And they are hated for the same reason: both reveal, unbearably, the real attitude of the white world, no matter how many liberal speeches are made, no matter how many lofty editorials are written, no matter how many civil-rights commissions are set up.

The projects are hideous, of course, there being a law, apparently respected throughout the world, that popular housing shall be as cheerless as a prison. They are lumped all over Harlem, colorless, bleak, high, and revolting. The wide windows look out on Harlem's invincible and indescribable squalor: the Park Avenue railroad tracks, around which, about forty years ago, the present dark community began; the unrehabilitated houses, bowed down, it would seem, under the great weight of frustration and bitterness they contain; the dark, the ominous schoolhouses from which the child may emerge maimed, blinded, hooked, or enraged for life; and the churches, churches, block upon block of churches, niched in the walls like cannon in the walls of a fortress. Even if the administration of the projects were not so insanely humiliating (for example: one must report raises in salary to the management, which will then eat up the profit by raising one's rent; the management has the right to know who is staying in your apartment; the management can ask you to leave, at their discretion), the projects would still be hated because they are an insult to the meanest intelligence.

Harlem got its first private project, Riverton*—which is now, naturally, a slum—about twelve years ago because at that time Negroes were not allowed to live in Stuyvesant Town. Harlem watched Riverton go up, therefore, in the most violent bitterness of spirit, and hated it long before the builders arrived. They began hating it at about the time people began moving out of their condemned houses to make room for this additional proof of how thoroughly the white world despised them. And they had scarcely moved in, naturally, before they began smashing windows, defacing walls, urinating in the elevators, and fornicating in the playgrounds.

---

*The inhabitants of Riverton were much embittered by this description; they have, apparently, forgotten how their project came into being; and have repeatedly informed me that I cannot possibly be referring to Riverton, but to another housing project which is directly across the street. It is quite clear, I think, that I have no interest in accusing any individuals or families of the depredations herein described: but neither can I deny the evidence of my own eyes. Nor do I blame anyone in Harlem for making the best of a dreadful bargain. But anyone who lives in Harlem and imagines that he has not struck this bargain, or that what he takes to be his status (in whose eyes?) protects him against the common pain, demoralization, and danger, is simply self-deluded.

Liberals, both white and black, were appalled at the spectacle. I was appalled by the liberal innocence—or cynicism, which comes out in practice as much the same thing. Other people were delighted to be able to point to proof positive that nothing could be done to better the lot of the colored people. They were, and are, right in one respect: that nothing can be done as long as they are treated like colored people. The people in Harlem know they are living there because white people do not think they are good enough to live anywhere else. No amount of "improvement" can sweeten this fact. Whatever money is now being earmarked to improve this, or any other ghetto, might as well be burnt. A ghetto can be improved in one way only: out of existence.

Similarly, the only way to police a ghetto is to be oppressive. None of the Police Commissioner's men, even with the best will in the world, have any way of understanding the lives led by the people they swagger about in twos and threes controlling. Their very presence is an insult, and it would be, even if they spent their entire day feeding gumdrops to children. They represent the force of the white world, and that world's real intentions are, simply, for that world's criminal profit and ease, to keep the black man corraled up here, in his place. The badge, the gun in the holster, and the swinging club make vivid what will happen should his rebellion become overt. Rare, indeed, is the Harlem citizen, from the most circumspect church member to the most shiftless adolescent, who does not have a long tale to tell of police incompetence, injustice, or brutality. I myself have witnessed and endured it more than once. The businessmen and racketeers also have a story. And so do the prostitutes. (And this is not, perhaps, the place to discuss Harlem's very complex attitude toward black policemen, nor the reasons, according to Harlem, that they are nearly all downtown.)

It is hard, on the other hand, to blame the policeman, blank, good-natured, thoughtless, and insuperably innocent, for being such a perfect representative of the people he serves. He, too, believes in good intentions and is astounded and offended when they are not taken for the deed. He has never, himself, done anything for which to be hated—which of us has?—and yet he is facing, daily and nightly, people who would gladly see him dead, and he knows it. There is no way for him not to know it: there are few things under heaven more unnerving than the silent, accumulating contempt and hatred of a people. He moves through Harlem, therefore, like an occupying soldier in a bitterly hostile country; which is precisely what, and where, he is, and is the reason he walks in twos and threes. And he is not the only one who knows why he is always in company: the people who are watching him know why, too. Any street meeting, sacred or secular, which he and his colleagues uneasily cover has as its explicit or implicit burden the cruelty and injustice of the white domination. And these days, of course, in terms increasingly vivid and jubilant, it speaks of the end of that domination. The white policeman standing on a Harlem street corner finds himself at the very center of the revolution now occurring in the world. He is not prepared for it—naturally, nobody is—and, what is possibly much more to the point, he is exposed, as few white people are, to the anguish of the black people around him. Even if he is gifted with the merest mustard grain of imagination, something must seep in. He cannot avoid observing that some of the children, in spite of their color, remind him of children he has known and loved, perhaps even of his own children. He knows that he certainly does not want *his* children living this way. He can retreat from his uneasiness in only one direction: into a callousness which very shortly becomes second nature. He becomes more callous, the population becomes more hostile, the situation grows more tense, and the police force is increased. One day, to everyone's astonishment, someone drops a match in the powder keg and everything blows up. Before the dust has settled or the blood congealed, editorials, speeches, and civil-rights commissions are loud in the land, demanding to know what happened. What happened is that Negroes want to be treated like men.

Negroes want to be treated like men: a perfectly straightforward statement, containing only seven words. People who have mastered Kant, Hegel, Shakespeare, Marx, Freud, and the Bible find this statement utterly impenetrable. The idea seems to threaten profound, barely conscious assumptions. A kind of panic paralyzes their features, as though they found themselves trapped on the edge of a steep place. I once tried to describe to a very well-known American intellectual the conditions among Negroes in the South. My recital disturbed him and made him indignant; and he asked me in perfect innocence, "Why don't all the Negroes in the South move North?" I tried to explain what *has* happened, unfailingly, whenever a significant body of Negroes move North. They do not escape Jim Crow: they merely encounter another, not-less-deadly variety. They do not move to Chicago, they move to the South Side; they do not move to New York, they move to Harlem. The pressure within the ghetto causes the ghetto walls to expand, and this expansion is always violent. White people hold the line as long as they can, and in as many ways as they can, from verbal intimidation to physical violence. But inevitably the border which has divided the ghetto from the rest of the world falls into the hands of the ghetto. The white people fall back bitterly before the black horde; the landlords make a tidy profit by raising the rent, chopping up the rooms, and all but dispensing with the upkeep; and what has once been a neighborhood turns into a "turf." This is precisely what happened when the Puerto Ricans arrived in their thousands— and the bitterness thus caused is, as I write, being fought out all up and down those streets.

Northerners indulge in an extremely dangerous luxury. They seem to feel that because they fought on the right side during the Civil War, and won, they have earned the right merely to deplore what is going on in the South, without taking any responsibility for it; and that they can ignore what is happening in Northern cities because what is happening in Little Rock or Birmingham is worse. Well, in the first place, it is not possible for anyone who has not endured both to know which is "worse." I know Negroes who prefer the South and white Southerners, because "At least there, you haven't got to play any guessing games!" The guessing games referred to have driven more than one Negro into the narcotics ward, the madhouse, or the river. I know another Negro, a man very dear to me, who says, with conviction and with truth, "The spirit of the South is the spirit of America." He was born in the

North and did his military training in the South. He did not, as far as I can gather, find the South "worse"; he found it, if anything, all too familiar. In the second place, though, even if Birmingham *is* worse, no doubt Johannesburg, South Africa, beats it by several miles, and Buchenwald was one of the worst things that ever happened in the entire history of the world. The world has never lacked for horrifying examples; but I do not believe that these examples are meant to be used as justification for our own crimes. This perpetual justification empties the heart of all human feeling. The emptier our hearts become, the greater will be our crimes. Thirdly, the South is not merely an embarrassingly backward region, but a part of this country, and what happens there concerns every one of us.

As far as the color problem is concerned, there is but one great difference between the Southern white and the Northerner: the Southerner remembers, historically and in his own psyche, a kind of Eden in which he loved black people and they loved him. Historically, the flaming sword laid across this Eden is the Civil War. Personally, it is the Southerner's sexual coming of age, when without any warning, unbreakable taboos are set up between himself and his past. Everything, thereafter, is permitted him except the love he remembers and has never ceased to need. The resulting, indescribable torment affects every Southern mind and is the basis of the Southern hysteria.

None of this is true for the Northerner. Negroes represent nothing to him personally, except, perhaps, the dangers of carnality. He never sees Negroes. Southerners see them all the time. Northerners never think about them whereas Southerners are never really thinking of anything else. Negroes are, therefore, ignored in the North and are under surveillance in the South, and suffer hideously in both places. Neither the Southerner nor the Northerner is able to look on the Negro simply as a man. It seems to be indispensable to the national self-esteem that the Negro be considered either as a kind of ward (in which case we are told how many Negroes, comparatively, bought Cadillacs last year and how few, comparatively, were lynched), or as a victim (in which case we are promised that he will never vote in our assemblies or go to school with our kids). They are two sides of the same coin and the South will not change— *cannot* change—until the North changes. The country will not change until it reexamines itself and discovers what it really means by freedom. In the meantime, generations keep being born, bitterness is increased by incompetence, pride, and folly, and the world shrinks around us.

It is a terrible, an inexorable, law that one cannot deny the humanity of another without diminishing one's own: in the face of one's victim, one sees oneself. Walk through the streets of Harlem and see what we, this nation, have become.

NORMAN MAILER

The Ninth Presidential Paper—
Totalitarianism

Two columns from *Esquire*:
"The Big Bite"—May and August, 1963

Totalitarianism has been the continuing preoccupation of this book, but one aspect of the subject might be underlined again—it is that totalitarianism is better understood if it is regarded as a plague rather than examined as a style of ideology. There was a time when simple totalitarianism could be found attached to Fascism, and perhaps to Bolshevism. It seemed synonymous with dictatorship; its syndrome was characteristic. Oppression was inflicted upon a nation through its leaders; people were forced to obey a governmental authority which was not only inhumane, but invariably antagonistic to the history of the nation's immediate past. A tension was still visible between the government as the oppressor and the people as the oppressed.

The kind of modern totalitarianism which we find in America, however, is as different from classical Fascism as is a plastic bomb from a hand grenade. The hand grenade makes an imprecise weapon. Thrown into a room full of people, one cannot know who will be hurt, who will be killed, who will escape. But the aggression is still direct: a man must throw *the grenade, and so, in the French sense of the word, he must "assist" at the performance of the act. He would have some idea of whom he was throwing it at. Whereas, the* bombe plastique, *used in the streets of Paris by terrorists in the O.A.S. toward the end of the Algerian War, consisted of a kind of putty which could be left in a trashbasket or stuck onto a wall. When it went off, an hour or two after its placement, only laws of chance were operating. The bomber*

67

*could not know whom he was killing for he was usually miles away.
Some of his own people might even be passing the intersection when the
explosion came. The actor was now wholly separated from his act.*

*So the crucial characteristic of modern totalitarianism is that it is a
moral disease which divorces us from guilt. It came into being as a
desire to escape the judgments of the past and our responsibility for past
injustice—in that sense it is a defense against eternity, an attempt to
destroy that part of eternity which is death, which is punishment or
reward. It arose from the excesses of theology, the exploitations of
theology, and the oppressions of theology, but in destroying theology, the
being of man and his vision may be reduced to a thousand year apathy,
or to extinction itself. The words are abstract, but the meaning by now
is I hope not altogether hidden. In our flight from the consequence of
our lives, in our flight from adventure, from danger, and from the
natural ravages of disease, in our burial of the primitive, it is death
the Twentieth Century is seeking to avoid.*

Let me close this introduction with a poem taken from Deaths for
the Ladies.

Death of a Lover Who Loved Death

> I find
>> that
>> most
>> of the people I
>>> know
>> are immature
>> and cannot
>>> cope
>>> with reality
>> said the suicide
> His death
>> followed
>> a slash on each wrist.
> Fit
> was this end
> for blood
>> in its flow

reveals
what a furnace
had burned
in the dungeon
of his unconscious

Burn and bleed

He coped with
reality
too well.

It was unreality
which waited
on a midnight trail
in that fierce
jungle of eternity
he heard murmuring
on the other side

Oh, night of the jungle,
God of mercy
wept the suicide
do not ask me
to reconnoiter
this
dark
trail
when I am now
without
hands.

The Big Bite—May, 1963

The act of traveling is never a casual act. It inspires an anxiety which no psychoanalyst can relieve in a hurry, for if travel is reminiscent of the trauma of birth, it is also suggestive of some possible migrations after death.

For most of us death may not be peace but an expedition into all the high terror and deep melancholy we sought to avoid in our lives. So the act of travel is a grave hour to some part of the unconscious, for it may be on a trip that we prepare a buried corner of ourselves to be ready for what happens once we are dead.

By this logic, the end of a trip is a critical moment of transition. Railroad stations in large cities should properly be monumental, heavy with dignity, reminiscent of the past. We learn little from travel, not nearly so much as we need to learn, if everywhere we are assaulted by the faceless plastic surfaces of everything which has been built in America since the war, that new architecture of giant weeds and giant boxes, of children's colors on billboards and jagged electric signs. Like the metastases of cancer cells, the plastic shacks, the motels, the drive-in theatres, the highway restaurants and the gas stations proliferate year by year until they are close to covering the highways of America with a new country which is laid over the old one the way a transparent sheet with new drawings is set upon the original plan. It is an architecture with no root to the past and no suggestion of the future, for one cannot conceive of a modern building growing old (does it turn dingy or will the colors stain?); there is no way to age, it can only cease to function. No doubt these buildings will live for twenty years and then crack in two. They will live like robots, or television sets which go out of order with one whistle of the wind.

In the suburbs it is worse. To live in leisure in a house much like other houses, to live in a landscape where it is meaningless to walk because each corner which is turned produces the same view, to live in comfort and be bored is a preparation for one condition: limbo.

The architectural face of the enemy has shifted. Twenty years ago Pennsylvania Station in New York City seemed a monstrosity, forbidding, old, dingy, unfunctional, wasteful of space, depressing in its passages and waiting rooms. The gloomy exploitative echoes of the industrial revolution sounded in its grey stone. And yet today the plan to demolish it is a small disaster.

Soon the planners will move in to tear down the majestic vaults of the old building in order to rear up in its place a new sports arena, a twenty-, thirty-, forty-story building. One can predict what the new building will look like. It will be made of steel, concrete and glass, it will have the appearance of a cardboard box which contains a tube of toothpaste, except that it will be literally one hundred million times larger in volume. In turn, the sports arena will have plastic seats painted in pastel colors, sky-blue, orange-pink, dead yellow. There will be a great deal of fluorescent lighting, an electronically operated scoreboard (which will break down frequently) and the acoustics will be particularly poor, as they invariably are in new auditoriums which have been designed to have good acoustics.

The new terminal will be underground. It will waste no space for high vaulted ceilings and monumental columns, it will look doubtless like the inside of a large airport. And one will feel the same subtle nausea coming into the city or waiting to depart from it that one feels now in such plastic catacombs as O'Hare's reception center in Chicago, at United or American Airlines in Idlewild, in the tunnels and ramps and blank gleaming corridors of Dallas' airport, which is probably one of the ten ugliest buildings in the world.

Now in the cities, an architectural plague is near upon us. For we have tried to settle the problem of slums by housing, and the void in education by new schools. So we have housing projects which look like prisons and prisons which look like hospitals which in turn look like schools, schools which look like luxury hotels, luxury hotels which seem to confuse themselves with airline terminals, and airline terminals which cannot be told apart from civic centers, and the civic centers look like factories. Even the new churches look like recreation centers at large ski resorts. One can no longer tell the purpose of a building by looking at its face. Modern buildings tend to look like call girls who came out of it intact except that their faces are a touch blank and the expression in their eyes is as lively as the tip on a filter cigarette.

Our modern architecture reminds me a little of cancer cells. Because the healthy cells of the lung have one appearance and those in the liver another. But if both are cancerous they tend to look a little more alike, they tend to look a little less like anything very definite.

Definition has a value. If an experience is precise, one can know a little more of what is happening to oneself. It is in those marriages and love affairs which are neither good nor bad, not quite interesting nor altogether awful that anxiety flows like a muddy river. It is in those housing projects which look like prisons that juvenile delinquency increases at a greater rate than it used to do in the slums.

Once I had the luck to have an argument with a United States Senator from New York. He was very proud of his Governor. What has Rockefeller done? I asked. What? cried the Senator. And the list came back. Education, roads, welfare, housing. But isn't it possible people can be happier living in slums than housing projects? I asked.

I might just as well have said to a devout Catholic that I thought all nuns should be violated. The Senator lost his temper. Listen, young man, went his theme, I grew up in a slum.

But then for years I too lived in a slum. I had a cold-water flat which was sixty feet long and varied in width from eight feet to eleven feet. I bought a stove and a refrigerator, and I spent two weeks putting in a sink and a bathtub and two gas heaters. The plaster was cracked and continued to develop its character as I lived there. I was as happy in that cold-water flat as I've been anywhere else. It was mine. When I stay in a modern apartment house for a few days, I feel as if I'm getting the plague walking down those blank halls.

So I tried to argue with the Senator. What if a government were to take a fraction of the money it cost to dispossess and relocate slum tenants, demolish buildings, erect twenty stories of massed barracks, and instead give a thousand or two thousand dollars to each slum tenant to spend on materials for improving his apartment and to pay for the wages of whatever skilled labor he needed for small specific jobs like a new toilet, a new window, a fireplace, new wiring, wallpaper, or a new wall. The tenant would be loaned or rented the tools he needed, he would be expected to work along with his labor. If he took the first hundred dollars he received and drank it up, he would get no more money.

By the time such a project was done, every slum apartment in the city would be different. Some would be worse, some would be improved, a few would be beautiful. But each man would know at least whether he wished to improve his home, or truly didn't care. And that might be better than moving into a scientifically allotted living space halfway between a hospital and a prison.

For the housing projects radiate depression in two directions. The people who live in them are deadened by receiving a gift which has no beauty. The people who go past the housing projects in their automobiles are gloomy for an instant, because the future, or that part of the future we sense in our architecture, is telling us that the powers who erected these buildings expect us to become more like one another as the years go by.

The conservatives cry out that the welfare state will reduce us to a low and dull common denominator. And indeed it will unless the welfare which reaches the poor can reach them directly in such a way that they can use their own hands to change their own life. What do you say, Senator Goldwater? Do you think the government could afford the funds to give a man who lives in a slum some money for his hammer and nails and a carpenter to work along with him, or do you think the housing projects ought to continue to be built, but only by private funds (somewhat higher rents), and no government interference? Just revenue for large real-estate interests and huge architectural firms who design edifices which reveal no more than the internal structure of a ten-million-dollar bill.

The Big Bite—August, 1963

Some of you will remember that the column for the May issue talked about the approaching destruction of Pennsylvania Station and the plague of modern architecture, a plague which sits like a plastic embodiment of cancer over our suburbs, office buildings, schools, prisons, factories, churches, hotels, motels, and airline terminals. A fair number of letters came in for that column, and I would like to quote from part of one:

> I'm curious about something. Why is it that [some] people have such strong dislike for a form of architecture which [other] people are able not only to accept, but to accept as positive values in our society—goals to try to achieve? My husband's answer is that nobody really likes the current building trend, but that few people think about it enough to define their own emotions. But I can't accept that as a full answer. [The fact remains] that some people react with... aversion to modern architecture... others... value it. Do you have an answer?

I think I do. But it rests on a premise most of you may find intolerable. The best short poem of the twentieth century, I would think, is Yeats' *The Second Coming*, which goes, in part:

> Things fall apart; the centre cannot hold;
> Mere anarchy is loosed upon the world,
> The blood-dimmed tide is loosed, and everywhere
> The ceremony of innocence is drowned;
> The best lack all conviction, while the worst
> Are full of passionate intensity.
>
> ...Somewhere in sands of the desert
> A shape with lion body and the head of a man,
> A gaze blank and pitiless as the sun,
> Is moving its slow thighs....

and ends:

> ...What rough beast, its hour come round at last,
> Slouches towards Bethlehem to be born?

That rough beast is a shapeless force, an obdurate emptiness, an annihilation of possibilities. It is totalitarianism: that totalitarianism which has haunted the twentieth century, haunted the efforts of intellectuals to define it, of politicians to withstand it, and of rebels to find a field of war where it could be given battle. Amoeboid, insidious, totalitarianism came close to conquering the world twenty years ago. In that first large upheaval the Nazis sang of blood and the deep roots of blood and then proceeded to show their respect for the roots of blood by annihilating their millions through the suffocations of the gas chamber. No wilder primitive song was ever sung by a modern power, no more cowardly way of exercising a collective will has been yet encountered in history. The Nazis came to power by suggesting they would return Germany to the primitive secrets of her barbaric age, and then proceeded to destroy the essential intuition of the primitive, the umbilical idea that death and the appropriate totems of burial are as essential to life as life itself.

That first huge wave of totalitarianism was like a tide which moved in two directions at once. It broke upon the incompatible military force of Russia and of America. But it was an ocean of plague. It contaminated whatever it touched. If Russia had been racing into totalitarianism before the war, it was pervasively totalitarian after the war, in the last half-mad years of Stalin's court. And America was altered from a nation of venture, exploitation, bigotry, initiative, strife, social justice and social injustice, into a vast central swamp of tasteless toneless authority whose dependable heroes were drawn from FBI men, doctors, television entertainers, corporation executives, and athletes who could cooperate with public-relations men. The creative mind gave way to the authoritative mind, the expert took over from the small businessman, the labor executive replaced the trade-union organizer, and that arbiter of morals, the novelist, was replaced by the psychoanalyst. Mental health had come to America. And cancer with it. The country had a collective odor which was reminiscent of a potato left to molder in a plastic box.

That period began with Truman and was continued by Eisenhower. It came to an historic fork with Kennedy's administration. America was faced with going back to its existential beginnings, its frontier psychology, where the future is unknown and one discovers the truth of the present by accepting the risks of the present; or America could continue to go on in its search for totalitarian security. It is characteristic of the President's major vice that he chose to go in both directions at once. But then his character contains a similar paradox. He is on the one hand possessed of personal bravery, some wit, some style, an aristocratic taste for variety. He is a consummate politician, and has a potentially dictatorial nose for the manipulation of newspapers and television. He is a hero. And yet he is a void. His mind seems never to have been seduced by a new idea. He is the embodiment of the American void, that great yawning empty American mind which cannot bear any question which takes longer than ten seconds to answer. Given his virtues, suffering his huge vice, his emptiness, his human emptiness, we have moved as a nation, under his regime, deeper into totalitarianism, far deeper than his predecessors could have dreamed, and have been granted (by the cavalier style of his personal life and the wistfulness of his appreciation for the arts) the possible beginnings of a Resistance to the American totalitarianism.

But first one must recognize the features of the plague. If it appeared first in Nazi Germany as a political juggernaut, and in the Soviet Union as a psychotization of ideology, totalitarianism has slipped into America with no specific political face. There are liberals who are totalitarian, and conservatives, radicals, rightists, fanatics, hordes of the well-adjusted. Totalitarianism has come to America with no concentration camps and no need for them, no political parties and no desire for new parties, no, totalitarianism has slipped into the body cells and psyche of each of us. It has been transported, modified, codified, and inserted into each of us by way of the popular arts, the social crafts, the political crafts, and the corporate techniques. It sits in the image of the commercials on television which use phallic and vaginal symbols to sell products which are otherwise useless for sex, it is heard in the jargon of educators, in the synthetic continuums of prose with which public-relations men learn to enclose the sense and smell of an event, it resides in the taste of frozen food, the pharmaceutical odor of tranquilizers, the planned obsolescence of automobiles, the lack of workmanship in the mass, it lives in the boredom of a good mind, in the sexual excess of lovers who love each other into apathy, it is the livid passion which takes us to sleeping pills, the mechanical action in every household appliance which breaks too soon, it vibrates in the sound of an air conditioner or the flicker of fluorescent lighting. And it proliferates in that new architecture which rests like an incubus upon the American landscape, that new architecture which cannot be called modern because it is not architecture but opposed to architecture. Modern architecture began with the desire to use the building materials of the twentieth century—steel, glass, reinforced concrete—and such techniques as cantilevered structure to increase the sculptural beauty of buildings while enlarging their function. It was the first art to be engulfed by the totalitarians who distorted the search of modern architecture for simplicity, and converted it to monotony. The essence of totalitarianism is that it beheads. It beheads individuality, variety, dissent, extreme possibility, romantic faith, it blinds vision, deadens instinct, it obliterates the past. Since it is also irrational, it puts up buildings with flat roofs and huge expanses of glass in northern climates and then suffocates the inhabitants with super-heating systems while the flat roof leaks under a weight of snow. Since totalitarianism is a cancer within the body of history, it obliterates distinctions. It makes factories look like college campuses or mental hospitals, where once factories had the specific beauty of revealing their huge and sometimes brutal function—beauty cannot exist without revelation, nor man maybe without beauty. It makes the new buildings on college campuses look like factories. It depresses the average American with the unconscious recognition that he is installed in a gelatin of totalitarian environment which is bound to deaden his most individual efforts. This new architecture, this totalitarian architecture, destroys the past. There is no trace of the forms which lived in the centuries before us, none of their arrogance, their privilege, their aspiration, their canniness, their creations, their vulgarities. We are left with less and less sense of the lives of men and women who came before us. So we are less able to judge the sheer psychotic values of the present: overkill, fallout shelters, and adjurations by the President to drink a glass of milk each day.

Totalitarianism came to birth at the moment man turned incapable of facing back into the accumulated wrath and horror of his historic past. We sink into cancer after we have gorged on all the medicines which cheated all the diseases we have fled in our life, we sink into cancer when the organs, deadened by chemical rescues manufactured outside the body, became too biologically muddled to dominate their cells. Departing from the function of the separate organs, cancer cells grow to look like one another. So, too, as society bogs into hypocrisies so elaborate they can no longer be traced, then do our buildings, those palpable artifacts of social cells, come to look like one another and cease to function with the art, beauty, and sometimes mysterious proportion of the past.

I can try to answer the lady who wrote the letter now: people who admire the new architecture find it of value because it obliterates the past. They are sufficiently totalitarian to wish to avoid the consequences of the past. Which of course is not to say that they see themselves as totalitarian. The totalitarian passion is an unconscious one. Which liberal fighting for bigger housing and additional cubic feet of air space in elementary schools does not see himself as a benefactor? Can he comprehend that the somewhat clammy pleasure he obtains from looking at the completion of the new school—that architectural horror!—is a reflection of a buried and ugly pleasure, a totalitarian glee that the Gothic knots and Romanesque oppressions which entered his psyche through the schoolhouses of his youth have now been excised. But those architectural wounds, those forms from his childhood not only shamed him and scored him, but marked upon him as well a wound from culture itself—its buried message of the cruelty and horror which were rooted in the majesties of the past. Now the flat surfaces, blank ornamentation and pastel colors of the new schoolhouses will maroon his children in an endless hallway of the present. A school is an arena to a child. Let it look like what it should be, mysterious, exciting, even gladiatorial, rather than a musical comedy's notion of a reception center for war brides. The totalitarian impulse not only washes away distinctions but looks for a style in buildings, in clothing, and in the ornamentations of tools, appliances, and daily objects which will diminish one's sense of function, and reduce one's sense of reality by reducing to the leaden formulations of jargon such emotions as awe, dread, beauty, pity, terror, calm, horror, and harmony. By dislocating us from the most powerful emotions of reality, totalitarianism leaves us further isolated in the empty landscapes of psychosis, precisely that inner landscape of void and dread which we flee by turning to totalitarian styles of life. The totalitarian liberal looks for new schools and more desks; the real (if vanishing) liberal looks for better books, more difficult books to force upon the curriculum. A high school can survive in a converted cow barn if the seniors are encouraged to read *Studs Lonigan* the same week they are handed *The Cardinal* or *The Seven Storey Mountain*.

Yes, the people who admire the new architecture are unconsciously totalitarian. They are looking to eject into their environment and landscape the same deadness and monotony life has put into them. A vast deadness and a huge monotony, a nausea without spasm, has been part of the profit of American life in the last fifteen years—we will pay in the next fifteen as this living death is disgorged into the buildings our totalitarian managers will manage to erect for us. The landscape of America will be stolen for half a century if a Resistance does not form. Indeed it may be stolen forever if we are not sufficiently courageous to enter the depression of contemplating what we have already lost and what we have yet to lose.

DWIGHT MACDONALD

Trotsky, Orwell, and Socialism

In the mid-thirties, two very different political thinkers wrote two very different books. During 1935, when he was in exile in France and then in Norway, Leon Trotsky kept a diary, which has now been published by the Harvard University Press. At about the same time, George Orwell wrote *The Road to Wigan Pier*, which has now been republished by Harcourt, Brace. Orwell and Trotsky were antithetical political types—the British empiricist versus the Russian-Jewish ideologue. Trotsky applied a consistent and taken-for-granted doctrine to each new situation, showing the greatest ingenuity in each application but never modifying the basic dogma. Orwell, a trueborn Englishman, had no talent for systematic thinking and, indeed, tended to regard over-all ideologies as either absurd or harmful, or both; he was always ready to abandon his most cherished beliefs if he came to the conclusion that they no longer "worked." Both were political moralists, but how differently! Orwell's code was a simple one, based on truth and "decency"; he was important—and original—because he insisted on applying that code to his own socialist comrades as well as to the class enemy. Trotsky's code was also simple, but the reverse of Orwell's; his was a class morality (more accurately, a party morality—the tendency to confuse one's own party with the proletariat seems to be endemic in Marxism), and truth and decency were relative terms, depending on the class-party interests involved. The left-wing politics of our time have been played out between the extremes represented by Trotsky and Orwell.

Trotsky's diary is brief (158 pages, plus 38 pages of editorial notes) and perfunctory. It can't be compared for biographical interest to his *My Life,* unfortunately long out of print. The first entry suggests what's wrong:

February 7, 1935: The diary is not a literary form I am especially fond of.... Lassalle wrote once that he would gladly leave unwritten what he *knew* if only he could accomplish at least a part of what he felt able to *do.* Any revolutionary would feel the same way. But one has to take the situation as it is. For the very reason that it fell to my lot to take part in greater events, my past now cuts me off from chances for action. I am reduced to interpreting events and trying to foresee their future course. At least this occupation is more satisfying than mere passive reading.

The crude contrast between knowing and doing, the notion of being "reduced" to interpreting events, the reference to "mere passive reading"—such is not the temper of the successful diarist. Still, the book is revealing. I was not prepared for the depth of Trotsky's feeling for his wife, Natalia—the love, gratitude, and admiration he expresses again and again. I was prepared for the rigidity of mind. Not that there aren't some very good things—after all, it's Trotsky. Such as his comment on the Norwegian socialists: "The war and the October Revolution, the upheavals of Fascism, have passed them by without a trace.... For them the future holds hot and cold showers." (Though, come to think of it, the Norwegians showed very different stuff once they *were* involved with war and fascism a few years later.) Or a lapidary note: "The radio reminds one how broad and varied life is and at the same time gives an extremely economical and compact expression to this variety. In short, it is an instrument perfectly suited to a prison." There are a few glints of self-awareness, such as his realization that his diary had taken a political-literary rather than a personal form. "And could it actually be otherwise? For politics and literature constitute in essence the content of my personal life. I need only take pen in hand and my thoughts of their own accord arrange themselves for *public* exposition.... You can't alter this, especially at fifty-five years of age."

But such flashes are rare. For all its vigor, Trotsky's mind was strait-jacketed by Marxism. "There is no creature more disgusting than a petty-bourgeois engaged in primary accumulation," he complains, apropos of his neighbors in provincial France. "I have never had the opportunity to observe this type as closely as I do now." Yet he feels no need to add any details; it is enough to classify the specimen in the Marxian catalogue. Nor is the political analysis any more perceptive. Is there a psychosociological law that once a man has tasted supreme power, he is doomed never to doubt his ideas again? Like Napoleon on St. Helena, Trotsky in exile was sure he still knew all the answers:

> I imagine an old doctor, devoid of neither education nor experience, who day after day has to watch quacks and charlatans doctor to death a person dear to him, knowing that this person could be certainly cured if only the elementary rules of medicine were observed. That would approximately be the way I feel as I watch the criminal work of the "leaders" of the French proletariat. Conceit? No, a deep and indestructible conviction.

But the trouble was precisely that his conviction *was* indestructible. One might think that after six years of reflection in exile he could have had doubts. He might have realized, for example, that his own prophecy, long before the October Revolution, about the totalitarian drift of Lenin's organizational methods had been fulfilled by Stalin, wherefore his own attempt to compete with Stalin as a pure Bolshevik, between 1924 and 1928, had been a mistake; after all, Stalin controlled the Party bureaucracy. And he might have realized that he and Lenin should have compromised with the Kronstadt sailors in 1921 instead of crushing them with troops led by Trotsky. Or that the dispersal by force of the Constituent Assembly, the reduction of the popular soviets to impotence, the outlawing of Shliapnikov's Workers' Opposition faction in the Party, and other such policies of Lenin and himself had taken power from the people and given it to the Party bureaucracy, and so had prepared the road for Stalin. Or, finally, that his whole estimate of Stalin had been wrong—he had seen Stalin as a man of the right and had worried about his restoring capitalism, but the danger lay in just the other direction. Once Stalin had sent Trotsky into foreign exile in 1929, he adopted Trotsky's own "Left" program of industrialization and agricultural collectivization, which was just what he needed to get the workers and the peasants under totalitarian control.

However, Trotsky resisted all such heretical thoughts; his Leninist convictions remained, to the end, "deep and indestructible." In twelve years of exile, he only once, as far as I recall, recognized even the possibility that Leninist Marxism might have to be revised—in his "The U.S.S.R. in War," in *The New International* for November, 1939. He used his enforced leisure, instead, in a desperate effort to fit an increasingly recalcitrant reality into his outworn formulae. He defended all the major actions of himself and Lenin from 1917 to 1923, including Kronstadt; he reached no more brilliant conclusion about Stalin's Russia than that it was "a degenerated workers' state" and therefore must be "supported," and he even justified the Russian invasion of Finland in 1939 on the ground that the Red Army was still a revolutionary force (slightly degenerated, chipped, and shopworn) that was liberating the Finnish masses from their bourgeois exploiters. (One of the many awkwardnesses of this position was that the Finnish masses, to a man, woman, and dog, fled from their liberators back into territory still held by Baron Mannerheim and their class enemies, leaving nobody to be freed from the shackles of capitalism.) He was quite willing to split the most important group of his adherents, the American Trotskyites, on this issue, and he denounced us with all the old papal fervor as "petty-bourgeois capitulators" when we couldn't see any difference in principle between Stalin's Russia invading Finland and Hitler's Germany invading Poland.

Trotsky's career poses an enigma. How, on the one hand, could the man of action who had important roles in both the 1905 and the 1917 Russian revolutions and who organized and led to victory the Red Army, the man who was a world-historical figure, be so easily deposed by the unknown Stalin? And, on the other hand, how explain the sterility and timidity of thought, after 1928, of the daring intellectual who, except for Lenin, was the only major leader to see that power could be taken and held by the Bolsheviks in 1917? Trotsky was a dazzling combination of the intellectual and the man of action, but he was not a genius; he was enormously able but he was not inspired, and the situations, practical or ideological, that he had to meet after Lenin's death were so novel and so extreme that they could be mastered only by a genius; that is, someone who was willing to violate all the rules and theories and principles. Stalin and Hitler were such, for all their mediocrtiy of character and intellect compared to the superlative Trotsky. I think it is also possible that Trotsky's unusual combination of talents was often a disadvantage. His intellectuality sometimes interfered with his effectiveness in action, as when he tried to fight Stalin, of all people, on principles (and mistaken principles, at that), while his practicality was too narrowly practical (intellectuals tend to go to extremes), so that he tried to solve political problems by administrative measures. A curious instance of the latter failure was his proposal for dealing with low productivity in the early years of the revolution by organizing "labor battalions" under quasi-military discipline—a solution that Lenin, a genius of the practical, rejected not on any principled grounds but simply because he saw it was politically impossible.*

"The depth and strength of a human character are defined by its moral *reserves*," Trotsky wrote in his diary on April 5, 1935. "People reveal themselves completely only when they are thrown out of the customary conditions of their life, for only then do they have to fall back on their reserves. N. and I have been together for almost thirty-three years (a third of a century!), and in tragic hours I am always amazed at the reserves of her character." Exile revealed in him plenty of certain kinds of moral reserves—courage,

*(1971) The close reader may have noted that in the preceding review of Sukhanov's memoirs, I called Trotsky "one of the two indisputable geniuses who were pushed to the top by the events of 1917." Let me herewith recant. Though not as to the other one, Lenin—if only he had *not* been a genius!

pride, faith—but also a startling deficiency in intellectual reserves and an almost complete lack of a quality that is partly moral and partly intellectual; namely, objectivity. He maintains a double standard throughout his diary, using one set of values for his side and another for the enemy. He makes great sport of bourgeois politicians for their fine phrases, yet he writes sentences like "In the blood of wars and revolts a new generation will rise, worthy of the epoch and its tasks." On page 24 he says, "In view of the prolonged decline in the international revolution, the victory of the bureaucracy—and consequently of Stalin—was foreordained." But eight pages later he refuses this alibi to Léon Blum, dismissing his excuse for not bringing about a revolution ("conditions were not yet ripe for socialization") as a "mechanistic, fatalistic conception." He points out that the October Revolution, after all, did take place, adding contemptuously, "Those parliamentary dilettantes have learned *nothing*." (Blum might have retorted that the degeneration of the October Revolution proved that conditions in Russia were not ripe for socialism.)

But the most extraordinary instance of double-standard thinking (and feeling) in the diary is implicit in the long entry of April ninth on the execution of the Czar and his family at Ekaterinburg. Trotsky reveals that the massacre was ordered by Lenin from Moscow. He notes that certain liberals had tried to exculpate Lenin by claiming that the executions were carried out by the local Bolsheviks on their own. Similarly, the present regime in Russia recently took pains to deny the story that Lenin had spared the life of Dora Kaplan, the young Social Revolutionary who had seriously wounded him in 1918. Mercy is a bourgeois weakness, it would seem, and Lenin was a sound Bolshevik.

Therefore, Trotsky not only takes the trouble to record Lenin's complicity in Ekaterinburg but also goes on to justify it: "The decision was not only expedient but necessary. The severity of this summary justice showed the world that we would continue to fight on mercilessly, stopping at nothing. The execution of the Czar's family was needed not only in order to frighten, horrify, and dishearten the enemy, but also in order to shake up our own ranks, to show them that there was no turning back, that ahead lay either complete victory or complete ruin." (So Hitler used Buchenwald and Dachau to frighten the enemy and to involve the Germans in blood guilt—"there was no turning back.") This entry is sandwiched in between many entries revealing Trotsky's anxiety about the fate of his son Seryozha, a nonpolitical engineer who had just been arrested by Stalin simply because Trotsky was his father. Trotsky thinks this is barbarous, which it was, and refers to Seryozha as "an innocent bystander," which he was, but it doesn't occur to him that the late Czar might have considered his fourteen-year-old son another innocent bystander, not to mention his four young daughters and the family servants. Trotsky would undoubtedly have been horrified if Stalin had justified Seryozha's imprisonment—and execution a year later—with the same *raison d'état* he thinks justified Ekaterinburg.* The next day he explains why Lenin had decided to shoot the Czar and his family without trial: "Under judicial procedures, of course, execution of the family would have been impossible." So, naturally, there was no alternative (except not to shoot them). Immediately after this, he writes, "No news about Seryozha." The unconsciousness of all this is amazing. One suspects that it never occurred to the diarist that the reason he thought about the fate of the Czar's family just then was his anxiety about his own son. For if he had been conscious of this, he would have been a different, and bigger, person, and he might not have been so addicted to the double standard.

The first half of George Orwell's *The Road to Wigan Pier* describes the life of the miners and the unemployed in Lancashire and Yorkshire in the mid-thirties. It is the best sociological reporting I know. The trouble with most such works—I am thinking of classics like Engels' *The Condition of the Working Classes in England in 1844*, Mayhew's volumes on the London poor, the Russell Sage Foun-

*(1971) Which was that if the Romanov, or the Trotsky, blood line was not completely extirpated down to infants, "pretenders" might arise later. (Cf. *Macbeth*.) But the servants were hardly a dynastic threat.

dation's *Pittsburgh Survey*, of 1909, and the Lynds' *Middletown* books—is that the writers are at a distance from their subjects in two ways. They exclude their own reactions, because of a mistaken idea of scientific objectivity—mistaken because the study of human behavior cannot, by its very nature, be scientific. And they maintain a psychological distance; they conscientiously spend much time in "the field," but it is always "the field." George Orwell, however, lived the life of the people he wrote about. When the Left Book Club commissioned him to do the volume, he simply went to Wigan and took a room in a cheap lodging house. He was no neophyte. He had already lived at the bottom—and not as a sociological "observer" but as a participant, a penniless tramp who survived on bread and tea between dishwashing jobs—and had written a remarkable book about it, *Down and Out in Paris and London*. What is even more notable about Orwell's safaris into lower-class life is that, while immersing himself in the most concrete, physical way, he never ceased to judge it by his own personal standards. The romanticism of poverty is a luxury idea, possible only to slummers from above, like Rousseau's concept of the noble savage; the poor are too busy keeping alive to feel romantic or, except occasionally, to realize fully the horror of their lives. Rarely does an observer come along who is neither a tourist nor a detached sociologist and who is able to submerge himself in the actual existence on the bottom without losing his bearings. Such was Jack London when he wrote *The People of the Abyss*, after living among the London poor at the turn of the century. Such was Simone Weil, who in the thirties worked for two years in the Renault and other factories in Paris and who has left us some explicit and disturbing commentaries in two of her books: *The Need for Roots* and *Factory Work*. And such was Orwell.

Perhaps the chief virtue of his reporting is that he combines indignation with specificity, as in his description of the boarding-house table:

> I never saw this table completely uncovered, but I saw its various wrappings at different times. At the bottom there was a layer of old

newspapers stained by Worcester sauce; above that a sheet of sticky white oilcloth; above that a green serge cloth; above that a coarse linen cloth, never changed and seldom taken off. Generally the crumbs from breakfast were still on the table at supper. I used to get to know individual crumbs by sight and watch their progress up and down the table from day to day.

Or the vignettes of two subscription-agents who were fellow lodgers:

The newspapers engage poor desperate wretches, out-of-work clerks and commercial travellers and the like, who for a while make frantic efforts and keep their sales up to the minimum; then as the deadly work wears them down they are sacked and fresh men are taken on. I got to know two who were employed by one of the more notorious weeklies. [What sociologist could permit himself the luxury of that "notorious," so emotional, so unscientific, so inspiriting!] Both of them were middle-aged men with families to support, and one of them was a grandfather. They were on their feet ten hours a day, "working" their appointed streets, and then busy late into the night filling in blank forms. . . . The fat one, the grandfather, used to fall asleep with his head on a pile of forms for some swindle their paper was running. . . . Neither of them could afford the pound a week which the Brookers charged for full board. They used to pay a small sum for their beds and make shamefaced meals in a corner of the kitchen off bacon and bread-and-margarine which they stored in their suitcases.

This kind of emotional identification with the people he lives among sometimes reaches an intensity that lights up the horror and injustice of a class society. Consider this glimpse as his train slowly trundles by "row after row of little grey slum houses":

At the back of one of the houses a young woman was kneeling on the stones, poking a stick up the leaden wastepipe which ran from the sink inside and which I suppose was blocked. I had time to see everything about her—her sacking apron, her clumsy clogs, her arms reddened by the cold. She looked up as the train passed, and

I was almost near enough to catch her eye. She had a round pale face, the usual exhausted face of the slum girl who is twenty-five and looks forty, thanks to miscarriages and drudgery; and it wore, for the second in which I saw it, the most desolate, hopeless expression I have ever seen. It struck me then that we are mistaken when we say that "It isn't the same for them as it would be for us," and that people bred in the slums can imagine nothing but the slums. For what I saw in her face was not the ignorant suffering of an animal. She knew well enough what was happening to her—understood as well as I did how dreadful a destiny it was to be kneeling there in the bitter cold, on the slimy stones of a slum backyard, poking a stick up a foul drainpipe.

There is a curiously similar passage in Trotsky's diary for April 27. Walking with Natalia "in a drizzling rain," he meets a young working-class woman, "in the very last stages of pregnancy," struggling along with a baby in her arms, pulling a goat with a kid, and trying to control a girl of two or three. The goat keeps trying to browse, the kid keeps getting tangled in the underbrush, and the little girl "would lag behind or run ahead." When he and Natalia turn back, they meet the group again: "They were slowly continuing their advance toward the village. In the still fresh face of the woman there was submission and patience. She was probably Spanish or Italian, perhaps even Polish—there are quite a few foreign working-class families here." Trotsky is not insensitive to the young mother's plight—this is one of the few glimpses his diary gives us of everyday life—but it doesn't occur to him to talk with her ("She was probably Spanish or Italian"). Unlike Orwell, who felt a compulsion that was almost neurotic (please note the "almost") to share the life of the masses, Trotsky approached the masses from above, with the abstract, generalizing view of the intellectual or with the utilitarian purpose of the man of action. When he actually ran into one of them on a country road, he was at a loss, for all his ideological sympathy. There may be some significance in the contrasting descriptions of the two young women's expressions—Orwell saw a consciousness of degradation, Trotsky merely "submission and patience."

Perhaps each saw what he was looking for. Trotsky, though he looked at the masses from above with the most benevolent intentions, still looked from above; the Marxian revolutionary and the social worker are not so far apart. But Orwell, looking up from below, in his second chapter makes it clear just how unbelievably difficult work in a mine is by no more esoteric a device than describing the effect on his own muscles of simply getting to the working face. He notes that when a miner leaves the elevator that takes him down into the mine, he must go through one to three miles of twisting corridors, nearly always stooping and sometimes crawling. He notes that the miner is not paid for this journey, which may take an hour each way, the fiction being that it is the same as the office worker's journey to work on the bus. (Portal-to-portal pay has been won by our own United Mine Workers, although the socialized mines of England have not got around to giving it.) This concern for the trivia of working-class life, which aren't so trivial if you are a worker, distinguishes Orwell's reporting. Thus, it does not escape him that old miners don't get their pension checks in the mail but must report once a week to the colliery office, waiting in line for hours and wasting an afternoon—not to mention the sixpence for bus fare, a trifling sum unless one measures one's income in six-pences.

> It is very different for a member of the bourgeoisie, even such a down-at-heel member as I am. Even when I am on the verge of starvation I have certain rights attaching to my bourgeois status. I do not earn much more than a miner earns, but I do at least get it paid into my bank in a gentlemanly manner.... This business of petty inconvenience and indignity, of being kept waiting about, of having to do everything at other people's convenience, is inherent in working-class life. A thousand influences constantly press a working man down into a *passive* rôle. He does not act, he is acted upon. He feels himself the slave of mysterious authority and has a firm conviction that "they" will never allow him to do this, that, and the other.

The second half of *The Road to Wigan Pier* is a general discussion of socialism that, at first glance, seems to have nothing to do with the first half but that, on second glance, is related to it by the sensitivity to class revealed in the foregoing quotation. Orwell begins this half, characteristically, with a painfully honest socio-biography that might be titled *Up from Snobbery*. He spares himself nothing. "Here you come to the real secret of class distinctions in the West," he writes, "the real reason why a European of bourgeois upbringing, even when he calls himself a Communist, cannot without a hard effort think of a working man as his equal. It is summed up in four frightful words which people nowadays are chary of uttering, but which were bandied about quite freely in my childhood. The words were: *'The lower classes smell.'*" Frightful words, certainly, and brave words for a socialist, but perhaps they tell us more about Orwell than about class distinctions. The point is not whether the lower classes smell—after all, everybody smells, according to our advertising—but why this is so important to him. (Orwell concludes, with his usual quiet reasonableness, that they don't smell intrinsically but do extrinsically, because they have less access to baths and laundering; all this should be put in the past tense now, considering the equalizing of living standards that has taken place in the last twenty years here and in England, and perhaps the very term "the lower classes" is happily obsolescent.) An interesting monograph could be written on "Olfactory Perceptions in the Writings of George Orwell," or, for the Luce papers, "Orwell & Smell." This is the most primitive and unanswerable of the senses—one can say "You sounded (or looked) bad" but not "You smelled bad"—and references to it are curiously frequent in Orwell's writings, as in his famous phrase about "the smelly little orthodoxies of the Left." I hazard that these references are merely the most obvious expression of a penchant for the painful, the demeaning, and the repulsive that runs through his work, from the crimson birthmark that disfigures the face of the protagonist of *Burmese Days* to the intimate dwelling on torture at the end of *1984*. In short, there is something masochistic about Orwell's personality, for all the moral courage and the penetration of his political thought, and there's no use blinking it (as he himself might have written). For he, too, had a double standard, though just the reverse of Trotsky's—he was tougher on himself and his own side than he was on the class enemy.

A good deal of this second half is devoted to an attempt to explain why socialism had not made more progress among the British masses. He blames the situation mostly on the socialists, whom he sees as health cranks, epicene pacifists, and, in general, "mingy little beasts." The rhetoric of abuse with which he overwhelms his comrades is more exuberant than anything he says about the bourgeoisie: "Socialism, *in the form in which it is now presented*, appeals chiefly to unsatisfactory or even inhuman types . . . that dreary tribe of high-minded women and sandal-wearers and bearded fruit-juice drinkers who come flocking toward the smell of 'progress' like bluebottles to a dead cat . . . the intellectual, tract-writing type of Socialist, with his pullover, his fuzzy hair, and his Marxian quotation. . . . The worst advertisement for Socialism is its adherents." Even to one who, like myself, no longer agrees that "Socialism is such elementary common sense," and even granting that Orwell, who had actually lived with the lower classes, had some right to be impatient with the middle-class romantics who preached socialism to "the masses" they knew nothing about, the abuse seems overdone.

However, it is better to turn the double standard against one's own side than against one's enemies, if the choice must be made, since it leads to more understanding. It is true that Orwell, like almost all political writers in the thirties, when Marxism permeated the air with illusions of omniscience, was often too quick on the draw with a prediction, as when he writes, "Of course it is obvious now that the upper middle class is done for." (In modern English prose, one puts in "of course" and "obvious" when the matter is not at all obvious, just as "undoubtedly" indicates doubt.) Or: "Under the capitalist system, in order that England may live in comparative comfort, a hundred million Indians must live on the verge of starvation—an evil state of affairs, but you acquiesce in it every time you step into a taxi or eat a plate of strawberries and cream." The British upper middle class is still very much with us, and although India has been freed, the British standard of living is higher than before,* and there are still lots of taxis and strawberries around. But while Trotsky was, so to speak, systematically wrong, much of Orwell is still fresh and to the point: his criticism of the socialist romanticism about industrial progress, for example, and his still disregarded advice that it is the exploited middle classes the socialists should try to recruit, and his debunking of the "liblab" (Liberal-Labour) cant idealizing the working class and the parallel cant of the proletarian intellectual, from the communists to D. H. Lawrence with his mystique of the potent gamekeeper and the eunuch landlord. He is also still to the point when he objects that modern socialists, bemused by Marx's historical materialism and by Stalin's Five-Year Plans, have forgotten the great moral goals, like Justice and Liberty, that have historically inspired their movement, and when he insists, with a side glance at the Communists, that "the real Socialist is one who wishes . . . to see tyranny overthrown."

Somebody at Harcourt, Brace had the happy idea of reprinting Victor Gollancz's Foreword to the original edition in 1937. "This Foreword is addressed to members of the Left Book Club (to whom *The Road to Wigan Pier* is being sent as the March Choice), and to them alone," it begins. "Members of the general public are asked to ignore it." Poor Mr. Gollancz, who had founded the Club earlier that year—with John Strachey and the late Harold Laski—was in a tough spot. The Club had commissioned Orwell to do a study of the unemployed in the North of England. He had done a masterly job, exactly what the Club had hoped for, but then, after exposing the horrors of capitalism, he had characteristically insisted on exposing the horrors of socialism. To their credit, the Messrs. Gollancz, Strachey, and Laski, although then (in those long-ago days) ardent Popular Fronters and sympathizers with the Soviet Union,

---

*(1974) Written in 1959, the good old days before the Tory-Labour stalemate became a mutual and national suicide pact.

printed the book as Orwell wrote it. (The British sense of fair play and open discussion has rarely been more agreeably demonstrated; one cannot imagine their American opposite numbers at the time acting so.) But the 38,000 members of the Left Book Club, hungry (and trusting) sheep looking up to be fed, had at least to be warned. British fair play is, after all, a human virtue, not an angelic one. So Mr. Gollancz, in the most reasonable and friendly style, defuses as many of Orwell's booby traps as he can. Sometimes he is acute ("Mr. Orwell calls himself a 'half-intellectual,' but the truth is that he is at one and the same time an extreme intellectual and a violent anti-intellectual"), sometimes he is persuasive (his defense of vegetarians, pacifists, and feminists), and sometimes he is absurd, as when he complains that "He even commits the curious indiscretion of referring to Russian commissars as 'half-gramophones, half-gangsters.'" But, given his dilemma, he didn't do badly. And he did produce what is now a most interesting historical document.

Another interesting, if depressing, document is *Voices of Dissent* (Grove Press, 1959), an anthology of pieces from *Dissent*, which has been appearing quarterly since 1954. *Dissent* is undoubtedly (see preceding gloss on this word) the best left-wing political magazine we have, which makes it all the more depressing. (Perhaps I should note that "left wing" includes among its meanings "anti-communist," our Communists having been for many years, *pace* the late Senator McCarthy, neither socialists nor revolutionaries.) Irving Howe, who, with Lewis Coser, has been the mainspring of the editorial board, defines *Dissent*'s purpose as providing of "a forum for the discussion of the ideals and problems of democratic socialism." If this formula sounds a little dusty, so do most of the articles here reprinted. Not that *Dissent* has been doctrinaire. It has tried to live up to its name, and has printed a great variety of socialist thinkers, and even a few nonsocialists. The difficulty seems to be that the very idea of socialism is no longer interesting; it is at once banal and ambiguous. It would take another Marx, God forbid, to redefine in the light of modern experience either "socialism" or "democracy." Meanwhile, *Dissent* keeps the franchise open, and perhaps this isn't a bad thing. But why is there such a lack of the individual accent in these articles, why do Orwell and Trotsky sound like men, while so many of these articles sound like the product of thinking machines? Is it because socialism is no longer, pro or con, connected with our actual life? There is a mandarin quality about this book: the writers are serious, they are in admirable revolt against our society, but they somehow deal with things at a distance; they are professors of revolution, members of the socialist academy. The few sharper, more direct articles merely emphasize the gray tone of the collection. Howe's "Stevenson and the Intellectuals" is incisive political criticism. Norman Mailer's whirling, breathless, earnest "The White Negro" is cockeyed but imaginative. He subtitles it "Superficial Reflections on the Hipster," but they aren't at all superficial; they are much too deep. William L. Neumann's "Historians in an Age of Acquiescence" is good old-fashioned cultural muckraking. And Czeslaw Milosz's open letter to Picasso, though it is only three pages, makes an impact because it is *felt*; one has the impression he is saying something that makes a real difference to him as a writer, and not just holding up the by now rather tattered banner of Socialism. There are three or four other nonmandarin pieces—those by Nicola Chiaromonte, Paul Goodman, and Harvey Swados come to mind—but the general tone is definitely gray. And there are far too many sentences like "Folded in the center of capitalist dynamics Marx detected a stasis in which completed being embodied itself continually."*

*(1973) This is still about the state of expectation in which I approach reading (or postponing reading) *Dissent*, to which I have been a fickle subscriber for years.

CHARLES REMBAR

How Much Due Process
Is Due a President?

Approve of the Nixon administration: 24%
Disapprove of the Nixon administration: 63%
July 1974

There is confusion, a dangerous confusion, in our talk about impeachment. In the year or so that there has been public discussion of the subject—since we began to allow ourselves to utter the unutterable—most of the discussion has been cast in concepts borrowed from the criminal law. It is said the President is to be presumed innocent until he is proved guilty, and that the evidence must establish guilt beyond a reasonable doubt; it has even been argued that the documents bearing on the matter that the President is asked to produce should be sheltered by the privilege against self-incrimination. We talk as though Richard Nixon, the man and citizen, were on trial, rather than the conduct of his office.

This is error. Impeachment is no closer to a criminal trial than it is to an election. It is not an election, of course, despite the fact that Vice-President Ford, when he was a Congressman (either cynically, he being a proponent of impeachment at the time, or, more likely, thoughtlessly), declared that an impeachable offense is whatever Congress says it is. The definition of impeachable transgressions is not the subject of this piece, which deals, rather, with the standards according to which Congress should arrive at its decision on whether such transgressions have occurred. But procedure here, as nearly everywhere, is hardly less significant than substance.

Impeachment is a unique political mechanism created by our Constitution, a proceeding *sui generis*. It therefore ought to have its own procedural standards, appropriate to its constitutional purpose. Models and forms taken from other parts of our governmental system have a limited utility. It is a mistake to import wholesale into the Constitution's provisions for expulsion from federal office—provisions that vest responsibility for the matter in the legislative branch—concepts peculiar to the functioning of the judiciary.

The confusion is natural. There are several reasons for it, all related. One is that impeachment of a President is virtually unprecedented. The House has voted Articles of Impeachment only twelve times in our history, and only four times has impeachment resulted in removal. Only once has a President been involved, and, though the Senate vote was notoriously close, the charges against Andrew Johnson were ludicrous. He was accused of two "high crimes and misdemeanors." One was making speeches disrespectful of the Congress. The other was firing his Secretary of War, in violation of a statute designed by Congress to provoke a confrontation, a statute obviously unconstitutional.

The charges against President Nixon provide a shocking contrast. Whether or not they are true, and whether or not they will lead to an impeachment, we have been forced to think about the gravest accusations, short of treason, that can be lodged against a Chief Executive: obstruction of justice, bribery, deliberate failure to check excesses of his principal subordinates, violation of his Constitutional duty to "take care that the laws be faithfully executed," secret abuse of Executive power—in short, subversion of the Constitution. No matter how inured we may be to political immorality, all this—if true—is of a different order, and creates a sense of crisis. We naturally turn to precedents in a crisis; the past has banked its wisdom and it is foolish not to draw on it. But since there are no precedents actually in point, we make the error of reaching for precedents not in point. And since the abuses charged, whatever they technically may be, are crimes in that larger sense of the word we often use, we tend to look for guidance to the criminal law.

Then there is the odd mixture in our emotional attitudes toward the Presidency. From the earliest days of the Republic we have felt free to criticize, even to revile, our Presidents, yet we have never thoroughly shed our old-world feelings of allegiance to a ruler. George Washington was asked by some to accept a crown rather than an office, and that sort of homage has never altogether disappeared. We are reluctant to be regicides.

Finally—and this, I think, is the principal reason for the confusion—the idea of judicial trial is root-deep in our culture. Most of those at the Capitol are lawyers (two-thirds of the Senators, more than half the Representatives), but this is a minor factor. All of us are lawyers in a sense. Law is more than an implement of government, more than an operating institution. It is as much a part of our culture as morals, art, technology. And the center of this aspect of our culture is the adversary trial, the age-old, well-loved struggle in the courtroom. The adversary trial is the method by which Americans (and Englishmen; other legal systems differ) settle disputes among themselves, and between themselves and their government. All of us, whether or not we practice law, are educated in it, have thoughts about it, feel strongly on what is right and wrong in the conduct of a trial. We pit antagonists against each other—trial by battle has never died—and we want to see a fair fight. Each contesting individual has procedural rights and privileges, which are given extra dimension when he is accused of crime.

These ideas and feelings find expression, tersely and powerfully, in our Constitution, in the phrase "due process of law." We look upon due process, along with the First Amendment's guaranties, as the basis of our freedom. And we are familiar with its rudiments. When the litigation is civil, our property is at stake, or certain personal rights the law tends to treat as property (reputation, privacy, domestic claims). When the litigation is criminal, it is our liberty, our property again, or even (rarely now) our lives. They are not to be taken from us, by force of law, except according to the system; that is, by the adversary process our culture tells us is our due.

But these are not the things at stake when an official is impeached. What is at stake, on both sides of the matter, is the filling of an office—and, when the office is high enough, the welfare of a nation. Whatever "high crimes and misdemeanors" may mean, the procedural standards by which the test is made need not be, and should not be, the standards of the courtroom. There is no "case" in the courtroom sense. The people are deciding for themselves, through their elected representatives, whether the President ought to stay in office.

If the distinction seems remote, too technical and abstract, let me give a few examples of how it bears on concrete problems. "Presumption of innocence" and "proof beyond a reasonable doubt" have been cited, on behalf of the President, as much by his liberal opponents as those who vociferously support him. Our criminal procedures are based on the premise that it is better that many of the guilty should escape than that one innocent be punished. Hence the guilty have the benefit of rules designed to protect the innocent; felons have a license to take advantage of the inhibitions we put upon enforcement of the penal law. But the proceedings for impeachment and removal, set forth in specific sections of the Constitution, are not penal. It cannot be supposed that the Founding Fathers thought it better that many office-holders who betray their office should nevertheless stay in office than that one of them, perhaps misjudged, should be expelled. Removal from the White House is not a punishment; it is a protection of the Presidency, and a safeguard to the people, created by the Constitution. Hence there is no room for favoring presumptions, no requirement of overwhelming proof. The familiar principles of the criminal law would be pertinent if an official, having been impeached and removed from office, were later prosecuted for violation of the penal code. But in acting on impeachment, each Senator must vote the way the evidence points; he should not vote against removal because he thinks there is, say, one chance in five that the official has not committed the extreme offenses he is charged with.

The same holds for the privilege against self-incrimination. The privilege comes from the Fifth Amendment, which states that "No person . . . shall be compelled in any criminal case to be a witness against himself." The proceedings in the Senate are not a criminal case. Indeed, Article I, Section 3 of the Constitution draws a distinction between impeachment, whose effects are carefully limited to removal and disqualification, and any criminal case that may come afterwards, which these provisions expressly mention. Self-incrimination therefore cannot be a ground on which an official subject to impeachment can keep evidence out of the hands of Congress. In a subsequent criminal prosecution, it might be argued that the yielding of certain evidence in the course of an impeachment invalidates the prosecution. But the possibility that criminal offenses might for this reason go unpunished is hardly relevant. Vindictiveness has no place here. Compliance with the Constitution, and the need that public servants perform responsibly and not abuse their powers, are incomparably more important than whether an individual who has committed crime gets his just deserts.

The concepts of the criminal law are incongruous in impeachment, and analogies drawn from civil litigation are scarcely better. It has been suggested that the model for the Senate proceedings should be the kind of litigation in which the beneficiary of a trust complains of his trustee's actions. But the Constitutional nature of impeachment excludes mechanical adherence to any courtroom standards. There is grave distortion when we view impeachment in the mirror of our courtroom adversary system, and see it as a struggle between an individual intent on preserving something that he claims belongs to him and another who seeks to take it from him.

Consider the manner in which the proceedings are to be conducted. Should they be televised? The Supreme Court, dividing five-to-four, has held that televising a criminal trial denies due process. One of the reasons given was that the defendant would be subjected to unwarranted additional strain. At a criminal trial, the defendant must be present in the courtroom; in impeachment, the President has an option, and the likelihood is he will not be present in the Senate chamber. If he chooses to, he will have made a judgment that his appearance will help his cause, a benefit magnified by television. Another factor in the majority's decision was the jury trial tradition that jurors must be insulated from public opinion; the Justices were concerned about the effects of television on the jurors' independence. In impeachment proceedings, the Senators and Representatives cannot be cut off from the people. They will not be insensitive to public opinion, and that opinion ought to be as well-informed as possible, an end toward which television can be a mighty aid. There are other dangers in the broadcast of a jury trail that have no relevance to impeachment; there is not space to list them all. If we keep in mind that the national welfare is involved—and not, as in the courtroom, the welfare of an individual—the answer is quite clear: everything possible should be done to subject what goes on to the closest national scrutiny. For this purpose, it is fortunate that we have lately had the means to give the people first-hand knowledge, without journalistic intermediation.

Take another important matter: the way the evidence and the argument are presented. The adversary tradition can be useful; having the evidence offered, and arguments made, from opposing points of view may help to reach right judgment. But there is a crucial difference. The Senate has a set of rules adopted when Andrew Johnson was impeached. The House of Representatives selects a group of its members, called "managers," to present the case for removal. The President is represented by counsel. I would suggest, instead, that both sides of the issue be presented by the House. Those who voted for impeachment would select the managers for removal; those who voted against impeachment would select the managers opposed. Each group should be free to employ outside counsel. But, given the public interest on both sides of an impeachment, it is inappropriate that the case for keeping the officeholder in office should be made by his private counsel. If it is not a matter of preserving personal rights, there should be no personal attorney.

Then there is the question of the kind and amount of evidence.

Here again the judicial adversary system should not be closely followed. Courtroom rules of evidence were developed with a view to protecting juries against whole categories of proof deemed not reliable enough. When a case is tried before a judge without a jury, the rules of evidence are more flexible, and much less is excluded. Rules are, of course, abstractions, and can work badly in specific cases. Whatever their value for the generality of jury trials, they should not uncritically be taken out of context. Since the question for decision involves the good of the whole country, and not the liberty or property of a single citizen, these traditional rules of evidence may be illuminating, but they cannot be controlling.

What has just been said would tend to enlarge the quantity of the evidence to be heard. Another need in this extraordinary situation points the other way; it might cut down the testimony. A long-continued Senate proceeding is obviously unhealthy. Stalling is a familiar tactic in courtroom litigation. Judges try to counter it, not always with success. Its capacity for mischief is infinitely greater here. There have been suggestions that the President means to stall, perhaps in the hope that some outside event will divert a current running against him. It has been suggested, on the other hand, that his opponents want to prolong proceedings which, whatever the final decision, would make the President look bad enough to affect the voting of the citizens in the following election. Neither stratagem, of course, should be aided or abetted. The snail's pace of litigation is too leisurely for impeachment. The "motions," "objections," points of the trial procedure—the adagio of the courtroom—can be too costly here.

I am not, of course, trying to prescribe specific rules of evidence and procedure. I am saying, rather, that what works best in the courtroom will not necessarily work best in the Senate chamber. Proceedings for impeachment and removal are not a judicial trial, and their conduct ought not be governed by the habits of the courtroom.

In the one previous instance of Presidential impeachment, its nature was grievously misunderstood (or deliberately distorted). It was not, however, the possibility of injustice to Andrew Johnson that made the event deplorable; it was Congress' failure to adhere to the Constitution. There would be another failure to adhere to the Constitution if Congress should now treat proceedings for removal as though they were a criminal trial or some other kind of litigation.

Sometimes President Nixon's presentation of the issue is consistent with a proper differentiation, as when he speaks about the Presidency. At other times, as when he promises to "fight like hell," he seems to view the White House as a personal possession of which assailants might deprive him.

The question is: has the Presidency, within the meaning of the Constitutional proscription, been abused? And the way to reach the answer, the way provided by special clauses in the Constitution— Sections 2 and 3 of Article I, Section 4 of Article II—is, as I have said, unique. The due process that is required is not the criminal due process that protects an accused's life, liberty and property, none of which is at hazard here. It is, rather, the due process that pervades the entire Constitution and our law. The damage to the country is minuscule when one criminal goes free. The damage to the country is critical when the abuses specified in Article II occur.

The words "fairness" and "due process" have a carapace of meaning, grown in another part of the law. The semantics are not properly transportable. The kind of fairness called for here is fairness to the people, whose concern to have the right conclusion reached is all that really matters. Richard Nixon's personal interest—the question whether Richard Nixon gains or loses—can have no weight in this extraordinary balance. It is, of course, a matter of dramatic interest, with rooters for and against. Nixon-opponents and Nixon-adherents have clothed the event with their feelings. But these competing feelings are trivial in relation to the vast importance of the issue. This is not a game we are watching.

If we are to think in adversary terms at all, we should think of these proceedings not as *The People* v. *Richard Nixon,* but as *The People* v. *The People.* It is the United States that is concerned, on either side of the "versus." The man who occupies the White House should be ejected if he has acted in a way the Constitution does not tolerate. He should stay if he has not. It is as important that an official who has not breached the Constitutional injunction should serve out his term as that one who has committed the trespass should be ousted. Either way, it is the welfare of the Republic that is the subject, not the welfare of Richard Nixon.

WILLIAM GASS

The Artist and Society

The tame bear's no better off than we are. You've seen how he sways in his cage. At first you might think him musical, but the staves are metal, and his movements are regular and even like the pulses of a pump. It's his nerves. Even when he claps his paws, rises like a man to his hind feet and full height, he looks awkward, feels strange, unsure (his private parts and underbelly are exposed); he trembles. Smiling (you remember the fawning eyeshine of the bear), he focuses his nose and waits for the marshmallow we're about to toss, alert to snap up the sweet cotton in his jaws. There's something terrible about the tame caged bear . . . all that wildness become marshmallow, terrible for his heart, his liver, his teeth (a diet so sugary and soft and unsubstantial, the bowels seek some new employment), and terrible for us—for what we've lost. His eyes, too, are filled with a movement that's not in the things he sees, but in himself. It is the movement of his own despair, his ineffectual rage.

My subject is the artist and society, not the tamed, trained bear, but in many ways the subjects are the same. Artists are as different as men are. It would be wrong to romanticize about them. In our society, indeed, they may live in narrower and more frightened corners than most of us do. We should not imitate their ways; they're not exemplary, and set no worthy fashions. Nor does the artist bear truth dead and drooping in his arms like a lovelorn maiden or a plump goose. His mouth hasn't the proper shape for prophecies. Pot or bottle ends or words or other mouths—whole catalogs of kissing—noisy singing, the folds of funny faces he's created and erased, an excess of bugling have spoiled it for philosophy. In the ancient quarrel between the poets and philosophers, Plato was surely right to think the poets liars. They lie quite roundly, unashamedly, with glee and gusto, since lies and fancies, figments and inventions, outrageous falsehoods are frequently more real, more emotionally pure, more continuously satisfying to them than the truth, which is likely to wear a vest, fancy bucket pudding, Technicolor movies, and long snoozes through Sunday.

W. H. Auden remarked quite recently, when pestered, I think it was, about Vietnam:

> Why writers should be canvassed for their opinion on controversial political issues I cannot imagine. Their views have no more authority than those of any reasonably well-educated citizen. Indeed, when read in bulk, the statements made by writers, including the greatest, would seem to indicate that literary talent and political common sense are rarely found together....

Israel makes war, and there are no symposia published by prize-fighters, no pronouncements from hairdressers, not a ding from the bellhops, from the dentists not even a drill's buzz, from the cabbies nary a horn beep, and from the bankers only the muffled chink of money. Composers, sculptors, painters, architects: they have no rolled-up magazine to megaphone themselves, and are, in consequence, ignored. But critics, poets, novelists, professors, journalists—those used to shooting off their mouths—they shoot (no danger, it's only their own mouth's wash they've wallowed their words in); and those used to print, they print; but neither wisdom nor goodwill nor magnanimity are the qualities which will win you your way to the rostrum . . . just plentiful friends in pushy places and a little verbal skill.

If it is pleasant to be thought an expert on croquet, imagine what bliss it is to be thought an authority on crime, on the clockwork of the human heart, the life of the city, peace and war. How hard to relinquish the certainty, which most of us have anyway, of *knowing.* How sweet it is always to be asked one's opinion. What a shame it is, when asked, not to have one.

Actually Auden's observation can be spread two ways: to include all artists, not writers merely, and to cover every topic not immediately related to their specialized and sometimes arcane talents. It's only the failed artist and his foolish public who would like to believe otherwise, for if they can honestly imagine that the purpose of art is to teach and to delight, to double the face of the world as though with a mirror, to penetrate those truths which nature is said to hold folded beneath her skirts and keeps modestly hidden from the eyes and paws of science, then they will be able to avoid art's actual impact altogether, and the artist's way of life can continue to seem outrageous, bohemian, quaint, a little sinful, irresponsible, hip, and charming, something to visit like the Breton peasants on a holiday, and not a challenge *to* and denial *of* their own manner of existence, an accusation concerning their own lack of reality.

Yet the social claims for art, and the interest normal people take in the lives of their artists, the examinations of the psychologists, the endless studies by endlessly energetic students of nearly everything, the theories of the philosophers, the deadly moral danger in which art is periodically presumed to place the young, unhappily married women, sacred institutions, tipsy souls, and unsteady parliaments, and all those nice persons in positions of power: these claims and interests are so regularly, so inevitably, so perfectly and purely irrelevant that one must begin to suspect that the tight-eyed, squeeze-eared, loin-lacking enemies of art are right; that in spite of everything that's reasonable, in spite of all the evidence, for example, that connoisseurs of yellowing marble statuary and greenish Roman coins are no more moral than the rest of us; that artists are a murky-headed, scurvy-living lot; that if art told the truth, truth must be polkadot; in spite, in short, of insuperable philosophical obstacles (and what obstacles, I ask you, could be more insuperable than those), art does tell us, in its manner, how to live, and artists are quite remarkable, even exemplary, men. We are right to keep them caged.

Thus I begin again, but this time on the other side.

Ronald Laing begins his extraordinary little book *The Politics of Experience* by saying:

Few books today are forgivable. Black on the canvas, silence on the
screen, an empty white sheet of paper, are perhaps feasible. There
is little conjunction of truth and social "reality." Around us are
pseudo-events, to which we adjust with a false consciousness adapted
to see these events as true and real, and even as beautiful. In the
society of men the truth resides now less in what things are than in
what they are not. Our social realities are so ugly if seen in the
light of exiled truth, and beauty is almost no longer possible if it
is not a lie.

You can measure the reality of an act, a man, an institution, custom,
work of art in many ways: by the constancy and quality of its effects,
the depth of the response which it demands, the kinds and range
of values it possesses, the actuality of its presence in space and time,
the multiplicity and reliability of the sensations it provides, its
particularity and uniqueness on the one hand, its abstract generality
on the other—I have no desire to legislate concerning these conditions, insist on them all.

We can rob these men, these acts and objects, of their reality by
refusing to acknowledge them. We pass them on the street but do
not see or speak. We have no Negro problem in our small Mid-
western towns. If someone has the experience of such a problem,
he is mistaken. What happened to him did not happen; what he
felt he did not feel; the urges he has are not the urges he has; what
he wants he does not want. Automatically I reply to my son, who
has expressed his desire for bubble gum: Oh, Peppy, you don't
want that. Number one, then: we deny. We nullify the consciousness
of others. We make their experiences unreal.

Put yourself in a public place, at a banquet—one perhaps at
which awards are made. Your fork is pushing crumbs about upon
your plate while someone is receiving silver in a bowler's shape
amid the social warmth of clapping hands. How would you feel if
at this moment a beautiful lady in a soft pink nightie should lead
among the tables a handsome poodle who puddled under them, and
there was a conspiracy among the rest of us not to notice? Suppose
we sat quietly; our expressions did not change; we looked straight
through her, herself as well as nightie, toward the fascinating figure

of the speaker; suppose, leaving, we stepped heedlessly in the pools, and afterward we did not even shake our shoes. And if you gave a cry, if you warned, explained, cajoled, implored; and we regarded you then with amazement, rejected with amusement, contempt, or scorn every one of your efforts, I think you would begin to doubt your senses and your very sanity. Well, that's the idea: with the weight of our numbers, our percentile normality, we create insanities: yours, as you progressively doubt more and more of your experience, hide it from others to avoid the shame, saying "There's that woman and her damn dog again," but now saying it silently, for your experience, you think, is private; and ours, as we begin to believe our own lies, and the lady and her nightie, the lady and her poodle, the lady and the poodle's puddles, all *do* disappear, expunged from consciousness like a stenographer's mistake.

If we don't deny, we mutilate, taking a part for the whole; or we rearrange things, exaggerating some, minimizing others. There was a lady, yes, but she was wearing a cocktail dress, and there was a dog, too, very small, and very quiet, who sat primly in her lap and made no awkward demonstrations. Or we invert values, and assume strange obligations, altogether neglecting the ones which are obvious and demanding: we rob the poor to give to the rich rich gifts, to kings their kingdoms, to congressmen bribes, to companies the inexpensive purchase of our lives. We rush to buy poodles with liquid nerves—it has become, like so much else, *the rage*. Teas are fun, we say, but necking's not nice. Imagine. We still *do* say that. Or we permit events to occur for some people but not for others. Women and children have no sexual drives; men don't either, thank god, after fifty—sixty? seventy-five? We discredit events by inserting in otherwise accurate accounts outrageous lies. It was the lady who made the mess, not the poodle. In short, we do what we can to destroy experience—our own and others'. But since we can only act according to the way we see things, "*if our experience is destroyed, our behavior will be destructive.*" We live in ruins, in bombed-out shells, in the basements of our buildings. In important ways, we are all mad. You don't believe it? This company, community, this state, our land, is normal? Healthy, is it? Laing has observed that normal healthy men have killed perhaps one hundred million of their fellow normal healthy men in the last fifty years.

Nudists get used to nakedness. We get used to murder.

Why are works of art so socially important? Not for the messages they may contain, not because they expose slavery or cry hurrah for the worker, although such messages in their place and time might be important, but because they insist more than most on their own reality; because of the absolute way in which they exist. Certainly, images exist, shadows and reflections, fakes exist and hypocrites, there are counterfeits (quite real) and grand illusions— but it is simply not true that the copies are as real as their originals, that they meet all of the tests which I suggested earlier. Soybean steak, by god, is soybean steak, and a pious fraud is a fraud. Reality is not a matter of fact, it is an achievement; and it is rare—rarer, let me say—than an undefeated football season. We live, most of us, amidst lies, deceits, and confusions. A work of art may not utter the truth, but it must be honest. It may champion a cause we deplore, but like Milton's Satan, it must in itself be noble; it must be *all there*. Works of art confront us the way few people dare to: completely, openly, at once. They construct, they comprise, our experience; they do not deny or destroy it; and they shame us, we fall so short of the quality of their Being. We live in Lafayette or Rutland—true. We take our breaths. We fornicate and feed. But Hamlet has his history in the heart, and none of us will ever be as real, as vital, as complex and living as he is—a total creature of the stage.

This is a difficult point to make if the reality or unreality of things has not been felt. Have you met a typical nonperson lately? Then say hello, now, to your neighbor. He may be male, but his facial expressions have been put on like lipstick and eyelashes. His greeting is inevitable; so is his interest in the weather. He always smiles; he speaks only in clichés; and his opinions (as bland as Cream of Wheat, as undefined, and—when sugared—just as sweet) are drearily predictable. He has nothing but good to say of people; he collects his wisdom like dung from a Digest; he likes to share his experiences with "folks," and recite the plots of movies. He is working up this saccharine soulside manner as part of his preparation for the ministry.

These are the "good" people. "Bad" people are unreal in the same way.

Nonpersons unperson persons. They kill. For them no one is human. Like cash registers, everyone's the same, should be addressed, approached, the same: all will go ding and their cash drawers slide out when you strike the right key.

So I don't think that it's the message of a work of art that gives it any lasting social value. On the contrary, insisting on this replaces the work with its interpretation, another way of robbing it of its reality. How would you like to be replaced by your medical dossier, your analyst's notes? They take much less space in the file. The analogy, I think, is precise. The aim of the artist ought to be to bring into the world objects which do not already exist there, and objects which are especially worthy of love. We meet people, grow to know them slowly, settle on some to companion our life. Do we value our friends for their social status, because they are burning in the public blaze? do we ask of our mistress her meaning? calculate the usefulness of our husband or wife? Only too often. Works of art are meant to be lived with and loved, and if we try to understand them, we should try to understand them as we try to understand anyone—in order to know *them* better, not in order to know something else.

Why do public officials, like those in the Soviet Union, object so strenuously to an art which has no images in it—which is wholly abstract, and says nothing? Because originals are dangerous to reproductions. For the same reason that a group of cosmetically constructed, teetotal lady-maidens is made uneasy by the addition of a boozy uncorseted madam. Because it is humiliating to be less interesting, less present, less moving, than an arrangement of enameled bedpans. Because, in a system of social relations based primarily on humbug, no real roaches must be permitted to wander. Because, though this may be simply my helpless optimism, your honest whore will outdraw, in the end, any sheaf you choose of dirty pictures.

Pornography is poor stuff, not because it promotes lascivious feelings, but because these feelings are released by and directed toward unreal things. The artist, in this sense, does not deal in dreams.

Of course there are many objects labeled works of art, I know, which are fakes—the paint, for instance, toupeed to the canvas— but I am thinking of the artist, now, as one who produces the honest article, and obviously, *he* is valuable to society if what he *produces* is valuable to it. He is presently valuable because in his shop or study he concocts amusements for our minds, foods for our souls— foods so purely spiritual and momentary they leave scarcely any stools. However, I wanted to say that despite the good reasons for wondering otherwise, the artist could be regarded an exemplary man—one whose ways are worthy of imitation. How can this be? The fellow sleeps with his models and paint jams the zipper on his trousers.

I think we can regard him as exemplary in this way: we judge it likely that a man's character will show up somewhere in his work; that if he is hot-tempered and impetuous, or reckless and gay . . . well, find somebody else to be your surgeon. And we regularly expect to see the imprint of the person in the deed, the body in the bedclothes. I think it is not unreasonable to suppose, too, that the work a man does works on him, that the brush he holds has his hand for its canvas, that the movements a man makes move the man who makes them just as much, and that the kind of ideals, dreams, perceptions, wishes his labor loves must, in him, love at least that labor.

Often enough we lead split lives, the artist as often as anybody; yet it isn't Dylan Thomas or D. H. Lawrence, the drunkard or sadist, I'm suggesting we admire, but the poets they were, and the men they had to be to be such poets. It would have been better if they had been able to assume in the world the virtues they possessed when they faced the page. They were unable. It's hard. And for that the world is partly to blame. It does not *want* its artists, after all. It especially does not want the virtues which artists must employ in the act of their work lifted out of prose and paint and plaster into life.

What are some of these virtues?

Honesty is one...the ability to see precisely what's been done...the ability to face up...because the artist wants his every line to be lovely—that's quite natural—he wants to think well of himself, and cover himself with his own praise like the sundae with its syrup. We all know that artists are vain. But they're not vain while working. We know, too, that they're defensive, insecure. But they dare not be defensive about a bad job, explain their mistakes away, substitute shouting for skill. If a runty tailor dresses himself in his dreams, he may measure for himself the suit of a wrestler. You can fill yourself with air, but will your skin hold it? They don't make balloons with the roughness and resiliency of genius.

Presence is one. The artist cannot create when out of focus. His is not another theatrical performance. There's no one to impress, no audience. He's lived with his work, doubtless, longer than he's had a wife, and it knows all about him in the thorough, hard-boiled way a wife knows. No poseur wrote "The Ballad of Reading Gaol." Presence is a state of concentration on another so complete it leaves you quite without defenses, altogether open; for walls face both ways, as do the bars of a cage. Inquire of the bears how it is. To erect bars is to be behind them. Withholding is not a requirement of poetry.

Unity is another. The artist does not create with something special called imagination which he has and you haven't. He can create with his body because that body has become a mind; he can create with his feelings because they've turned into sensations. He thinks in roughness, loudness, and in color. A painter's hands are magnified eyes. He *is* those fingers—he becomes his medium—and as many fingers close simply in a single fist, so all our faculties can close, and hold everything in one clasp as the petals close in a rose or metal edges crimp.

Awareness is another. Honesty, concentration, unity of being: these allow, in the artist, the world to be *seen*—an unimaginable thing to most of us—to fully take in a tree, a tower, a hill, a graceful arm. If you've ever had an artist's eyes fall on you, you'll know what I mean. Only through such openings may the world pass to existence.

Sensuality is another. Painting and poetry (to name just two) are sexual acts. The artist is a lover, and he must woo his medium till she opens to him; until the richness in her rises to the surface like a blush. Could we adore one another the way the poet adores his words or the painter his colors—what would be the astonishing result?

Totality is still another. I mean that the artist dare not fail to see the whole when he sees with the whole of him. He sees the ant in the jam, yet the jam remains sweet. He must fall evenly on all sides, like a cloak. If he stops to sing a single feeling, he can do so well because he knows how feelings move; he knows the fish is offset from its shadow; knows the peck of the crow does not disturb the beauty of its beak or the dent it makes in the carrion. There is, it seems to me, in the works of the great, an inner measure, wound to beat, a balance which extends through the limbs like bones, an accurate and profound assessment of the proportion and value of things.

Naturally the artist is an enemy of the state. He cannot play politics, succumb to slogans and other simplifications, worship heroes, ally himself with any party, suck on some politician's program like a sweet. He is also an enemy of every ordinary revolution. As a man he may long for action; he may feel injustice like a burn; and certainly he may speak out. But the torn-up street is too simple for him when he sculpts or paints. He undermines everything. Even when, convinced of the rightness of a cause, he dedicates his skills to a movement, he cannot simplify, he cannot overlook, he cannot forget, omit, or falsify. In the end the movement must reject or even destroy him. The evidence of history is nearly unanimous on this point.

The artist's revolutionary activity is of a different kind. He is concerned with consciousness, and he makes his changes there. His inaction is only a blind, for his books and buildings go off under everything—not once but a thousand times. How often has Homer remade men's minds?

An uncorrupted consciousness . . . what a dangerous thing it is.

One could compile, I do not doubt, another list. These are

examples, although central ones. I could so easily be wrong that no one's going to pay me any mind, and so I shall suggest most irresponsibly that we and our world might use more virtues of this kind—the artist's kind—for they are bound to the possibility of Being itself; and occasionally it strikes me as even almost tragic that there should be artists who were able, from concrete, speech, or metal, to release a brilliant life, who nevertheless could not release themselves, either from their own cage, or from ours . . . there is no difference. After all, we are—artists and society—both swaying bears *and* rigid bars. Again, it may be that the *bars* are moving, and the bears, in terror—stricken—are standing behind them . . . no, in front of them—among them—quite, quite still.

RALPH ELLISON

The Golden Age, Time Past

That which we do is what we are. That which we remember is, more often than not, that which we would like to have been; or that which we hope to be. Thus our memory and our identity are ever at odds; our history ever a tall tale told by inattentive idealists.

It has been a long time now, and not many remember how it was in the old days; not really. Not even those who were there to see and hear as it happened, who were pressed in the crowds beneath the dim rosy lights of the bar in the smoke-veiled room, and who shared, night after night, the mysterious spell created by the talk, the laughter, grease paint, powder, perfume, sweat, alcohol and food—all blended and simmering, like a stew on the restaurant range, and brought to a sustained moment of elusive meaning by the timbres and accents of musical instruments locked in passionate recitative. It has been too long now, some seventeen years.

Above the bandstand there later appeared a mural depicting a group of jazzmen holding a jam session in a narrow Harlem bedroom. While an exhausted girl with shapely legs sleeps on her stomach in a big brass bed, they bend to their music in a quiet concatenation of unheard sound: a trumpeter, a guitarist, a clarinetist, a drummer; their only audience a small, cock-eared dog. The clarinetist is white. The guitarist strums with an enigmatic smile. The trumpet is muted. The barefooted drummer, beating a folded newspaper with whisk-brooms in lieu of a drum, stirs the eye's ear like a blast of brasses in a midnight street. A bottle of

116

port rests on a dresser, but it, like the girl, is ignored. The artist, Charles Graham, adds mystery to, as well as illumination within, the scene by having them play by the light of a kerosene lamp. The painting, executed in a harsh documentary style reminiscent of W.P.A. art, conveys a feeling of musical effort caught in timeless and unrhetorical suspension, the sad remoteness of a scene observed through a wall of crystal.

Except for the lamp, the room might well have been one in the Hotel Cecil, the building on 118th Street in which Minton's Playhouse is located, and although painted in 1946, some time after the revolutionary doings there had begun, the mural should help recall the old days vividly. But the décor of the place has been changed and now it is covered, most of the time, by draperies. These require a tricky skill of those who would draw them aside. And even then there will still only be the girl who must sleep forever unhearing, and the men who must forever gesture the same soundless tune. Besides, the time it celebrates is dead and gone and perhaps not even those who came when it was still fresh and new remember those days as they were.

Neither do those remember who knew Henry Minton, who gave the place his name. Nor those who shared in the noisy lostness of New York the rediscovered community of the feasts, evocative of home, of South, of good times, the best and most unself-conscious of times, created by the generous portions of Negro American cuisine—the hash, grits, fried chicken, the ham-seasoned vegetables, the hot biscuits and rolls and the free whiskey—with which, each Monday night, Teddy Hill honored the entire cast of current Apollo Theatre shows. They were gathered here from all parts of America and they broke bread together and there was a sense of good feeling and promise, but what shape the fulfilled promise would take they did not know, and few except the more restless of the younger musicians even questioned. Yet it was an exceptional moment and the world was swinging with change.

Most of them, black and white alike, were hardly aware of where they were or what time it was; nor did they wish to be. They thought of Minton's as a sanctuary, where in an atmosphere blended of nostalgia and a music-and-drink-lulled suspension of time they could retreat like a death blow glimpsed from the corner of the eye, the revolutionary rumpus sounding like a series of flubbed notes blasting the talk with discord. So that the events which made Minton's *Minton's* arrived in conflict and ran their course—then the heat was gone and all that is left to mark its passage is the controlled fury of the music itself, sealed pure and irrevocable, banalities and excellencies alike, in the early recordings; or swept along by our restless quest for the new, to be diluted in more recent styles, the best of it absorbed like drops of fully distilled technique, mood and emotions into the great stream of jazz.

Left also to confuse our sense of what happened is the word "bop," hardly more than a nonsense syllable, by which the music synthesized at Minton's came to be known. A most inadequate word which does little, really, to help us remember. A word which throws up its hands in clownish self-deprecation before all the complexity of sound and rhythm and self-assertive passion which it pretends to name; a mask-word for the charged ambiguities of the new sound, hiding the serious face of art.

Nor does it help that so much has come to pass in the meantime. There have been two hot wars and that which continues, called "cold." And the unknown young men who brought a new edge to the sound of jazz and who scrambled the rhythms of those who used the small clear space at Minton's for dancing are no longer so young or unknown; indeed, they are referred to now by nickname in even the remotest of places. And in Paris and Munich and Tokyo they'll tell you the details of how, after years of trying, "Dizzy" (meaning John Birks Gillespie) vanquished "Roy" (meaning Roy Eldridge) during a jam session at Minton's, to become thereby the new king of trumpeters. Or how, later, while jetting over the world on the blasts of his special tilt-belled horn, he jammed with a snake charmer in Pakistan. "Sent the bloody cobra, man," they'll tell you in London's Soho. So their subsequent fame has blurred the sharp, ugly lines of their rebellion even in the memories of those who found them most strange and distasteful.

What's more, our memory of some of the more brilliant young

men has been touched by the aura of death, and we feel guilt that the fury of their passing was the price paid for the art they left us to enjoy unscathed: Charlie Christian, burned out by tuberculosis like a guitar consumed in a tenement fire; Fats Navarro, wrecked by the tensions and needling temptations of his orgiastic trade, a big man physically as well as musically, shrunken to nothingness; and, most notably of all, Charlie Parker, called "Bird," now deified, worshiped and studied and, like any fertility god, mangled by his admirers and imitators, who coughed up his life and died—as incredibly as the leopard which Hemingway tells us was found "dried and frozen" near the summit of Mount Kilimanjaro—in the hotel suite of a Baroness. (Nor has any one explained what a "yardbird" was seeking at that social altitude, though we know that ideally anything is possible within a democracy, and we know quite well that upper-class Europeans were seriously interested in jazz long before Newport became hospitable.) All this is too much for memory; the dry facts are too easily lost in legend and glamour. (With jazz we are yet not in the age of history, but linger in that of folklore.) We know for certain only that the strange sounds which they and their fellows threw against the hum and buzz of vague signification that seethed in the drinking crowd at Minton's and which, like disgruntled conspirators meeting fatefully to assemble the random parts of a bomb, they joined here and beat and blew into a new jazz style—these sounds we know now to have become the cliché, the technical exercises and the standard of achievement not only for fledgling musicians all over the United States, but for Dutchmen and Swedes, Italians and Frenchmen, Germans and Belgians, and even Japanese. All these, in places which came to mind during the Minton days only as points where the war was in progress and where one might soon be sent to fight and die, are now spotted with young men who study the discs on which the revolution hatched in Minton's is preserved with all the intensity that young American painters bring to the works, say, of Kandinsky, Picasso and Klee. Surely this is an odd swing of the cultural tide. Yet Stravinsky, Webern and Berg notwithstanding, or, more recently, Boulez or Stockhausen—such young men (many of them

excellent musicians in the highest European tradition) find in the
music made articulate at Minton's some key to a fuller freedom of
self-realization. Indeed for many young Europeans the developments which took place here and the careers of those who brought
it about have become the latest episodes in the great American epic.
They collect the recordings and thrive on the legends as eagerly,
perhaps, as young Americans.

Today the bartenders at Minton's will tell you how they come
fresh off the ships or planes, bringing their brightly expectant
and—in this Harlem atmosphere—startlingly innocent European
faces, to buy drinks and stand looking about for the source of the
mystery. They try to reconcile the quiet reality of the place with
the events which fired, at such long range, their imaginations. They
come as to a shrine; as we to the Louvre, Notre Dame or St. Peter's;
as young Americans hurry to the Café Flore, the Deux Magots,
the Rotonde or the Café du Dôme in Paris. For some years now
they have been coming to ask, with all the solemnity of pilgrims
inquiring of a sacred relic, to see the nicotine-stained amplifier
which Teddy Hill provided for Charlie Christian's guitar. And
this is quite proper, for every shrine should have its relic.

Perhaps Minton's has more meaning for European jazz fans than
for Americans, even for those who regularly went there. Certainly
it has a *different* meaning. For them it is associated with those
continental cafés in which great changes, political and artistic, have
been plotted; it is to modern jazz what the Café Voltaire in Zurich
is to the Dadaist phase of modern literature and painting. Few of
those who visited Harlem during the forties would associate it so,
but there is a context of meaning in which Minton's and the musical
activities which took place there can be meaningfully placed.

Jazz, for all the insistence of the legends, has been far more
closely associated with cabarets and dance halls than with brothels,
and it was these which provided both the employment for the
musicians and an audience initiated and aware of the overtones of
the music; which knew the language of riffs, the unstated meanings
of the blues idiom, and the dance steps developed from, and complementary to, its rhythms. And in the beginning it was in the

Negro dance hall and night club that jazz was most completely a part of a total cultural expression; and in which it was freest and most satisfying, both for the musicians and for those in whose lives it played a major role. As a night club in a Negro community then, Minton's was part of a national pattern.

But in the old days Minton's was far more than this; it was also a rendezvous for musicians. As such, and although it was not formally organized, it goes back historically to the first New York center of Negro musicians, the Clef Club. Organized in 1910, during the start of the great migration of Negroes northward, by James Reese Europe, the director whom Irene Castle credits with having invented the fox trot, the Clef Club was set up on West 53rd Street to serve as a meeting place and booking office for Negro musicians and entertainers. Here wage scales were regulated, musical styles and techniques worked out, and entertainment was supplied for such establishments as Rector's and Delmonico's, and for such producers as Florenz Ziegfeld and Oscar Hammerstein. Later, when Harlem evolved into a Negro section, a similar function was served by the Rhythm Club, located then in the old Lafayette Theatre building on 132nd Street and Seventh Avenue. Henry Minton, a former saxophonist and officer of the Rhythm Club, became the first Negro delegate to Local 802 of the American Federation of Musicians and was thus doubly aware of the needs, artistic as well as economic, of jazzmen. He was generous with loans, was fond of food himself and, as an old acquaintance recalled, "loved to put a pot on the range" to share with unemployed friends. Naturally when he opened Minton's Playhouse many musicians made it their own.

Henry Minton also provided, as did the Clef and Rhythm clubs, a necessity more important to jazz musicians than food: a place in which to hold their interminable jam sessions. And it is here that Minton's becomes most important to the development of modern jazz. It is here, too, that it joins up with all the countless rooms, private and public, in which jazzmen have worked out the secrets of their craft. Today jam sessions are offered as entertainment by night clubs and on radio and television, and some are quite exciting;

but what is seen and heard is only one aspect of the true jam session: the "cutting session," or contest of improvisational skill and physical endurance between two or more musicians. But the jam session is far more than this, and when carried out by musicians, in the privacy of small rooms (as in the mural at Minton's) or in such places as Halley Richardson's shoeshine parlor in Oklahoma City— where I first heard Lester Young jamming in a shine chair, his head thrown back, his horn even then outthrust, his feet working the footrests, as he played with and against Lem Johnson, Ben Webster (this was 1929) and other members of the old Blue Devils Orchestra—or during the after hours in Piney Brown's old Sunset Club in Kansas City; in such places as these with only musicians and jazzmen present, then the jam session is revealed as the jazzman's true academy.

It is here that he learns tradition, group techniques and style. For although since the twenties many jazzmen have had conservatory training and were well grounded in formal theory and instrumental technique, when we approach jazz we are entering quite a different sphere of training. Here it is more meaningful to speak, not of courses of study, of grades and degrees, but of apprenticeship, ordeals, initiation ceremonies, of rebirth. For after the jazzman has learned the fundamentals of his instrument and the traditional techniques of jazz—the intonations, the mute work, manipulation of timbre, the body of traditional styles—he must then "find himself," must be reborn, must find, as it were, his soul. All this through achieving that subtle identification between his instrument and his deepest drives which will allow him to express his own unique ideas and his own unique voice. He must achieve, in short, his self-determined identity.

In this his instructors are his fellow musicians, especially the acknowledged masters, and his recognition of manhood depends upon their acceptance of his ability as having reached a standard which is all the more difficult for not having been rigidly codified. This does not depend upon his ability to simply hold a job but upon his power to express an individuality in tone. Nor is his status ever unquestioned, for the health of jazz and the unceasing attraction which it holds for the musicians themselves lies in the ceaseless warfare for mastery and recognition—not among the general public, though commercial success is not spurned, but among their artistic peers. And even the greatest can never rest on past accomplishments, for, as with the fast guns of the old West, there is always someone waiting in a jam session to blow him literally, not only down, but into shame and discouragement.

By making his club hospitable to jam sessions even to the point that customers who were not musicians were crowded out, Henry Minton provided a retreat, a homogeneous community where a collectivity of common experience could find continuity and meaningful expression. Thus the stage was set for the birth of bop.

In 1941 Mr. Minton handed over his management to Teddy Hill, the saxophonist and former band leader, and Hill turned the Playhouse into a musical dueling ground. Not only did he continue Minton's policies, he expanded them. It was Hill who established the Monday Celebrity Nights, the house band which included such members from his own disbanded orchestra as Kenny Clark, Dizzy Gillespie, along with Thelonious Monk, sometimes with Joe Guy, and, later, Charlie Christian and Charlie Parker; and it was Hill who allowed the musicians free rein to play whatever they liked. Perhaps no other club except Clarke Monroe's Uptown House was so permissive, and with the hospitality extended to musicians of all schools the news spread swiftly. Minton's became the focal point for musicians all over the country.

Herman Pritchard, who presided over the bar in the old days, tells us that every time they came, "Lester Young and Ben Webster used to tie up in battle like dogs in the road. They'd fight on those saxophones until they were tired out, then they'd put in long-distance calls to their mothers, both of whom lived in Kansas City, and tell them about it."

And most of the masters of jazz came either to observe or to participate and be influenced and listen to their own discoveries transformed; and the aspiring stars sought to win their approval,

as the younger tenor men tried to win the esteem of Coleman
Hawkins. Or they tried to vanquish them in jamming contests as
Gillespie is said to have outblown his idol, Roy Eldridge. It was
during this period that Eddie "Lockjaw" Davis underwent an ordeal
of jeering rejection until finally he came through as an admired
tenor man.

In the perspective of time we now see that what was happening
at Minton's was a continuing symposium of jazz, a summation of
all the styles, personal and traditional, of jazz. Here it was possible
to hear its resources of technique, ideas, harmonic structure, melodic phrasing and rhythmical possibilities explored more thoroughly than was ever possible before. It was also possible to hear
the first attempts toward a conscious statement of the sensibility of
the younger generation of musicians as they worked out the techniques, structures and rhythmical patterns with which to express
themselves. Part of this was arbitrary, a revolt of the younger against
the established stylists, part of it was inevitable. For jazz had reached
a crisis and new paths were certain to be searched for and found.
An increasing number of the younger men were formally trained
and the post Depression developments in the country had made for
quite a break between their experience and that of the older men.
Many were even of a different physical build. Often they were
quiet and of a reserve which contrasted sharply with the exuberant
and outgoing lyricism of the older men, and they were intensely
concerned that their identity as Negroes placed no restriction upon
the music they played or the manner in which they used their talent.
They were concerned, they said, with art, not entertainment. Especially were they resentful of Louis Armstrong, whom (confusing
the spirit of his music with his clowning) they considered an Uncle
Tom.

But they too, some of them, had their own myths and miscon-
ceptions: That theirs was the only generation of Negro musicians
who listened to or enjoyed the classics; that to be truly free they
must act exactly the opposite of what white people might believe,
rightly or wrongly, a Negro to be; that the performing artist can
be completely and absolutely free of the obligations of the enter-
tainer, and that they could play jazz with dignity only by frowning

and treating the audience with aggressive contempt; and that to be in control, artistically and personally, one must be so cool as to quench one's own human fire.

Nor should we overlook the despair which must have swept Minton's before the technical mastery, the tonal authenticity, the authority and the fecundity of imagination of such men as Hawkins, Young, Goodman, Tatum, Teagarden, Ellington and Waller. Despair, after all, is ever an important force in revolutions.

They were also responding to the non-musical pressures affecting jazz. It was a time of big bands, and the greatest prestige and economic returns were falling outside the Negro community— often to leaders whose popularity grew from the compositions and arrangements of Negroes—to white instrumentalists whose only originality lay in the enterprise with which they rushed to market with some Negro musician's hard-won style. Still there was no policy of racial discrimination at Minton's. Indeed, it was very much like those Negro cabarets of the twenties and thirties in which a megaphone was placed on the piano so that anyone with the urge could sing a blues. Nevertheless, the inside dopesters will tell you that the "changes" or chord progressions and the melodic inversions worked out by the creators of bop sprang partially from their desire to create a jazz which could not be so easily imitated and exploited by white musicians to whom the market was more open simply *because* of their whiteness. They wished to receive credit for what they created, and besides, it was easier to "get rid of the trash" who crowded the bandstand with inept playing and thus make room for the real musicians, whether white or black. Nevertheless, white musicians like Tony Scott, Remo Palmieri and Al Haig who were part of the development at Minton's became so by passing a test of musicianship, sincerity and temperament. Later, it is said, the boppers became engrossed in solving the musical problems which they set themselves. Except for a few sympathetic older musicians it was they who best knew the promise of the Minton moment, and it was they, caught like the rest in all the complex forces of American life which comes to focus in jazz, who made the most of it. Now the tall tales told as history must feed on the results of their efforts.

GUY DAVENPORT

The Geography of the Imagination

The difference between the Parthenon and the World Trade Center, between a French wine glass and a German beer mug, between Bach and John Philip Sousa, betweeen Sophocles and Shakespeare, between a bicycle and a horse, though explicable by historical moment, necessity, and destiny, is before all a difference of imagination.

Man was first a hunter, and an artist: his earliest vestiges tell us that alone. But he must always have dreamed, and recognized and guessed and supposed, all skills of the imagination. Language itself is continuously an imaginative act. Rational discourse outside our familiar territory of Greek logic sounds to our ears like the wildest imagination. The Dogon, a people of West Africa, will tell you that a white fox named Ogo frequently weaves himself a hat of string bean hulls, puts it on his impudent head, and dances in the okra to insult and infuriate God Almighty, and that there's nothing we can do about it except abide him in faith and patience.

This is not folklore, or a quaint custom, but as serious a matter to the Dogon as a filling station to us Americans. The imagination; that is, the way we shape and use the world, indeed the way we *see* the world, has geographical boundaries like islands, continents, and countries. These boundaries can be crossed. That Dogon fox and his impudent dance come to live with us, but in a different body, and to serve a different mode of the imagination. We call him Brer Rabbit.

We in America are more sensitive than most to boundaries of the imagination. Our arrival was a second one; the misnamed first arrivers must all bear a name from the imagination of certain

Renaissance men, who for almost a century could not break out of the notion that these two vast continents were the Indies, itself a name so vague as to include China, India, and even Turkey, for which they named our most delicious bird.

The imagination has a history, as yet unwritten, and it has a geography, as yet only dimly seen. History and geography are inextricable disciplines. They have different shelves in the library, and different offices at the university, but they cannot get along for a minute without consulting the other. Geography is the wife of history, as space is the wife of time.

When Heraclitus said that everything passes steadily along, he was not inciting us to make the best of the moment, an idea unseemly to his placid mind, but to pay attention to the pace of things. Each has its own rhythm: the nap of a dog, the precession of the equinoxes, the dances of Lydia, the majestically slow beat of the drums at Dodona, the swift runners at Olympia.

The imagination, like all things in time, is metamorphic. It is also rooted in a ground, a geography. The Latin word for the sacredness of a place is *cultus*, the dwelling of a god, the place where a rite is valid. *Cultus* becomes our word *culture*, not in the portentous sense it now has, but in a much humbler sense. For ancient people the sacred was the vernacular ordinariness of things: the hearth, primarily; the bed, the wall around the yard. The temple was too sacred to be entered. Washing the feet of a guest was as religious an act as sharing one's meals with the gods.

When Europeans came to the new world, they learned nothing on the way, as if they came through a dark tunnel. Plymouth, Lisbon, Amsterdam, then the rolling Atlantic for three months, then the rocks and pines, sand and palms of Cathay, the Indies, the wilderness. A German cartographer working in Paris decided to translate the first name of Amerigo Vespucci into Latin, for reasons best known to himself, and call the whole thing America. In geography you have maps, and maps must have the names of places on them.

We new-world settlers, then, brought the imagination of other countries to transplant it in a different geography. We have been here scarcely a quarter of the time that the pharaohs ruled Egypt. We brought many things across the Atlantic, and the Pacific; many things we left behind: a critical choice to live with forever. The imagination is like the drunk man who lost his watch, and must get drunk again to find it. It is as intimate as speech and custom, and to trace its ways we need to reeducate our eyes. In 1840—when Cooper's *The Pathfinder* was a bestseller, and photography had just been made practical—an essay called "The Philosophy of Furniture" appeared in an American magazine. Dickens made fun of Americans for attending lectures on the philosophy of anything, the philosophy of crime on Monday, the philosophy of government on Wednesday, the philosophy of the soul on Thursday, as Martin Chuzzlewit learned from Mrs. Brick. The English, also, we know from Thomas Love Peacock's satirical novels, were addicted to the lecture. The great French encyclopedia, its imitators, and the periodical press had done their work, and audiences were eager to hear anybody on any subject. Crowds attended the lectures of Louis Agassiz on zoology and geology (in 1840 he was explaining the Ice Age and the nature of glaciers, which he had just discovered); of Emerson, of transcendentalists, utopians, home-grown scientists like John Cleve Symmes, of Cincinnati, who explained that the globe is open at the poles and another world and another humanity resident on the concavity of a hollow earth; and even Thoreau, who gave lectures in the basements of churches.

This "Philsophy of Furniture" was by an unlikely writer: Edgar Allan Poe. In it he explains how rooms should be decorated. "We have no aristocracy of the blood," says this author who was educated at a university founded by Thomas Jefferson, "and having therefore as a natural, and indeed as an inevitable thing, fashioned for ourselves an aristocracy of dollars, the *display of wealth* has here to take the place and perform the office of the heraldic display in monarchial countries."

We are familiar with Poe's anxiety about good taste, about the fidelity of the United States to European models. What we want to see in this essay is a clue to the structure of Poe's imagination, which Charles Baudelaire thought the greatest of the century, an imagination so fine that Paul Valéry said it was incapable of making a mistake.

Poe's sense of good taste in decoration was in harmony with the best English style of the early Victorian period; we recognize his ideal room as one in which we might find the young Carlyles, those strenuous aesthetes, or George Eliot and Elizabeth Gaskell— a glory of wallpaper, figured rugs, marble-top tables, tall narrow windows with dark red curtains, sofas, antimacassars, vases, unfading wax flowers under bell jars, a rosewood piano, and a cozy fireplace. The amazing thing is that Poe emphasizes lightness and grace, color and clarity; whereas we associate his imagination with the most claustrophobic, dark, Gothic interiors in all of literature.

On our walls, Poe says, we should have many paintings to relieve the expanse of wallpaper—"a glossy paper of silvery-grey tint, spotted with small arabesque devices of a fainter hue." "These are," he dictates, "chiefly landscapes of an imaginative cast—such as the fairy grottoes of Stanfield, or the lake of the Dismal Swamp of Chapman. There are, nevertheless, three or four female heads, of an ethereal beauty—portraits in the manner of Sully."

In another evocation of an ideal room, in a sketch called "Landor's Cottage" he again describes a wall with pictures: ". . . three of Julien's exquisite lithographs à *trois crayons*, fastened to the wall without frames. One of these drawings was a scene of Oriental luxury, or rather voluptuousness; another was a 'carnival piece,' spirited beyond compare; the third was a Greek female head—a face so divinely beautiful, and yet of an expression so provokingly indeterminate, never before arrested my attention."

Poe titled the collection of his stories published that year *Tales of the Grotesque and Arabesque.* These two adjectives have given critics trouble for years. *Grotesque,* as Poe found it in the writings of Sir Walter Scott, means something close to *Gothic,* an adjective designating the Goths and their architecture, and what the neoclassical eighteenth century thought of mediaeval art in general, that it was ugly but grand. It was the fanciful decoration by the

Italians of grottoes, or caves, with shells, and statues of ogres and giants from the realm of legend, that gave the word *grotesque* its meaning of *freakish, monstrous, misshapen.*

Arabesque clearly means the intricate, nonrepresentational, infinitely graceful decorative style of Islam, best known to us in their carpets, the geometric tile-work of their mosques, and their calligraphy.

Had Poe wanted to designate the components of his imagination more accurately, his title would have been, *Tales of the Grotesque, Arabesque, and Classical.* For Poe in all his writing divided all his imagery up into three distinct species.

Look back at the pictures on the wall in his ideal rooms. In one we have grottoes and a view of the Dismal Swamp: this is the grotesque mode. Then female heads in the manner of Sully: this is the classical mode. The wallpaper against which they hang is arabesque.

In the other room we had a scene of oriental luxury: the arabesque, a carnival piece spirited beyond compare (Poe means masked and costumed people, at Mardi Gras, as in "The Cask of Amontillado" and "The Masque of the Red Death"): the grotesque, and a Greek female head: the classical.

A thorough inspection of Poe's work will disclose that he performs variations and mutations of these three vocabularies of imagery. We can readily recognize those works in which a particular idiom is dominant. The great octosyllabic sonnet "To Helen," for instance, is classical, "The Fall of the House of Usher" is grotesque, and the poem "Israfel" is arabesque.

But no work is restricted to one mode; the other two are there also. We all know the beautiful "To Helen," written when he was still a boy:

> Helen, thy beauty is to me
> Like those Nicaean barks of yore,
> That gently, o'er a perfumed sea,
> The weary, way-worn wanderer bore
> To his own native shore.

On desperate seas long wont to roam,
Thy hyacinth hair, thy classic face,
Thy Naiad airs have brought me home
To the glory that was Greece
And the grandeur that was Rome.

Lo! in yon brilliant window niche
How statue-like I see thee stand,
The agate lamp within thy hand!
Ah, Psyche, from the regions which
Are Holy Land!

The words are as magic as Keats, but what is the sense? Sappho, whom Poe is imitating, had compared a woman's beauty to a fleet of ships. Byron had previously written lines that Poe outbyrons Byron with, in "the glory that was Greece / And the grandeur that was Rome." But how is Helen also Psyche; who is the wanderer coming home? Scholars are not sure. In fact, the poem is not easy to defend against the strictures of critics. We can point out that *Nicaean* is not, as has been charged, a pretty bit of gibberish, but the adjective for the city of Nice, where a major shipworks was: Marc Antony's fleet was built there. We can defend *perfumed sea,* which has been called silly, by noting that classical ships never left sight of land, and could smell orchards on shore, that perfumed oil was an extensive industry in classical times and that ships laden with it would smell better than your shipload of sheep. Poe is normally far more exact than he is given credit for.

That window-niche, however, slipped in from Northern Europe; it is Gothic, a slight tone of the grotto in this almost wholly classical poem. And the closing words, "Holy Land," belong to the Levant, to the arabesque.

In "The Raven" we have a dominant grotesque key, with a vision of an arabesque Eden, "perfumed from an unseen censer / Swung by Seraphim whose footfalls tinkled on the tufted floor," and a grotesque raven sits on a classical bust of Pallas Athene. That raven was the device on the flag of Alaric the Visigoth, whose torch at Eleusis was the beginning of the end of Pallas's reign over the mind of men. Lenore (a name Walter Scott brought from Germany for his horse) is a mutation of Eleanor, a French mutation of Helen.

Were we to follow the metamorphoses of these images through all of Poe—grotesque, or Gothic; arabesque, or Islamic; classical, or Graeco-Roman—we would discover an articulate grammar of symbols, a new, as yet unread Poe. What we shall need to understand is the meaning of the symbols, and why they are constantly being translated from one imagistic idiom to another.

The clues are not difficult, or particularly arcane. Israfel for instance is an arabesque, and Roderick Usher a grotesque Orpheus; Orpheus himself does not appear in Poe in his native Greek self. But once we see Orpheus in Usher, we can then see that this masterpiece is a retelling of his myth from a point of view informed by a modern understanding of neuroses, of the inexplicable perverseness of the human will. That lute, that speaking guitar, all those books on Usher's table about journeys underground and rites held in darkness—all fit into a translation by Poe of a classical text into a Gothic one. "The Gold Bug," as Northrop Frye has seen, is strangely like the marriage of Danaë; the old black who lowers the gold bug is named Jupiter. Danaë was shut up in a treasure house and a riddle put her there.

Where do these images come from? The Mediterranean in the time of Columbus was from its western end and along its northern shore Graeco-Roman, what historians call the Latin culture, and at its eastern end, and along its southern shore, Islamic. So two thirds of Poe's triple imagery sums up the Mediterranean, and fed his imagination with its most congenial and rich portion. The Gothic style has its home in northern Europe, "my Germany of the soul" as Poe put it. He was always ambiguous about the culture with which, ironically, he is identified. Death, corruption, and dreariness inhere in the Gothic. Poe relates it to melancholia, hypersensitivity, madness, obsession, awful whirlpools in the cold sea, ancient houses spent and crumbling. Is there some pattern here from his own life? There is a real House of Usher, still standing, not in a gloomy Transylvanian valley by a black tarn, but in Boston, Massachusetts, where Poe was born, and where his barely remembered mother played the first Ophelia on an American stage, a rôle definitively Gothic in Poe's scheme of modes.*

Poe's sense of Islam, which we can trace to Byron and Shelley, derived as well from the explorers Burckhardt, Volney, and John Lloyd Stephens. The angel Israfel is not, as Poe wants us to believe, in the Koran, but from George Sale's introduction to his translation of the *Koran* by way of Thomas Moore.

The classical was being restated before Poe's eyes in Charlottesville by an old man who said he loved a particular Greek temple as if it were his mistress. Jefferson had the undergraduates up to dinner at Monticello two at a time, in alphabetical order. *P* is deep in the alphabet; Poe was expelled and the old man dead before the two most astute readers of Alexander von Humboldt in the United States could face each other over a platter of Virginia ham.

Poe's imagination was perfectly at home in geographies he had no knowledge of except what his imagination appropriated from other writers. We might assume, in ignorance, that he knew Paris like a Parisian, that Italy and Spain were familiar to him, and even Antarctica and the face of the moon.

The brothers Goncourt wrote in their journal as early as 1856 that Poe was a new kind of man writing a new kind of literature. We have still to learn that his sensibility was radically intelligent rather than emotional.

When he compares the eyes of Ligeia to stars, they are the binary stars that Herschel discovered and explained in the year of Poe's birth (the spectroscopic double Beta Lyra and the double double Epsilon Lyra, to be exact), not the generalized stars of Petrarchan tradition. We have paid too little attention to this metaphysical Poe; and we scarcely understand Europeans when they speak of the passion they find in his poetry. What are we to think of the Russian

---

*Fiske Kimball, *Domestic Architecture of the American Colonies and of the Early Republic* (New York: Dover, 1966), p. 275.

translator of Poe, Vladimir Pyast, who, while reciting "Ulalume" in a St. Petersburg theater, went stark raving mad? Russians treasure the memory of that evening.

Night after night, from 1912 to 1917, a man who might have been the invention of Poe sat in a long, almost empty room in a working-class district of Berlin, writing a book by candle light. *Might have been the invention of Poe*—he was basically a classicist, his doctoral thesis was on Heraclitus, his mind was shaped by Goethe, Nietzsche, von Humboldt, and Leo Frobenius, the anthropologist and cultural morphologist. Like Poe, he thought in symbols.

He was Oswald Spengler. His big book, *The Decline of the West*, was meant to parallel the military campaigns of the Wehrmacht in 1914–1918, which by pedantic adherence to tactics and heroic fervor was to impose German regularity and destiny upon Europe. Spengler's book, like the Wehrmacht, imposed only a tragic sense that history is independent of our will, ironically perverse, and a nightmare.

The value of *The Decline of the West* is in its poetry of vision, its intuition of the rise, growth, and decline of cultures. By culture Spengler meant the formative energy of a people, lasting for thousands of years. A civilization is the maturity of a culture, and inevitably its decline. His feeling for the effeteness of a finished culture was precisely that of Poe in "The Fall of the House of Usher" and "The Murders in the Rue Morgue"—both stories about the vulnerability of order and civilized achievement.

Spengler's most useful intuition was to divide world cultures into three major styles: the Apollonian, or Graeco-Roman; the Faustian, or Western-Northern European; and the Magian, or Asian and Islamic. Historians instantly complained that the cultures of our world may not be divided into three but into seventy-six distinct groups.

What interests us, however, is that Spengler's categories are exactly those of Edgar Allan Poe.

And those of James Joyce. Look at the first three stories of Joyce's *Dubliners*. The first is concerned with a violation of rites that derive from deep in Latin culture by way of the Roman Mass, the second takes its symbols from chivalry, the moral codes of Northern knighthood, and the third is named "Araby." This triad of symbolic patterns is repeated four more times, to achieve fifteen stories. The first three chapters of *Ulysses* also follow this structure, even more complexly; and the simplest shape to which we can summarize *Ulysses* is to say that it is about a man, Leopold Bloom, in a northern European, a Faustian-technological context, who is by heritage a Jew of Spengler's Magian culture, who is made to act out the adventures of Ulysses, exemplar of classical man.

"We have museum catalogues but no artistic atlases," the great French historian and cultural geographer Fernand Braudel complains in his *The Mediterranean and the Mediterranean World in the Age of Philip II*, "We have histories of art and literature but none of civilization."

He suspects that such a map of the arts would disclose the same kind of historical structure that he has demonstrated for food, clothing, trade routes, industrial and banking centers; and that our understanding of our imaginative life would take on as yet unguessed coherence and hitherto uncomprehended behavior.

Such a map would presumably display such phenomena as the contours of the worship of Demeter and Persephone, coinciding with grain-producing terrain, and with the contours of Catholicism. This would not surprise us. It might also show how the structure of psychology and drama nourished by grain-producing cultures persists outside that terrain, continuing to act as if it were inside, because its imaginative authority refuses to abdicate.

How else can we explain a story like O. Henry's "The Church with the Overshot Wheel"? In this poignant little tale, set in the pinewoods of North Carolina, a miller's daughter named Aglaia (a name commensurate with the style of naming girls in the Fancy Names Belt) is kidnapped by shiftless rovers who take her to Atlanta. The miller in his grief moves away to the Northwest, becomes prosperous and a philanthropist, naming his best brand of flour for his lost daughter whom he supposes to be dead. In her memory he has his old mill rebuilt as a church, endowing it handsomely,

but keeping its overshot wheel. The community becomes a summer
resort for people of modest means; and of course O. Henry has
the orphan daughter come to it as a grown woman, and in a typical
denouement, her memory of a song she used to sing as a child,
together with an accidental spill of flour over her father, who is
visiting the old mill, reunites them. O. Henry, perhaps unconsciously, has retold the myth of Persephone, using a name, Aglaia,
"the bright girl," which was one of the epithets of Persephone,
deification of wheat, and all the elements of the myth, transposed
to twentieth-century America: the rape that brought devastation,
the return and reunion that brought healing and regeneration.

I find an explanation of this story according to the theory of
Jungian archetypes—patterns imprinted in the mind—unsatisfactory. It is better to trace O. Henry's plot and symbols backward
along geographical lines, through myths brought across the Atlantic
from the Mediterranean, through books and schoolrooms, through
libraries and traditions, and to assess his story as a detail in the
structure of a culture of strong vitality which decided on the ex-
pressiveness of certain symbols five thousand years ago, and finds
them undiminished and still full of human significance.

The appeal of popular literature must lie precisely in its faith-
fulness to ancient traditions. The charming little children's book
by Carlo Collodi, *Le Avventuri di Pinocchio,* can scarcely claim to
be included in a history of Italian literature, and yet to a geographer
of the imagination it is a more elegant paradigm of the narrative
art of the Mediterranean than any other book since Ovid's *Metamorphoses,* rehearses all the central myths, and adds its own to the
rich stock of its tradition. It reaches back to a Gnostic theme known
to both Shakespeare and Emily Dickinson: "Split the stick," said
Jesus, "and I am there." It combines Pygmalion, Ovid, the book
of Jonah, the Commedia dell'Arte, and Apuleius; and will continue
to be a touchstone of the imagination.

The discovery of America, its settlement, and economic development, were activities of the Renaissance and the Reformation,
Mediterranean tradition and northern acumen. The continuities of
that double heritage have been longlasting. The *Pequod* set out from
Joppa, the first Thoreau was named Diogenes, Whitman is a con-

temporary of Socrates, the *Spoon River Anthology* was first written in Alexandria; for thirty years now our greatest living writer, Eudora Welty, has been rewriting Ovid in Mississippi. "The Jumping Frog of Calaveras County" was a turn for a fifth-century Athenian mime.

A geography of the imagination would extend the shores of the Mediterranean all the way to Iowa.

Eldon, Iowa—where in 1929 Grant Wood sketched a farmhouse as the background for a double portrait of his sister Nan and his dentist, Dr. B. H. McKeeby, who donned overalls for the occasion and held a rake. Forces that arose three millennia ago in the Mediterranean changed the rake to a pitchfork, as we shall see.

Let us look at this painting to which we are blinded by familiarity and parody. In the remotest distance against this perfect blue of a fine harvest sky, there is the Gothic spire of a country church, as if to seal the Protestant sobriety and industry of the subjects. Next there are trees, seven of them, as along the porch of Solomon's temple, symbols of prudence and wisdom.

Next, still reading from background to foreground, is the house that gives the primary meaning of the title, *American Gothic*, a style of architecture. It is an example of a revolution in domestic building that made possible the rapid rise of American cities after the Civil War and dotted the prairies with decent, neat farmhouses. It is what was first called in derision a balloon-frame house, so easy to build that a father and his son could put it up. It is an elegant geometry of light timber posts and rafters requiring no deep foundation, and is nailed together. Technically, it is, like the clothes of the farmer and his wife, a mail-order house, as the design comes out of a pattern-book, this one from those of Alexander Davis and Andrew Downing, the architects who modified details of the Gothic Revival for American farmhouses. The balloon-frame house was invented in Chicago in 1833 by George Washington Snow, who was orchestrating in his invention a century of mechanization that provided the nails, wirescreen, sash-windows, tin roof, lathe-turned posts for the porch, doorknobs, locks, and hinges—all standard pieces from factories.

We can see a bamboo sunscreen—out of China by way of Sears,

Roebuck—that rolls up like a sail: nautical technology applied to the prairie. We can see that distinctly American feature, the screen door. The sash-windows are European in origin, their glass panes from Venetian technology as perfected by the English, a luxury that was a marvel of the eighteenth century, and now as common as the farmer's spectacles, another revolution in technology that would have seemed a miracle to previous ages. Spectacles begin in the thirteenth century, the invention of either Salvino degl'Armati or Alessandro della Spina; the first portrait of a person wearing specs is of Cardinal Ugone di Provenza, in a fresco of 1352 by Tommaso Barisino di Modena. We might note, as we are trying to see the geographical focus that this painting gathers together, that the center for lens grinding from which eyeglasses diffused to the rest of civilization was the same part of Holland from which the style of the painting itself derives.

Another thirteenth-century invention prominent in our painting is the buttonhole. Buttons themselves are prehistoric, but they were shoulder-fasteners that engaged with loops. Modern clothing begins with the buttonhole. The farmer's wife secures her Dutch Calvinist collar with a cameo brooch, an heirloom passed down the generations, an eighteenth-century or Victorian copy of a design that goes back to the sixth century B.C.

She is a product of the ages, this modest Iowa farm wife: she has the hair-do of a mediaeval madonna, a Reformation collar, a Greek cameo, a nineteenth-century pinafore.

Martin Luther put her a step behind her husband; John Knox squared her shoulders; the stock-market crash of 1929 put that look in her eyes.

The train that brought her clothes—paper pattern, bolt cloth, needle, thread, scissors—also brought her husband's bib overalls, which were originally, in the 1870s, trainmen's workclothes designed in Europe, manufactured here by J. C. Penney, and disseminated across the United States as the railroads connected city with city. The cloth is denim, from Nîmes in France, introduced by Levi Strauss of blue-jean fame. The design can be traced to no less a person than Herbert Spencer, who thought he was creating a utilitarian one-piece suit for everybody to wear. His own example was of tweed, with buttons from crotch to neck, and his female relatives somehow survived the mortification of his sporting it one Sunday in St. James's Park.

His jacket is the modification of that of a Scots shepherd which we all still wear.

Grant Wood's Iowans stand, as we might guess, in a pose dictated by the Brownie box camera, close together in front of their house, the farmer looking at the lens with solemn honesty, his wife with modestly averted eyes. But that will not account for the pitchfork held as assertively as a minuteman's rifle. The pose is rather that of the Egyptian prince Rahotep, holding the flail of Osiris, beside his wife Nufrit—strict with pious rectitude, poised in absolute dignity, mediators between heaven and earth, givers of grain, obedient to the gods.

This formal pose lasts out 3000 years of Egyptian history, passes to some of the classical cultures—Etruscan couples in terra cotta, for instance—but does not attract Greece and Rome. It recommences in northern Europe, where (to the dismay of the Romans) Gaulish wives rode beside their husbands in the war chariot. Kings and eventually the merchants of the North repeated the Egyptian double portrait of husband and wife: van Eyck's Meester and Frouw Arnolfini; Rubens and his wife Helena. It was this Netherlandish tradition of painting middle-class folk with honor and precision that turned Grant Wood from Montparnasse, where he spent two years in the 1920s trying to be an American post-Impressionist, back to Iowa, to be our Hans Memling.

If Van Gogh could ask, "Where is my Japan?" and be told by Toulouse-Lautrec that it was Provence, Wood asked himself the whereabouts of his Holland, and found it in Iowa.

Just thirty years before Wood's painting, Edwin Markham's poem "The Man with the Hoe" had pictured the farmer as a peasant with a life scarcely different from that of an ox, and called on the working men of the world to unite, as they had nothing to lose but their chains. The painting that inspired Markham was one of a series of agricultural subjects by Jean François Millet, whose work also inspired Van Gogh. A digging fork appears in five of Van Gogh's pictures, three of them variations of themes by Millet, and all of them are studies of grinding labor and poverty.

And yet the Independent Farmer had edged out the idle aristocrat for the hand of the girl in Royal Tyler's "The Contrast," the first native American comedy for the stage, and in Emerson's "Concord Hymn" it is a battle-line of farmers who fire the shot heard round the world. George III, indeed, referred to his American colonies as "the farms," and the two Georges of the Revolution, Hanover and Washington, were proudly farmers by etymology and in reality.

The window curtains and apron in this painting are both calico printed in a reticular design, the curtains of rhombuses, the apron of circles and dots, the configuration Sir Thomas Browne traced through nature and art in his *Garden of Cyrus*, the quincunxial arrangement of trees in orchards, perhaps the first human imitation of phyllotaxis, acknowledging the symmetry, justice, and divine organization of nature.

Curtains and aprons are as old as civilization itself, but their presence here in Iowa implies a cotton mill, a dye works, a roller press that prints calico, and a wholesale-retail distribution system involving a post office, a train, its tracks, and, in short, the Industrial Revolution.

That revolution came to America in the astounding memory of one man, Samuel Slater, who arrived in Philadelphia in 1789 with the plans of all Arkwright's, Crompton's, and Hargreaves's machinery in his head, put himself at the service of the rich Quaker Moses Brown, and built the first American factory at Pawtucket, Rhode Island.

The apron is trimmed with rickrack ribbon, a machine-made substitute for lace. The curtains are bordered in a variant of the egg-and-dart design that comes from Nabataea, the Biblical Edom, in Syria, a design which the architect Hiram incorporated into the entablatures of Solomon's temple—"and the chapiters upon the two pillars had pomegranates also above, over against the belly which was by the network: and the pomegranates were two hundred in rows round about" (1 Kings 7:20) and which formed the border of the high priest's dress, a frieze of "pomegranates of blue, and of purple, and of scarlet, round about the hem thereof; and bells of gold between them round about" (Exodus 28:33).

The brass button that secures the farmer's collar is an unassertive, puritanical understatement of Matthew Boulton's eighteenth-century cut-steel button made in the factory of James Watt. His shirt button is mother-of-pearl, made by James Boepple from Mississippi fresh-water mussel shell, and his jacket button is of South American vegetable ivory passing for horn.

The farmer and his wife are attended by symbols, she by two plants on the porch, a potted geranium and sanseveria, both tropical and alien to Iowa; he by the three-tined American pitchfork whose triune shape is repeated throughout the painting, in the bib of the overalls, the windows, the faces, the siding of the house, to give it a formal organization of impeccable harmony.

If this painting is primarily a statement about Protestant diligence on the American frontier, carrying in its style and subject a wealth of information about imported technology, psychology, and aesthetics, it still does not turn away from a pervasive cultural theme of Mediterranean origin—a tension between the growing and the ungrowing, between vegetable and mineral, organic and inorganic, wheat and iron.

Transposed back into its native geography, this icon of the lord of metals with his iron sceptre, head wreathed with glass and silver, buckled in tin and brass, and a chaste bride who has already taken on the metallic thraldom of her plight in the gold ovals of her hair and brooch, are Dis and Persephone posed in a royal portrait among the attributes of the first Mediterranean trinity, Zeus in the blue sky and lightning rod, Poseidon in the trident of the pitchfork, Hades in the metals. It is a picture of a sheaf of golden grain, female and cyclical, perennial and the mother of civilization; and of metal shaped into scythe and hoe: nature and technology, earth and farmer, man and world, and their achievement together.

STEPHEN JAY GOULD

The Misnamed, Mistreated, and Misunderstood Irish Elk

Nature herself seems by the vast magnitude and stately horns, she has given this creature, to have singled it out as it were, and showed it such regard, with a design to distinguish it remarkably from the common herd of all other smaller quadrupeds.

THOMAS MOLYNEUX, 1697

The Irish Elk, the Holy Roman Empire, and the English Horn form a strange ensemble indeed. But they share the common distinction of their completely inappropriate names. The Holy Roman Empire, Voltaire tells us, was neither holy, nor Roman, nor an empire. The English horn is a continental oboe; the original versions were curved, hence "angular" (corrupted to English) horn. The Irish Elk was neither exclusively Irish, nor an elk. It was the largest deer that ever lived. Its enormous antlers were even more impressive. Dr. Molyneux marveled at "these spacious horns" in the first published description of 1697. In 1842, Rathke described them in a language unexcelled for the expression of enormity as *bewunderungswuerdig*. Although *The Guinness Book of World Records* ignores fossils and honors the American moose, the antlers of the Irish Elk have never been exceeded, or even approached, in the history of life. Reliable estimates of their total span range up to 12 feet. This figure seems all the more impressive when we recognize that the antlers were probably shed and regrown annually, as in all other true deer.

Fossil antlers of the giant deer have long been known in Ireland, where they occur in lake sediments underneath peat deposits. Before attracting the attention of scientists, they had been used as gateposts,

142

and even as a temporary bridge to span a rivulet in County Tyrone. One story, probably apocryphal, tells of a huge bonfire made of their bones and antlers in County Antrim to celebrate the victory over Napoleon at Waterloo. They were called elk because the European moose (an "elk" to Englishmen) was the only familiar animal with antlers that even approached those of the giant deer in size.

The first known drawing of giant deer antlers dates from 1588. Nearly a century later, Charles II received a pair of antlers and (according to Dr. Molyneux) "valued them so highly for their prodigious largeness" that he set them up in the horn gallery of Hampton Court, where they "so vastly exceed" all others in size "that the rest appear to lose much of their curiosity."

Ireland's exclusive claim vanished in 1746 (although the name stuck) when a skull and antlers were unearthed in Yorkshire, England. The first continental discovery followed in 1781 from Germany, while the first complete skeleton (still standing in the museum of Edinburgh University) was exhumed from the Isle of Man in the 1820s.

We now know that the giant deer ranged as far east as Siberia and China and as far south as northern Africa. Specimens from England and Eurasia are almost always fragmentary, and nearly all the fine specimens that adorn so many museums throughout the world come from Ireland. The giant deer evolved during the glacial period of the last few million years and may have survived to historic times in continental Europe, but it became extinct in Ireland about 11,000 years ago.

"Among the fossils of the British empire," wrote James Parkinson in 1811, "none are more calculated to excite astonishment." And so it has been throughout the history of paleontology. Putting aside both the curious anecdotes and the sheer wonder that immensity always inspires, the importance of the giant deer lies in its contribution to debates about evolutionary theory. Every great evolutionist has used the giant deer to defend his favored views. The controversy has centered around two main issues: (1) Could antlers of such bulk be of any use? and (2) Why did the giant deer become extinct?

Since debate on the Irish Elk has long centered on the reasons for its extinction, it is ironic that the primary purpose of Molyneux's original article was to argue that it must still be alive. Many seventeenth-century scientists maintained that the extinction of any species would be inconsistent with God's goodness and perfection. Dr. Molyneux's article of 1697 begins:

> That no real species of living creatures is so utterly extinct, as to be lost entirely out of the World, since it was first created, is the opinion of many naturalists; and 'tis grounded on so good a principle of Providence taking care in general of all its animal productions, that it deserves our assent.

Yet the giant deer no longer inhabited Ireland, and Molyneux was forced to search elsewhere. After reading travelers' reports of antler size in the American moose, he concluded that the Irish Elk must be the same animal; the tendency toward exaggeration in such accounts is apparently universal and timeless. Since he could find neither figure nor an accurate description of the moose, his conclusions are not as absurd as modern knowledge would indicate. Molyneax attributed the giant deer's demise in Ireland to an "epidemick distemper," caused by "a certain ill constitution of air."

For the next century arguments raged along Molyneux's line— to which modern species did the giant deer belong? Opinion was equally divided between the moose and the reindeer.

As eighteenth-century geologists unraveled the fossil record of ancient life, it became more and more difficult to argue that the odd and unknown creatures revealed by fossils were all still living in some remote portion of the globe. Perhaps God had not created just once and for all time; perhaps He had experimented continually in both creation and destruction. If so, the world was surely older than the six thousand years that literalists allowed.

The question of extinction was the first great battleground of modern paleontology. In America, Thomas Jefferson maintained the old view, while Georges Cuvier, the great French paleontologist, was using the Irish Elk to prove that extinction did occur. By 1812 Cuvier had resolved two pressing issues: by minute anatomical description, he proved that the Irish Elk was not like any modern animal; and by placing it among many fossil mammals with no modern counterparts, he established the fact of extinction and set the basis for a geologic time scale.

Once the fact of extinction had been settled, debate moved to the time of the event: in particular, had the Irish Elk survived the flood? This was no idle matter, for if the flood or some previous catastrophe had wiped out the giant deer, then its demise had natural (or supernatural) causes. Archdeacon Maunsell, a dedicated amateur, wrote in 1825: "I apprehended they must have been destroyed by some overwhelming deluge." A certain Dr. MacCulloch even believed that the fossils were found standing erect, noses elevated — a final gesture to the rising flood, as well as a final plea: don't make waves.

If, however, they had survived the flood, then their exterminating angel could only have been the naked ape himself. Gideon Mantell, writing in 1851, blamed Celtic tribes; in 1830, Hibbert implicated the Romans and the extravagant slaughters of their public games. Lest we assume that our destructive potential was recognized only recently, Hibbert wrote in 1830: "Sir Thomas Molyneux conceived that a sort of distemper, or pestilential murrain, might have cut off the Irish Elks. . . . It is, however, questionable, if the human race has not occasionally proved as formidable as a pestilence in exterminating from various districts, whole races of wild animals."

In 1846, Britain's greatest paleontologist, Sir Richard Owen, reviewed the evidence and concluded that in Ireland at least, the giant deer had perished before man's arrival. By this time, Noah's flood as a serious geologic proposition had passed from the scene. What then had wiped out the giant deer?

Charles Darwin published the *Origin of Species* in 1859. Within ten years virtually all scientists had accepted the *fact* of evolution. But the debate about causes and mechanisms was not resolved (in Darwin's favor) until the 1940s. Darwin's theory of natural selection requires that evolutionary changes be adaptive—that is, that they be useful to the organism. Therefore, anti-Darwinians searched the fossil record for cases of evolution that could not have benefited the animals involved.

The theory of orthogenesis became a touchstone for anti-Darwinian paleontologists, for it claimed that evolution proceeded in straight lines that natural selection could not regulate. Certain trends, once started, could not be stopped even if they led to extinction. Thus certain oysters, it was said, coiled their valves upon each other until they sealed the animal permanently within; saber-toothed "tigers" could not stop growing their teeth or mammoths their tusks.

But by far the most famous example of orthogenesis was the Irish Elk itself. The giant deer had evolved from small forms with even smaller antlers. Although the antlers were useful at first, their growth could not be contained and, like the sorcerer's apprentice, the giant deer discovered only too late that even good things have their limits. Bowed by the weight of their cranial excrescences, caught in the trees or mired in the ponds, they died. What wiped out the Irish Elk? They themselves or, rather, their own antlers did.

In 1925, the American paleontologist R. S. Lull invoked the giant deer to attack Darwinism: "Natural selection will not account for overspecialization, for it is manifest that, while an organ can be brought to the point of perfection by selection, it would never be carried to a condition where it is an actual menace to survival... [as in] the great branching antlers of the extinct Irish deer."

Darwinians, led by Julian Huxley, launched a counterattack in the 1930s. Huxley noted that as deer get larger—either during their own growth or in the comparison of related adults of different sizes—the antlers do not increase in the same proportion as body size; they increase faster, so that the antlers of large deer are not only absolutely larger but also relatively larger than those of small deer. For such regular and orderly change of shape with increasing size, Huxley used the term allometry.

Allometry provided a comfortable explanation for the giant deer's antlers. Since the Irish Elk had the largest body size of any deer, its relatively enormous antlers could have been a simple result of the allometric relationship present among all deer. We need only assume that increased body size was favored by natural selection; the large antlers might have been an automatic consequence. They might even have been slightly harmful in themselves, but this disadvantage was more than compensated by the benefits of larger size, and the trend continued. Of course, when problems of larger antlers outweighed the advantages of larger bodies, the trend would cease since it could no longer be favored by natural selection.

Almost every modern textbook of evolution presents the Irish Elk in this light, citing the allometric explanation to counter orthogenetic theories. As a trusting student, I had assumed that such constant repetition must be firmly based on copious data. Later I discovered that textbook dogma is self-perpetuating; therefore, three years ago I was disappointed, but not really surprised, to discover that this widely touted explanation was based on no data whatsoever. Aside from a few desultory attempts to find the largest set of antlers, no one had ever measured an Irish Elk. Yardstick in hand, I resolved to rectify this situation.

The National Museum of Ireland in Dublin has seventeen specimens on display and many more, piled antler upon antler, in a nearby warehouse. Most large museums in western Europe and America own an Irish Elk, and the giant deer adorns many trophy rooms of English and Irish gentry. The largest antlers grace the entranceway to Adare Manor, home of the Earl of Dunraven. The sorriest skeleton sits in the cellar of Bunratty Castle, where many merry and slightly inebriated tourists repair for coffee each evening after a medieval banquet. This poor fellow, when I met him early the morning after, was smoking a cigar, missing two teeth, and carrying three coffee cups on the tines of his antlers. For those who enjoy invidious comparisons, the largest antlers in America are at Yale; the smallest in the world at Harvard.

To determine if the giant deer's antlers increased allometrically, I compared antler and body size. For antler size, I used a compounded measure of antler length, antler width, and the lengths of major tines. Body length, or the length and width of major bones, might be the most appropriate measure of body size, but I could not use it because the vast majority of specimens consist only of a skull and its attached antlers. Moreover, the few complete skeletons are invariably made up of several animals, much plaster, and an occasional ersatz (the first skeleton in Edinburgh once sported a horse's pelvis). Skull length therefore served as my measure of overall size. The skull reaches its final length at a very early age (all my specimens are older) and does not vary thereafter; it is, therefore, a good indicator of body size. My sample included seventy-nine skulls and antlers from museums and homes in Ireland, Britain, continental Europe, and the United States.

My measurements showed a strong positive correlation between antler size and body size, with the antlers increasing in size two and one-half times faster than body size from small to large males. This is not a plot of individual growth; it is a relationship among adults of different body size. Thus, the allometric hypothesis is affirmed. If natural selection favored large deer, then relatively larger antlers would appear as a correlated result of no necessary significance in itself.

Yet, even as I affirmed the allometric relationship, I began to doubt the traditional explanation—for it contained a curious remnant of the older, orthogenetic view. It assumed that the antlers are not adaptive in themselves and were tolerated only because the advantages of increased body size were so great. But why must we assume that the immense antlers had no primary function? The opposite interpretation is equally possible: that selection operated primarily to increase antler size, thus yielding increased body size as a secondary consequence. The case for inadaptive antlers has never rested on more than subjective wonderment born of their immensity.

Views long abandoned often continue to exert their influence in subtle ways. The orthogenetic argument lived on in the allometric context proposed to replace it. I believe that the supposed problem of "unwieldy" or "cumbersome" antlers is an illusion rooted in a notion now abandoned by students of animal behavior.

To nineteenth-century Darwinians, the natural world was a cruel

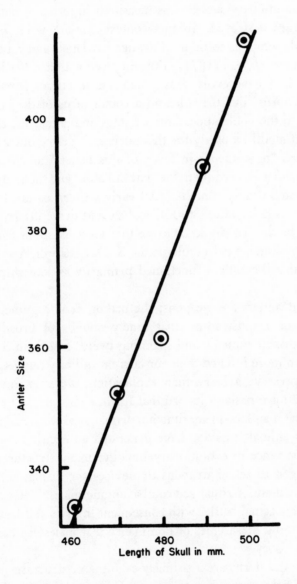

Graph showing relative increase in antler size with increasing skull length in Irish Elks. Each point is the average for all skulls in a 10 mm. interval of length; the actual data include 81 individuals. Antler size increases more than 2½ times as fast as skull length—a line with a slope of 1.0 (45 degree angle with the x-axis) would indicate equal rates of increase on these logarithmic scales. The slope here is obviously very much higher.

place. Evolutionary success was measured in terms of battles won and enemies destroyed. In this context, antlers were viewed as formidable weapons to be used against predators and rival males. In his *Descent of Man* (1871), Darwin toyed with another idea: that antlers might have evolved as ornaments to attract females. "If, then, the horns, like the splendid accouterments of the knights of old, add to the noble appearance of stags and antelopes, they may have been modified partly for this purpose." Yet he quickly added that he had "no evidence in favor of this belief," and went on to interpret antlers according to the "law of battle" and their advantages in "reiterated deadly contests." All early writers assumed that the Irish Elk used its antlers to kill wolves and drive off rival males in fierce battle. To my knowledge this view has been challenged only by the Russian paleontologist L. S. Davitashvili, who asserted in 1961 that the antlers functioned primarily as courtship signals to females.

Now, if antlers are weapons, the orthogenetic argument is appealing, for I must admit that ninety pounds of broad-palmed antler, regrown annually and spanning twelve feet from tip to tip, seems even more inflated than our current military budget. Therefore, to preserve a Darwinian explanation, we must invoke the allometric hypothesis in its original form.

But what if antlers do not function primarily as weapons? Modern studies of animal behavior have generated an exciting concept of great importance to evolutionary biology: many structures previously judged as actual weapons or devices for display to females are actually used for ritualized combat among males. Their function is to prevent actual battle (with consequent injuries and loss of life) by establishing hierarchies of dominance that males can easily recognize and obey.

Antlers and horns are a primary example of structures used for ritualized behavior. They serve, according to Valerius Geist, as "visual dominance-rank symbols." Large antlers confer high status and access to females. Since there can be no evolutionary advantage more potent than a guarantee of successful reproduction, selective pressures for larger antlers must often be intense. As more and more horned animals are observed in their natural environment, older ideas of deadly battle are yielding to evidence of purely ritualized display without body contact, or fighting in ways clearly designed to prevent bodily injury. This has been observed in red deer by Beninde and Darling, caribou by Kelsall, and in mountain sheep by Geist.

As devices for display among males, the enormous antlers of the Irish Elk finally make sense as structures adaptive in themselves. Moreover, as R. Coope of Birmingham University pointed out to me, the detailed morphology of the antlers can be explained, for the first time, in this context. Deer with broad-palmed antlers tend to show the full width of their antlers in display. The modern fallow deer (considered by many as the Irish Elk's nearest living relative) must rotate its head from side to side in order to show its palm. This would have created great problems for giant deer, since the torque produced by swinging ninety-pound antlers would have been immense. But the antlers of the Irish Elk were arranged to display the palm fully when the animal looked straight ahead. Both the unusual configuration and the enormous size of the antlers can be explained by postulating that they were used for display rather than for combat.

If the antlers were adaptive, why did the Irish Elk become extinct (at least in Ireland)? The probable answer to this old dilemma is, I am afraid, rather commonplace. The giant deer flourished in Ireland for only the briefest of times—during the so-called Alleröd interstadial phase at the end of the last glaciation. This period, a minor warm phase between two colder epochs, lasted for about 1,000 years, from 12,000 to 11,000 years before the present. (The Irish Elk had migrated to Ireland during the previous glacial phase when lower sea levels established a connection between Ireland and continental Europe.) Although it was well adapted to the grassy, sparsely wooded, open country of Alleröd times, it apparently could not adapt either to the subarctic tundra that followed in the next cold epoch or to the heavy forestation that developed after the final retreat of the ice sheet.

Extinction is the fate of most species, usually because they fail to adapt rapidly enough to changing conditions of climate or competition. Darwinian evolution decrees that no animal shall actively develop a harmful structure, but it offers no guarantee that useful structures will continue to be adaptive in changed circumstances. The Irish Elk was probably a victim of its own previous success. *Sic transit gloria mundi.*

LEWIS THOMAS

Computers

You can make computers that are almost human. In some respects they are superhuman; they can beat most of us at chess, memorize whole telephone books at a glance, compose music of a certain kind and write obscure poetry, diagnose heart ailments, send personal invitations to vast parties, even go transiently crazy. No one has yet programmed a computer to be of two minds about a hard problem, or to burst out laughing, but that may come. Sooner or later, there will be real human hardware, great whirring, clicking cabinets intelligent enough to read magazines and vote, able to think rings around the rest of us.

Well, maybe, but not for a while anyway. Before we begin organizing sanctuaries and reservations for our software selves, lest we vanish like the whales, here is a thought to relax with.

Even when technology succeeds in manufacturing a machine as big as Texas to do everything we recognize as human, it will still be, at best, a single individual. This amounts to nothing, practically speaking. To match what we can do, there would have to be 3 billion of them with more coming down the assembly line, and I doubt that anyone will put up the money, much less make room. And even so, they would all have to be wired together, intricately and delicately, as we are, communicating with each other, talking incessantly, listening. If they weren't *at* each other this way, all their waking hours, they wouldn't be anything like human, after all. I think we're safe, for a long time ahead.

It is in our collective behavior that we are most mysterious. We won't be able to construct machines like ourselves until we've understood this, and we're not even close. All we know is the phenomenon:

we spend our time sending messages to each other, talking and trying to listen at the same time, exchanging information. This seems to be our most urgent biological function; it is what we do with our lives. By the time we reach the end, each of us has taken in a staggering store, enough to exhaust any computer, much of it incomprehensible, and we generally manage to put out even more than we take in. Information is our source of energy; we are driven by it. It has become a tremendous enterprise, a kind of energy system on its own. All 3 billion of us are being connected by telephones, radios, television sets, airplanes, satellites, harangues on public-address systems, newspapers, magazines, leaflets dropped from great heights, words got in edgewise. We are becoming a grid, a circuitry around the earth. If we keep at it, we will become a computer to end all computers, capable of fusing all the thoughts of the world into a syncytium.

Already, there are no closed, two-way conversations. Any word you speak this afternoon will radiate out in all directions, around town before tomorrow, out and around the world before Tuesday, accelerating to the speed of light, modulating as it goes, shaping new and unexpected messages, emerging at the end as an enormously funny Hungarian joke, a fluctuation in the money market, a poem, or simply a long pause in someone's conversation in Brazil.

We do a lot of collective thinking, probably more than any other social species, although it goes on in something like secrecy. We don't acknowledge the gift publicly, and we are not as celebrated as the insects, but we do it. Effortlessly, without giving it a moment's thought, we are capable of changing our language, music, manners, morals, entertainment, even the way we dress, all around the earth in a year's turning. We seem to do this by general agreement, without voting or even polling. We simply think our way along, pass information around, exchange codes disguised as art, change our minds, transform ourselves.

Computers cannot deal with such levels of improbability, and it is just as well. Otherwise, we might be tempted to take over the control of ourselves in order to make long-range plans, and that would surely be the end of us. It would mean that some group or other, marvelously intelligent and superbly informed, undoubtedly guided by a computer, would begin deciding what human society ought to be like, say, over the next five hundred years or so, and the rest of us would be persuaded, one way or another, to go along. The process of social evolution would then grind to a standstill, and we'd be stuck in today's rut for a millennium.

Much better we work our way out of it on our own, without governance. The future is too interesting and dangerous to be entrusted to any predictable, reliable agency. We need all the fallibility we can get. Most of all, we need to preserve the absolute unpredictability and total improbability of our connected minds. That way we can keep open all the options, as we have in the past.

It would be nice to have better ways of monitoring what we're up to so that we could recognize change while it is occurring, instead of waking up as we do now to the astonished realization that the whole century just past wasn't what we thought it was, at all. Maybe computers can be used to help in this, although I rather doubt it. You can make simulation models of cities, but what you learn is that they seem to be beyond the reach of intelligent analysis; if you try to use common sense to make predictions, things get more botched up than ever. This is interesting, since a city is the most concentrated aggregation of humans, all exerting whatever influence they can bring to bear. The city seems to have a life of its own. If we cannot understand how this works, we are not likely to get very far with human society at large.

Still, you'd think there would be some way in. Joined together, the great mass of human minds around the earth seems to behave like a coherent, living system. The trouble is that the flow of information is mostly one-way. We are all obsessed by the need to feed information in, as fast as we can, but we lack sensing mechanisms for getting anything much back. I will confess that I have no more sense of what goes on in the mind of mankind than I have for the mind of an ant. Come to think of it, this might be a good place to start.

ROBERT FINCH

Very Like a Whale

One day last week at sunset I went back to Corporation Beach in Dennis to see what traces, if any, might be left of the great, dead finback whale that had washed up there several weeks before. The beach was not as hospitable as it had been that sunny Saturday morning after Thanksgiving when thousands of us streamed over the sand to gaze and look. A few cars were parked in the lot, but these kept their inhabitants. Bundled up against a sharp wind, I set off along the twelve-foot swath of trampled beach grass, a raw highway made in a few hours by ten thousand feet that day.

I came to the spot where the whale had beached and marveled that such a magnitude of flesh could have been there one day and gone the next. But the carcass had been hauled off and the tide had smoothed and licked clean whatever vestiges had remained. The cold, salt wind had lifted from the sands the last trace of that pervasive stench of decay that clung to our clothes for days, and now blew clean and sharp into my nostrils.

The only sign that anything unusual had been there was that the beach was a little too clean, not quite so pebbly and littered as the surrounding areas, as the grass above a new grave is always fresher and greener. What had so manifestly occupied this space a short while ago was now utterly gone. And yet the whale still lay heavily on my mind; a question lingered, like a persistent odor in the air. And its dark shape, though now sunken somewhere beneath the waves, still loomed before me, beckoning, asking something.

What was it? What had we seen? Even the several thousand of us that managed to get down to the beach before it was closed off did not see much. Whales, dead or alive, are protected these days under the Federal Marine Mammals Act, and shortly after we arrived, local police kept anyone from actually touching the whale. I could hardly regret this, since in the past beached whales, still alive, have had cigarettes put out in their eyes and bits of flesh hacked off with pocket knives by souvenir seekers. And so, kept at a distance, we looked on while the specialists worked, white-coated, plastic-gloved autopsists from the New England Aquarium, hacking open the thick hide with carving knives and plumbing its depth for samples to be shipped to Canada for analysis and deter-mination of causes of death. What was it they were pulling out? What fetid mystery would they pluck from that huge coffin of dead flesh? We would have to trust them for the answer.

But as the crowds continued to grow around the whale's body like flies around carrion, the question seemed to me, and still seems, not so much why did the whale die, as why had we come to see it? What made this dark bulk such a human magnet, spilling us over onto private lawns and fields? I watched electricians and oil truck drivers pulling their vehicles off the road and clambering down to the beach. Women in high heels and pearls, on their way to Filene's, stumbled through the loose sand to gaze at a corpse. The normal human pattern was broken and a carnival atmosphere was created, appropriate enough in the literal sense of "a farewell to the flesh." But there was also a sense of pilgrimage in those trekking across the beach, an obligation to view such a thing. But for what? Are we really such novices to death? Or so reverent toward it?

I could understand my own semiprofessional interest in the whale, but what had drawn these hordes? There are some obvious answers, of course: a break in the dull routine, "something different." An old human desire to associate ourselves with great and extraordinary events. We placed children and sweethearts in front of the corpse and clicked cameras. "Ruthie and the whale." "Having a whale of a time on Cape Cod."

Curiosity, the simplest answer, doesn't really answer anything. What, after all, did we learn by being there? We were more like children at a zoo, pointing and poking, or Indians on a pristine beach, gazing in innocent wonder at strange European ships come

ashore. Yet, as the biologists looted it with vials and plastic bags
and the press captured it on film, the spectators also tried to *make*
something of the whale. Circling around it as though for some hold
on its slippery bulk, we grappled it with metaphors, lashed similes
around its immense girth. It lay upside down, overturned "like a
trailer truck." Its black skin was cracked and peeling, red underneath, "like a used tire." The distended, corrugated lower jaw, "a
giant accordion," was afloat with the gas of putrefaction and, when
pushed, oscillated slowly "like an enormous waterbed." Like our
primitive ancestors, we still tend to make images to try to comprehend the unknown.

But what were we looking at? Or more to the point, from what
perspective were we looking at it? What did we see in it that might
tell us why we had come? A male finback whale—*Balaenoptera
physalus*—a baleen cetacean. The second largest creature ever to
live on earth. An intelligent and complex mammal. A cause for
conservationists. A remarkably adapted swimming and eating machine. Perfume, pet food, engineering oil. A magnificent scientific
specimen. A tourist attraction. A media event, a "day to remember."
A health menace, a "possible carrier of a communicable disease."
A municipal headache and a navigational hazard. Material for an
essay.

On the whale's own hide seemed to be written its life history,
which we could remark but not read. The right fluke was almost
entirely gone, lost in some distant accident or battle and now healed
over with a white scar. The red eye, unexpectedly small and mam-
malian, gazed out at us with fiery blankness. Like the glacial
scratches sometimes found on our boulders, there were strange
marks or grooves in the skin around the anal area, perhaps caused
by scraping the ocean bottom.

Yet we could not seem to scratch its surface. The whale—dead,
immobile, in full view—nonetheless shifted kaleidoscopically before our eyes. The following morning it was gone, efficiently and
sanitarily removed, like the week's garbage. What was it we saw?
I have a theory, though probably (as they say in New England) it
hardly does.

There is a tendency these days to defend whales and other endangered animals by pointing out their similarities to human beings. Cetaceans, we are told, are very intelligent. They possess a highly complex language and have developed sophisticated communications systems that transmit over long distances. They form family groups, develop social structures and personal relationships, and express loyalty and affection toward one another. Much of their behavior seems to be recreational: they sing, they play. And so on.

These are not sentimental claims. Whales apparently do these things, at least as far as our sketchy information about their habits warrants such interpretations. And for my money, any argument that helps to preserve these magnificent creatures can't be all bad.

I take exception to this approach not because it is wrong, but because it is wrongheaded and misleading. It is exclusive, anthropocentric, and does not recognize nature in its own right. It implies that whales and other creatures have value only insofar as they reflect man himself and conform to his ideas of beauty and achievement. This attitude is not really far removed from that of the whalers themselves. To consume whales solely for their nourishment of human values is only a step from consuming them for meat and corset staves. It is not only presumptuous and patronizing, but it is misleading and does both whales and men a grave disservice. Whales have an inalienable right to exist, not because they resemble man *or* because they are useful to him, but simply because they do exist, because they have a proven fitness to the exactitudes of being on a global scale matched by few other species. If they deserve our admiration and respect, it is because, as Henry Beston put it, "They are other nations, caught with ourselves in the net of life and time, fellow prisoners of the splendour and travail of life."

But that still doesn't explain the throngs who came pell-mell to stare and conjecture at the dead whale that washed up at Corporation Beach and dominated it for a day like some extravagant *memento mori*. Surely we were not flattering ourselves, consciously or unconsciously, with any human comparisons to that rotting hulk. Nor was there much, in its degenerate state, that it had to teach us. And yet we came—why?

The answer may be so obvious that we have ceased to recognize it. Man, I believe, has a crying need to confront otherness in the universe. Call it nature, wilderness, the "great outdoors," or what you will—we crave to look out and behold something other than our own human faces staring back at us, expectantly and increasingly frustrated. What the human spirit wants, as Robert Frost said, "Is not its own love back in copy-speech, / But counter-love, original response."

This sense of otherness is, I feel, as necessary a requirement to our personalities as food and warmth are to our bodies. Just as an individual, cut off from human contact and stimulation, may atrophy and die of loneliness and neglect, so mankind is today in a similar, though more subtle, danger of cutting himself off from the natural world he shares with all creatures. If our physical survival depends upon our devising a proper use of earth's materials and produce, our growth as a species depends equally upon our establishing a vital and generative relationship with what surrounds us.

We need plants, animals, weather, unfettered shores and unbroken woodland, not merely for a stable and healthy environment, but as an antidote to introversion, a preventive against human inbreeding. Here in particular, in the splendor of natural life, we have an extraordinary reservoir of the Cape's untapped possibilities and modes of being, ways of experiencing life, of knowing wind and wave. After all, how many neighborhoods have whales wash up in their backyards? To confine this world in zoos or in exclusive human terms does injustice not only to nature, but to ourselves as well.

Ever since his beginnings, when primitive man adopted totems and animal spirits to himself and assumed their shapes in ritual dance, *Homo sapiens* has been a superbly imitative animal. He has looked out across the fields and seen and learned. Somewhere along the line, though, he decided that nature was his enemy, not his ally, and needed to be confined and controlled. He abstracted nature and lost sight of it. Only now are we slowly realizing that nature can be confined only by narrowing our own concepts of it, which in turn narrows us. That is why we came to see the whale.

We substitute human myth for natural reality and wonder why we starve for nourishment. "Your Cape" becomes "your Mall," as the local radio jingle has it. Thoreau's "huge and real Cape Cod . . . a wild, rank place with no flattery in it," becomes the Chamber of Commerce's "Rural Seaside Charm"—until forty tons of dead flesh wash ashore and give the lie to such thin, flattering conceptions, flesh whose stench is still the stench of life that stirs us to reaction and response. That is why we came to see the whale. Its mute, immobile bulk represented that ultimate, unknowable otherness that we both seek and recoil from, and shouted at us louder than the policeman's bullhorn that the universe is fraught, not merely with response or indifference, but incarnate assertion.

Later that day the Dennis Board of Health declared the whale carcass to be a "health menace" and warned us off the beach. A health menace? More likely an intoxicating, if strong, medicine that might literally bring us to our senses.

But if those of us in the crowd failed to grasp the whale that day, others did not have much better luck. Even in death the whale escaped us: the tissue samples taken in the autopsy proved insufficient for analysis and the biologists concluded, "We will never know why the whale died." The carcass, being towed tail-first by a Coast Guard cutter for a final dumping beyond Provincetown, snapped a six-inch hawser. Eluding further attempts to reattach it, it finally sank from sight. Even our powers of disposal, it seemed, were questioned that day.

And so, while we are left on shore with the memory of a deflated and stinking carcass and of bullhorns that blared and scattered us like flies, somewhere out beyond the rolled waters and the shining winter sun, the whale sings its own death in matchless, sirenian strains.

EDWARD HOAGLAND

Hailing the Elusory
Mountain Lion

The swan song sounded by the wilderness grows fainter, ever more constricted, until only sharp ears can catch it at all. It fades to a nearly inaudible level, and yet there never is going to be any one time when we can say right *now* it is gone. Wolves meet their maker in wholesale lots, but coyotes infiltrate eastward, northward, southeastward. Woodland caribou and bighorn sheep are vanishing fast, but moose have expanded their range in some areas.

Mountain lions used to have practically the run of the Western Hemisphere, and they still do occur from Cape Horn to the Big Muddy River at the boundary of the Yukon and on the coasts of both oceans, so that they are the most versatile land mammal in the New World, probably taking in more latitudes than any other four-footed wild creature anywhere. There are perhaps only four to six thousand left in the United States, though there is no place that they didn't once go, eating deer, elk, pikas, porcupines, grasshoppers, and dead fish on the beach. They were called mountain lions in the Rockies, pumas (originally an Incan word) in the Southwestern states, cougars (a naturalist's corruption of an Amazonian Indian word) in the Northwest, panthers in the traditionalist East— "painters" in dialect-proud New England—or catamounts. The Dutchmen of New Netherland called them tigers, red tigers, deer tigers, and the Spaniards *leones* or *leopardos*. They liked to eat horses—wolves preferred beef and black bears favored pork—but as adversaries of mankind they were overshadowed at first because bears appeared more formidable and wolves in their howling packs were more flamboyant and more damaging financially. Yet this panoply of names is itself quite a tribute, and somehow the legends about "panthers" have lingered longer than bear or wolf tales, helped by the animal's own limber, far-traveling stealth and as a carryover from the immense mythic force of the great cats of the Old World. Though only Florida among the Eastern states is known for certain to have any left, no wild knot of mountains or swamp is without rumors of panthers; nowadays people delight in these, keeping their eyes peeled. It's wishful, and the wandering, secretive nature of the beast ensures that even Eastern panthers will not soon be certifiably extinct. An informal census among experts in 1963 indicated that an island of twenty-five or more may have survived in the New Brunswick–Maine–Quebec region, and Louisiana may still have a handful, and perhaps eight live isolated in the Black Hills of South Dakota, and the Oklahoma panhandle may have a small colony—all outside the established range in Florida, Texas, and the Far West. As with the blue whale, who will be able to say when they have been eliminated?

"Mexican lion" is another name for mountain lions in the border states—a name that might imply a meager second-best rating there yet ties to the majestic African beasts. Lions are at least twice as big as mountain lions, measuring by weight, though they are nearly the same in length because of the mountain lion's superb long tail. Both animals sometimes pair up affectionately with mates and hunt in tandem, but mountain lions go winding through life in ones and twos, whereas the lion is a harem-keeper, harem-dweller, the males eventually becoming stay-at-homes, heavy figureheads. Lions enjoy the grassy flatlands, forested along the streams, and they stay put, engrossed in communal events—roaring, grunting, growling with a racket like the noise of gears being stripped—unless the game moves on. They sun themselves, preside over the numerous kibbutz young, sneeze from the dust, and bask in dreams, occasionally waking up to issue reverberating, guttural pronouncements which serve notice that they are now awake.

Mountain lions spirit themselves away in saw-toothed canyons and on escarpments instead, and when conversing with their mates they coo like pigeons, sob like women, emit a flat slight shriek, a popping bubbling growl, or mew, or yowl. They growl and suddenly caterwaul into falsetto—the famous scarifying, metallic scream functioning as a kind of hunting cry close up, to terrorize and start the game. They ramble as much as twenty-five miles in a night, maintaining a large loop of territory which they cover every week or two. It's a solitary, busy life, involving a survey of several valleys, many deer herds. Like tigers and leopards, mountain lions are not sociably inclined and don't converse at length with the whole waiting world, but they are even less noisy; they seem to speak most eloquently with their feet. Where a tiger would roar, a mountain lion screams like a castrato. Where a mountain lion hisses, a leopard would snarl like a truck stuck in snow.

Leopards are the best counterpart to mountain lions in physique and in the tenor of their lives. Supple, fierce creatures, skilled at concealment but with great self-assurance and drive, leopards are bolder when facing human beings than the American cats. Basically they are hot-land beasts and not such remarkable travelers individually, though as a race they once inhabited the broad Eurasian land mass all the way from Great Britain to Malaysia, as well as Africa. As late as the 1960s, a few were said to be still holding out on the shore of the Mediterranean at Mount Mycale, Turkey. (During a forest fire twenty years ago a yearling swam the narrow straits to the Greek island Samos and holed up in a cave, where he was duly killed—perhaps the last leopard ever to set foot in Europe on his own.) Leopards are thicker and shorter than adult mountain lions and seem to lead an athlete's indolent, incurious life much of the time, testing their perfected bodies by clawing tree trunks, chewing on old skulls, executing acrobatic leaps, and then rousing themselves to the semiweekly antelope kill. Built with supreme hardness and economy, they make little allowance for man—they don't see him as different. They relish the flesh of his dogs, and they run up a tree when hunted and then sometimes spring down, as heavy as a chunk of iron wrapped in a flag. With stunning, gorgeous coats, their tight, dervish faces carved in a snarl, they head for the hereafter as if it were just one more extra-emphatic leap—as impersonal in death as the crack of the rifle was.

The American leopard, the jaguar, is a powerfully built, serious fellow, who, before white men arrived, wandered as far north as the Carolinas, but his best home is the humid basin of the Amazon. Mountain lions penetrate these ultimate jungles too, but rather thinly, thriving better in the cooler, drier climate of the untenanted pampas and on the mountain slopes. They are blessed with a pleasant but undazzling coat, tan except for a white belly, mouth and throat, and some black behind the ears, on the tip of the tail and at the sides of the nose, and so they are hunted as symbols, not for their fur. The cubs are spotted, leopardlike, much as lion cubs are. If all of the big cats developed from a common ancestry, the mountain lions' specialization has been unpresumptuous—away from bulk and savagery to traveling light. Toward deer, their prey, they may be as ferocious as leopards, but not toward chance acquaintances such as man. They sometimes break their necks, their jaws, their teeth, springing against the necks of quarry they have crept close to—a fate in part resulting from the circumstance that they can't ferret out the weaker individuals in a herd by the device of a long chase, the way wolves do; they have to take the luck of the draw. None of the cats possess enough lung capacity for gruelling runs. They depend upon shock tactics, bursts of speed, sledge-hammer leaps, strong collarbones for hitting power, and shearing dentition, whereas wolves employ all the advantages of time in killing their quarry, as well as the numbers and gaiety of the pack, biting the beast's nose and rump—the technique of a thousand cuts—lapping the bloody snow. Wolves sometimes even have a cheering section of flapping ravens accompanying them, eager to scavenge after the brawl.

It's a risky business for the mountain lion, staking the strength and impact of his neck against the strength of the prey animal's neck. Necessarily, he is concentrated and fierce; yet legends exist that mountain lions have irritably defended men and women lost in the wilderness against marauding jaguars, who are no friends of theirs, and (with a good deal more supporting evidence) that they are susceptible to an odd kind of fascination with human beings. Sometimes they will tentatively seek an association, hanging about a campground or following a hiker out of curiosity, perhaps, circling around and bounding up on a ledge above to watch him pass. This mild modesty has helped preserve them from extinction. If they have been unable to make any adjustments to the advent of man, they haven't suicidally opposed him either, as the buffalo, wolves and grizzlies did. In fact, at close quarters they seem bewildered. When treed, they don't breathe a hundred-proof ferocity but puzzle over what to do. They're too light-bodied to bear down on the hunter and kill him easily, even if they should attack—a course they seem to have no inclination for. In this century in the United States only one person, a child of thirteen, has been killed by a mountain lion; that was in 1924. And they're informal animals. Lolling in an informal sprawl on a high limb, they can't seem to summon any Enobarbus-like front of resistance for long. Daring men occasionally climb up and toss lassos about a cat and haul him down, strangling him by pulling from two directions, while the lion, mortified, appalled, never does muster his fighting aplomb. Although he could fight off a pack of wolves, he hasn't worked out a posture to assume toward man and his dogs. Impotently, he stiffens, as the dinosaurs must have when the atmosphere grew cold.

Someday hunting big game may come to be regarded as a form of vandalism, and the remaining big creatures of the wilderness will skulk through restricted reserves wearing radio transmitters and numbered collars, or bearing stripes of dye, as many elephants already do, to aid the busy biologists who track them from the air. Like a vanishing race of trolls, more report and memory than a reality, they will inhabit children's books and nostalgic articles, a special glamour attaching to those, like mountain lions, that are geographically incalculable and may still be sighted away from the preserves. Already we've become enthusiasts. We want game about us—at least at a summer house; it's part of privileged living. There is a precious privacy about seeing wildlife, too. Like meeting a fantastically dressed mute on the road, the fact that no words are exchanged and that *he's* not going to give an account makes the experience light-hearted; it's wholly ours. Besides, if anything out of the ordinary happened, we know we can't expect to be believed, and since it's rather fun to be disbelieved—fishermen know this—

the privacy is even more complete. Deer, otter, foxes are messengers from another condition of life, another mentality, and bring us tidings of places where we don't go.

Ten years ago at Vavenby, a sawmill town on the North Thompson River in British Columbia, a frolicsome mountain lion used to appear at dusk every ten days or so in a bluegrass field alongside the river. Deer congregated there, the river was silky and swift, cooling the summer air, and it was a festive spot for a lion to be. She was thought to be a female, and reputedly left tracks around an enormous territory to the north and west—Raft Mountain, Battle Mountain, the Trophy Range, the Murtle River, and Mahood Lake—territory on an upended, pelagic scale, much of it scarcely accessible to a man by trail, where the tiger lilies grew four feet tall. She would materialize in this field among the deer five minutes before dark, as if checking in again, a habit that may have resulted in her death eventually, though for the present the farmer who observed her visits was keeping his mouth shut about it. This was pioneer country; there were people alive who could remember the time when poisoning the carcass of a cow would net a man a pile of dead predators—a family of mountain lions to bounty, maybe half a dozen wolves, and both black bears and grizzlies. The Indians considered lion meat a delicacy, but they had clans which drew their origins at the Creation from ancestral mountain lions, or wolves or bears, so these massacres amazed them. They thought the outright bounty hunters were crazy men.

Even before Columbus, mountain lions were probably not distributed in saturation numbers anywhere, as wolves may have been. Except for the family unit—a female with her half-grown cubs— each lion seems to occupy its own spread of territory, not as a result of fights with intruders but because the young transients share the same instinct for solitude and soon sheer off to find vacant mountains and valleys. A mature lion kills only one deer every week or two, according to a study by Maurice Hornocker in Idaho, and therefore is not really a notable factor in controlling the local deer population. Rather, it keeps watch contentedly as that population grows, sometimes benefitting the herds by scaring them onto new wintering grounds that are not overbrowsed, and by its very presence warding off other lions.

This thin distribution, coupled with the mountain lion's taciturn habits, makes sighting one a matter of luck, even for game officials located in likely country. One warden in Colorado I talked to had indeed seen a pair of them fraternizing during the breeding season. He was driving a jeep over an abandoned mining road, and he passed two brown animals sitting peaceably in the grass, their heads close together. For a moment he thought they were coyotes and kept driving, when all of a sudden the picture registered that they were *cougars*! He braked and backed up, but of course they were gone. He was an old-timer, a man who had crawled inside bear dens to pull out the cubs, and knew where to find clusters of buffalo skulls in the recesses of the Rockies where the last bands had hidden; yet this cryptic instant when he was turning his jeep round a curve was the only glimpse—unprovable—that he ever got of a mountain lion.

Such glimpses usually are cryptic. During a summer I spent in Wyoming in my boyhood, I managed to see two coyotes, but both occasions were so fleeting that it required an act of faith on my part afterward to feel sure I had seen them. One of the animals vanished between rolls of ground; the other, in rougher, stonier, wooded country, cast his startled gray face in my direction and simply was gone. Hunching, he swerved for cover, and the brush closed over him. I used to climb to a vantage point above a high basin at twilight and watch the mule deer steal into the meadows to feed. The grass grew higher than their stomachs, the steep forest was close at hand, and they were as small and fragile-looking as filaments at that distance, quite human in coloring, gait and form. It was possible to visualize them as a naked Indian hunting party a hundred years before—or not to believe in their existence at all, either as Indians or deer. Minute, aphid-sized, they stepped so carefully in emerging, hundreds of feet below, that, straining my eyes, I needed to tell myself constantly that they were deer; my imagination, left to its own devices with the dusk settling down, would have made of them a dozen other creatures.

Recently, walking at night on the woods road that passes my house in Vermont, I heard footsteps in the leaves and windfalls. I waited, listening—they sounded too heavy to be anything less than a man, a large deer or a bear. A man wouldn't have been in the woods so late, my dog stood respectfully silent and still, and they did seem to shuffle portentously. Sure enough, after pausing at the edge of the road, a fully grown bear appeared, visible only in dimmest outline, staring in my direction for four or five seconds. The darkness lent a faintly red tinge to his coat; he was well built. Then, turning, he ambled off, almost immediately lost to view, though I heard the noise of his passage, interrupted by several pauses. It was all as concise as a vision, and since I had wanted to see a bear close to my own house, being a person who likes to live in a melting pot, whether in the city or country, and since it was too dark to pick out his tracks, I was grateful when the dog inquisitively urinated along the bear's path, thereby confirming that at least I had witnessed *something*. The dog seemed unsurprised, however, as if the scent were not all that remarkable, and, sure enough, the next week in the car I encountered a yearling bear in daylight two miles downhill, and a cub a month later. My farmer neighbors were politely skeptical of my accounts, having themselves caught sight of only perhaps a couple of bears in all their lives.

So it's with sympathy as well as an awareness of the tricks that enthusiasm and nightfall may play that I have been going to nearby towns seeking out people who have claimed at one time or another to have seen a mountain lion. The experts of the state—game wardens, taxidermists, the most accomplished hunters—emphatically discount the claims, but the believers are unshaken. They include some summer people who were enjoying a drink on the back terrace when the apparition of a great-tailed cat moved out along the fringe of the woods on a deer path; a boy who was hunting with his .22 years ago near the village dump and saw the animal across a gully and fired blindly, then ran away and brought back a search party, which found a tuft of toast-colored fur; and a state forestry employee, a sober woodsman, who caught the cat in his headlights while driving through Victory Bog in the wildest corner of the Northeast Kingdom. Gordon Hickok, who works for a furniture factory and has shot one or two mountain lions on hunting trips in the West, saw one cross U.S. 5 at a place called Auger Hole near Mount Hor. He tracked it with dogs a short distance, finding a fawn with its head gnawed off. A high-school English teacher reported seeing a mountain lion cross another road, near Runaway Pond, but the hunters who quickly went out decided that the prints were those of a big bobcat, splayed impressively in the mud and snow. Fifteen years ago a watchman in the fire tower on top of Bald Mountain had left grain scattered in the grooves of a flat rock under the tower to feed several deer. One night, looking down just as the dusk turned murky, he saw two slim long-tailed lions creep out of the scrubby border of spruce and inspect the rock, sniffing deer droppings and dried deer saliva. The next night, when he was in his cabin, the dog barked and, looking out the window, again he saw the vague shape of a lion just vanishing.

A dozen loggers and woodsmen told me such stories. In the Adirondacks I've also heard some persuasive avowals—one by an old dog-sled driver and trapper, a French Canadian; another by the owner of a tourist zoo, who was exhibiting a Western cougar. In Vermont perhaps the most eager rumor buffs are some of the farmers. After all, now that packaged semen has replaced the awesome farm bull and so many procedures have been mechanized, who wants to lose *all* the adventure of farming? Until recently the last mountain lion known to have been killed in the Northeast was recorded in 1881 in Barnard, Vermont. However, it has been learned that probably another one was shot from a tree in 1931 in Mundleville, New Brunswick, and still another trapped seven years later in Somerset County in Maine. Bruce S. Wright, director of the Northeastern Wildlife Station (which is operated at the University of New Brunswick with international funding), is convinced that though they are exceedingly rare, mountain lions are still part of the fauna of the region; in fact, he has plaster casts of tracks to prove it, as well as a compilation of hundreds of reported sightings. Some people may have mistaken a golden retriever for a lion, or may have intended to foment a hoax, but all in all the evidence does seem promising. Indeed, after almost twenty years of search and study, Wright himself finally saw one.

The way these sightings crop up in groups has often been pooh-poohed as greenhorn fare or as a sympathetic hysteria among neighbors, but it is just as easily explained by the habit mountain lions have of establishing a territory that they scout through at intervals, visiting an auspicious deer-ridden swamp or remote ledgy mountain. Even at such a site a successful hunt could not be mounted without trained dogs, and if the population of the big cats was extremely sparse, requiring of them long journeys during the mating season, and yet with plenty of deer all over, they might not stay for long. One or two hundred miles is no obstacle to a Western cougar. The cat might inhabit a mountain ridge one year, and then never again.

Fifteen years ago, Francis Perry, who is an ebullient muffin of a man, a farmer all his life in Brownington, Vermont, saw a mountain lion "larger and taller than a collie, and grayish yellow" (he had seen them in circuses). Having set a trap for a woodchuck, he was on his way to visit the spot when he came over a rise and, at a distance of fifty yards, saw the beast engaged in eating the dead woodchuck. It bounded off, but Perry set four light fox traps for it around the woodchuck. Apparently, a night or two later the cat returned and got caught in three of these, but they couldn't hold it; it pulled free, leaving the marks of a struggle. Noel Perry, his brother, remembers how scared Francis looked when he came home from the first episode. Noel himself saw the cat (which may have meant that Brownington Swamp was one of its haunts that summer), once when it crossed a cow pasture on another farm the brothers owned, and once when it fled past his rabbit dogs through underbrush while he was training them—he thought for a second that its big streaking form was one of the dogs. A neighbor, Robert Chase, also saw the animal that year. Then again last summer, for the first time in fifteen years, Noel Perry saw a track as big as a bear's but round like a mountain lion's, and Robert's brother, Larry Chase, saw the actual cat several times one summer evening, playing a chummy hide-and-seek with him in the fields.

Elmer and Elizabeth Ambler are in their forties, populists politically, and have bought a farm in Glover to live the good life, though he is a truck driver in Massachusetts on weekdays and must drive hard in order to be home when he can. He's bald, with large eyebrows, handsome teeth and a low forehead, but altogether a strong-looking, clear, humane face. He is an informational kind of man who will give you the history of various breeds of cattle or a talk about taxation in a slow and musical voice, and both he and his wife, a purposeful, self-sufficient redhead, are fascinated by the possibility that they live in the wilderness. Beavers inhabit the river that flows past their house. The Amblers say that on Black Mountain nearby hunters "disappear" from time to time, and bears frequent the berry patches in their back field—they see them, their visitors see them, people on the road see them, their German shepherds meet them and run back drooling with fright. They've stocked their farm with horned Herefords instead of the polled variety so that the creatures can "defend themselves." Ambler is intrigued by the thought that apart from the danger of bears, someday "a cat" might prey on one of his cows. Last year, looking out the back window, his wife saw through binoculars an animal with a flowing tail and "a cat's gallop" following a line of trees where the deer go, several hundred yards uphill behind the house. Later, Ambler went up on snowshoes and found tracks as big as their shepherds'; the dogs obligingly ran alongside. He saw walking tracks, leaping tracks and deer tracks marked with blood going toward higher ground. He wonders whether the cat will ever attack him. There are plenty of bobcats around, but they both say they know the difference. The splendid, nervous *tail* is what people must have identified in order to claim they have seen a mountain lion.

I, too, cherish the notion that I may have seen a lion. Mine was crouched on an overlook above a grass-grown, steeply pitched wash in the Alberta Rockies—a much more likely setting than anywhere in New England. It was late afternoon on my last day at Maligne Lake, where I had been staying with my father at a national-park chalet. I was twenty; I could walk forever or could climb endlessly in a sanguine scramble, going out every day as far as my legs carried me, swinging around for home before the sun went down.

Earlier, in the valley of the Athabasca, I had found several winter-starved or wolf-killed deer, well picked and scattered, and an area with many elk antlers strewn on the ground where the herds had wintered safely, dropping their antlers but not their bones. Here, much higher up, in the bright plenitude of the summer, I had watched two wolves and a stately bull moose in one mountain basin, and had been up on the caribou barrens on the ridge west of the lake and brought back the talons of a hawk I'd found dead on the ground. Whenever I was watching game, a sort of stopwatch in me started running. These were moments of intense importance and intimacy, of new intimations and aptitudes. Time had a jam-packed character, as it does during a mile run.

I was good at moving quietly through the woods and at spotting game, and was appropriately exuberant. The finest, longest day of my stay was the last. Going east, climbing through a luxuriant terrain of up-and-down boulders, brief brilliant glades, sudden potholes fifty feet deep—a forest of moss-hung lodgepole pines and firs and spare, gaunt spruce with the black lower branches broken off—I came upon the remains of a young bear, which had been torn up and shredded. Perhaps wolves had cornered it during some imprudent excursion in the early spring. (Bears often wake up while the snow is still deep, dig themselves out and rummage around in the neighborhood sleepily for a day or two before bedding down again under a fallen tree.) I took the skull along so that I could extract the teeth when I got hold of some tools. Discoveries like this represent a superfluity of wildlife and show how many beasts there are scouting about.

I went higher. The marmots whistled familiarly; the tall trees wilted to stubs of themselves. A pretty stream led down a defile from a series of openings in front of the ultimate barrier of a vast mountain wall which I had been looking at from a distance each day on my outings. It wasn't too steep to be climbed, but it was a barrier because my energies were not sufficient to scale it and bring me back the same night. Besides, it stretched so majestically, surf-like above the lesser ridges, that I liked to think of it as the Continental Divide.

On my left as I went up this wash was an abrupt, grassy slope that enjoyed a southern exposure and was sunny and windblown all winter, which kept it fairly free of snow. The ranger at the lake had told me it served as a wintering ground for a few bighorn sheep and for a band of mountain goats, three of which were in sight. As I approached laboriously, these white, pointy-horned fellows drifted up over a rise, managing to combine their retreat with some nippy good grazing as they went, not to give any pursuer the impression that they had been pushed into flight. I took my time too, climbing to locate the spring in a precipitous cleft of rock where the band did most of its drinking, and finding the shallow, high-ceilinged cave where the goats had sheltered from storms, presumably for generations. The floor was layered with rubbery droppings, tramped down and sprinkled with tufts of shed fur, and the black wall was checkered with footholds where the goats liked to clamber and perch. Here and there was a horn lying loose— a memento for me to add to my collection from an old individual that had died a natural death, secure in the band's winter stronghold. A bold, thriving family of pack rats emerged to observe me. They lived mainly on the nutritives in the droppings, and were used to the goats' tolerance; they seemed astonished when I tossed a stone.

I kept scrabbling along the side of the slope to a section of outcroppings where the going was harder. After perhaps half an hour, crawling around a corner, I found myself faced with a bighorn ram who was taking his ease on several square yards of bare earth between large rocks, a little above the level of my head. Just as surprised as I, he stood up. He must have construed the sounds of my advance to be those of another sheep or goat. His horns had made a complete curl and then some; they were thick, massive and bunched together like a high Roman helmet, and he himself was muscly and military, with a grave-looking nose. A squared-off, middle-aged, trophy-type ram, full of imposing professionalism, he was at the stage of life when rams sometimes stop herding and live as rogues.

He turned and tried a couple of possible exits from the pocket where I had found him, but the ground was badly pitched and would require a reeling gait and loss of dignity. Since we were within a national park and obviously I was unarmed, he simply was not inclined to put himself to so much trouble. He stood fifteen or twenty feet above me, pushing his tongue out through his teeth, shaking his head slightly and dipping it into charging position as I moved closer by a step or two, raising my hand slowly toward him in what I proposed as a friendly greeting. The day had been a banner one since the beginning, so while I recognized immediately that this meeting would be a valued memory, I felt as natural in his company as if he were a friend of mine reincarnated in a shag suit. I saw also that he was going to knock me for a loop, head over heels down the steep slope, if I sidled nearer, because he did not by any means feel as expansive and exuberant at our encounter as I did. That was the chief difference between us. I was talking to him with easy gladness, and beaming; he was not. He was unsettled and on his mettle, waiting for me to move along, the way a bighorn sheep waits for a predator to move on in wildlife movies when each would be evenly matched in a contest of strength and position. Although his warlike nose and high bone helmet, blocky and beautiful as weaponry, kept me from giving in to my sense that we were brothers, I knew I could stand there for a long while. His coat was a down-to-earth brown, edgy with muscle, his head was that of an unsmiling veteran standing to arms, and despite my reluctance to treat him as some sort of boxed-in prize, I might have stayed on for half the afternoon if I hadn't realized that I had other sights to see. It was not a day to dawdle.

I trudged up the wash and continued until, past tree line, the terrain widened and flattened in front of a preliminary ridge that formed an obstacle before the great roaring, silent, surflike mountain wall that I liked to think of as the Continental Divide, although it wasn't. A cirque separated the preliminary ridge from the ultimate divide, which I still hoped to climb to and look over. The opening into this was roomy enough, except for being littered with enormous boulders, and I began trying to make my way across them. Each was boat-sized and rested upon under-boulders; it was like running in place. After tussling with this landscape for an hour or two, I was limp and sweating, pinching my cramped legs. The sun had gone so low that I knew I would be finding my way home by moonlight in any case, and I could see into the cirque, which was big and symmetrical and presented a view of sheer barbarism; everywhere were these cruel boat-sized boulders.

Giving up and descending to the goats' draw again, I had a drink from the stream and bathed before climbing farther downward. The grass was green, sweet-smelling, and I felt safely close to life after that sea of dead boulders. I knew I would never be physically younger or in finer country; even then the wilderness was singing its swan song. I had no other challenges in mind, and though very tired, I liked looking up at the routes where I'd climbed. The trio of goats had not returned, but I could see their wintering cave and the cleft in the rocks where the spring was. Curiously, the bighorn ram had not left; he had only withdrawn upward, shifting away from the outcroppings to an open sweep of space where every avenue of escape was available. He was lying on a carpet of grass and, lonely pirate that he was, had his head turned in my direction.

It was from this same wash that looking up, I spotted the animal I took to be a mountain lion. He was skulking among some outcroppings at a point lower on the mountainside than the ledges where the ram originally had been. A pair of hawks or eagles were swooping at him by turns, as if he were close to a nest. The slant between us was steep, but the light of evening was still more than adequate. I did not really see the wonderful tail—that special medallion—nor was he particularly big for a lion. He was gloriously catlike and slinky, however, and so indifferent to the swooping birds as to seem oblivious of them. There are plenty of creatures he wasn't: he wasn't a marmot, a goat or other grass-eater, a badger, a wolf or coyote or fisher. He *may* have been a big bobcat or a wolverine, although he looked ideally lion-colored. He had a cat's strong collarbone structure for hitting, powerful haunches for vaulting, and the almost mystically small head mountain lions possess, with the gooseberry eyes. Anyway, I believed him to be a mountain lion, and standing quietly I watched him as he inspected in leisurely fashion the ledge that he was on and the one under him savory with every trace of goat—frosty-colored with the white hairs they'd shed.

The sight was so dramatic that it seemed to be happening close to me, though in fact he and the hawks or eagles, whatever they were, were miniaturized by distance.

If I'd kept motionless, eventually I could have seen whether he had the proper tail, but such scientific questions had no weight next to my need to essay some kind of communication with him. It had been exactly the same when I'd watched the two wolves playing together a couple of days before. They were above me, absorbed in their game of noses-and-paws. I had recognized that I might never witness such a scene again, yet I couldn't hold myself in. Instead of talking and raising my arm to them, as I had with the ram, I'd shuffled forward impetuously as if to say *Here I am!* Now, with the lion, I tried hard to dampen my impulse and restrained myself as long as I could. Then I stepped toward him, just barely squelching a cry in my throat but lifting my hand—as clumsy as anyone is who is trying to attract attention.

At that, of course, he swerved aside instantly and was gone. Even the two birds vanished. Foolish, triumphant and disappointed, I hiked on down into the lower forests, gargantuanly tangled, another life zone—not one which would exclude a lion but one where he would not be seen. I'd got my second wind and walked lightly and softly, letting the silvery darkness settle around me. The blowdowns were as black as whales; my feet sank in the moss. Clearly this was as crowded a day as I would ever have, and I knew my real problem would not be to make myself believed but rather to make myself understood at all, simply in reporting the story, and that I must at least keep the memory straight for myself. I was so happy that I was unerring in distinguishing the deer trails going my way. The forest's night beauty was supreme in its promise, and I didn't hurry.

JOHN UPDIKE

Eclipse

I went out into the backyard and the usually roundish spots of dappled sunlight underneath the trees were all shaped like feathers, crescent in the same direction, from left to right. Though it was five o'clock on a summer afternoon, the birds were singing good-bye to the day, and their merged song seemed to soak the strange air in an additional strangeness. A kind of silence prevailed. Few cars were moving on the streets of the town. Of my children only the baby dared come into the yard with me. She wore only under-pants, and as she stood beneath a tree, bulging her belly toward me in the mood of jolly flirtation she has grown into at the age of two, her bare skin was awash with pale crescents. It crossed my mind that she might be harmed, but I couldn't think how. *Cancer?*

The eclipse was to be over 90 percent in our latitude and the newspapers and television for days had been warning us not to look at it. I looked up, a split-second Prometheus, and looked away. The bitten silhouette of the sun lingered redly on my retinas. The day was half-cloudy, and my impression had been of the sun strug-gling, amid a furious knotted huddle of black and silver clouds, with an enemy too dreadful to be seen, with an eater as ghostly and hungry as time. Every blade of grass cast a long bluish-brown shadow, as at dawn.

My wife shouted from behind the kitchen screen door that as long as I was out there I might as well burn the wastepaper. She darted from the house, eyes downcast, with the wastebasket, and darted back again, leaving the naked baby and me to wander up through the strained sunlight to the wire trash barrel. After my forbidden peek at the sun, the flames dancing transparently from the blackening paper—yesterday's Boston *Globe*, a milk carton, a Hi-Ho cracker box—seemed dimmer than shadows, and in the teeth of all the warnings I looked up again. The clouds seemed bunched and twirled as if to plug a hole in the sky, and the burning afterimage was the shape of a near-new moon, horns pointed down. It was gigantically unnatural, and I lingered in the yard under the vague apprehension that in some future life I might be called before a cosmic court to testify to this assault. I seemed to be the sole witness. The town around my yard was hushed, all but the singing of the birds, who were invisible. The feathers under the trees had changed direction, and curved from right to left.

Then I saw my neighbor sitting on her porch. My neighbor is a widow, with white hair and brown skin; she has in her yard an aluminum-and-nylon-net chaise longue on which she lies at every opportunity, head back, arms spread, prostrate under the sun. Now she hunched dismally on her porch steps in the shade, which was scarcely darker than the light. I walked toward her and hailed her as a visitor to the moon might salute a survivor of a previous expedition. "How do you like the eclipse?" I called over the fence that distinguished our holdings on this suddenly insubstantial and lunar earth.

"I don't like it," she answered, shading her face with a hand. "They say you shouldn't go out in it."

"I thought it was just you shouldn't look at it."

"There's something in the rays," she explained, in a voice far louder than it needed to be, for silence framed us. "I shut all the windows on that side of the house and had to come out for some air."

"I think it'll pass," I told her.

"Don't let the baby look up," she warned, and turned away from talking to me, as if the open use of her voice exposed her more fatally to the rays.

Superstition, I thought, walking back through my yard, clutching my child's hand as tightly as a good-luck token. There was no question in her touch. Day, night, twilight, noon were all wonders to her, unscheduled, free from all bondage of prediction. The sun was being restored to itself and soon would radiate influence as brazenly as ever—and in this sense my daughter's blind trust was vindicated. Nevertheless, I was glad that the eclipse had passed, as it were, over her head; for in my own life I felt a certain assurance evaporate forever under the reality of the sun's disgrace.

A. J. LIEBLING

Ahab and Nemesis

Back in 1922, the late Heywood Broun, who is not remembered primarily as a boxing writer, wrote a durable account of a combat between the late Benny Leonard and the late Rocky Kansas for the lightweight championship of the world. Leonard was the greatest practitioner of the era, Kansas just a rough, optimistic fellow. In the early rounds Kansas messed Leonard about, and Broun was profoundly disturbed. A radical in politics, he was a conservative in the arts, and Kansas made him think of Gertrude Stein, *les Six*, and nonrepresentational painting, all novelties that irritated him.

"With the opening gong, Rocky Kansas tore into Leonard," he wrote. "He was gauche and inaccurate, but terribly persistent." The classic verities prevailed, however. After a few rounds, during which Broun continued to yearn for a return to a culture with fixed values, he was enabled to record: "The young child of nature who was challenging for the championship dropped his guard, and Leonard hooked a powerful and entirely orthodox blow to the conventional point of the jaw. Down went Rocky Kansas. His past life flashed before him during the nine seconds in which he remained on the floor, and he wished that he had been more faithful as a child in heeding the advice of his boxing teacher. After all, the old masters did know something. There is still a kick in style, and tradition carries a nasty wallop."

I have often thought of Broun's words in the years since Rocky Marciano, the reigning heavyweight champion, scaled the fistic summits, as they say in *Journal-Americanese*, by beating Jersey Joe Walcott. The current Rocky is gauche and inaccurate, but besides being persistent he is a dreadfully severe hitter with either hand.

181

The predominative nature of this asset has been well stated by Pierce Egan, the Edward Gibbon and Sir Thomas Malory of the old London prize ring, who was less preoccupied than Broun with ultimate implications. Writing in 1821 of a milling cove named Bill Neat, the Bristol Butcher, Egan said, "He possesses a requisite above all the art that *teaching* can achieve for any boxer; namely, *one hit* from his right hand, given in proper distance, can gain a victory; but three of them are positively enough to dispose of a giant." This is true not only of Marciano's right hand but of his left hand, too—provided he doesn't miss the giant entirely. Egan doubted the advisability of changing Neat's style, and he would have approved of Marciano's. The champion has an apparently unlimited absorptive capacity for percussion (Egan would have called him an "insatiable glutton") and inexhaustible energy ("a prime bottom fighter"). "Shifting," or moving to the side, and "milling in retreat," or moving back, are innovations of the late eighteenth century that Rocky's advisers have carefully kept from his knowledge, lest they spoil his natural prehistoric style. Egan excused these tactics only in boxers of feeble constitution.

Archie Moore, the light-heavyweight champion of the world, who hibernates in San Diego, California, and estivates in Toledo, Ohio, is a Brounian rather than an Eganite in his thinking about style, but he naturally has to do more than think about it. Since the rise of Marciano, Moore, a cerebral and hyper-experienced light-colored pugilist who has been active since 1936, has suffered the pangs of a supreme exponent of *bel canto* who sees himself crowded out of the opera house by a guy who can only shout. As a sequel to a favorable review I wrote of one of his infrequent New York appearances, when his fee was restricted to a measly five figures, I received a sad little note signed "The most unappreciated fighter in the world, Archie Moore." A fellow who has as much style as Moore tends to overestimate the intellect—he develops the kind of Faustian mind that will throw itself against the problem of perpetual motion, or of how to pick horses first, second, third, *and* fourth in every race. Archie's note made it plain to me that he was honing his harpoon for the White Whale.

When I read newspaper items about Moore's decisioning a large, playful porpoise of a Cuban heavyweight named Nino Valdes and scoop-netting a minnow like Bobo Olsen, the middleweight champion, for practice, I thought of him as a lonely Ahab, rehearsing to buck Herman Melville, Pierce Egan, and the betting odds. I did not think that he could bring it off, but I wanted to be there when he tried. What would *Moby Dick* be if Ahab had succeeded? Just another fish story. The thing that is eternally diverting is the struggle of man against history—or what Albert Camus, who used to be an amateur middleweight, has called the Myth of Sisyphus. (Camus would have been a great man to cover the fight, but none of the syndicates thought of it.) When I heard that the boys had been made for September 20, 1955, at the Yankee Stadium, I shortened my stay abroad in order not to miss the Encounter of the Two Heroes, as Egan would have styled the rendezvous.

In London on the night of September thirteenth, a week before the date set for the Encounter, I tried to get my eye in for fight-watching by attending a bout at the White City greyhound track between Valdes, who had been imported for the occasion, and the British Empire heavyweight champion, Don Cockell, a fat man whose gift for public suffering has enlisted the sympathy of a sentimental people. Since Valdes had gone fifteen rounds with Moore in Las Vegas the previous May, and Cockell had excruciated for nine rounds before being knocked out by Marciano in San Francisco in the same month, the bout offered a dim opportunity for establishing what racing people call a "line" between Moore and Marciano. I didn't get much of an optical workout, because Valdes disposed of Cockell in three rounds. It was evident that Moore and Marciano had not been fighting the same class of people this season.

This was the only fight I ever attended in a steady rainstorm. It had begun in the middle of the afternoon, and, while there was a canopy over the ring, the spectators were as wet as speckled trout. "The weather, it is well known, has no terrors to the admirers of Pugilism of Life," Egan once wrote, and on his old stamping ground this still holds true. As I took my seat in a rock pool that had collected in the hollow of my chair, a South African giant named Ewart Potgieter, whose weight had been announced as twenty-two stone ten, was ignoring the doctrine of Apartheid by leaning on a Jamaican colored man who weighed a mere sixteen stone, and by the time I had transposed these statistics to three hundred and eighteen pounds and two hundred and twenty-four pounds, respectively, the exhausted Jamaican had acquiesced in resegregation and retired. The giant had not struck a blow, properly speaking, but had shoved downward a number of times, like a man trying to close an overfilled trunk.

The main bout proved an even less grueling contest. Valdes, eager to get out of the chill, struck Cockell more vindictively than is his wont, and after a few gestures invocative of commiseration the fat man settled in one corner of the ring as heavily as suet pudding upon the unaccustomed gastric system. He had received what Egan would have called a "ribber" and a "nobber," and when he arose it was seen that the latter had raised a cut on his forehead. At the end of the third round, his manager withdrew him from competition. It was not an inspiring occasion, but after the armistice eight or nine shivering Cubans appeared in the runway behind the press section and jumped up and down to register emotion and restore circulation. "*Ahora Marciano!*" they yelled. "Now for Marciano!" Instead of being grateful for the distraction, the other spectators took a poor view of it. "Sit down, you chaps!" one of them cried. "We want to see the next do!" They were still parked out there in the rain when I tottered into the Shepherd's Bush underground station and collapsed, sneezing, on a train that eventually disgorged me at Oxford Circus, with just enough time left to buy a revivifying draught before eleven o'clock, when the pubs closed. How the mugs I left behind cured themselves I never knew. They had to do it on Bovril.

Because I had engagements that kept me in England until a few days before the Encounter, I had no opportunity to visit the training camps of the rival American Heroes. I knew all the members of both factions, however, and I could imagine what they were thinking. In the plane on the way home, I tried to envision the rival patterns of ratiocination. I could be sure that Marciano, a kind, quiet, imperturbable fellow, would plan to go after Moore and make him fight continuously until he tired enough to become an accessible target. After that he would expect concussion to accentuate exhaustion and exhaustion to facilitate concussion, until Moore came away from his consciousness, like everybody else Rocky had ever fought. He would try to remember to minimize damage to himself in the beginning, while there was still snap in Moore's arms, because Moore is a sharp puncher. (Like Bill Neat of old, Marciano hits at his opponent's arms when he cannot hit past them. "In one instance, the arm of Oliver [a Neat adversary] received so paralyzing a shock in stopping the blow that it appeared almost useless," Egan once wrote.) Charlie Goldman would have instructed Marciano in some rudimentary maneuver to throw Moore's first shots off, I felt sure, but after a few minutes Rocky would forget it, or Archie would figure it out. But there would always be Freddie Brown, the "cut man," in the champion's corner to repair superficial damage. One reason Goldman is a great teacher is that he doesn't try to teach a boxer more than he can learn. What he had taught Rocky in the four years since I had first seen him fight was to shorten the arc of most of his blows without losing power thereby, and always to follow one hard blow with another—"for insurance"—delivered with the other hand, instead of recoiling to watch the victim fall. The champion had also gained confidence and presence of mind; he has a good fighting head, which is not the same thing as being a good mechanical practitioner. "A *boxer* requires a *nob* as well as a *statesman* does a HEAD, coolness and calculation being essential to *second* his efforts," Egan wrote, and the old historiographer was never more correct. Rocky was thirty-one, not in the first flush of youth for a boxer, but Moore was only a few days short of thirty-nine, so age promised to be in the champion's favor if he kept pressing.

Moore's strategic problem, I reflected on the plane, offered more choices and, as a corollary, infinitely more chances for error. It was possible, but not probable, that jabbing and defensive skill would carry him through fifteen rounds, even on those old legs, but I knew that the mere notion of such a *gambade* would revolt Moore. He is not what Egan would have called a shy fighter. Besides, would Ahab have been content merely to go the distance with the White Whale? I felt sure that Archie planned to knock the champion out, so that he could sign his next batch of letters "The most appreciated and deeply opulent fighter in the world." I surmised that this project would prove a mistake, like Mr. Churchill's attempt to take Gallipoli in 1915, but it would be the kind of mistake that would look good in his memoirs. The basic of what I rightly anticipated would prove a miscalculation went back to Archie's academic background. As a young fighter of conventional tutelage, he must have heard his preceptors say hundreds of times, "They will all go if you hit them right." If a fighter did not believe that, he would be in the position of a Euclidian without faith in the hundred-and-eighty-degree triangle. Moore's strategy, therefore, would be based on working Marciano into a position where he could hit him right. He would not go in and slug with him, because that would be wasteful, distasteful, and injudicious, but he might try to cut him up, in an effort to slow him down so he could hit him right, or else try to hit him right and then cut him up. The puzzle he reserved for me—and Marciano—was the tactic by which he would attempt to attain his strategic objective. In the formation of his views, I believed, Moore would be handicapped, rather than aided, by his active, skeptical mind. One of the odd things about Marciano is that he isn't terribly big. It is hard for a man like Moore, just under six feet tall and weighing about a hundred and eighty pounds, to imagine that a man approximately the same size can be immeasurably stronger than he is. This is particularly true when, like the light-heavyweight champion, he has spent his whole professional life contending with boxers—some of them considerably bigger—whose strength has proved so near his own that he could move their arms and bodies by cunning pressures. The old classicist would consequently refuse to believe what he was up against.

. . .

The light-heavyweight limit is a hundred and seventy-five pounds, and Moore can get down to that when he must, in order to defend his title, but in a heavyweight match each Hero is allowed to weigh whatever he pleases. I was back in time to attend the weighing-in ceremonies, held in the lobby of Madison Square Garden at noon on the day set for the Encounter, and learned that Moore weighed 188 and Marciano 188¼—a lack of disparity that figured to encourage the rationalist's illusions. I also learned that, in contrast to Jack Solomons, the London promoter who held the Valdes-Cockell match in the rain, the I.B.C., which was promoting the Encounter, had decided to postpone it for twenty-four hours, although the weather was clear. The decision was based on apprehension of Hurricane Ione, which, although apparently veering away from New York, might come around again like a lazy left hook and drop in on the point of the Stadium's jaw late in the evening. Nothing like that happened, but the postponement brought the town's theaters and bars another evening of good business from the out-of-town fight trade, such as they always get on the eve of a memorable Encounter. ("Not a bed could be had at any of the villages at an early hour on the preceding evening; and Uxbridge was crowded beyond all former precedent," Egan wrote of the night before Neat beat Oliver.) There was no doubt that the fight had caught the public imagination, ever sensitive to a meeting between Hubris and Nemesis, as the boys on the quarterlies would say, and the bookies were laying 18–5 on Nemesis, according to the boys on the dailies, who always seem to hear. (A friend of mine up from Maryland with a whim and a five-dollar bill couldn't get ten against it in ordinary barroom money anywhere, although he wanted Ahab.)

The enormous—by recent precedent—advance sale of tickets had so elated the I.B.C. that it had decided to replace the usual card of bad preliminary fights with some not worth watching at all, so there was less distraction than usual as we awaited the appearance of the Heroes on the fateful evening. The press seats had been so closely juxtaposed that I could fit in only sidewise between two colleagues—the extra compression having been caused by the injection of a prewar number of movie stars and politicos. The tight quarters were an advantage, in a way, since they facilitated

my conversation with Peter Wilson, an English prize-ring correspondent, who happened to be in the row behind me. I had last
seen Mr. Wilson at White City the week before, at a time when
the water level had already reached his shredded-Latakia mustache.
I had feared that he had drowned at ringside, but when I saw him
at the Stadium, he assured me that by buttoning the collar of his
mackintosh tightly over his nostrils he had been able to make the
garment serve as a diving lung, and so survive. Like all British
fight writers when they are relieved of the duty of watching British
fighters, he was in a holiday mood, and we chatted happily. There
is something about the approach of a good fight that renders the
spirit insensitive to annoyance; it is only when the amateur of the
Sweet Science has some doubts as to how good the main bout will
turn out to be that he is avid for the satisfaction to be had from
the preliminaries. This is because after the evening is over, he may
have only a good supporting fight to remember. There were no
such doubts—even in the minds of the mugs who had paid for
their seats—on the evening of September twenty-first.

At about ten-thirty the champion and his faction entered the ring.
It is not customary for the champion to come in first, but Marciano
has never been a stickler for protocol. He is a humble, kindly
fellow, who even now will approach an acquaintance on the street
and say bashfully, "Remember me? I'm Rocky Marciano." The
champion doesn't mind waiting five or ten minutes to give anybody
a punch in the nose. In any case, once launched from his dressing
room under the grandstand, he could not have arrested his progress
to the ring, because he had about forty policemen pushing behind
him, and three more clearing a path in front of him. Marciano,
tucked in behind the third cop like a football ball-carrier behind
his interference, had to run or be trampled to death. Wrapped in
a heavy blue bathrobe and with a blue monk's cowl pulled over his
head, he climbed the steps to the ring with the cumbrous agility
of a medieval executioner ascending the scaffold. Under the hood
he seemed to be trying to look serious. He has an intellectual
appreciation of the anxieties of a champion, but he has a hard time
forgetting how strong he is; while he remembers that, he can't

worry as much as he knows a champion should. His attendants—quick, battered little Goldman; Al Weill, the stout, excitable manager, always stricken just before the bell with the suspicion that he may have made a bad match; Al Columbo—are all as familiar to the crowd as he is.

Ahab's party arrived in the ring a minute or so later, and Charlie Johnston, his manager—a calm sparrow hawk of a man, as old and wise in the game as Weill—went over to watch Goldman put on the champion's gloves. Freddie Brown went to Moore's corner to watch *his* gloves being put on. Moore wore a splendid black silk robe with a gold lamé collar and belt. He sports a full mustache above an imperial, and his hair, sleeked down under pomade when he opens operations, invariably rises during the contest, as it gets water sloshed on it between rounds and the lacquer washes off, until it is standing up like the top of a shaving brush. Seated in his corner in the shadow of his personal trainer, a brown man called Cheerful Norman, who weighs two hundred and thirty-five pounds, Moore looked like an old Japanese print I have of a "Shogun Engaged in Strategic Contemplation in the Midst of War." The third member of his group was Bertie Briscoe, a rough, chipper little trainer, whose more usual charge is Sandy Saddler, the featherweight champion—also a Johnston fighter. Mr. Moore's features in repose rather resemble those of Orson Welles, and he was reposing with intensity.

The procession of other fighters and former fighters to be introduced was longer than usual. The full galaxy was on hand, including Jack Dempsey, Gene Tunney, and Joe Louis, *têtes de cuvée* of former-champion society; ordinary former heavyweight champions, like Max Baer and Jim Braddock, slipped through the ropes practically unnoticed. After all the celebrities had been in and out of the ring, an odd dwarf, advertising something or other—possibly himself—was lifted into the ring by an accomplice and ran across it before he could be shooed out. The referee, a large, craggy, oldish man named Harry Kessler, who, unlike some of his better-known colleagues, is not an ex-fighter, called the men to the center of the ring. This was his moment; he had the microphone.

"Now Archie and Rocky, I want a nice, clean fight," he said, and I heard a peal of silvery laughter behind me from Mr. Wilson, who had seen both of them fight before. "Protect yourself at all times," Mr. Kessler cautioned them unnecessarily. When the principals shook hands, I could see Mr. Moore's eyebrows rising like storm clouds over the Sea of Azov. His whiskers bristled and his eyes glowed like dark coals as he scrunched his eyebrows down again and enveloped the Whale with the Look, which was intended to dominate his will power. Mr. Wilson and I were sitting behind Marciano's corner, and as the champion came back to it I observed his expression, to determine what effect the Look had had upon him. More than ever, he resembled a Great Dane who has heard the word "bone."

A moment later the bell rang and the Heroes came out for the first round. Marciano, training in the sun for weeks, had tanned to a slightly deeper tint than Moore's old ivory, and Moore, at 188, looked, if anything, bigger and more muscular than Marciano; much of the champion's weight is in his legs, and his shoulders slope. Marciano advanced, but Moore didn't go far away. As usual, he stood up nicely, his arms close to his body and his feet not too far apart, ready to go anywhere but not without a reason—the picture of a powerful, decisive intellect unfettered by preconceptions. Marciano, pulling his left arm back from the shoulder, flung a left hook. He missed, but not by enough to discourage him, and then walked in and hooked again. All through the round he threw those hooks, and some of them grazed Moore's whiskers; one even hit him on the side of the head. Moore didn't try much offensively; he held a couple of times when Marciano worked in close.

Marciano came back to his corner as he always does, unimpassioned. He hadn't expected to catch Moore with those left hooks anyway, I imagine; all he had wanted was to move him around. Moore went to his corner inscrutable. They came out for the second, and Marciano went after him in brisker fashion. In the first round he had been throwing the left hook, missing with it, and then throwing a right and missing with that, too. In the second he tried a variation—throwing a right and then pulling a shoulder back to throw the left. It appeared for a moment to have Moore confused, as a matador might be confused by a bull who walked in on his hind legs. Marciano landed a couple of those awkward hooks, but not squarely. He backed Moore over toward the side of the ring farthest from me, and then Moore knocked him down.

Some of the reporters, describing the blow in the morning papers, called it a "sneak punch," which is journalese for one the reporter didn't see but technically means a lead thrown before the other man has warmed up or while he is musing about the gate receipts. This had been no lead, and although I certainly hadn't seen Moore throw the punch, I knew that it had landed inside the arc of Marciano's left hook. ("Marciano missed with the right, trun the left, and Moore stepped inside it," my private eye, Whitey Bimstein, said next day, confirming my diagnosis, and the film of the fight bore both of us out.) So Ahab had his harpoon in the Whale. He had hit him right if ever I saw a boxer hit right, with a classic brevity and conciseness. Marciano stayed down for two seconds. I do not know what took place in Mr. Moore's breast when he saw him get up. He may have felt, for the moment, like Don Giovanni when the Commendatore's statue grabbed at him— startled because he thought he had killed the guy already—or like Ahab when he saw the Whale take down Fedallah, harpoons and all. Anyway, he hesitated a couple of seconds, and that was reasonable. A man who took nine to come up after a punch like that would be doing well, and the correct tactic would be to go straight in and finish him. But a fellow who came up on two was so strong he would bear investigation.

After that, Moore did go in, but not in a crazy way. He hit Marciano some good, hard, classic shots, and inevitably Marciano, a trader, hit him a few devastating swipes, which slowed him. When the round ended, the edge of Moore's speed was gone, and he knew that he would have to set a new and completely different trap, with diminished resources. After being knocked down, Marciano had stopped throwing that patterned right-and-left combination; he has a good nob. "He never trun it again in the fight," Whitey said next day, but I differ. He threw it in the fifth, and again Moore hit him a peach of a right inside it, but the steam was gone; this time Ahab couldn't even stagger him. Anyway, there was Moore at the end of the second, dragging his shattered faith in the unities and humanities back to his corner. He had hit a guy right, and the guy hadn't gone. But there is no geezer in Moore, any more than there was in the master of the Pequod.

Both came out for the third very gay, as Egan would have said. Marciano had been hit and cut, so he felt acclimated, and Moore was so mad at himself for not having knocked Marciano out that he almost displayed animosity toward him. He may have thought that perhaps he had not hit Marciano *just* right; the true artist is always prone to self-reproach. He would try again. A minute's attention from his squires had raised his spirits and slicked down his hair. At this point, Marciano set about him. He waddled in, hurling his fists with a sublime disregard of probabilities, content to hit an elbow, a biceps, a shoulder, the top of a head—the last supposed to be the least profitable target in the business, since, as every beginner learns, "the head is the hardest part of the human body," and a boxer will only break his hands on it. Many boxers make the systematic presentation of the cranium part of their defensive scheme. The crowd, basically anti-intellectual, screamed encouragement. There was Moore, riding punches, picking them off, slipping them, rolling with them, ducking them, coming gracefully out of his defensive efforts with sharp, patterned blows—and just about holding this parody even on points. His face, emerging at instants from under the storm of arms—his own and Rocky's— looked like that of a swimming walrus. When the round ended, I could see that he was thinking deeply. Marciano came back to his corner at a kind of suppressed dogtrot. He didn't have a worry in the world.

It was in the fourth, though, that I think Sisyphus began to get the idea he couldn't roll back the Rock. Marciano pushed him against the ropes and swung at him for what seemed a full minute without ever landing a punch that a boxer with Moore's background would consider a credit to his workmanship. He kept them coming so fast, though, that Moore tired just getting out of the way. One newspaper account I saw said that at this point Moore "swayed uncertainly," but his motions were about as uncertain as Margot Fonteyn's, or Arthur Rubinstein's. He is the most premeditated and best-synchronized swayer in his profession. After the bell rang for the end of the round, the champion hit him a right for good measure—he usually manages to have something on the way all the time—and then pulled back to disclaim any uncouth intention. Moore, no man to be conned, hit him a corker of a punch in return, when he wasn't expecting it. It was a gesture of moral reprobation and also a punch that would give any normal man something to think about between rounds. It was a good thing Moore couldn't see Marciano's face as he came back to his corner, though, because the champion was laughing.

The fifth was a successful round for Moore, and I had him ahead on points that far in the fight. But it took no expert to know where the strength lay. There was even a moment in the round when Moore set himself against the ropes and encouraged Marciano to swing at him, in the hope the champion would swing himself tired. It was a confession that he himself was too tired to do much hitting.

In the sixth Marciano knocked Moore down twice—once, early in the round, for four seconds, and once, late in the round, for eight seconds, with Moore getting up just before the bell rang. In the seventh, after that near approach to obliteration, the embattled intellect put up its finest stand. Marciano piled out of his corner to finish Moore, and the stylist made him miss so often that it looked, for a fleeting moment, as if the champion were indeed punching himself arm-weary. In fact, Moore began to beat him to the punch. It was Moore's round, certainly, but an old-timer I talked to later averred that one of the body blows Marciano landed in that round was the hardest of the fight.

It was the eighth that ended the competitive phase of the fight. They fought all the way, and in the last third of the round the champion simply overflowed Archie. He knocked him down with a right six seconds before the bell, and I don't think Moore could have got up by ten if the round had lasted that long. The fight by then reminded me of something that Sam Langford, one of the most profound thinkers—and, according to all accounts, one of the greatest doers—of the prize ring, once said to me: "Whatever that other man wants to do, don't let him do it." Merely by moving in all the time and punching continually, Marciano achieves the same strategic effect that Langford gained by finesse. It is impossible to think, or to impose your thought, if you have to keep on avoiding punches.

Moore's "game," as old Egan would have called his courage, was beyond reproach. He came out proudly for the ninth, and stood and fought back with all he had, but Marciano slugged him down, and he was counted out with his left arm hooked over the middle rope as he tried to rise. It was a crushing defeat for the higher faculties and a lesson in intellectual humility, but he had made a hell of a fight.

The fight was no sooner over than hundreds of unsavory young yokels with New England accents began a kind of mountain-goat immigration from the bleachers to ringside. They leaped from chair to chair and, after they reached the press section, from typewriter shelf to typewriter shelf and, I hope, from movie star to movie star. "Rocky!" they yelled. "Brockton!" Two of them, as dismal a pair of civic ambassadors as I have ever seen since I worked on the Providence *Journal & Evening Bulletin,* stood on Wilson's typewriter and yelled "Providence!" After the fighters and the hick delinquents had gone away, I made my way out to Jerome Avenue, where the crowd milled, impenetrable, under the "El" structure.

If you are not in a great hurry to get home (and why should you be at eleven-thirty or twelve on a fight night?), the best plan is to walk up to the station north of the stadium and have a beer in a saloon, or a cup of tea in the 167th Street Cafeteria, and wait until the whole mess clears away. By that time you may even get a taxi. After this particular fight I chose the cafeteria, being in a contemplative rather than a convivial mood. The place is of a genre you would expect to find nearer Carnegie Hall, with blond woodwork and modern functional furniture imported from Italy—an appropriate background for the evaluation of an aesthetic experience. I got my tea and a smoked-salmon sandwich on a soft onion roll at the counter and made my way to a table, where I found myself between two young policemen who were talking about why Walt Disney has never attempted a screen version of Kafka's "Metamorphosis." As I did not feel qualified to join in that one, I got out my copy of the official program of the fights and began to read the high-class feature articles as I munched my sandwich.

One reminded me that I had seen the first boxing show ever held in Yankee Stadium—on May 12, 1923. I had forgotten that it *was* the first show, and even that 1923 was the year the Stadium opened. In my true youth the Yankees used to share the Polo Grounds with the Giants, and I had forgotten that, too, because I never cared much about baseball, although, come to think of it, I used to see the Yankees play occasionally in the nineteen-'teens, and should have remembered. I remembered the boxing show itself very well, though. It happened during the spring of my second suspension from college, and I paid five dollars for a high-grandstand seat. The program merely said that it had been "an all-star heavyweight bill promoted by Tex Rickard for the Hearst Milk Fund," but I found that I could still remember every man and every bout on the card. One of the main events was between old Jess Willard, the former heavyweight champion of the world, who had lost the title to Jack Dempsey in 1919, and a young heavyweight named Floyd Johnson. Willard had been coaxed from retirement to make a comeback because there was such a dearth of heavyweight material that Rickard thought he could still get by, but as I remember the old fellow, he couldn't fight a lick. He had a fair left jab and a right uppercut that a fellow had to walk into to get hurt by, and he was big and soft. Johnson was a mauler worse than Rex Layne, and the old man knocked him out. The other main event, *ex aequo*, had Luis Angel Firpo opposing a fellow named Jack McAuliffe II, from Detroit, who had had only fifteen fights and had never beaten anybody, and had a glass jaw. The two winners, of whose identity there was infinitesimal preliminary doubt, were to fight each other for the right to meet the great Jack Dempsey.

Firpo was so crude that Marciano would be a Fancy Dan in comparison. He could hit with only one hand—his right—he hadn't the faintest idea of what to do in close, and he never cared much for the business anyway. He knocked McAuliffe out, of course, and then, in a later "elimination" bout, stopped poor old Willard. He subsequently became a legend by going one and a half sensational rounds with Dempsey, in a time that is now represented to us as the golden age of American pugilism.

I reflected with satisfaction that old Ahab Moore could have whipped all four principals on that card within fifteen rounds, and that while Dempsey may have been a great champion, he had less to beat than Marciano. I felt the satisfaction because it proved that the world isn't going backward, if you can just stay young enough to remember what it was really like when you were really young.

EUDORA WELTY

A Sweet Devouring

When I used to ask my mother which we were, rich or poor, she refused to tell me. I was nine years old and of course what I was dying to hear was that we were poor. I was reading a book called *Five Little Peppers* and my heart was set on baking a cake for my mother in a stove with a hole in it. Some version of rich, crusty old Mr. King—up till that time not living on our street—was sure to come down the hill in his wheelchair and rescue me if anything went wrong. But before I could start a cake at all I had to find out if we were poor, and poor *enough;* and my mother wouldn't tell me, she said she was too busy. I couldn't wait too long; I had to go on reading and soon Polly Pepper got into more trouble, some that was a little harder on her and easier on me.

Trouble, the backbone of literature, was still to me the original property of the fairy tale, and as long as there was plenty of trouble for everybody and the rewards for it were falling in the right spots, reading was all smooth sailing. At that age a child reads with higher appetite and gratification, and with those two stars sailing closer together, than ever again in his growing up. The home shelves had been providing me all along with the usual books, and I read them with love—but snap, I finished them. I read everything just alike— snap. I even came to the *Tales from Maria Edgeworth* and went right ahead, without feeling the bump—then. It *was* noticeable that when her characters suffered she punished them for it, instead of rewarding them as a reader had rather been led to hope. In her stories, the children had to make their choice between being un- happy and good about it and being unhappy and bad about it, and then she helped them to choose wrong. In *The Purple Jar,* it will be remembered, there was the little girl being taken through the shops by her mother and her downfall coming when she chooses to buy something beautiful instead of something necessary. The purple jar, when the shop sends it out, proves to have been purple only so long as it was filled with purple water, and her mother knew it all the time. They don't deliver the water. That's only the cue for stones to start coming through the hole in the victim's worn-out shoe. She bravely agrees she must keep walking on stones until such time as she is offered another choice between the beautiful and the useful. Her father tells her as far as he is concerned she can stay in the house. If I had been at all easy to disappoint, that story would have disappointed me. Of course, I did feel, what is the good of walking on rocks if they are going to let the water out of the jar too? And it seemed to me that even the illustrator fell down on the characters in that book, not alone Maria Edgeworth, for when a rich, crusty old gentleman gave Simple Susan a guinea for some kind deed she'd done him, there was a picture of the transaction and where was the guinea? I couldn't make out a feather. But I liked *reading* the book all right—except that I finished it.

My mother took me to the Public Library and introduced me: "Let her have any book she wants, except *Elsie Dinsmore*." I looked for the book I couldn't have and it was a row. That was how I learned about the Series Books. The *Five Little Peppers* belonged, so did *The Wizard of Oz*, so did *The Little Colonel*, so did *The Green Fairy Book*. There were many of everything, generations of everybody, instead of one. I wasn't coming to the end of reading, after all—I was saved.

Our library in those days was a big rotunda lined with shelves. A copy of *V. V.'s Eyes* seemed to follow you wherever you went, even after you'd read it. I didn't know what I liked, I just knew what there was a lot of. After *Randy's Spring* there came *Randy's Summer* and *Randy's Fall* and *Randy's Winter*. True, I didn't care very much myself for her spring, but it didn't occur to me that I might not care for her summer, and then her summer didn't prejudice me against her fall, and I still had hopes as I moved on to her winter. I was disappointed in her whole year, as it turned out, but a thing like that didn't keep me from wanting to read every word of it. The pleasures of reading itself—who doesn't remember?—were like those of a Christmas cake, a sweet devouring. The "Randy Books" failed chiefly in being so soon over. Four seasons doesn't make a series.

All that summer I used to put on a second petticoat (our librarian wouldn't let you past the front door if she could see through you), ride my bicycle up the hill and "through the Capitol" (shortcut) to the library with my two read books in the basket (two was the limit you could take out at one time when you were a child and also as long as you lived), and tiptoe in ("Silence") and exchange them for two more in two minutes. Selection was no object. I coasted the two new books home, jumped out of my petticoat, read (I suppose I ate and bathed and answered questions put to me), then in all hope put my petticoat back on and rode those two books back to the library to get my next two.

The librarian was the lady in town who wanted to be it. She called me by my full name and said, "Does your mother know where you are? You know good and well the fixed rule of this library: *Nobody is going to come running back here with any book on the same day they took it out.* Get those things out of here and don't come back till tomorrow. And I can practically see through you."

My great-aunt in Virginia, who understood better about needing more to read than you *could* read, sent me a book so big it had to be read on the floor—a bound volume of six or eight issues of *St. Nicholas* from a previous year. In the very first pages a serial began: *The Lucky Stone* by Abbie Farwell Brown. The illustrations were right down my alley: a heroine so poor she was ragged, a witch with an extremely pointed hat, a rich, crusty old gentleman in— better than a wheelchair—a runaway carriage; and I set to. I gobbled up installment after installment through the whole luxurious book, through the last one, and then came the words, turning me to *un*lucky stone: "To be concluded." The book had come to an end and *The Lucky Stone* wasn't finished! The witch had it! I couldn't believe this infidelity from my aunt. I still had my secret childhood feeling that if you hunted long enough in a book's pages, you could find what you were looking for, and long after I knew books better than that, I used to hunt again for the end of *The Lucky Stone*. It never occurred to me that the story had an existence anywhere else outside the pages of that single green-bound book. The last chapter was just something I would have to do without. Polly Pepper could do it. And then suddenly I tried something—I read it again, as much as I had of it. I was in love with books at least partly for what they looked like; I loved the printed page.

In my little circle books were almost never given for Christmas, they cost too much. But the year before, I'd been given a book and got a shock. It was from the same classmate who had told me there was no Santa Claus. She gave me a book, all right—*Poems by Another Little Girl*. It looked like a real book, was printed like a real book—but it was *by her*. *Homemade* poems? Illusion-dispelling was her favorite game. She was in such a hurry, she had such a pile to get rid of—her mother's electric runabout was stacked to the bud vases with copies—that she hadn't even time to say, "Merry Christmas!" With only the same raucous laugh with which she had told me, "Been filling my own stocking for years!" she shot me her book, received my Japanese pencil box with a moonlight scene on the lid and a sharpened pencil inside, jumped back into the car and was sped away by her mother. I stood right where they had left me, on the curb in my Little Nurse's uniform, and read that book, and I had no better way to prove when I got through than I had when I started that this was not a real book. But of course it wasn't. The printed page is not absolutely everything.

Then this Christmas was coming, and my grandfather in Ohio sent along in his box of presents an envelope with money in it for me to buy myself the book I wanted.

I went to Kress's. Not everybody knew Kress's sold books, but children just before Christmas know everything Kress's ever sold or will sell. My father had showed us the mirror he was giving my mother to hang above her desk, and Kress's is where my brother and I went to reproduce that by buying a mirror together to give her ourselves, and where our little brother then made us take him and he bought her one his size for fifteen cents. Kress's had also its version of the Series Books, called, exactly like another series, "The Camp Fire Girls," beginning with *The Camp Fire Girls in the Woods.*

I believe they were ten cents each and I had a dollar. But they weren't all that easy to buy, because the series stuck, and to buy some of it was like breaking into a loaf of French bread. Then after you got home, each single book was as hard to open as a box stuck in its varnish, and when it gave way it popped like a fire-cracker. The covers once prized apart would never close; those books once opened stayed open and lay on their backs helplessly fluttering their leaves like a turned-over June bug. They were as light as a matchbox. They were printed on yellowed paper with corners that crumbled, if you pinched on them too hard, like old graham crackers, and they smelled like attic trunks, caramelized glue, their own confinement with one another and, over all, the Kress's smell—bandannas, peanuts and sandalwood from the incense counter. Even without reading them I loved them. It was hard, that year, that Christmas is a day you can't read.

What could have happened to those books?—but I can tell you about the leading character. His name was Mr. Holmes. He was not a Camp Fire Girl: he wanted to catch one. Through every book of the series he gave chase. He pursued Bessie and Zara—those were the Camp Fire Girls—and kept scooping them up in his touring car, while they just as regularly got away from him. Once Bessie escaped from the second floor of a strange inn by climbing down a gutter pipe. Once she escaped by driving away from Mr. Holmes in his own automobile, which she had learned to drive by watching him. What Mr. Holmes wanted with them—either Bessie or Zara would do—didn't give me pause; I was too young to be a Camp Fire Girl; I was just keeping up. I wasn't alarmed by Mr. Holmes—when I cared for a chill, I knew to go to Dr. Fu Manchu, who had his own series in the library. I wasn't fascinated either. There was one thing I wanted from those books, and that was for me to have ten to read at one blow.

Who in the world wrote those books? I knew all the time they were the false "Camp Fire Girls" and the ones in the library were the authorized. But book reviewers sometimes say of a book that if anyone else had written it, it might not have been this good, and I found it out as a child—their warning is justified. This was a proven case, although a case of the true not being as good as the false. In the true series the characters were either totally different or missing (Mr. Holmes was missing), and there was too much time given to teamwork. The Kress's Campers, besides getting into a more reliable kind of trouble than the Carnegie Campers, had adventures that even they themselves weren't aware of: the pages were in wrong. There were transposed pages, repeated pages, and whole sections in upside down. There was no way of telling if there was anything missing. But if you knew your way in the woods at all, you could enjoy yourself tracking it down. I read the library "Camp Fire Girls," since that's what they were there for, but though they could be read by poorer light they were not as good.

And yet, in a way, the false Campers were no better either. I wonder whether I felt some flaw at the heart of things or whether I was just tired of not having any taste; but it seemed to me when I had finished that the last nine of those books weren't as good as the first one. And the same went for all Series Books. As long as they are keeping a series going, I was afraid, nothing can really happen. The whole thing is one grand prevention. For my greed, I might have unwittingly dealt with myself in the same way Maria Edgeworth dealt with the one who put her all into the purple jar— I had received word it was just colored water.

And then I went again to the home shelves and my lucky hand reached and found Mark Twain—twenty-four volumes, not a series, and good all the way through.

M. F. K. FISHER

Once a Tramp, Always . . .

There is a mistaken idea, ancient but still with us, that an overdose of anything from fornication to hot chocolate will teach restraint by the very results of its abuse. A righteous and worried father, feeling broad-minded and full of manly understanding, will urge a rich cigar upon his fledgling and almost force him to be sick, to show him how to smoke properly. Another, learning that his sons have been nipping dago red, will chain them psychologically to the dinner table and drink them under it, to teach them how to handle their liquor like gentlemen. Such methods are drastic and of dubious worth, I think. People continue to smoke and to drink, and to be excessive or moderate according to their own needs. Their good manners are a matter more of innate taste than of outward training.

Craving—the actual and continued need for something—is another matter. Sometimes it lasts for one's lifetime. There is no satisfying it, except temporarily, and that can spell death or ruin. At least three people I know very well, children of alcoholic parents, were literally born drunk, and after sad experience they face the hideous fact that one more nip will destroy them. But they dream of it. Another of my friends dreams of chocolate, and is haunted by sensory fantasies of the taste and smell of chocolate, and occasionally talks of chocolate the way some people talk of their mistresses, but one Hershey bar would damn him and his liver too. (Members of A.A. pray to God daily to keep them from taking that First Drink. A first candy bar can be as dangerous.) These people choose to live, no matter how cautiously, because they know they can never be satisfied. For them real satiety, the inner spiritual kind, is impossible. They are, although in a noble way, cheating:

an *honest* satyr will risk death from exhaustion, still happily aware that there will always be more women in the world than he can possibly accommodate.

Somewhere between the extremes of putative training in self-control and unflagging discipline against wild cravings lie the sensual and voluptuous gastronomical favorites-of-a-lifetime, the nostalgic yearnings for flavors once met in early days—the smell or taste of a gooseberry pie on a summer noon at Peachblow Farm, the whiff of anise from a Marseille bar. Old or moderately young, of any sex, most of us can forgo the analyst's couch at will and call up some such flavors. It is better thus. Kept verbal, there is small danger of indigestion, and in truth, a gooseberry pie can be a horror (those pale beady acid fruits, the sugar never masking their mean acidity, the crust sogging . . . my father rhapsodized occasionally about the ones at Peachblow and we tried to recapture their magic for him, but it was impossible). And a glass of *pastis* at the wrong time and with the wrong people can turn into a first-class emetic, no matter how it used to make the mind and body rejoice in Provence. Most people like to talk, once steered onto the right track, about their lifetime favorites in food. It does not matter if they have only dreamed of them for the past countless decades: favorites remain, and mankind is basically a faithful bunch of fellows. If you loved Gaby Deslys or Fanny Brice, from no matter how far afar, you still can and do. And why not? There is, in this happily insatiable fantasizing, no saturation point, no moment at which the body must cry: *Help!*

Of course, the average person has not actually possessed a famous beauty, and it is there that gastronomy serves as a kind of surrogate, to ease our longings. One does not need to be a king or mogul to indulge most, if at all, of his senses with the heady enjoyment of a dish—speaking in culinary terms, that is. I myself, to come right down to it, have never been in love from afar, except perhaps for a handful of fleeting moments when a flickering shot of Wallace Reid driving over a cliff would make me feel queer. I know of women who have really mooned, and for years, over some such glamorous shadow, and it is highly possible that my own immunity is due to my sensual satisfaction, even vicarious, in such things as potato chips and Beluga caviar. This realization is cruelly matter-of-fact to anyone of romantic sensitivity, and I feel vaguely apologetic about it. At the same time, I am relieved. I am free from any regrets that Clark Marlon Barrymore has never smiled at me. I know that even though I eat potato chips perhaps once every three years, I can, whenever I wish to, tap an almost unlimited fountain of them not five hundred feet from my own door. It is not quite the same thing with caviar, of course, and I have dug into a one-pound tin of it, fresh and pearly gray, not more than eight or nine times in my life. But I know that for a while longer the Acipensers of the Black and Caspian seas will be able to carry out their fertility rites and that I may even partake again of their delectable fruits. Meanwhile, stern about potato chips on the one hand and optimistic about Beluga on the other, I can savor with my mind's palate their strange familiarity.

It is said that a few connoisseurs, such as old George Saintsbury, can recall *physically* the bouquet of certain great vintages a half century after tasting them. I am a mouse among elephants now, but I can say just as surely that this minute, in a northern California valley, I can taste-smell-hear-see and then feel between my teeth the potato chips I ate slowly one November afternoon in 1936, in the bar of the Lausanne Palace. They were uneven in both thickness and color, probably made by a new apprentice in the hotel kitchen, and almost surely they smelled faintly of either chicken or fish, for that was always the case there. They were a little too salty, to encourage me to drink. They were ineffable. I am still nourished by them. That is probably why I can be so firm about not eating my way through barrels, tunnels, mountains more of them here in the land where they hang like square cellophane fruit on wire trees in all the grocery stores, to tempt me sharply every time I pass them.

As for the caviar, I can wait. I know I cannot possibly, *ever*, eat enough of it to satisfy my hunger, my unreasonable lust, so I think back with what is almost placidity upon the times I could attack a tub of it and take five minutes or so for every small

voluptuous mouthful. Again, why not? Being carnal, such dreams
are perforce sinful in some vocabularies. Other ways of thinking
might call them merely foolish, or Freudian "substitutes." It is all
right; I know that I can cultivate restraint, or accept it patiently
when it is thrust upon me—just as I know that I can walk right
down Main Street this minute and buy almost as many Macadamia
nuts as I would like to eat, and certainly enough to make me feel
very sick for a time, but that I shan't do so.

I have some of the same twinges of basic craving for those salty
gnarled little nuts from Hawaii as the ones I keep ruthlessly at bay
for the vulgar fried potatoes and the costly fish eggs. Just writing
of my small steady passion for them makes my mouth water in a
reassuringly controlled way, and I am glad there are dozens of jars
of them in the local goodies shoppe, for me not to buy. I cannot
remember when I first ate a Macadamia, but I was hooked from
that moment. I think it was about thirty years ago. The Prince of
Wales was said to have invested in a ranch in Hawaii which raised
them in small quantities, so that the name stuck in my mind because
he did, but I doubt that royal business cunning had much to do
with my immediate delectation. The last time I ate one was about
four months ago, in New York. I surprised my *belle-soeur* and
almost embarrassed myself by letting a small moan escape me when
she put a bowl of them beside my chair; they were beautiful—so
lumpy, Macadamian, salty, golden! And I ate one, to save face.
One. I can still sense its peculiar crispness and its complete Mac-
adamianimity. How fortunate I am!

Many of the things we batten on in our fantasies are part of our
childhoods, although none of mine has been, so far in this list. I
was perhaps twenty-three when I first ate almost enough caviar—
not to mention any caviar at all that I can now remember. It was
one of the best, brightest days of my whole life with my parents,
and lunching in the quiet back room at the Café de la Paix was
only a part of the luminous whole. My mother ate fresh foie gras,
sternly forbidden to her liver, but she loved the cathedral at Stras-
bourg enough to risk almost any kind of retribution, and this
truffled slab was so plainly the best of her lifetime that we all agreed

it could do her nothing but good, which it did. My father and I ate caviar, probably Sevruga, with green-black smallish beads and a superb challenge of flavor for the iced grassy vodka we used to cleanse our happy palates. We ate three portions apiece, tacitly knowing it could never happen again that anything would be quite so mysteriously perfect in both time and space. The headwaiter sensed all this, which is, of course, why he was world-known, and the portions got larger, and at our third blissful command he simply put the tin in its ice bowl upon our table. It was a regal gesture, like being tapped on the shoulder with a sword. We bowed, served ourselves exactly as he would have done, grain for grain, and had no need for any more. It was reward enough to sit in the almost empty room, chaste rococo in the slanting June sunlight, with the generous tub of pure delight between us, Mother purring there, the vodka seeping slyly through our veins, and real wood strawberries to come, to make us feel like children again and not near-gods. That was a fine introduction to what I hope is a reasonably long life of such occasional bliss.

As for potato chips, I do not remember them earlier than my twenty-first year, when I once ate stupidly and well of them in a small, stylish restaurant in Germany, where we had to wait downstairs in the tavern while our meal was being readied to eat upstairs. Beside me on a table was a bowl of exquisitely fresh and delicate chips, and when we finally sat down I could not face the heavily excellent dinner we had ordered. I was ashamed of my gluttony, for it is never commendable, even when based on ignorance. Perhaps *that* is why I am so stern today about not eating many of the devilish temptations?

There is one other thing I know I shall never get enough of— champagne. I cannot say when I drank my first prickly, delicious glass of it. I was raised in Prohibition, which meant that my father was very careful about his bootleggers, but the general adult drinking stayed around pinch-bottle Scotch as safest in those days, and I think I probably started my lifelong affair with Dom Pérignon's discovery in 1929, when I first went to France. It does not matter. I would gladly ask for the same end as a poor peasant's there, who is given a glass of champagne on his deathbed to cheer him on his way.

I used to think, in my Russian-novel days, that I would cherish a lover who managed through thick and thin, snow and sleet, to have a bunch of Parma violets on my breakfast tray each morning—also rain or shine, Christmas or August, and onward into complete Neverland. Later, I shifted my dream plan—a split of cold champagne, one half hour *before* the tray! Violets, sparkling wine, and trays themselves were as nonexistent as the lover(s), of course, but once again, why not? By now, I sip a mug of vegetable broth and count myself fortunate, while my mind's nose and eyes feast on the pungency of the purple blossoms, and the champagne stings my sleepy tongue . . . and on feast days I drink a little glass of California "dry Sauterne" from the icebox . . . and it is much easier to get out of bed to go to work if there is not that silly tray there.

Mayonnaise, real mayonnaise, good mayonnaise, is something I can dream of any time, almost, and not because I ate it when I was little but because I did not. My maternal grandmother, whose Victorian neuroses dictated our family table tastes until I was about twelve, found salads generally suspect but would tolerate the occasional serving of some watery lettuce in a dish beside each plate (those crescents one still sees now and then in English and Swiss boardinghouses and the mansions of American Anglophiles). On it would be a dab or lump or blob, depending on the current cook, of what was quietly referred to as Boiled Dressing. It seemed dreadful stuff—enough to harm one's soul.

I do not have my grandmother's own recipe, although I am sure she seared it into many an illiterate mind in her kitchens, but I have found an approximation, which I feel strangely forced to give. It is from Miss Parloa's *New Cook Book,* copyrighted in Boston in 1880 by Estes and Lauriat:

Three eggs, one tablespoon each of sugar, oil and salt, a scant tablespoon of mustard, a cupful of milk and one of vinegar. Stir oil, mustard, salt and sugar in a bowl until perfectly smooth. Add the eggs, and beat well; then add the vinegar, and finally the milk.

Place the bowl in a basin of boiling water, and stir the dressing until it thickens like soft custard. . . . The dressing will keep two weeks if bottled tightly and put in a cool place.

On second thought, I think Grandmother's receipt, as I am sure it was called, may have used one egg instead of three, skimped on the sugar and oil, left out the mustard, and perhaps eliminated the milk as well. It was a kind of sour whitish gravy and . . . Yes! Patience is its own reward; I have looked in dozens of cookbooks without finding her abysmal secret, and now I have it: she did not use eggs at all, but *flour*. This is it. Flour thickened the vinegar— no need to waste eggs and sugar . . . Battle Creek frowned on oil, and she spent yearly periods at that health resort . . . mustard was a heathen spice . . . salt was cheap, and good cider vinegar came by the gallon. . . . And (here I can hear words as clearly as I can see the limp wet lettuce under its load of Boiled Dressing): "Salad is roughage and a French idea."

As proof of the strange hold childhood remembrance has on us, I think I am justified to print once, and only once, my considered analysis of the reason I must live for the rest of my life with an almost painful craving for mayonnaise made with fresh eggs and lemon juice and good olive oil:

Grandmother's Boiled Dressing

1 cup cider vinegar
Enough flour to make thin paste
Salt to taste

Mix well, boil slowly fifteen minutes or until done, and serve with wet shredded lettuce.

Unlike any other recipe I have ever given, this one has never been tested and never shall be, nor is it recommended for anything but passing thought.

Some of the foods that are of passionate interest in childhood, as potently desirable as drink to a toper, with time lose everything but a cool intellectuality. For about three years, when I was around

six, we sometimes ate hot milk toast for Sunday night supper, but
made with rich cocoa, and I would start waiting for the next time
as soon as I had swallowed the last crumbly buttery brown spoonful
of it. I am thankful I need have no real fear of ever being faced
with another bowl of the stuff, but equally happy that I can still
understand how its warmth and savor satisfied my senses then. I
feel much the same grateful relief when I conjure, no matter how
seldom, the four or five years when I was in boarding schools and
existed—sensually, at least—from one private slow orgy to the
next, of saltines and Hershey bars, bite for bite.

There is one concoction, or whatever it should be called, that I
was never allowed to eat, and that I dreamed of almost viciously
for perhaps seventeen years, until I was about twenty-two and
married. I made it then and ate every bit of it and enjoyed it
enormously and have never tasted it since, except in the happy
reaches of my gastronomical mind. And not long ago, when I found
a distinctly literary reference to it, I beamed and glowed. I love
the reality of Mark Twain almost as much as I love the dream
image of this dish, and when he included it, just as I myself would
have, in a list of American foods he planned to eat—"a modest,
private affair," all to himself—I could hardly believe the mirac-
ulous coincidence: my ambrosia, my god's!

In *A Tramp Abroad*, Twain grouses about the food he found in
Europe in 1878 (even a god can sound a little limited at times)
and makes a list of the foods he has missed the most and most
poignantly awaits on his return. It starts out "Radishes," which is
indeed either blind or chauvinistic, since I myself always seem to
eat five times as many of them when I am a tramp abroad as when
I am home. He then names eighty separate dishes and ends, "All
sorts of American pastry. Fresh American Fruits. . . . Ice water."
Love is *not* blind, and I do feel sorry about a certain lack of divinity
in this utterance, but my faith and loyalty are forever strengthened
by items 57 and 58: "Mashed Potatoes. Catsup."

These two things were printed on the same line, and I feel—in
fact, I *know*—that he meant "Mashed Potatoes *and* Catsup," or
perhaps "Mashed Potatoes *with* Catsup." This certainty springs

from the fact that there is, in my own mind and plainly in his, an affinity there. The two belong together. I have known this since I was about five, or perhaps even younger. I have proved it—only once, but very thoroughly, I am willing to try to again, preferably in "a modest, private affair, all to myself," but in public if I should ever be challenged.

We often ate mashed potatoes at home. Grandmother liked what my mother secretly scoffed at as "slip-and-go-easies": custards, junkets, strained stewed tomatoes, things like that, with mashed potatoes, of course, at the head of the list as a necessity alongside any decent cut of meat. But—and here is the secret, perhaps, of my lifelong craving—we were never allowed to taste catsup. Never. It was spicy and bad for us, and "common" in bottles. (This is an odd fact, chronologically, for all the housekeepers of my beldam's vintage prided themselves on their special receipts for "ketchups," made of everything from oysters to walnuts and including the plentiful love apple.)

I remember that once when Grandmother was gone off to a religious convention, Mother asked each of us what we would most like to eat before the awesome Nervous Stomach took over our menus again. My father immediately said he would pick a large salad of watercress from the Rio Hondo and make a dressing of olive oil and wine vinegar—a double cock-snoot, since olive oil was an exotic smelly stuff kept only to rub on the navels of the new babies that seemed to arrive fairly often, and watercress grew along the banks of a stream that might well be . . . er . . . *used* by cows. When my turn came, I said, "Mashed potatoes and catsup." I forget exactly what went on next, except that Father was for letting me eat all I wanted of the crazy mixture and I never did get to. Ah, well . . . I loved watercress, too, and whatever forbidden fruits we bit into during that and similar gastric respites, and I did not need to stop dreaming.

My one deliberate challenge to myself was delicious. I was alone, which seems to be indicated for many such sensual rites. The potatoes were light, whipped to a firm cloud with rich hot milk, faintly yellow from ample butter. I put them in a big warmed bowl, made a dent about the size of a respectable coffee cup, and filled it to the brim with catsup from a large, full, *vulgar* bottle that stood beside my table mat where a wineglass would be at an ordinary, commonplace, everyday banquet. Mine was, as I have said, delicious. I would, as I have also said, gladly do it again if I were dared to. But I prefer to nourish myself with the knowledge that it is not impossible (potato chips), not too improbable (fresh Beluga caviar). And now I am sharing it with a friend. I could not manage to serve forth to Mark Twain the "Sheep-head and croakers, from New Orleans," or the "Prairie hens, from Illinois," that he dreamed of in European boardinghouses ninety years ago, but mashed potatoes *with* catsup are ready to hand when he says the word.

JOAN DIDION

On Keeping a Notebook

"'That woman Estelle,'" the note reads, "'is partly the reason why George Sharp and I are separated today.' *Dirty crepe-de-Chine wrapper, hotel bar, Wilmington RR, 9:45 a.m. August Monday morning.*"

Since the note is in my notebook, it presumably has some meaning to me. I study it for a long while. At first I have only the most general notion of what I was doing on an August Monday morning in the bar of the hotel across from the Pennsylvania Railroad station in Wilmington, Delaware (waiting for a train? missing one? 1960? 1961? why Wilmington?), but I do remember being there. The woman in the dirty crepe-de-Chine wrapper had come down from her room for a beer, and the bartender had heard before the reason why George Sharp and she were separated today. "Sure," he said, and went on mopping the floor. "You told me." At the other end of the bar is a girl. She is talking, pointedly, not to the man beside her but to a cat lying in the triangle of sunlight cast through the open door. She is wearing a plaid silk dress from Peck & Peck, and the hem is coming down.

Here is what it is: the girl has been on the Eastern Shore, and now she is going back to the city, leaving the man beside her, and all she can see ahead are the viscous summer sidewalks and the 3 a.m. long-distance calls that will make her lie awake and then sleep drugged through all the steaming mornings left in August (1960? 1961?). Because she must go directly from the train to lunch in New York, she wishes that she had a safety pin for the hem of the plaid silk dress, and she also wishes that she could forget about the hem and the lunch and stay in the cool bar that smells of disinfectant and malt and make friends with the woman in the crepe-de-Chine

213

wrapper. She is afflicted by a little self-pity, and she wants to compare Estelles. That is what that was all about.

Why did I write it down? In order to remember, of course, but exactly what was it I wanted to remember? How much of it actually happened? Did any of it? Why do I keep a notebook at all? It is easy to deceive oneself on all those scores. The impulse to write things down is a peculiarly compulsive one, inexplicable to those who do not share it, useful only accidentally, only secondarily, in the way that any compulsion tries to justify itself. I suppose that it begins or does not begin in the cradle. Although I have felt compelled to write things down since I was five years old, I doubt that my daughter ever will, for she is a singularly blessed and accepting child, delighted with life exactly as life presents itself to her, unafraid to go to sleep and unafraid to wake up. Keepers of private notebooks are a different breed altogether, lonely and resistant rearrangers of things, anxious malcontents, children afflicted apparently at birth with some presentiment of loss.

My first notebook was a Big Five tablet, given to me by my mother with the sensible suggestion that I stop whining and learn to amuse myself by writing down my thoughts. She returned the tablet to me a few years ago; the first entry is an account of a woman who believed herself to be freezing to death in the Arctic night, only to find, when day broke, that she had stumbled onto the Sahara Desert, where she would die of the heat before lunch. I have no idea what turn of a five-year-old's mind could have prompted so insistently "ironic" and exotic a story, but it does reveal a certain predilection for the extreme which has dogged me into adult life; perhaps if I were analytically inclined I would find it a truer story than any I might have told about Donald Johnson's birthday party or the day my cousin Brenda put Kitty Litter in the aquarium.

So the point of my keeping a notebook has never been, nor is it now, to have an accurate factual record of what I have been doing or thinking. That would be a different impulse entirely, an instinct for reality which I sometimes envy but do not possess. At no point have I ever been able successfully to keep a diary; my approach to daily life ranges from the grossly negligent to the merely absent, and on those few occasions when I have tried dutifully to record a day's events, boredom has so overcome me that the results are mysterious at best. What is this business about "shopping, typing piece, dinner with E, depressed"? Shopping for what? Typing what piece? Who is E? Was this "E" depressed, or was I depressed? Who cares?

In fact I have abandoned altogether that kind of pointless entry; instead I tell what some would call lies. "That's simply not true," the members of my family frequently tell me when they come up against my memory of a shared event. "The party was *not* for you, the spider was *not* a black widow, *it wasn't that way at all.*" Very likely they are right, for not only have I always had trouble distinguishing between what happened and what merely might have happened, but I remain unconvinced that the distinction, for my purposes, matters. The cracked crab that I recall having for lunch the day my father came home from Detroit in 1945 must certainly be embroidery, worked into the day's pattern to lend verisimilitude; I was ten years old and would not now remember the cracked crab. The day's events did not turn on cracked crab. And yet it is precisely that fictitious crab that makes me see the afternoon all over again, a home movie run all too often, the father bearing gifts, the child weeping, an exercise in family love and guilt. Or that is what it was to me. Similarly, perhaps it never did snow that August in Vermont; perhaps there never were flurries in the night wind, and maybe no one else felt the ground hardening and summer already dead even as we pretended to bask in it, but that was how it felt to me, and it might as well have snowed, could have snowed, did snow.

How it felt to me: that is getting closer to the truth about a notebook. I sometimes delude myself about why I keep a notebook, imagine that some thrifty virtue derives from preserving everything observed. See enough and write it down, I tell myself, and then some morning when the world seems drained of wonder, some day when I am only going through the motions of doing what I am

supposed to do, which is write—on that bankrupt morning I will
simply open my notebook and there it will all be, a forgotten account
with accumulated interest, paid passage back to the world out there:
dialogue overheard in hotels and elevators and at the hat-check
counter in Pavillon (one middle-aged man shows his hat check to
another and says, "That's my old football number"); impressions
of Bettina Aptheker and Benjamin Sonnenberg and Teddy ("Mr.
Acapulco") Stauffer; careful *aperçus* about tennis bums and failed
fashion models and Greek shipping heiresses, one of whom taught
me a significant lesson (a lesson I could have learned from F. Scott
Fitzgerald, but perhaps we all must meet the very rich for ourselves)
by asking, when I arrived to interview her in her orchid-filled
sitting room on the second day of a paralyzing New York blizzard,
whether it was snowing outside.

I imagine, in other words, that the notebook is about other people.
But of course it is not. I have no real business with what one
stranger said to another at the hat-check counter in Pavillon; in fact
I suspect that the line "That's my old football number" touched not
my own imagination at all, but merely some memory of something
once read, probably "The Eighty-Yard Run." Nor is my concern
with a woman in a dirty crepe-de-Chine wrapper in a Wilmington
bar. My stake is always, of course, in the unmentioned girl in the
plaid silk dress. *Remember what it was to be me:* that is always the
point.

It is a difficult point to admit. We are brought up in the ethic that
others, any others, all others, are by definition more interesting
than ourselves; taught to be diffident, just this side of self-effacing.
("You're the least important person in the room and don't forget
it," Jessica Mitford's governess would hiss in her ear on the advent
of any social occasion; I copied that into my notebook because it is
only recently that I have been able to enter a room without hearing
some such phrase in my inner ear.) Only the very young and the
very old may recount their dreams at breakfast, dwell upon self,
interrupt with memories of beach picnics and favorite Liberty lawn

dresses and the rainbow trout in a creek near Colorado Springs. The rest of us are expected, rightly, to affect absorption in other people's favorite dresses, other people's trout.

And so we do. But our notebooks give us away, for however dutifully we record what we see around us, the common denominator of all we see is always, transparently, shamelessly, the implacable "I." We are not talking here about the kind of notebook that is patently for public consumption, a structural conceit for binding together a series of graceful *pensées;* we are talking about something private, about bits of the mind's string too short to use, an indiscriminate and erratic assemblage with meaning only for its maker.

And sometimes even the maker has difficulty with the meaning. There does not seem to be, for example, any point in my knowing for the rest of my life that, during 1964, 720 tons of soot fell on every square mile of New York City, yet there it is in my notebook, labeled "FACT." Nor do I really need to remember that Ambrose Bierce liked to spell Leland Stanford's name "£eland $tanford" or that "smart women almost always wear black in Cuba," a fashion hint without much potential for practical application. And does not the relevance of these notes seem marginal at best?:

In the basement museum of the Inyo County Courthouse in Independence, California, sign pinned to a mandarin coat: "This MANDARIN COAT was often worn by Mrs. Minnie S. Brooks when giving lectures on her TEAPOT COLLECTION."

Redhead getting out of car in front of Beverly Wilshire Hotel, chinchilla stole, Vuitton bags with tags reading:

> MRS. LOU FOX
> HOTEL SAHARA
> VEGAS

Well, perhaps not entirely marginal. As a matter of fact, Mrs. Minnie S. Brooks and her MANDARIN COAT pull me back into my own childhood, for although I never knew Mrs. Brooks and did not visit Inyo County until I was thirty, I grew up in just such a world, in houses cluttered with Indian relics and bits of gold ore and ambergris and the souvenirs my Aunt Mercy Farnsworth brought back from the Orient. It is a long way from that world to Mrs. Lou Fox's world, where we all live now, and is it not just as well to remember that? Might not Mrs. Minnie S. Brooks help me to remember what I am? Might not Mrs. Lou Fox help me to remember what I am not?

But sometimes the point is harder to discern. What exactly did I have in mind when I noted down that it cost the father of someone I know $650 a month to light the place on the Hudson in which he lived before the Crash? What use was I planning to make of this line by Jimmy Hoffa: "I may have my faults, but being wrong ain't one of them"? And although I think it interesting to know where the girls who travel with the Syndicate have their hair done when they find themselves on the West Coast, will I ever make suitable use of it? Might I not be better off just passing it on to John O'Hara? What is a recipe for sauerkraut doing in my note-book? What kind of magpie keeps this notebook? *"He was born the night the Titanic went down."* That seems a nice enough line, and I even recall who said it, but is it not really a better line in life than it could ever be in fiction?

But of course that is exactly it: not that I should ever use the line, but that I should remember the woman who said it and the afternoon I heard it. We were on her terrace by the sea, and we were finishing the wine left from lunch, trying to get what sun there was, a California winter sun. The woman whose husband was born the night the *Titanic* went down wanted to rent her house, wanted to go back to her children in Paris. I remember wishing that I could afford the house, which cost $1,000 a month. "Someday you will," she said lazily. "Someday it all comes." There in the sun on her terrace it seemed easy to believe in someday, but later I had a low-grade afternoon hangover and ran over a black snake on the way to the supermarket and was flooded with inexplicable fear when

I heard the checkout clerk explaining to the man ahead of me why she was finally divorcing her husband. "He left me no choice," she said over and over as she punched the register. "He has a little seven-month-old baby by her, he left me no choice." I would like to believe that my dread then was for the human condition, but of course it was for me, because I wanted a baby and did not then have one and because I wanted to own a house that cost $1,000 a month to rent and because I had a hangover.

It all comes back. Perhaps it is difficult to see the value in having one's self back in that kind of mood, but I do see it; I think we are well advised to keep on nodding terms with the people we used to be, whether we find them attractive company or not. Otherwise they turn up unannounced and surprise us, come hammering on the mind's door at 4 a.m. of a bad night and demand to know who deserted them, who betrayed them, who is going to make amends. We forget all too soon the things we thought we could never forget. We forget the loves and the betrayals alike, forget what we whispered and what we screamed, forget who we were. I have already lost touch with a couple of people I used to be; one of them, a seventeen-year-old, presents little threat, although it would be of some interest to me to know again what it feels like to sit on a river levee drinking vodka-and-orange-juice and listening to Les Paul and Mary Ford and their echoes sing "How High the Moon" on the car radio. (You see I still have the scenes, but I no longer perceive myself among those present, no longer could even improvise the dialogue.) The other one, a twenty-three-year-old, bothers me more. She was always a good deal of trouble, and I suspect she will reappear when I least want to see her, skirts too long, shy to the point of aggravation, always the injured party, full of recriminations and little hurts and stories I do not want to hear again, at once saddening me and angering me with her vulnerability and ignorance, an apparition all the more insistent for being so long banished.

It is a good idea, then, to keep in touch, and I suppose that keeping in touch is what notebooks are all about. And we are all on our own when it comes to keeping those lines open to ourselves:

your notebook will never help me, nor mine you. *"So what's new in the whiskey business?"* What could that possibly mean to you? To me it means a blonde in a Pucci bathing suit sitting with a couple of fat men by the pool at the Beverly Hills Hotel. Another man approaches, and they all regard one another in silence for a while. "So what's new in the whiskey business?" one of the fat men finally says by way of welcome, and the blonde stands up, arches one foot and dips it in the pool, looking all the while at the cabaña where Baby Pignatari is talking on the telephone. That is all there is to that, except that several years later I saw the blonde coming out of Saks Fifth Avenue in New York with her California complexion and a voluminous mink coat. In the harsh wind that day she looked old and irrevocably tired to me, and even the skins in the mink coat were not worked the way they were doing them that year, not the way she would have wanted them done, and there is the point of the story. For a while after that I did not like to look in the mirror, and my eyes would skim the newspapers and pick out only the deaths, the cancer victims, the premature coronaries, the suicides, and I stopped riding the Lexington Avenue IRT because I noticed for the first time that all the strangers I had seen for years— the man with the Seeing Eye dog, the spinster who read the classified pages every day, the fat girl who always got off with me at Grand Central—looked older than they once had.

It all comes back. Even that recipe for sauerkraut: even that brings it back. I was on Fire Island when I first made that sauerkraut, and it was raining, and we drank a lot of bourbon and ate the sauerkraut and went to bed at ten, and I listened to the rain and the Atlantic and felt safe. I made the sauerkraut again last night and it did not make me feel any safer, but that is, as they say, another story.

HOWARD MOSS

Jean: Some Fragments

I met her by subletting an apartment in New York, hers and Robert
Lowell's, in the early forties. The war was on; I had been hired
by the Office of War Information on 57th Street and was looking
for a place to stay. Cal was still in jail, serving out his term as a
conscientious objector; Jean had finished *Boston Adventure* and was
waiting for it to be published. She was going away somewhere for
a few months—England, I think—but maybe it was Boston. I
don't remember. The apartment, in a brownstone on 17th Street
overlooking Stuyvesant Park, was graceful and old-fashioned and
full of things Jean loved: Victorian sofas, lamps with pleated shades,
deep engulfing chairs, small objects on tables, and books, books,
books. Those in the bedroom bookcase were mainly religious; she
was a Catholic convert at the time, or at least receiving instruction.
She had a weakness for mechanical toys: a bear that turned the
pages of a book (named after a well-known critic), a fire truck that
turned at sharp right angles and raced across the floor at great
speed. When Jean returned from England (or Boston), she would
visit me occasionally, always bringing a pint of whiskey in a brown
paper bag—either as a matter of scrupulous courtesy or because
she felt she couldn't count on my supply—and we would drink
and talk. And laugh. A demure quality about her alternated with
a kind of Western no-nonsense toughness, and she shed years every
time she laughed, showing her gums like a child or an ancient.
Funny and sharp about people, she loved gossip. We became friends.

We developed, over the years, a tendency to make elaborate plans
that were never carried out. This was particularly true of travel,

221

which we both dreaded. Europe eluded us at least six times. We
did get to Boston once for a Thanksgiving weekend, but even then
something went wrong. We were to meet on the train but never
did. We found each other, finally, in South Station, exhausted and
bewildered.

I remember seeing a life mask of Jean—Jean the way she looked
before the car accident that changed her face forever. (I had
known her only since the accident, which occurred while she was
married to Lowell.) A handsome woman, she had once been
beautiful in a more conventional way, or so the mask suggested.
"The Interior Castle" describes the surgical procedure with chilling
exactitude; its central conceit is of the brain as a castle probed
and assaulted by alien forces. I often forgot that Jean had been
through this traumatic ordeal, and the long adjustment that must
have been necessary afterwards. That fact, when I remembered
it, always made the killing of the girl (rather than the boy) in
The Mountain Lion more poignant. It also cast a light on Jean's
predilection for masks and disguises. She liked to dress up—but
in the manner of a child at a Halloween party. Once she came
to my house for drinks and emerged from the kitchen wearing
a joke mask with a big red nose. Another time I visited her in
East Hampton and she answered the door dressed as a cocktail
waitress, or something very close.

On her back door, there was a warning sign forbidding entrance
to anyone who used the word "hopefully" incorrectly.

A noted hypochondriac, she outdid everyone in real and imagined
illnesses. I was waiting for her outside Longchamps at 48th and
Madison (bygone days!) when I noticed her suddenly across the
street on crutches. It was snowing, I think, a nice, light New York
snow. Astonished, I walked over to help her—she was already in

the middle of the street by the time I got to her. She was wearing a red plaid cape, very stylish, peculiarly suited to crutches—no sleeves got in the way. When we were safely back on the sidewalk, she said, "Look! Look at these!" and showed me her wrist. Little white blotches were appearing, a sort of albino rash. "What is it?" I asked. "I don't know." She hobbled into lunch. I hadn't even had time to ask about the crutches before she'd been stricken by something new. I never did get the story about the crutches straight. A hypochondriac myself, I was outclassed.

Jean enjoyed medical discussions, symptoms, diagnoses, horror stories, freak accidents, diseases, cures. She owned a Merck's Manual and a gruesome textbook we would sometimes pore over, looking at the more hideous skin diseases in color. She was an amateur authority on ailments, including her own.

Although she was easily influenced, she was the least imitative person I knew. Older women of distinction became her friends— at least twice—and she would bank her originality in a deference of a peculiar kind, as if a mother with standards—a woman of impeccable authority—had been in the back of her mind all the while. But in dress, manner, and ideas she was independent and crotchety, and about writers her opinions were her own and unshakable. She adored cats, old furniture—Biedermeier especially— books, bourbon, odd clothes. Like the dress she used to wear that looked like a man's tuxedo and seemed to have a watch pinned to the lapel. The plaid cape. Fawn slacks and sweaters. She was a special mixture of the outlandish and the decorous. She paid great respect to the civilized, but something ingrained and Western in her mocked it at the same time. Think of Henry James being brought up in Colorado. . . .

Her favorite cat, George Eliot, used to sit under a lamp, eyes closed, basking in the warmth. Jean was proud of that, as if it were some extraordinary feline accomplishment.

. . .

In Westport, before she married for the second time, she had her own apartment for a while. I noticed two typewriters, one big, one small. I asked her about them. "The big one's for the novel and the little one's for short stories."

We were going to a cocktail party for St.-Jean Perse. I called for her. We had a drink and then another. Then—and how many times this happened between us!—one of us asked the fatal question: "Do you *really* want to go?" We never got there.

The Met. An opera box. Jean and I turned to each other after the first act of *Andrea Chénier*. This time, the fatal question remained unspoken. We got up and left.

Guilty dawdling became a kind of game between us, as well as a safety valve. If I secretly didn't want to go somewhere, I knew I could always stop off at Jean's and that would be a guarantee of never arriving at my original destination. In any case—or every— Jean was more interesting than anywhere I might be going.

A stitched sampler with the words "God Bless America" hung over her television screen.

She had a dream, a dream in which Arran Island (the one off Scotland, where her forebears came from, not the Aran Islands off Ireland) and the Greek island of Samothrace were historically con- nected. She paid a visit to Arran Island, and, eventually, she and A. J. Liebling, her third and last husband, went to Samothrace. She began to read seriously in anthropology and archaeology, particularly Lehman on the digs in Samothrace. But I think the broad view of ancient history and mythology required to complete a project mainly intuitive and then oddly confirmed by fact became too complicated and technical for her. What she had started to write with so much enthusiasm couldn't be finished. I stopped asking her about it the way I later stopped asking her about the novel in which her father was the chief character. But one day she let me read what she had of the Samothrace piece—about forty pages—and it was some of the most extraordinary prose I'd ever read. After I'd finished it, I looked at her and said something like, "My God, Jean, if you don't go on with it, at least publish *this*. . . ." I don't know what happened to it. Although Joe Liebling did everything to encourage Jean to write, she was intimidated by his swiftness, versatility, and excellence as a reporter. She shot off in journalistic directions of her own—the book on Oswald's mother, for instance. One day, Joe and I were riding up together in the elevator at *The New Yorker*. I told Joe I'd read the Samothrace piece and how good I thought it was. "I know," he said, "I wish you'd tell her." "I *have*," I said. And added, "I wish I could write prose like *that*. . . ." Joe, about to get off at his floor, turned to me and said, "I wish *I* could. . . ."

She was a born writer, and if certain mannerisms entered her prose later on, there was no question, in my mind at least, that she was one of the most naturally gifted writers I'd ever known. She simply couldn't write a bad sentence, excellence was a matter of personal integrity, the style was the woman. She couldn't stand the half-baked, the almost-good, the so-so. She made her views clear in a series of brilliant book reviews, still uncollected. They are all of a piece throughout, united by a single sensibility and an unwavering intelligence. And the annual round-up reviews of children's books she did for *The New Yorker* were scalpel-like attacks on mediocrity, commercial greed, stupidity, and cant.

. . .

One of her qualities hardest to get down on paper was the young girl always present in the civilized and cultivated woman. The balance was delicate and impossible to pin down. Like her conversation, it vanished into smoke. But what smoke!

A strangely momentous occasion: when she and Joe Liebling took an apartment on Fifth Avenue and 11th Street—an elegant, rambling apartment in a house built by Stanford White—before they moved in, Jean and Elizabeth Bowen and I walked about the rooms, talking about rugs, draperies, and so on. One of the rare times in New York City when people were dwarfed by space. Steve Goodyear gave Jean two plants. One, a rubber plant, had leaves that scraped the ceiling—eighteen, maybe twenty feet high.

Jean and I (at Fifth and 11th) sometimes would take out her Ouija board when I came over early for a drink. (This must have been in the late fifties.) The person always summoned up by Jean was her brother Dick, killed in the Second World War. The board would begin to shake, she would become excited by the message she read. . . . But these sessions never lasted long. Joe Liebling didn't like Jean using the Ouija board, and when we heard his key in the door, the board was hastily put away.

The farmhouse Joe Liebling bought in the thirties was first his, then theirs, then hers. It brought her enormous pleasure. She embarked on a long series of renovations, mostly of the interior; each change was a great source of satisfaction, perhaps too much so, for a writer discovers—especially a writer who lives alone—that a house can become a formidable enemy of work. Creative energy is drained off in redecorated guest rooms, expanded gardens, kitchens designed and redesigned to be more practical, new wallpaper, decking, house plants—the list is endless. In Jean's case, off the downstairs dining room she built a new bathroom in one direction and a new study–*cum*–guest room in another; a second new study appeared upstairs. The kitchen was revamped. The thirty or so acres surrounding the farmhouse boasted a particularly beautiful meadow some distance behind her house, a greensward worthy of a château. The shingled farmhouse was ample but modest. Its small living room had a fireplace set at an angle so that no one could ever quite face it. There was a larger dining room and a kitchen and pantry. Farmers didn't waste their money on unnecessary fuel, and, originally, the living room had been a concession to formality rather than a social center. The Liebling-Stafford house had been built for practicality (close to the road in case of a snowstorm), snugness, and warmth. It was a comfortable house and Jean fell in love with it—slowly, I think. It became—in the end—her refuge and her garrison, the place she holed up in and from which she viewed the world. The literal view was pretty enough because, from the front window, across Fire Place Road, you could see the water of an inlet, often intensely blue. There was an apple tree in the backyard, seemingly dead. It developed a new twisted limb and became grotesquely lovely. Behind it, there were many yucca plants with their white desert flowers, and in front of the house a mimosa tree that bloomed each spring.

In spite of a certain reputation for waspishness, the result of a sharply honed and witty tongue, Jean was generous and courageous. When she was accused of being the leader of the supposedly quixotic NBA jury that chose Walker Percy's *The Moviegoer* as the best novel of the year (no one had ever heard of Walker Percy before), she stood up for herself, and for him. And the same thing was true when John Williams's Prix de Rome was withdrawn. She spoke up for anyone she admired. Her nervous but good-natured allure derived from a special combination of the tart and the sweet. She was a surprisingly fine cook, liked entertaining and being entertained (at least for the better part of her life), and, above all, enjoyed good conversation.

. . .

She could resist a good writer if she disliked his person, but she was far more open to affection and the giving of it than seems generally known. She put herself out for people she liked and did nothing at all for people she didn't.

Youthfulness of manner was belied by the satiric thrust of her language, the slightly breathless drawl of her speech, the odd sense that she was searching for the next installment of words, another piece of the story, some phrase that would precisely focus what she had in mind—habits of speech cruelly underlined by her stroke, when she became unsure—she, of all people!—of her words. It was unfair and particularly cruel to be stricken at the very center of her being: talk, words, speech. It was not unlike—in the meanness of the affliction undercutting the essential person—Beethoven's going deaf.

She was anecdotal in the extreme, turning everything into a story. This became, later on, and long before the stroke, somewhat edgy. A certain amount of complaining, of being the great-lady-offended had become habitual. Something on the order of "And do you know who had the *nerve* to invite me to dinner last Wednesday?" And so on. But then it would turn out that she had *gone* to dinner, so that the point of the complaint seemed muddled. Once she had taken a real distaste to someone, she refused any invitation, any offer of friendship. And she made enemies easily by being outspoken, o-pinionated, strict in her standards. Once she took a real scunner to someone, she rarely changed her mind.

She felt abandoned by her friends, sometimes, and they, sometimes, by her. She would forget you for a time and then be hurt and surprised that she had been temporarily forgotten. People I think she liked without qualification: Mrs. Rattray, Saul Steinberg, John Stonehill, Peter Taylor, Elizabeth Bowen, Peter De Vries.

. . .

We had dinner together for the last time on July 13, 1978, in East Hampton, at a restaurant called Michael's. I called for Jean. Not being able to drive had once united us; now I had a driver's license. Convenient as it was, I'm not sure Jean approved of it. We arrived—down dark paths to a restaurant on the water. Jean, who had been drinking at home, ordered another bourbon. The question of what to order loomed. No menu came to hand; a young waitress reeled off the available fish of the day. Jean deferring, I ordered striped bass. Then Jean said, "I cannot do striped bass." But she didn't seem to be able to do anything else, either, and, after some confusion, I asked the waitress to give us a few minutes. I went over again what fish were available. The waitress came back. Jean said, "Striped bass." I asked her if she was *sure,* considering that she'd said she couldn't do striped bass, and she said she was *absolutely* sure. But when her fish came, she said, "This isn't what I wanted." I wanted to send it back; Jean said not to. Then she added, "What I really wanted was the finnan haddie." There hadn't been any finnan haddie; it had never been mentioned. And I realized we were in some kind of trouble, though most of the conversation was rational, pleasant, at times funny. Suddenly she said, "What do you think of friends?" I was surprised, but babbled on about how they might be the most important people in one's life, not the same as lovers, of course, but desperately needed, a second family, essential. . . . Jean said, lighting a cigarette, "Yes. I must give them up. I'm going to give up smoking." And it became clear she had meant the word "cigarettes" or "smokes" when she said "friends." And I suddenly remembered something: years ago, way back, a mutual friend had described cigarettes as "twenty little friends in a pack—twenty friends always available. . . ." I thought: Could there be a memory behind the choice of every mistaken word?

We talked on the phone twice while she was in New York Hospital. I called again on the afternoon of March 26 because I was going up to see my doctor on East 68th Street and thought I'd stop by and see her. The voice on the phone told me she was no

longer there. They had no forwarding address, no information. I
called East Hampton. No answer—odd, because there had always
been a phone machine where you could leave a message. I couldn't
figure out where she'd gone. To the Rusk Rehabilitation Center,
it turned out later, a special outpost of the hospital. I found out
the next day she had died that afternoon.

PAUL FUSSELL

My War

Over the past few years I find I've written a great deal about war, which is odd because I'm supposed to be a professor of English literature. And I find I've given the Second World War a uniformly bad press, rejecting all attempts to depict it as a sensible proceeding or to mitigate its cruelty and swinishness. I have rubbed readers' noses in some very noisome materials—corpses, maddened dogs, deserters and looters, pain, Auschwitz, weeping, scandal, coward-ice, mistakes and defeats, sadism, hangings, horrible wounds, fear and panic. Whenever I deliver this unhappy view of the war, especially when I try to pass it through a protective screen of irony, I hear from outraged readers. Speaking of some ironic aesthetic observations I once made on a photograph of a mangled sailor on his ruined gunmount, for example, a woman from Brooklyn found me "callous," and accused me of an "overwhelming deficiency in human compassion." Another reader, who I suspect has had as little empirical contact with the actualities of war face to face as the correspondent from Brooklyn, found the same essay "black and monstrous" and concluded that the magazine publishing it (*Har-per's*, actually) "disgraced itself."

How did I pick up this dark, ironical, flip view of the war? Why do I enjoy exhibiting it? The answer is that I contracted it in the infantry. Even when I write professionally about Walt Whitman or Samuel Johnson, about the theory of comparative literature or the problems facing the literary biographer, the voice that's audible is that of the pissed-off infantryman, disguised as a literary and cultural commentator. He is embittered that the Air Corps had beds to sleep in, that Patton's Third Army got all the credit, that noncombatants of the Medical Administrative and Quartermaster Corps wore the same battle stars as he, that soon after the war the "enemy" he had labored to destroy had been rearmed by his own government and positioned to oppose one of his old allies. "We broke our ass for nothin'," says Sergeant Croft in *The Naked and the Dead*. These are this speaker's residual complaints while he is affecting to be annoyed primarily by someone's bad writing or slipshod logic or lazy editing or pretentious ideas. As Louis Simpson says, "The war made me a foot-soldier for the rest of my life," and after any war foot soldiers are touchy.

My war is virtually synonymous with my life. I entered the war when I was nineteen, and I have been in it ever since. Melville's Ishmael says that a whale ship was his Yale College and his Harvard. An infantry division was mine, the 103rd, whose dispirited personnel wore a colorful green-and-yellow cactus on their left shoulders. These hillbillies and Okies, drop-outs and used-car salesmen and petty criminals were my teachers and friends.

How did an upper-middle-class young gentleman find himself in so unseemly a place? Why wasn't he in the Navy, at least, or in the OSS or Air Corps administration or editing *Stars and Stripes* or being a general's aide? The answer is comic: at the age of twenty I found myself leading forty riflemen over the Vosges Mountains and watching them being torn apart by German artillery and machine guns because when I was sixteen, in junior college, I was fat and flabby, with feminine tits and a big behind. For years the thing I'd hated most about school was gym, for there I was obliged to strip and shower communally. Thus I chose to join the ROTC (infantry, as it happened) because that was a way to get out of gym, which meant you never had to take off your clothes and invite— indeed, compel—ridicule. You rationalized by noting that this was 1939 and that a little "military training" might not, in the long run, be wasted. Besides, if you worked up to be a cadet officer, you got to wear a Sam Browne belt, from which depended a nifty saber.

When I went on to college, it was natural to continue my technique for not exposing my naked person, and luckily my college had an infantry ROTC unit, where I was welcomed as something of an experienced hand. This was in 1941. When the war began for the United States, college students were solicited by various "programs" of the Navy and Marine Corps and Coast Guard with plans for transforming them into officers. But people enrolled in the ROTC unit were felt to have committed themselves already. They had opted for the infantry, most of them all unaware, and that's where they were going to stay. Thus, while shrewder friends were enrolling in Navy V-1 or signing up for the pacific exercises of the Naval Japanese Language Program or the Air Corps Meteorological Program, I signed up for the Infantry Enlisted Reserve Corps, an act guaranteeing me one extra semester in college before I was called. After basic training, advancement to officer training was promised, and that seemed a desirable thing, even if the crossed rifles on the collar did seem to betoken some hard physical exertion and discomfort—marching, sleeping outdoors, that sort of thing. But it would help "build you up," and besides, officers, even in the infantry, got to wear those wonderful pink trousers and receive constant salutes.

It was such imagery of future grandeur that, in spring 1943, sustained me through eighteen weeks of basic training in hundred-degree heat at dreary Camp Roberts, California, where, to toughen us—it was said—water was forbidden from 8:00 A.M. to 5:00 P.M. ("water discipline," this was called). Within a few weeks I'd lost all my flab and with it the whole ironic "reason" I found myself there at all. It was abundantly clear already that "infantry" had been a big mistake: it was not just stupid and boring and bloody, it was athletic, and thus not at all for me. But supported by vanity and pride I somehow managed to march thirty-five miles and tumble through the obstacle course, and a few months later I found myself at the Infantry School, Fort Benning, Georgia, where, training to become an officer, I went through virtually the same thing over again.

As a second lieutenant of infantry I "graduated" in the spring of

1944 and was assigned to the 103rd Division at Camp Howze, Texas, the local equivalent of Camp Roberts, only worse: Roberts had white-painted two-story clapboard barracks, Howze, one-story tarpaper shacks. But the heat was the same, and the boredom, and the local whore culture, and the hillbilly songs:

> Who's that gal with the red dress on?
> Some folks call her Dinah.
> She stole my heart away,
> Down in Carolina.

The 103rd Division had never been overseas, and all the time I was putting my rifle platoon through its futile exercises we were being prepared for the invasion of southern France, which followed the landings in Normandy. Of course we didn't know this, and assumed from the training ("water discipline" again) that we were destined for the South Pacific. There were some exercises involving towed gliders that seemed to portend nothing but self-immolation, we were so inept with these devices. In October 1944, we were all conveyed by troop transports to Marseilles.

It was my first experience of abroad, and my lifelong affair with France dates from the moment I first experienced such un-American phenomena as: formal manners and a respect for the language; a well-founded skepticism; the pollarded plane trees on the Avenue R. Schumann; the red wine and real bread; the *pissoirs* in the streets; the international traffic signs and the visual public language hinting at a special French understanding of things—*Hôtel de Ville*, *Défense d'afficher*; the smell of Turkish tobacco when one has been brought up on Virginia and burley. An intimation of what we might be opposing was supplied by the aluminum Vichy coinage. On one side, a fasces and *État Français*. No more Republic. On the other, *Liberté, Égalité, Fraternité* replaced by *Travail* (as in *Arbeit Macht Frei,*) *Famille,* and *Patrie* (as in *Vaterland*). But before we had time to contemplate all this, we were moving rapidly northeast.

After a truck ride up the Rhône valley, still pleasant with girls and flowers and wine, our civilized period came to an abrupt end. On the night of November 11 (nice irony there) we were introduced into the line at St. Dié, in Alsace.

We were in "combat." I find the word embarrassing, carrying as it does false chivalric overtones (as in "single combat"). But synonyms are worse: "fighting" is not accurate, because much of the time you are being shelled, which is not fighting but suffering; "battle" is too high and remote; "in action" is a euphemism suited more to dire telegrams than description. "Combat" will have to do, and my first hours of it I recall daily, even now. They fueled, and they still fuel, my view of things.

Everyone knows that a night relief is among the most difficult of infantry maneuvers. But we didn't know it, and in our innocence we expected it to go according to plan. We and the company we were replacing were cleverly and severely shelled; it was as if the Germans a few hundred feet away could see us in the dark and through the thick pine growth. When the shelling finally stopped, at about midnight, we realized that although near the place we were supposed to be, until daylight we were hopelessly lost. The order came down to stop where we were, lie down among the trees, and get some sleep. We would finish the relief at first light. Scattered over several hundred yards, the 250 of us in F Company lay down in a darkness so thick we could see nothing at all. Despite the terror of our first shelling (and several people had been hit), we slept as soundly as babes. At dawn I awoke, and what I saw all around were numerous objects I'd miraculously not tripped over in the dark. These objects were dozens of dead German boys in greenish-gray uniforms, killed a day or two before by the company we were relieving. If darkness had hidden them from us, dawn disclosed them with open eyes and greenish-white faces like marble, still clutching their rifles and machine pistols in their seventeen-year-old hands, fixed where they had fallen. (For the first time I understood the German phrase for the war dead: *die Gefallenen*.) Michelangelo could have made something beautiful out of these forms, in the Dying Gaul tradition, and I was startled to find that at first, in a way I couldn't understand, they struck me as beautiful. But after a moment, no feeling but shock and horror. My adolescent illusions, largely intact to that moment, fell away all at once, and I suddenly knew I was not and never would be in a world that was reasonable or just. The scene was less apocalyptic than shabbily ironic: it sorted so ill with modern popular assumptions about the idea of progress and attendant improvements in public health, social welfare, and social justice. To transform guiltless boys into cold marble after passing them through unbearable fear and humiliation and pain and contempt seemed to do them an interesting injustice. I decided to ponder these things. In 1917, shocked by the Battle of the Somme and recovering from neurasthenia, Wilfred Owen was reading a life of Tennyson. He wrote his mother: "Tennyson, it seems, was always a great child. So should I have been, but for Baumont Hamel." So should I have been, but for St. Dié.

After that, one day was much like another: attack at dawn, run and fall and crawl and sweat and worry and shoot and be shot at and cower from mortar shells, always keeping up a jaunty carriage in front of one's platoon; and at night, "consolidate" the objective, usually another hill, sometimes a small town, and plan the attack for the next morning. Before we knew it we'd lost half the company, and we all realized then that for us there would be no way out until the war ended but sickness, wounds, or oblivion. And the war would end only as we pressed our painful daily advance. Getting it over was our sole motive. Yes, we knew about the Jews. But our skins seemed to us more valuable at the time.

The word for the German defense all along was "clever," a word that never could have been applied to our procedures. It was my first experience, to be repeated many times in later years, of the cunning ways of Europe versus the blunter ways of the New World. Although manned largely by tired thirty-year-old veterans (but sharp enough to have gotten out of Normandy alive), old men, and crazy youths, the German infantry was officered superbly, and their defense, which we experienced for many months, was disciplined and orderly. My people would have run, or at least "snaked off." But the Germans didn't, until the very end. Their uniforms were a scandal—rags and beat-up boots and unauthorized articles—but somehow they held together. Nazis or not, they did themselves credit. Lacking our lavish means, they compensated by patience and shrewdness. It was not until well after the war that I discovered that many times when they unaccountably located us hidden in deep woods and shelled us accurately, they had done so by inferring electronically the precise positions of the radios over which we innocently conversed.

As the war went on, the destruction of people became its sole means. I felt sorry for the Germans I saw killed in quantity everywhere—along the roads, in cellars, on rooftops—for many reasons. They were losing, for one thing, and their deaths meant nothing, though they had been persuaded that resistance might "win the war." And they were so pitifully dressed and accoutered: that was touching. Boys with raggedy ad hoc uniforms and Panzerfausts and too few comrades. What were they doing? They were killing themselves; and for me, who couldn't imagine being killed, for people my age voluntarily to get themselves killed caused my mouth to drop open.

Irony describes the emotion, whatever it is, occasioned by perceiving some great gulf, half-comic, half-tragic, between what one expects and what one finds. It's not quite "disillusion," but it's adjacent to it. My experience in the war was ironic because my previous innocence had prepared me to encounter in it something like the same reasonableness that governed prewar life. This, after all, was the tone dominating the American relation to the war: talk of "the future," allotments and bond purchases carefully sent home, hopeful fantasies of the "postwar world." I assumed, in short, that everyone would behave according to the clear advantages offered by reason. I had assumed that in war, like chess, when you were beaten you "resigned"; that when outnumbered and outgunned you retreated; that when you were surrounded you surrendered. I found out differently, and with a vengeance. What I found was people obeying fatuous and murderous "orders" for no reason I could understand, killing themselves because someone "told them to," prolonging the war when it was hopelessly lost because—because it was unreasonable to do so. It was my introduction to the shakiness of civilization. It was my first experience of the profoundly irrational element, and it made ridiculous all talk of plans and preparations for the future and goodwill and intelligent arrangements. Why did the red-haired young German machine-gunner firing at us in the woods not go on living—marrying, going to university, going to the beach, laughing, smiling—but keep firing long after he had made his point, and so require us to kill him with a grenade?

Before we knew it it was winter, and the winter in 1944–1945 was the coldest in Europe for twenty-five years. For the ground troops conditions were unspeakable, and even the official history admits the disaster, imputing the failure to provide adequate winter clothing—analogous to the similar German oversight when the Russian winter of 1941–1942 surprised the planners—to optimism, innocence, and "confidence":

> Confidence born of the rapid sweep across Europe in the summer of 1944 and the conviction on the part of many that the successes of Allied arms would be rewarded by victory before the onset of winter contributed to the unpreparedness for winter combat.

The result was 64,008 casualties from "cold injury"—not wounds but pneumonia and trench foot. The official history sums up: "This constitutes more than four 15,000-man divisions. Approximately 90 percent of cold casualties involved riflemen and there were about 4,000 riflemen per infantry division. Thus closer to thirteen divisions were critically disabled for combat." We can appreciate those figures by recalling that the invasion of Normandy was initially accomplished by only six divisions (nine if we add the airborne). Thus crucial were little things like decent mittens and gloves, fur-lined parkas, thermal underwear—all of which any normal peacetime hiker or skier would demand as protection against prolonged exposure. But "the winter campaign in Europe was fought by most combat personnel in a uniform that did not give proper protection": we wore silly long overcoats, right out of the nineteenth century; thin field jackets, designed to convey an image of manliness at Fort Bragg; and wool dress trousers. We wore the same shirts and huddled under the same blankets as Pershing's troops in the expedition against Pancho Villa in 1916. Of the 64,008 who suffered "cold injury" I was one. During February 1945, I was back in various hospitals for a month with pneumonia. I told my parents it was flu.

That month away from the line helped me survive for four weeks more but it broke the rhythm and, never badly scared before, when I returned to the line early in March I found for the first time that I was terrified, unwilling to take the chances that before had seemed rather sporting. My month of safety had renewed my interest in survival, and I was psychologically and morally ill prepared to lead my platoon in the great Seventh Army attack of March 15, 1945. But lead it I did, or rather push it, staying as far in the rear as was barely decent. And before the day was over I had been severely rebuked by a sharp-eyed lieutenant-colonel who threatened court martial if I didn't pull myself together. Before that day was over I was sprayed with the contents of a soldier's torso when I was lying behind him and he knelt to fire at a machine gun holding us up: he was struck in the heart, and out of the holes in the back of his field jacket flew little clouds of tissue, blood, and powdered cloth. Near him another man raised himself to fire, but the machine gun caught him in the mouth, and as he fell he looked back at me with surprise, blood and teeth dribbling out onto the leaves. He was one to whom early on I had given the Silver Star for heroism, and he didn't want to let me down.

As if in retribution for my cowardice, in the late afternoon, near Ingwiller, Alsace, clearing a woods full of Germans cleverly dug in, my platoon was raked by shells from an .88, and I was hit in the back and leg by shell fragments. They felt like red-hot knives going in, but I was as interested in the few quiet moans, like those of a hurt child drifting off to sleep, of my thirty-seven-year-old platoon sergeant—we'd been together since Camp Howze—killed instantly by the same shell. We were lying together, and his immediate neighbor on the other side, a lieutenant in charge of a section of heavy machine guns, was killed instantly too. My platoon was virtually wiped away. I was in disgrace, I was hurt, I was clearly expendable—while I lay there the supply sergeant removed my issue wristwatch to pass on to my replacement—and I was twenty years old.

I bore up all right while being removed from "the field" and passed back through the first-aid stations where I was known. I was deeply on morphine, and managed brave smiles as called for. But when I got to the evacuation hospital thirty miles behind the lines and was coming out of the anesthetic from my first operation, all my affectations of control collapsed, and I did what I'd wanted to do for months. I cried, noisily and publicly, and for hours. I was the scandal of the war. There were lots of tears back there: in the operating room I saw a nurse dissolve in shoulder-shaking sobs when a boy died with great stertorous gasps on the operating table she was attending. That was the first time I'd seen anyone cry in the whole European theater of operations, and I must have cried because I felt that there, out of "combat," tears were licensed. I was crying because I was ashamed and because I'd let my men be killed and because my sergeant had been killed and because I recognized as never before that he might have been me and that statistically if in no other way he was me, and that I had been killed too. But ironically I had saved my life by almost losing it, for my leg wound providentially became infected, and by the time it was healed and I was ready for duty again, the European war was over, and I journeyed back up through a silent Germany to rejoin my reconstituted platoon "occupying" a lovely Tyrolean valley near Innsbruck. For the infantry there was still the Japanese war to sweat out, and I was destined for it, despite the dramatic gash in my leg. But, thank God, the Bomb was dropped while I was on my way there, with the result that I can write this.

That day in mid-March that ended me was the worst of all for

F Company. We knew it was going to be bad when it began at
dawn, just like an episode from the First World War, with an
hour-long artillery preparation and a smokescreen for us to attack
through. What got us going and carried us through was the conviction that, suffer as we might, we were at least "making history."
But we didn't even do that. Liddell-Hart's 766-page *History of the
Second World War* never heard of us. It mentions neither March
15 nor the 103rd Infantry Division. The only satisfaction history
has offered is the evidence that we caused Joseph Goebbels some
extra anxiety. The day after our attack he entered in his log under
"Military Situation":

> In the West the enemy has now gone over to the attack in the sector
> between Saarbrücken and Hagenau in addition to the previous flash-
> points. . . . His objective is undoubtedly to drive in our front on
> the Saar and capture the entire region south of the Moselle and west
> of the Rhine.

And he goes on satisfyingly: "Mail received testifies to a deep-seated
lethargy throughout the German people degenerating almost into
hopelessness. There is very sharp criticism of the . . . entire national
leadership." One reason: "The Moselle front is giving way." But
a person my age whom I met thirty years later couldn't believe that
there was still any infantry fighting in France in the spring of 1945,
and, puzzled by my dedicating a book of mine to my dead platoon
sergeant with the date March 15, 1945, confessed that he couldn't
figure out what had happened to him.

To become disillusioned you must earlier have been illusioned.
Evidence of the illusions suffered by the youth I was is sadly
available in the letters he sent, in unbelievable profusion, to his
parents. They radiate a terrible naïveté, together with a pathetic
disposition to be pleased in the face of boredom and, finally, horror.
The young man had heard a lot about the importance of "morale"
and ceaselessly labored to sustain his own by sustaining his addressees'. Thus: "We spent all of Saturday on motor maintenance,"

he writes from Fort Benning; "a very interesting subject." At Benning he believes all he's told and fails to perceive that he's being prepared for one thing only, and that a nasty, hazardous job, whose performers on the line have a life expectancy of six weeks. He assures his parents: "I can get all sorts of assignments from here: . . . battalion staff officer, mess officer, rifle-platoon leader, weapons-platoon leader, company executive officer, communications officer, motor officer, etc." (Was it an instinct for protecting himself from a truth half-sensed that made him bury *rifle-platoon leader* in the middle of this list?) Like a bright schoolboy, he is pleased when grown-ups tell him he's done well. "I got a compliment on my clean rifle tonight. The lieutenant said, 'Very good.' I said, 'Thank you, sir.'" His satisfaction in making Expert Rifleman is touching; it is "the highest possible rating," he announces. And although he is constantly jokey, always on the lookout for what he terms "laffs," he seems to have no sense of humor:

> We're having a very interesting week . . . taking up the carbine, automatic rifle, rifle grenade, and the famous "bazooka." We had the bazooka today, and it was very enjoyable, although we could not fire it because of lack of ammunition.

He has the most impossible standards of military excellence, and he enlists his critical impulse in the service of optimistic self-deception. Appalled by the ineptitude of the 103rd Division in training, he writes: "As I told you last time, this is a very messed up division. It will never go overseas as a unit, and is now serving mainly as a replacement training center, disguised as a combat division."

Because the image of himself actually leading troops through bullets and shellfire is secretly unthinkable, fatuous hope easily comes to his assistance. In August 1944, with his division preparing to ship abroad, he asserts that the Germans seem to be "on their last legs." Indeed, he reports, "bets are being made . . . that the European war will be over in six weeks." But October finds him on the transport heading for the incredible, and now he "expects," he says, that "this war will end some time in November or December," adding, "I feel very confident and safe." After the epiphanies of the line in November and December, he still entertains hopes for an early end, for the Germans are rational people, and what rational people would persist in immolating themselves once it's clear that they've lost the war? "This *can't* last much longer," he finds.

The letters written during combat are full of requests for food packages from home, and interpretation of this obsession is not quite as simple as it seems. The C and K rations were tedious, to be sure, and as readers of *All Quiet on the Western Front* and *The Middle Parts of Fortune* know, soldiers of all times and places are fixated on food. But how explain this young man's requests for "fantastic items" like gherkins, olives, candy-coated peanuts (the kind "we used to get out of slot-machines at the beach"), cans of chili and tamales, cashew nuts, deviled ham, and fig pudding? The lust for a little swank is the explanation, I think, the need for some exotic counterweight to the uniformity, the dullness, the lack of point and distinction he sensed everywhere. These items also asserted an unbroken contact with home, and a home defined as the sort of place fertile not in corned-beef hash and meat-and-vegetable stew but gum drops and canned chicken. In short, an upper-middle-class venue.

Upper middle class too, I suspect, is the unimaginative cruelty of some of these letters, clear evidence of arrested emotional development. "Period" anti-Semitic remarks are not infrequent, and they remain unrebuked by any of his addressees. His understanding of the American South (he's writing from Georgia) can be gauged from his remark "Everybody down here is illiterate." In combat some of his bravado is a device necessary to his emotional survival, but some bespeaks a genuine insensitivity:

Feb. 1, 1945

Dear Mother and Dad:
Today is the division's 84th consecutive day on line. The average is 90–100 days, although one division went 136 without being relieved. . . .

This house we're staying in used to be the headquarters of a local German Motor Corps unit, and it's full of printed matter, uniforms, propaganda, and pictures of Der Führer. I am not collecting any souveniers [sic], although I have had ample opportunity to pick up helmets, flags, weapons, etc. The only thing I have kept is a Belgian pistol, which one German was carrying who was unfortunate enough to walk right into my platoon. That is the first one I had the job of shooting. I have kept the pistol as a souvenier of my first Kraut.

It is odd how hard one becomes after a little bit of this stuff, but it gets to be more like killing mad dogs than people. . . .

Love to all,
Paul

The only comfort I can take today in contemplating these letters is the ease with which their author can be rationalized as a stranger. Even the handwriting is not now my own. There are constant shows of dutifulness to parents, and even grandparents, and mentions of churchgoing, surely anomalous in a leader of assault troops. Parental approval is indispensable: "This week I was 'Class A Agent Officer' for Co. F, paying a $6000 payroll without losing a cent! I felt very proud of myself!" And the complacency! The twittiness! From the hospital, where for a time he's been in an enlisted men's ward: "Sometimes I enjoy being with the men just as much as associating with the officers." (*Associating* is good.) The letter-writer is more pretentious than literate ("Alright," "thank's," "curiousity"), and his taste is terrible. He is thrilled to read Bruce Barton's *The Man Nobody Knows* ("It presents Christ in a very human light"), Maugham's *The Summing Up,* and the short stories of Erskine Caldwell. Even his often-sketched fantasies of the postwar heaven are grimly conventional: he will get married (to whom?); he will buy a thirty-five-foot sloop and live on it; he will take a year of nonserious literary graduate study at Columbia; he will edit a magazine for yachtsmen. He seems unable to perceive what is happening, constantly telling his addressee what will please rather than what he feels. He was never more mistaken than when he assured his parents while recovering from his wounds, "Please try not to worry, as no permanent damage has been done."

But the shock of these wounds and the long period recovering from them seem to have matured him a tiny bit, and some of his last letters from the hospital suggest that one or two scales are beginning to fall from his eyes:

> One of the most amazing things about this war is the way the bizarre and unnatural become the normal after a short time. Take this hospital and its atmosphere: after a long talk with him, an eighteen-year-old boy without legs seems like the *normal* eighteen-year-old. You might even be surprised if a boy of the same age should walk in on both his legs. He would seem the freak and the object of pity. It is easy to imagine, after seeing some of these men, that *all* young men are arriving on this planet with stumps instead of limbs.
>
> The same holds true with life at the front. The same horrible unrealness that is so hard to describe.... I think I'll have to write a book about all this sometime.

But even here, he can't conclude without reverting to cliché and twerpy optimism:

> Enough for this morning. I'm feeling well and I'm very comfortable, and the food is improving. We had chicken and ice cream yesterday!

He has not read Swift yet, but in the vision of the young men with their stumps there's perhaps a hint that he's going to. And indeed, when he enrolled in graduate school later, the first course he was attracted to was on Swift and Pope. And ever since he's been trying to understand satire, and even to experiment with it himself.

It was in the army that I discovered my calling. I hadn't known that I was a teacher, but I found I could explain things: the operation of flamethrowers, map-reading, small-arms firing, "field sanitation." I found I could "lecture" and organize and make things clear. I could start at the beginning of a topic and lead an audience to the end. When the war was over, being trained for nothing useful, I naturally fell into the course that would require largely a mere continuation of this act. In becoming a college teacher of literature I was aware of lots of company: thousands of veterans swarmed to graduate school to study literature, persuaded that poetry and prose could save the world, or at least help wash away some of the intellectual shame of the years we'd been through. From this generation came John Berryman and Randall Jarrell and Delmore Schwartz and Saul Bellow and Louis Simpson and Richard Wilbur and William Meredith and all the others who, afire with the precepts of the New Criticism, embraced literature, and the teaching of it, as quasi-religious obligation.

To this day I tend to think of all hierarchies, especially the academic one, as military. The undergraduate students, at the "bottom," are the recruits and draftees, privates all. Teaching assistants and graduate students are the noncoms, with grades (only officers have "ranks") varying according to seniority: a G-4 is more important than a G-1, etc. Instructors, where they still exist, are the second and first lieutenants, and together with the assistant professors (captains) make up the company-grade officers. When we move up to the tenured ranks, associate professors answer to field-grade officers, majors and colonels. Professors are generals, beginning with brigadier—that's a newly promoted one. Most are major-generals, and upon retirement they will be advanced to lieutenant-general ("professor emeritus"). The main academic administration is less like a higher authority in the same structure than an adjacent echelon, like a group of powerful congressmen, for example, or people from the judge advocate's or inspector general's departments. The board of trustees, empowered to make professorial appointments and thus confer academic ranks and privileges, is the equivalent of the president of the United States, who signs commissions very like letters of academic appointment: "Reposing special trust and confidence in the . . . abilities of——, I do appoint him," etc. It is not hard to see also that the military principle crudely registered in the axiom "rank has its privileges" operates in academic life, where there are such plums to be plucked as frequent leaves of absence, single-occupant offices, light teaching loads, and convenient, all-weather parking spaces.

I think this generally unconscious way of conceiving of the academic hierarchy is common among people who went to graduate school immediately after the war, and who went on the G.I. Bill. Perhaps many were attracted to university teaching as a postwar profession because in part they felt they understood its mechanisms already. Hence their ambitiousness, their sense that if to be a first lieutenant is fine, to work up to lieutenant-general is wonderful. And I suspect that their conception of instruction is still, like mine, tinged with Army. I think all of us of that vintage feel uneasy with forms of teaching that don't recognize a clear hierarchy—team-teaching, for example, or even the seminar, which assumes the fiction that leader and participants possess roughly equal knowledge and authority. For students (that is, enlisted men) to prosecute a rebellion, as in the Sixties and early Seventies, is tantamount to mutiny, an offense, as the Articles of War indicate, "to be punished by death, or such other punishment as a court-martial shall direct." I have never been an enthusiast for the Movement.

In addition to remaining rank-conscious, I persist in the army habit of exact personnel classification. For me, everyone still has an invisible "spec number" indicating what his job is or what he's supposed to be doing. Thus a certain impatience with people of ambiguous identity or, worse, people who don't seem to do anything, like self-proclaimed novelists and poets who generate no apprehensible product. These seem to me the T-5s of the postwar world, mere technicians fifth grade, parasites, drones, noncombatants.

Twenty years after the First World War Siegfried Sassoon reports that he is still having dreams about it, dreams less of terror than of obligation. He dreams that

the War is still going on and I have got to return to the Front. I complain bitterly to myself because it hasn't stopped yet. I am worried because I can't find my active-service kit. I am worried because I have forgotten how to be an officer. I feel that I can't face it again, and sometimes I burst into tears and say, "It's no good, I can't do it." But I know that I can't escape going back, and search frantically for my lost equipment.

That's uniquely the dream of a junior officer. I had such dreams too, and mine persisted until about 1960, when I was thirty-six, past recall age.

Those who actually fought on the line in the war, especially if they were wounded, constitute an in-group forever separate from those who did not. Praise or blame does not attach: rather, there is the accidental possession of a special empirical knowledge, a feeling of a mysterious shared ironic awareness manifesting itself in an instinctive skepticism about pretension, publicly enunciated truths, the vanities of learning, and the pomp of authority. Those who fought know a secret about themselves, and it's not very nice. As Frederic Manning said in 1929, remembering 1914–1918: "War is waged by men; not by beasts, or by gods. It is a peculiarly human activity. To call it a crime against mankind is to miss at least half its significance; it is also the punishment of a crime."

And now that those who fought have grown much older, we must wonder at the frantic avidity with which we struggled then to avoid death, digging our foxholes like madmen, running from danger with burning lungs and pounding hearts. What, really, were we so frightened of? Sometimes now the feeling comes over us that Housman's lines, which in our boyhood we thought attractively cynical, are really just:

> Life, to be sure, is nothing much to lose;
> But young men think it is, and we were young.

ELIZABETH HARDWICK

Boston: The Lost Ideal

With Boston and its mysteriously enduring reputation, "the reverberation is longer than the thunderclap," as Emerson observed about the tenacious fame of certain artists. Boston—wrinkled, spindly-legged, depleted of nearly all her spiritual and cutaneous oils, provincial, self-esteeming—has gone on spending and spending her inflated bills of pure reputation decade after decade. Now, one supposes it is all over at last. The old jokes embarrass, the anecdotes are so many thrice-squeezed lemons, and no new fruit hangs on the boughs.

All the American regions are breaking up, ground down to a standard American corn meal. And why not Boston, which would have been the most difficult to maintain? There has never been anything quite like Boston as a creation of the American imagination, or perhaps one should say as a creation of the American scene. Some of the legend was once real, surely. Our utilitarian, fluid landscape has produced a handful of regional conceptions, popular images, brief and naked; the conservative Vermonter, the boastful Texan, the honeyed Southerner. "Graciousness is ours," brays a coarsened South; and the sheiks of Texas cruise around in their desert.

The Boston image is more complex. The city is felt to have, in the end, a pure and special nature, absurd no doubt but somehow valuable. An author can hardly fail to turn a penny or two on this magical subject. Everyone will consent to be informed on it, to be slyly entertained by it. The image lends itself to exaggerations, to dreams of social and ethnic purity, to notions of grand old families still existing as grand old families are supposed to exist. *Actual*

Boston, the living city, is governed largely by people of Irish descent and more and more, recently, by men of Italian descent. Not long ago, the old Yankee, Senator Saltonstall, remarked wistfully that there were still a good many Anglo-Saxons in Massachusetts, his own family among them. Extinction is foreshadowed in the defense.

Plainness and pretension restlessly feuding and combining; wealth and respectability and firmness of character ending in the production of a number of diverting individual tics or, at the best, instances of high culture. Something of that sort is the legendary Boston soul or so one supposes without full confidence because the old citizens of Boston vehemently hold to the notion that the city and their character are ineffable, unknowable. When asked for an opinion on the admirable novel, *Boston Adventure*, or even the light social history, *The Proper Bostonians*, the answer invariably comes, "Not Boston." The descriptive intelligence, the speculative mind, the fresh or even the merely open eye are felt to discover nothing but errors here, be they errors of praise or censure. Still, wrong-headedness flourishes, the subject fascinates, and the Athenaeum's list of written productions on this topic is nearly endless.

The best book on Boston is Henry James's novel, *The Bostonians*. By the bald and bold use of the place name, the unity of situation and person is dramatized. But poor James, of course, was roundly and importantly informed by everyone, including his brother William, that this too was "not Boston," and, stricken, he pushed aside a superb creation, and left the impregnable, unfathomable Boston to its mysteries. James's attitude toward the city's intellectual consequence and social charm is one of absolute impiety. A view of the Charles River reveals ". . . an horizon indented at empty intervals with wooden spires, the masts of lonely boats, the chimneys of dirty 'works,' over a brackish expanse of anomalous character, which is too big for a river and too small for a bay." A certain house has "a peculiar look of being both new and faded—a kind of modern fatigue—like certain articles of commerce which are sold at a reduction as shopworn." However, there is little natural landscape in James's novel. The picture is, rather, of the psychological Boston of the 1870s, a confused scene, slightly mad with

neurotic repressions, provincialism, and earnestness without intellectual seriousness.

James's view of Boston is not the usual one, although his irony
and dissatisfaction are shared by Henry Adams, who says that "a
simpler manner of life and thought could hardly exist, short of
cave-dwelling," and by Santayana who spoke of Boston as a "moral
and intellectual nursery, always busy applying first principles to
trifles." The great majority of the writings on Boston are in another
spirit altogether—frankly unctuous, for the town has always attracted men of quiet and timid and tasteful opinion, men interested
in old families and things, in the charms of times recently past,
collectors of anecdotes about those Boston worthies hardly anyone
can still clearly identify, men who spoke and preached and whose
style and fame deteriorated quickly. Rufus Choate, Dr. Channing,
Edward Everett Hale, Phillips Brooks, and Theodore Parker: names
that remain in one's mind, without producing an image or a fact,
as the marks are left on the wall after the picture has been removed.
William Dean Howells held a more usual view than Henry James
or Adams or Santayana. Indeed Howells' original enthusiasm for
garden and edifice, person and setting, is more than a little *exalté*.
The first sight of the Chapel at Mount Auburn Cemetery moved
him more than the "Acropolis, Westminster Abbey, and Santa Croce
in one." The massive, gray stones of "the Public Library and the
Athenaeum are hardly eclipsed by the Vatican and the Pitti." And
so on.

The importance of Boston was intellectual and as its intellectual
donations to the country have diminished, so it has declined from
its lofty symbolic meaning, to become a more lowly image, a sort
of farce of conservative exclusiveness and snobbish humor. Mar-
quand's George Apley is a figure of the decline—fussy, sentimental,
farcically mannered, archaic. He cannot be imagined as an Abo-
litionist, an author, a speaker; he is merely a "character," a very
idiosyncratic and simple-minded one. The old Boston had something of the spirit of Bloomsbury: clannish, worldly, and intellec-
tually serious. About the historian, Prescott, Van Wyck Brooks
could say, " . . . for at least ten years, Prescott had been hard at

work, harder, perhaps, than any Boston merchant."

History, indeed, with its long, leisurely, gentlemanly labors, the books arriving by post, the cards to be kept and filed, the sections to be copied, the documents to be checked, is the ideal pursuit for the New England mind. All the Adamses spent a good deal of their lives on one kind of history or another. The eccentricity, studiousness, and study-window slow pace of life of the historical gentleman lay everywhere about the Boston scene. For money, society, fashion, extravagance, one went to New York. But now, the descendants of the old, intellectual aristocracy live in the respectable suburbs and lead the healthy, restless, outdoor life that atrophies the sedentary nerves of culture. The blue-stocking, the eccentric, the intransigent bring a blush of uncertainty and embarrassment to the healthy young couple's cheek.

Boston today can still provide a fairly stimulating atmosphere for the banker, the broker, for doctors and lawyers. "Open end" investments prosper, the fish come in at the dock, the wool market continues, and workers are employed in the shoe factories in the nearby towns. For the engineer, the physicist, the industrial designer, for all the highly trained specialists of the electronic age, Boston and its area are of seemingly unlimited promise. Sleek, well-designed factories and research centers pop up everywhere; the companies plead, in the Sunday papers, for more chemists, more engineers, and humbly relate the executive benefits of salary and pension and advancement they are prepared to offer.

But otherwise, for the artist, the architect, the composer, the writer, the philosopher, the historian, for those humane pursuits for which the town was once noted and even for the delights of entertainment, for dancing, acting, cooking, Boston is a bewildering place. There is, first of all, the question of Boston or New York. (The question is not new; indeed it was answered in the last decades of the last century in favor of New York as the cultural center of America.) It is, in our day, only a private and personal question: where or which of the two Eastern cities should one try to live and work in? It is a one-sided problem. For the New Yorker, San Francisco or Florida, perhaps—Boston, never. In Boston, New York tantalizes; one of the advantages of Boston is said, wistfully, to be its nearness to New York. It is a bad sign when a man who has come to Boston or Cambridge, Massachusetts, from another place begins to show an undivided acceptance of his new town. Smugness is the great vice of the two places. Between puffy self-satisfaction and the fatiguing wonder if one wouldn't be happier, more productive, more appreciated in New York a thoughtful man makes his choice.

Boston is not a small New York, as they say a child is not a small adult but is, rather, a specially organized small creature with its small-creature's temperature, balance, and distribution of fat. In Boston there is an utter absence of that wild electric beauty of New York, of the marvelous, excited rush of people in taxicabs at twilight, of the great Avenues and Streets, the restaurants, theatres, bars, hotels, delicatessens, shops. In Boston the night comes down with an incredibly heavy, small-town finality. The cows come home; the chickens go to roost; the meadow is dark. Nearly every Bostonian is in his own house or in someone else's house, dining at the home board, enjoying domestic and social privacy. The "nice little dinner party"—for this the Bostonian would sell his soul. In the evenings, the old "accommodators" dart about the city, carrying their black uniforms and white aprons in a paper bag. They are on call to go, anywhere, to cook and serve dinners. Many of these women are former cooks and maids, now living on Social Security retirement pensions, supplemented by the fees for these evening "accommodations" to the community. Their style and the bland respectability of their cuisine keep up the social tone of the town. They are like those old slaves who stuck to their places and, even in the greatest deprivation, graciously went on toting things to the Massa.

There is a curious flimsiness and indifference in the commercial life of Boston. The restaurants are, charitably, to be called mediocre, the famous sea food is only palatable when raw. Otherwise it usually has to endure the deep-fry method that makes everything taste like those breaded pork chops of the Middle West, which in turn taste like the fried sole of Boston. Here, French restaurants quickly become tea-roomy, as if some sort of rapid naturalization had taken place. There is not a single attractive eating place on the water front. An old downtown restaurant of considerable celebrity, Locke-Ober's, has been expanded, let out, and "costumed" by one of the American restaurant decorators whose productions have a ready-made look, as if the designs had been chosen from a catalogue. But for the purest eccentricity, there is the "famous" restaurant, Durgin-Park, which is run like a boarding house in a mining town. And so it goes.

Downtown Boston at night is a dreary jungle of honky-tonks for sailors, dreary department-store windows, Loew's movie houses, hillbilly bands, strippers, parking lots, undistinguished new buildings. Midtown Boston—small, expensive shops, the inevitable Elizabeth Arden and Helena Rubinstein "salons," Brooks Brothers—is deserted at night, except for people going in and out of the Ritz Carlton Hotel, the only public place in Boston that could be called "smart." The merchandise in the Newbury Street shops is designed in a high fashion, elaborate, furred and sequined, but it is never seen anywhere. Perhaps it is for out-of-town use, like a traveling man's mistress.

Just as there is no smart life, so there is no Soho, no Greenwich Village. Recently a man was murdered in a parking lot in the Chinatown area. His address was given as the South End, a lower-class section, and he was said to be a free-spender, making enough money as a summer bartender on Cape Cod to lead a free-wheeling life the rest of the year. One paper referred to the unfortunate man as a "member of the Beacon Hill Bohemia set." This designation is of considerable interest because there is no "Bohemia" in Boston, neither upper nor lower; the detergent of bourgeois Boston cleans everything, effortlessly, completely. If there *were* a Bohemia, its members would indeed live on Beacon Hill, the most beautiful part of Boston and, like the older parts of most cities, fundamentally classless, providing space for the rich in the noble mansions and for the people with little money in the run-down alleys. For both of these groups the walled gardens of Beacon Hill, the mews, the coach houses, the river views, the cobblestone streets are a necessity and the yellow-brick, sensible structures of the Fenway—a plausible but unpoetical residential section near the Art Museum—are poison. Espresso bars have sprung up, or rather dug down in basements, but no summer of wild Bohemia is ushered into town. This reluctance is due to the Boston legend and its endurance as a lost ideal, a romantic quest.

Something transcendental is always expected in Boston. There is, one imagines, behind the drapery on Mount Vernon Street a person of democratic curiosity and originality of expression, someone alas— and this is the tiresome Boston note—*well-born*. It is likely to be, even in imagination, a she, since women now and not the men provide the links with the old traditions. Of her, then, one expects a certain unprofessionalism, but it is not expected that she will be superficial; she is profoundly conventional in manner of life but capable of radical insights. To live in Boston means to seek some connection with this famous local excellence, the regional type and special creation of the city. An angry disappointment attends the romantic soul bent upon this quest. When the archaeological diggings do turn up an authentic specimen it will be someone old, nearly gone, "whom you should have known when she was young"— and still could hear.

The younger Bostonians seem in revolt against the old excellence, with its indulgent, unfettered development of the self. Revolt, however, is too active a word for a passive failure to perpetuate the ideal high-mindedness and intellectual effort. With the fashionable young women of Boston, one might just as well be on Long Island. Only in the nervous, shy, earnest women is there a lingering hint of the peculiar local development. Terrible *faux pas* are constantly being made by this reasonable, honorable person, followed by blushes and more false steps and explanations and the final blinking, retreating blush.

Among the men, the equivalent of the blushing, blurting, sensitive, and often "fine" woman, is a person who exists everywhere perhaps but nowhere else with such elaboration of type, such purity of example. This is the well-born failure, the amateur not by choice but from some fatal reticence of temperament. They are often descendants of intellectual Boston, odd-ball grandsons, charming and sensitive, puzzlingly complicated, living on a "small income." These unhappy men carry on their conscience the weight of unpublished novels, half-finished paintings, impossible historical projects, old-fashioned poems, unproduced plays. Their inevitable "small income" is a sort of dynastic flaw, like hemophilia. Much money seems often to impose obligations of energetic management; from great fortunes the living cells receive the hints of the possibilities of genuine power, enough to make some enormously rich Americans endure the humiliations and fatigues of political office. Only the most decadent and spoiled think of living in idleness on millions; but this notion does occur to the man afflicted with ten thousand a year. He will commit himself with a dreamy courage to whatever traces of talent he may have and live to see himself punished by the New England conscience which demands accomplishments, duties performed, responsibilities noted, and energies sensibly used. The dying will accuses and the result is a queer kind of Boston incoherence. It is literally impossible much of the time to tell what some of the most attractive men in Boston are talking about. Half-uttered witticisms, grave and fascinating obfuscations, points incredibly qualified, hesitations infinitely refined—one staggers about, charmed and confused, by the twilight.

But this person, with his longings, connects with the old possibilities and, in spite of his practical failure, keeps alive the memory of the best days. He may have a brother who has retained the mercantile robustness of nature and easy capacity for action and yet has lost all belief in anything except money and class, who may practice private charities, but entertain profoundly trivial national and world views. A Roosevelt, Harriman, or Stevenson is impossible to imagine as a member of the Boston aristocracy; in Boston the vein of self-satisfaction and conservatism cuts too deeply.

. . .

Harvard (across the river in Cambridge) and Boston are two ends of one mustache. Harvard is now so large and international it has altogether avoided the whimsical stagnation of Boston. But the two places need each other, as we knowingly say of a mismatched couple. Without the faculty, the visitors, the events that Harvard brings to the life here, Boston would be intolerable to anyone except genealogists, antique dealers, and those who find repletion in a closed local society. Unfortunately, Harvard, like Boston, has "tradition" and in America this always carries with it the risk of a special staleness of attitude, and of pride, incredibly and comically swollen like the traits of hypocrisy, selfishness, or lust in the old dramas. At Harvard some of the vices of "society" exist, of Boston society that is—arrogance and the blinding dazzle of being, *being at Harvard*.

The moral and social temptations of Harvard's unique position in American academic life are great and the pathos is seen in those young faculty members who are presently at Harvard but whose appointments are not permanent and so they may be thrown down, banished from the beatific condition. The young teacher in this position lives in a dazed state of love and hatred, pride and fear; their faces have a look of desperate yearning, for they would rather serve in heaven than reign in hell. For those who are not banished, for the American at least, since the many distinguished foreigners at Harvard need not endure these piercing and fascinating complications, something of Boston seems to seep into their characters. They may come from anywhere in America and yet to be at Harvard unites them with the transcendental, legendary Boston, with New England in flower. They begin to revere the old worthies, the houses, the paths trod by so many before, and they feel a throb of romantic sympathy for the directly-gazing portraits on the walls, for the old graves and old names in the Mount Auburn Cemetery. All of this has charm and may even have a degree of social and intellectual value—and then again it may not. Devious parochialisms, irrelevant snobberies, a bemused exaggeration of one's own productions, pimple the soul of a man upholding tradition in a forest of relaxation, such as most of America is thought to be.

Henry James's observation in his book on Hawthorne bears on this:

> ... it is only in a country where newness and change and brevity of tenure are the common substance of life, that the fact of one's ancestors having lived for a hundred and seventy years in a single spot would become an element of one's morality. It is only an imaginative American that would feel urged to keep reverting to this circumstance, to keep analyzing and cunningly considering it.

If the old things of Boston are too heavy and plushy, the new either hasn't been born or is appallingly shabby and poor. As early as Thanksgiving, Christmas decorations unequaled for cheap ugliness go up in the Public Garden and on the Boston Common. Year after year, the city fathers bring out crèches and camels and Mother and Child so badly made and of such tasteless colors they verge on blasphemy, or would seem to do so if it were not for the equally dismal, although secular, little men blowing horns and the canes of peppermint hanging on the lamps. The shock of the first sight is the most interesting; later the critical senses are stilled as year after year the same bits are brought forth and gradually one realizes that the whole thing is a permanent exhibition.

Recently the dying downtown shopping section of Boston was to be graced with flowers, an idea perhaps in imitation of the charming potted geraniums and tulips along Fifth Avenue in New York. Commercial Boston produced a really amazing display: old, gray square bins, in which were stuck a few bits of yellowing, drying evergreen. It had the look of exhausted greenery thrown out in the garbage and soon the dust-bins were full of other bits of junk and discard—people had not realized or recognized the decorative hope and saw only the rubbishy result.

The municipal, civic backwardness of Boston does not seem to bother its more fortunate residents. For them and for the observer, Boston's beauty is serene and private, an enclosed, intense personal life, rich with domestic variation, interesting stuffs and things, showing the hearthside vitality of a Dutch genre painting. Of an evening the spirits quicken, not to public entertainment, but instead to the sights behind the draperies, the glimpses of drawing-rooms on Louisburg Square, paneled walls, and French chandeliers on Commonwealth Avenue, bookshelves and flower-filled bays on Beacon Street. Boston is a winter city. Every apartment has a fireplace. In the town houses, old persons climb steps without complaint, four or five floors of them, cope with the maintenance of roof and gutter, and survive the impractical kitchen and resign themselves to the useless parlors. This is life: the house, the dinner party, the charming gardens, one's high ceilings, fine windows, lacy grillings, magnolia trees, inside shutters, glassed-in studios on the top of what were once stables, outlook on the "river side." Setting is serious.

When it is not serious, when a splendid old private house passes into less dedicated hands, an almost exuberant swiftness of deterioration can be noticed. A rooming house, although privately owned, is no longer in the purest sense a private house and soon it partakes of some of the reckless, ugly municipal neglect. The contrasts are startling. One of two houses of almost identical exterior design will have shining windows, a bright brass door-knocker, and its twin will show a "Rooms" sign peering out of dingy glass, curtained by those lengths of flowered plastic used in the shower bath. Garbage lies about in the alleys behind the rooming houses, discarded furniture blocks old garden gateways. The vulnerability of Boston's way of life, the meanness of most things that fall outside the needs of the upper classes are shown with a bleak and terrible fullness in the rooming houses on Beacon Street. And even some of the best houses show a spirit of mere "maintenance," which, while useful for the individual with money, leads to civic dullness, architectural torpor, and stagnation. In the Back Bay area, a voluntary, casual association of property owners exists for the purpose of trying to keep the alleys clean, the streets lighted beyond their present medieval darkness, and to pursue other worthy items of neighborhood value. And yet this same group will "protest" against the attractive Café Florian on Newbury Street (smell of coffee too strong!) and against the brilliantly exciting Boston Arts Festival held in the beautiful Public Garden for two weeks in June. The idea that Boston might be a vivacious, convenient place to live in is not uppermost in most residents' thoughts. Trying to buy groceries in the best sections of the Back Bay region is an interesting study in commercial apathy.

A great many of the young Bostonians leave town, often taking off with a sullen demand for a freer, more energetic air. And yet many of them return later, if not to the city itself, to the beautiful sea towns and old villages around it. For the city itself, who will live in it after the present human landmarks are gone? No doubt, some of the young people there at the moment will persevere, and as a reward for their fidelity and endurance will themselves later become monuments, old types interesting to students of what our colleges call American Civilization. Boston is defective, out-of-date, vain, and lazy, but if you're not in a hurry it has a deep, secret appeal. Or, more accurately, those who like it may make of its appeal a secret. The weight of the Boston legend, the tedium of its largely fraudulent posture of traditionalism, the disillusionment of the Boston present as a cultural force, make quick minds hesitate to embrace a region so deeply compromised. They are on their guard against falling for it, but meanwhile they can enjoy its very defects, its backwardness, its slowness, its position as one of the large, possible cities on the Eastern seacoast, its private, residential charm. They speak of going to New York and yet another season finds them holding back, positively enjoying the Boston life. . . .

. . . Outside it is winter, dark. The curtains are drawn, the wood is on the fire, the table has been checked, and in the stillness one waits for the guests who come stamping in out of the snow. There are lectures in Cambridge, excellent concerts in Symphony Hall, bad plays being tried out for the hungry sheep of Boston before going to the hungry sheep of New York. Arnold Toynbee or T. S. Eliot or Robert Frost or Robert Oppenheimer or Barbara Ward is in town again. The cars are double-parked so thickly along the narrow streets that a moving vehicle can scarcely maneuver; the pedestrians stumble over the cobbles; in the back alleys a cat cries and the rats, enormously fat, run in front of the car lights creeping into the parking spots. Inside it is cozy, Victorian, and gossipy. Someone else has *not* been kept on at Harvard. The old Irish "accommodator" puffs up stairs she had never seen before a few hours previously and announces that dinner is ready. A Swedish journalist is just getting off the train at the Back Bay Station. He has been exhausted by cocktails, reality, life, taxis, telephones, bad connections in New York and Chicago, pulverized by "a good time." Sighing, he alights, seeking old Boston, a culture that hasn't been alive for a long time . . . and rest.

KATHERINE ANNE PORTER

St. Augustine and the Bullfight

Adventure. The word has become a little stale to me, because it has been applied too often to the dull physical exploits of professional "adventurers" who write books about it, if they know how to write; if not, they hire ghosts who quite often can't write either.

I don't read them, but rumors of them echo, and re-echo. The book business at least is full of heroes who spend their time, money and energy worrying other animals, manifestly their betters such as lions and tigers, to death in trackless jungles and deserts only to be crossed by the stoutest motorcar; or another feeds hooks to an inedible fish like the tarpon; another crosses the ocean on a raft, living on plankton and seaweed, why ever, I wonder? And always always, somebody is out climbing mountains, and writing books about it, which are read by quite millions of persons who feel, apparently, that the next best thing to going there yourself is to hear from somebody who went. And I have heard more than one young woman remark that, though she did not want to get married, still, she would like to have a baby, for the adventure: not lately though. That was a pose of the 1920s and very early '30s. Several of them did it, too, but I do not know of any who wrote a book about it—good for them.

W. B. Yeats remarked—I cannot find the passage now, so must say it in other words—that the unhappy man (unfortunate?) was one whose adventures outran his capacity for experience, capacity for experience being, I should say, roughly equal to the faculty for understanding what has happened to one. The difference then between mere adventure and a real experience might be this? That adventure is something you seek for pleasure, or even for profit, like a gold rush or invading a country; for the illusion of being more alive than ordinarily, the thing you will to occur; but experience is what really happens to you in the long run; the truth that finally overtakes you.

Adventure is sometimes fun, but not too often. Not if you can remember what really happened; all of it. It passes, seems to lead nowhere much, is something to tell friends to amuse them, maybe. "Once upon a time," I can hear myself saying, for I once said it, "I scaled a cliff in Boulder, Colorado, with my bare hands, and in Indian moccasins, bare-legged. And at nearly the top, after six hours of feeling for toe- and fingerholds, and the gayest feeling in the world that when I got to the top I should see something wonderful, something that sounded awfully like a bear growled out of a cave, and I scuttled down out of there in a hurry." This is a fact. I had never climbed a mountain in my life, never had the least wish to climb one. But there I was, for perfectly good reasons, in a hut on a mountainside in heavenly sunny though sometimes stormy weather, so I went out one morning and scaled a very minor cliff; alone, unsuitably clad, in the season when rattlesnakes are casting their skins; and if it was not a bear in that cave, it was some kind of unfriendly animal who growls at people; and this ridiculous escapade, which was nearly six hours of the hardest work I ever did in my life, toeholds and fingerholds on a cliff, put me to bed for just nine days with a complaint the local people called "muscle poisoning." I don't know exactly what they meant, but I do remember clearly that I could not turn over in bed without help and in great agony. And did it teach me anything? I think not, for three years later I was climbing a volcano in Mexico, that celebrated unpronounceably named volcano, Popocatepetl which everybody who comes near it climbs sooner or later; but was that any reason for me to climb it? No. And I was knocked out for weeks, and that finally did teach me: I am not supposed to go climbing things. Why did I not know in the first place? For me, this sort of thing must come under the head of Adventure.

I think it is pastime of rather an inferior sort; yet I have heard men tell yarns like this only a very little better: their mountains were higher, or their sea was wider, or their bear was bigger and noisier, or their cliff was steeper and taller, yet there was no point whatever to any of it except that it had happened. This is not enough. May it not be, perhaps, that experience, that is, the thing that happens to a person living from day to day, is anything at all that sinks in? is, without making any claims, a part of your growing and changing life? what it is that happens in your mind, your heart?

Adventure hardly ever seems to be that at the time it is happening: not under that name, at least. Adventure may be an afterthought, something that happens in the memory with imaginative trimmings if not downright lying, so that one should suppress it entirely, or go the whole way and make honest fiction of it. My own habit of writing fiction has provided a wholesome exercise to my natural, incurable tendency to try to wangle the sprawling mess of our existence in this bloody world into some kind of shape: almost any shape will do, just so it is recognizably made with human hands, one small proof the more of the validity and reality of the human imagination. But even within the most limited frame what utter confusion shall prevail if you cannot take hold firmly, and draw the exact line between what really happened, and what you have since imagined about it. Perhaps my soul will be saved after all in spite of myself because now and then I take some unmanageable, indigestible fact and turn it into fiction; cause things to happen with some kind of logic—my own logic, of course—and everything ends as I think it should end and no back talk, or very little, from anybody about it. Otherwise, and except for this safety device, I should be the greatest liar unhung. (When was the last time anybody was hanged for lying?) What is Truth? I often ask myself. Who knows?

A publisher asked me a great while ago to write a kind of autobiography, and I was delighted to begin; it sounded very easy when he said, "Just start, and tell everything you remember until now!" I wrote about a hundred pages before I realized, or admitted, the hideous booby trap into which I had fallen. First place, I remember quite a lot of stupid and boring things: there were other times when my life seemed merely an endurance test, or a quite mysterious but not very interesting and often monotonous effort at survival on the most primitive terms. There are dozens of things that might be entertaining but I have no intention of telling them, because they are nobody's business; and endless little gossipy incidents that might entertain indulgent friends for a minute, but in print they look as silly as they really are. Then, there are the tremendous, unmistakable, life-and-death crises, the scalding, the bone-breaking events, the lightnings that shatter the landscape of the soul—who would write that by request? No, that is for a secretly written manuscript to be left with your papers, and if your executor is a good friend, who has probably been brought up on St. Augustine's *Confessions*, he will read it with love and attention and gently burn it to ashes for your sake.

Yet I intend to write something about my life, here and now, and so far as I am able without one touch of fiction, and I hope to keep it as shapeless and unforeseen as the events of life itself from day to day. Yet, look! I have already betrayed my occupation, and dropped a clue in what would be the right place if this were fiction, by mentioning St. Augustine when I hadn't meant to until it came in its right place in life, not in art. Literary art, at least, is the business of setting human events to rights and giving them meanings that, in fact, they do not possess, or not obviously, or not the meanings the artist feels they should have—we do understand so little of what is really happening to us in any given moment. Only by remembering, comparing, waiting to know the consequences can we sometimes, in a flash of light, see what a certain event really meant, what it was trying to tell us. So this will be notes on a fateful thing that happened to me when I was young and did not know much about the world or about myself. I had been reading St. Augustine's *Confessions* since I was able to read at all, and I thought I had read every word, perhaps because I did know certain favorite passages by heart. But then, it was something like having read the Adventures of Gargantua by Rabelais when I was twelve and enjoying it; when I read it again at thirty-odd, I was astounded at how much I had overlooked in the earlier reading, and wondered what I thought I had seen there.

So it was with St. Augustine and my first bullfight. Looking back nearly thirty-five years on my earliest days in Mexico, it strikes me that, for a fairly serious young woman who was in the country for the express purpose of attending a Revolution, and studying Mayan people art, I fell in with a most lordly gang of fashionable international hoodlums. Of course I had Revolutionist friends and artist friends, and they were gay and easy and poor as I was. This other mob was different: they were French, Spanish, Italian, Polish, and they all had titles and good names: a duke, a count, a marquess, a baron, and they all were in some flashy money-getting enterprise like importing cognac wholesale, or selling sports cars to newly rich politicians; and they all drank like fish and played fast games like polo or tennis or jai alai; they haunted the wings of theaters, drove slick cars like maniacs, but expert maniacs, never missed a bullfight or a boxing match; all were reasonably young and they had ladies to match, mostly imported and all speaking French. These persons stalked pleasure as if it were big game—they took their fun exactly where they found it, and the way they liked it, and they worked themselves to exhaustion at it. A fast, tough, expensive, elegant, high lowlife they led, for the ladies and gentlemen each in turn had other friends you would have had to see to believe; and from time to time, without being in any way involved or engaged, I ran with this crowd of shady characters and liked their company and ways very much. I don't like gloomy sinners, but the merry ones charm me. And one of them introduced me to Shelley. And Shelley, whom I knew in the most superficial way, who remained essentially a stranger to me to the very end, led me, without in the least ever knowing what he had done, into one of the most important and lasting experiences of my life.

He was British, a member of the poet's family; said to be authentic great-great-nephew; he was rich and willful, and had come to Mexico young and wild, and mad about horses, of course. Coldly mad— he bred them and raced them and sold them with the stony detachment and merciless appraisal of the true horse lover—they call it love, and it could be that: but he did not like them. "What is there to like about a horse but his good points? If he has a vice, shoot him or send him to the bullring; that is the only way to work a vice out of the breed!"

Once, during a riding trip while visiting a ranch, my host gave me a stallion to ride, who instantly took the bit in his teeth and bolted down a steep mountain trail. I managed to stick on, held an easy rein, and he finally ran himself to a standstill in an open field. My disgrace with Shelley was nearly complete. Why? Because the stallion was not a good horse. I should have refused to mount him. I said it was a question how to refuse the horse your host offered you—Shelley thought it no question at all. "A lady," he reminded me, "can always excuse herself gracefully from anything she doesn't wish to do." I said, "I wish that were really true," for the argument about the bullfight was already well started. But the peak of his disapproval of me, my motives, my temperament, my ideas, my ways, was reached when, to provide a diversion and end a dull discussion, I told him the truth: that I had liked being run away with, it had been fun and the kind of thing that had to happen unexpectedly, you couldn't arrange for it. I tried to convey to him my exhilaration, my pure joy when this half-broken, crazy beast took off down that trail with just a hoofhold between a cliff on one side and a thousand-foot drop on the other. He said merely that such utter frivolity surprised him in someone whom he had mistaken for a well-balanced, intelligent girl; and I remember thinking how revoltingly fatherly he sounded, exactly like my own father in his stuffier moments.

He was a stocky, red-faced, muscular man with broad shoulders, hard-jowled, with bright blue eyes glinting from puffy lids; his hair was a grizzled tan, and I guessed him about fifty years old, which seemed a great age to me then. But he mentioned that his Mexican wife had "died young" about three years before, and that his eldest son was only eleven years old. His whole appearance was so remarkably like the typical horsy, landed-gentry sort of Englishman one meets in books by Frenchmen or Americans, if this were fiction I should feel obliged to change his looks altogether, thus falling into one stereotype to avoid falling into another. However, so Shelley did look, and his clothes were magnificent and right beyond words, and never new-looking and never noticeable at all except one could not help observing sooner or later that he was beyond argument the best-dressed man in America, North or South; it was that kind of typical British inconspicuous good taste: he had it, superlatively. He was evidently leading a fairly rakish life, or trying to, but he was of a cast-iron conventionality even in that. We did not fall in love—far from it. We struck up a hands-off, quaint, farfetched, tetchy kind of friendship which consisted largely of good advice about worldly things from him, mingled with critical marginal notes on my character—a character of which I could not recognize a single trait; and if I said, helplessly, "But I am not in the least like that," he would answer, "Well, you should be!" or "Yes, you are, but you don't know it."

This man took me to my first bullfight. I'll tell you later how St. Augustine comes into it. It was the first bullfight of that season; Covadonga Day; April; clear, hot blue sky; and a long procession of women in flower-covered carriages; wearing their finest lace veils and highest combs and gauziest fans; but I shan't describe a bullfight. By now surely there is no excuse for anyone who can read or even hear or see not to know pretty well what goes on in a bullring. I shall say only that Sánchez Mejías and Rudolfo Gaona each killed a bull that day; but before the Grand March of the toreros, Hattie Weston rode her thoroughbred High School gelding into the ring to thunders of shouts and brassy music.

She was Shelley's idol. "Look at that girl, for God's sake," and his voice thickened with feeling, "the finest rider in the world," he said in his dogmatic way, and it is true I have not seen better since.

She was a fine buxom figure of a woman, a highly colored blonde with a sweet, childish face; probably forty years old, and perfectly rounded in all directions; a big round bust, and that is the word, there was nothing plural about it, just a fine, warm-looking bolster straight across her front from armpit to armpit; fine firm round hips—again, why the plural? It was an ample seat born to a side-saddle, as solid and undivided as the bust, only more of it. She was tightly laced and her waist was small. She wore a hard-brimmed dark gray Spanish sailor hat, sitting straight and shallow over her large golden knot of hair; a light gray bolero and a darker gray riding skirt—not a Spanish woman's riding dress, nor yet a man's, but something tight and fit and formal and appropriate. And there she went, the most elegant woman in the saddle I have ever seen, graceful and composed in her perfect style, with her wonderful, lightly dancing, learned horse, black and glossy as shoe polish, perfectly under control—no, not under control at all, you might have thought, but just dancing and showing off his paces by himself for his own pleasure.

"She makes the bullfight seem like an anticlimax," said Shelley, tenderly.

I had not wanted to come to this bullfight. I had never intended to see a bullfight at all. I do not like the slaughtering of animals as sport. I am carnivorous, I love all the red juicy meats and all the fishes. Seeing animals killed for food on the farm in summers shocked and grieved me sincerely, but it did not cure my taste for flesh. My family for as far back as I know anything about them, only about 450 years, were the huntin', shootin', fishin' sort: their houses were arsenals and their dominion over the animal kingdom was complete and unchallenged. When I was older, my father remarked on my tiresome timidity, or was I just pretending to finer feelings than those of the society around me? He hardly knew which was the more tiresome. But that was perhaps only a personal matter. Morally, if I wished to eat meat I should be able to kill the animal—otherwise it appeared that I was willing to nourish myself on other people's sins? For he supposed I considered it a sin. Otherwise why bother about it? Or was it just something unpleasant I wished to avoid? Maintaining my own purity—and a very doubtful kind of purity he found it, too—at the expense of the guilt of others? Altogether, my father managed to make a very sticky question of it, and for some years at intervals I made it a matter of conscience to kill an animal or bird, something I intended to eat. I gave myself and the beasts some horrible times, through fright and awkwardness, and to my shame, nothing cured me of my taste for flesh. All forms of cruelty offend me bitterly, and this repugnance is inborn, absolutely impervious to any arguments, or even insults, at which the red-blooded lovers of blood sports are very expert; they don't admire me at all, any more than I admire them. . . . Ah, me, the contradictions, the paradoxes! I was once perfectly capable of keeping a calf for a pet until he outgrew the yard in the country and had to be sent to the pastures. His subsequent fate I leave you to guess. Yes, it is all revoltingly sentimental and, worse than that, confused. My defense is that no matter whatever else this world seemed to promise me, never once did it promise to be simple.

So, for a great tangle of emotional reasons I had no intention of going to a bullfight. But Shelley was so persistently unpleasant about my cowardice, as he called it flatly, I just wasn't able to take the thrashing any longer. Partly, too, it was his natural snobbery: smart people of the world did not have such feelings; it was to him a peculiarly provincial if not downright Quakerish attitude. "I have some Quaker ancestors," I told him. "How absurd of you!" he said, and really meant it.

The bullfight question kept popping up and had a way of spoiling other occasions that should have been delightful. Shelley was one of those men, of whose company I feel sometimes that I have had more than my fair share, who simply do not know how to drop a subject, or abandon a position once they have declared it. Constitutionally incapable of admitting defeat, or even its possibility, even when he had not the faintest shadow of right to expect a victory— for why should he make a contest of my refusal to go to a bull- fight?—he would start an argument during the theater intermis- sions, at the fronton, at a street fair, on a stroll in the Alameda, at a good restaurant over coffee and brandy; there was no occasion so pleasant that he could not shatter it with his favorite gambit: "If you would only see one, you'd get over this nonsense."

So there I was, at the bullfight, with cold hands, trembling innerly, with painful tinglings in the wrists and collarbone: yet my excitement was not altogether painful; and in my happiness at Hattie Weston's performance I was calmed and off guard when the heavy barred gate to the corral burst open and the first bull charged

through. The bulls were from the Duke of Veragua's* ranch, as
enormous and brave and handsome as any I ever saw afterward.
(This is not a short story, so I don't have to maintain any suspense.)
This first bull was a beautiful monster of brute courage: his hide
was a fine pattern of black and white, much enhanced by the goad
with fluttering green ribbons stabbed into his shoulder as he entered
the ring; this in turn furnished an interesting design in thin rivulets
of blood, the enlivening touch of scarlet in his sober color scheme,
with highly aesthetic effect.

He rushed at the waiting horse, blindfolded in one eye and
standing at the proper angle for the convenience of his horns, the
picador making only the smallest pretense of staving him off, and
disemboweled the horse with one sweep of his head. The horse trod
in his own guts. It happens at least once every bullfight. I could
not pretend not to have expected it; but I had not been able to
imagine it. I sat back and covered my eyes. Shelley, very deliberately and as inconspicuously as he could, took both my wrists and
held my hands down on my knees. I shut my eyes and turned my
face away, away from the arena, away from him, but not before I
had seen in his eyes a look of real, acute concern and almost loving
anxiety for me—he really believed that my feelings were the sign
of a grave flaw of character, or at least an unbecoming, unworthy
weakness that he was determined to overcome in me. He couldn't
shoot me, alas, or turn me over to the bullring; he had to deal with
me in human terms, and he did it according to his lights. His voice
was hoarse and fierce: "Don't you dare come here and then do this!
You must face it!"

Part of his fury was shame, no doubt, at being seen with a girl
who would behave in such a pawky way. But at this point he was,
of course, right. Only he had been wrong before to nag me into
this, and I was altogether wrong to have let him persuade me. Or
so I felt then. "You have got to face this!" By then he was right;
and I did look and I did face it, though not for years and years.

During those years I saw perhaps a hundred bullfights, all in

*Lineal descendant of Christopher Columbus.

Mexico City, with the finest bulls from Spain and the greatest
bullfighters—but not with Shelley—never again with Shelley, for
we were not comfortable together after that day. Our odd, mismatched sort of friendship declined and neither made any effort to
revive it. There was bloodguilt between us, we shared an evil secret,
a hateful revelation. He hated what he had revealed in me to himself,
and I hated what he had revealed to me about myself, and each of
us for entirely opposite reasons; but there was nothing more to say
or do, and we stopped seeing each other.

I took to the bullfights with my Mexican and Indian friends. I
sat with them in the cafés where the bullfighters appeared; more
than once went at two o'clock in the morning with a crowd to see
the bulls brought into the city; I visited the corral back of the ring
where they could be seen before the corrida. Always, of course, I
was in the company of impassioned adorers of the sport, with their
special vocabulary and mannerisms and contempt for all others who
did not belong to their charmed and chosen cult. Quite literally
there were those among them I never heard speak of anything else;
and I heard then all that can be said—the topic is limited, after
all, like any other—in love and praise of bullfighting. But it can
be tiresome, too. And I did not really live in that world, so narrow
and so trivial, so cruel and so unconscious; I was a mere visitor.
There was something deeply, irreparably wrong with my being
there at all, something against the grain of my life; except for this
(and here was the falseness I had finally to uncover): I loved the
spectacle of the bullfights, I was drunk on it, I was in a strange,
wild dream from which I did not want to be awakened. I was now
drawn irresistibly to the bullring as before I had been drawn to
the race tracks and the polo fields at home. But this had death in
it, and it was the death in it that I loved. . . . And I was bitterly
ashamed of this evil in me, and believed it to be in me only—no
one had fallen so far into cruelty as this! These bullfight buffs I
truly believed did not know what they were doing—but I did, and
I knew better because I had once known better; so that spiritual
pride got in and did its deadly work, too. How could I face the
cold fact that at heart I was just a killer, like any other, that some

deep corner of my soul consented not just willingly but with rapture?
I still clung obstinately to my flattering view of myself as a unique
case, as a humane, blood-avoiding civilized being, somehow a fallen
angel, perhaps? Just the same, what was I doing there? And why
was I beginning secretly to abhor Shelley as if he had done me a
great injury, when in fact he had done me the terrible and dangerous
favor of helping me to find myself out?

In the meantime I was reading St. Augustine; and if Shelley had
helped me find myself out, St. Augustine helped me find myself
again. I read for the first time then his story of a friend of his, a
young man from the provinces who came to Rome and was taken
up by the gang of clever, wellborn young hoodlums Augustine
then ran with; and this young man, also wellborn but severely
brought up, refused to go with the crowd to the gladiatorial combats;
he was opposed to them on the simple grounds that they were cruel
and criminal. His friends naturally ridiculed such dowdy senti-
ments; they nagged him slyly, bedeviled him openly, and, of course,
finally some part of him consented—but only to a degree. He
would go with them, he said, but he would not watch the games.
And he did not, until the time for the first slaughter, when the
howling of the crowd brought him to his feet, staring: and afterward
he was more bloodthirsty than any.

Why, of course: oh, it might be a commonplace of human nature,
it might be it could happen to anyone! I longed to be free of my
uniqueness, to be a fellow-sinner at least with someone: I could not
bear my guilt alone—and here was this student, this boy at Rome
in the fourth century, somebody I felt I knew well on sight, who
had been weak enough to be led into adventure but strong enough
to turn it into experience. For no matter how we both attempted
to deceive ourselves, our acts had all the earmarks of adventure:
violence of motive, events taking place at top speed, at sustained
intensity, under powerful stimulus and a willful seeking for pure
sensation; willful, I say, because I was not kidnapped and forced,
after all, nor was that young friend of St. Augustine's. We both
proceeded under the power of our own weakness. When the time
came to kill the splendid black and white bull, I who had pitied

him when he first came into the ring stood straining on tiptoe to see everything, yet almost blinded with excitement, and crying out when the crowd roared, and kissing Shelley on the cheekbone when he shook my elbow and shouted in the voice of one justified: "Didn't I tell you? Didn't I?"

Notes on the Contributors

Formerly a reporter for *Life* magazine, MICHAEL J. ARLEN has been a regular contributor to *The New Yorker* since 1966. His essays on television for that magazine have been collected in three volumes: *Living Room War* (1969), *The View from Highway 1* (1976), and *The Camera Age* (1981). He is also the author of *Exiles* (1960), *An American Verdict* (1973), *Passage to Ararat* (1975), which won a National Book Award, and *Thirty Seconds* (1980), an account of the making of a television commercial.

LESLIE FIEDLER's best-known work, *Love and Death in the American Novel* (1960), earned him the sobriquet "the wildman of American criticism." He has sustained that reputation for original and often outrageous commentary on literary and popular culture and the political scene for more than thirty years with such works as *An End to Innocence* (1955), *No! In Thunder* (1960), *Waiting for the End* (1964), *The Return of the Vanishing American* (1967), *Freaks* (1977), and *What Was Literature?* (1982). He has taught in many universities in the United States and Europe and is currently Samuel L. Clemens Professor at the State University of New York at Buffalo.

A former Jesuit seminarian with a Ph.D. in classics from Yale, GARRY WILLS began his journalistic career as one of the brilliant cadre of writers recruited by William F. Buckley for his fledgling *National Review*; in the 1960s he was a contributing editor for *Esquire* magazine. In his numerous books and articles, Wills brings enormous erudition and an academic rigor to subjects both sensational and abstruse. His best-known publications include *Jack Ruby* (1968), the best-selling *Nixon Agonistes* (1970), *Bare Ruined Choirs* (1972), *Inventing America* (1978), which won the National Book Award, *Confessions of a Conservative* (1979), *The Kennedy Imprisonment* (1982), and his collection *Lead Time* (1982). He teaches at Northwestern University and writes a nationally syndicated column.

LILLIAN ROSS has been a regular contributor to *The New Yorker* since 1948, writing fiction, reportage, profiles, and, most famously, her highly objective and beautifully crafted "Talk of the Town" pieces, of which "Halloween Party" is one. Her nonfiction books are *Picture* (1952), *Portrait of Hemingway* (1961), *Reporting* (1964), *Adlai Stevenson* (1966), *Reporting Two* (1969), *Moments with Chaplin* (1978), and her omnibus collection of "Talk" pieces, *Takes* (1983).

RUSSELL BAKER began his career at *The New York Times* as a member of its Washington bureau in 1954, and since 1962 has written his syndicated column of humorous commentary and political satire for that paper. He won the Pulitzer Prize for Commentary in 1979. His newspaper columns have been collected in *An American in Washington* (1961), *No Cause for Panic* (1964), *All Things Considered* (1965), *Poor Russell's Almanac* (1972), *So This Is Depravity* (1980), and *The Rescue of Miss Yaskell and Other Disasters* (1983). His touching autobiography, *Growing Up* (1982), has been widely acclaimed.

DONALD BARTHELME's first collection of stories, *Come Back, Dr. Caligari* (1964), established his reputation as a master of an experimental fiction with roots in absurdism, surrealism, collage, and Pop. He has continued his production of greatly admired fictions of intricacy and irony in such collections as *City Life* (1970), *Sadness* (1972), *Amateurs* (1976), and *Overnight to Many Distant Cities* (1983), and the novels *Snow White* (1967) and *The Dead Father* (1975). His only nonfiction work, a collection of parodies, satires, essays, and fables, *Guilty Pleasures*, was published in 1974.

JAMES BALDWIN was born in Harlem in 1924, the son of a minister. His reputation as perhaps the most eloquent black writer, in both his fiction and his essays, on themes of racism and the American experience was established in the 1950s by his first novels, *Go Tell It on the Mountain* (1953) and *Giovanni's Room* (1956), and his collection of autobiographical essays, *Notes of a Native Son* (1955). In the late 1950s and the 1960s Baldwin took an active role in the civil rights movement, an involvement reflected in his two great collections, *Nobody Knows My Name* (1961) and *The Fire Next Time* (1963). His most recent nonfiction works are *No Name in the Street* (1972) and *The Devil Finds Work* (1976).

NORMAN MAILER was catapulted to instant literary celebrity with the publication of his 1948 World War II novel, *The Naked and the Dead*, and he has conducted his subsequent career as one of our grandest writers, a celebrity, and an aging *enfant terrible* in the unending glare of national publicity. In addition to his novels, he has published his observations on modern life in *The White Negro* (1958), *Advertisements for Myself* (1959), *The Presidential Papers* (1963), *Cannibals and Christians* (1966), *The Armies of the Night* (1968), which received the National Book Award, *Miami and the Siege of Chicago* (1968), *The Prisoner of Sex* (1971), *Existential Errands* (1972), and *Pieces and Pontifications* (1982).

DWIGHT MACDONALD began writing for Henry Luce's *Fortune* in 1929. In 1937 he became an editor of *Partisan Review* and from 1944 to 1949 he was editor and publisher of *Politics*. From 1951 to 1965 he was a staff writer for *The New Yorker*, and from 1969 through 1966 the film critic of *Esquire*. His talents as a devastatingly witty critic, student of popular culture, and political thinker and activist can be seen to best advantage in his collections *Against the American Grain* (1962), *Dwight Macdonald on Movies* (1969), and *Discriminations* (1974). He died in 1982.

CHARLES REMBAR is an attorney widely known for his battles, both within the courts and in print, for freedom of expression. His best-known book, *The End of Obscenity* (1968), received the George Polk Memorial award for best book of the year, an award to recognize the best reporter, writer, or photographer of exceptional bravery and enterprise abroad or in the United States. His collection of articles, *Perspectives*, was published in 1975, and *The Law of the Land*, a study of the evolution of our legal system, in 1980. A graduate of Harvard College and Columbia Law School, he is currently in private practice in New York City.

WILLIAM GASS began his academic career as a trained philosopher, and he is currently a philosophy professor at Washington University in St. Louis. In both his novels and his story collections—*Omensetter's Luck* (1966), *In the Heart of the Heart of the Country* (1968), *Willie Master's Lonesome Wife* (1968)—and his critical and philosophical essays, he combines a dazzling speculative intelligence with a sensual use of language rarely found in contemporary American writing. His nonfiction books are *Fiction and the Figures of Life* (1971), *On Being Blue* (1976), and *The World Within the Word* (1978).

RALPH ELLISON's middle name is "Waldo"—he was, in fact, named after Emerson. He studied music at the Tuskegee Institute but found his novelist's vocation when he met Richard Wright while working for the Federal Writers' Project. His one novel, *Invisible Man* (1952), won the National Book Award and was cited in one survey of writers and critics as the most distinguished American novel of the postwar era. He has published one collection of nonfiction, *Shadow and Act* (1964).

GUY DAVENPORT studied at Duke University, at Oxford University as a Rhodes Scholar, and at Harvard, where he received his Ph.D. He is professor of English at the University of Kentucky, and he enjoys a superb reputation as, among other things, a critic, classicist, translator, and short story writer. He is the author of two story collections widely acclaimed for their intellectual virtuosity, *DaVinci's Bicycle* (1979) and *Eclogues* (1981), and an essay collection, *The Geography of the Imagination* (1981).

STEPHEN JAY GOULD, a professor of biology at Harvard University, is one of the most highly respected paleontologists in the country. He is equally well regarded as a popular writer on scientific subjects and has gained an ardent following through his columns in *Natural History* and his collections: *Ontogeny and Phylogeny* (1977), *Ever Since Darwin* (1977), *The Panda's Thumb* (1980), which received the National Book Award, *The Mismeasure of Man* (1981), which received the National Book Critics Circle Award, and *Hen's Teeth and Horse's Toes* (1983).

For most of his life, medicine has been LEWIS THOMAS's primary career—he is a physician, has been a teacher, was dean of the Yale Medical School, and recently retired as chancellor of the Memorial–Sloan Kettering Cancer Center. It was only in 1970 that he began writing occasional essays for *The New England Journal of Medicine*; his first collection of those pieces, *The Lives of a Cell* (1974), instantly made his reputation as a humanist speaking from the world of science. His subsequent collections are *The Medusa and the Snail* (1979), *The Youngest Science* (1983), and *Late Night Thoughts on Listening to Mahler's Ninth Symphony* (1983).

ROBERT FINCH currently serves as publications director for the Cape Cod Museum of Natural History and as a staff member of the Bread Loaf Writers' Conference at Middlebury College. His first book, *Common Ground: A Naturalist's Cape Cod* (1981), brought his sensitive and beautiful prose wide recognition, as did *The Primal Place* (1983). He lives in Brewster, Massachusetts, on Cape Cod.

EDWARD HOAGLAND is a graduate of Harvard and has for many years divided his time between New York City and rural Vermont—poles that roughly mark off the range of his essayistic subject matter. Whether he is writing about urban life or about nature, Hoagland's essays are distinguished by a strongly personal flavor, and many regard him as the best essayist of his generation. He is the author of two novels, *Cat Man* (1956) and *The Circle Home* (1960); a travel book, *African Calliope* (1979); and the collections *The Courage of Turtles* (1971), *Walking the Dead Diamond River* (1973), *Red Wolves and Black Bears* (1976), *The Tugman's Passage* (1982), and *The Edward Hoagland Reader* (1983).

Since his graduation from Harvard and attendance at the Ruskin School of Drawing at Oxford in the mid-1950s, JOHN UPDIKE has consistently been associated with *The New Yorker*, which has published his stories, essays, poems, and reviews. Updike is perhaps best known for his novels, among them the Rabbit trilogy—*Rabbit Run* (1960), *Rabbit Redux* (1971), and *Rabbit Is Rich* (1981)—*The Centaur* (1963), *Of the Farm* (1965), *Couples* (1968), *Bech: A Book* (1970), and *The Coup* (1978). In recent years he has also consolidated his reputation as a skilled and versatile critic, most recently with his collection *Hugging the Shore* (1983). His other collections of nonfiction are *Assorted Prose* (1965) and *Picked Up Pieces* (1976).

A. J. LIEBLING was one of this century's legendary reporters, famous for his gusto for lowlife, his crusading individualism, his delicious gastronomical writing, and his considerable girth. He began his journalistic career on newspapers, but from the late 1930s until his death in 1963 he wrote primarily for *The New Yorker*. Among his best-known books are *The Telephone Booth Indian* (1942), *The Wayward Pressman* (1947), *The Sweet Science* (1951), *Chicago: The Second City* (1952), *The Earl of Louisiana* (1961), and *The Jollity Building* (1962).

EUDORA WELTY was born in Jackson, Mississippi, in 1909, and some seventy-five years later she continues to make it her home. She published her first collection of stories, *A Curtain of Green and Other Stories*, in 1941, and her subsequent collections and novels, among them *The Ponder Heart* (1954), *Losing Battles* (1970), *The Optimist's Daughter* (1972), and *The Collected Stories* (1980), have made her perhaps the most admired living Southern writer. She also enjoys a reputation as one of America's finest essayists and students of the art of fiction, as seen in *The Eye of the Story: Selected Essays and Reviews* (1979) and *One Writer's Beginnings* (1984).

M. F. K. FISHER is generally regarded as the premier American writer on food, and as being among the finest American writers of prose, no matter what the topic. Her first book, *Serve It Forth*, was published in 1937, and has been followed over the years by such works as *Consider the Oyster* (1941), *How to Cook a Wolf* (1942), *An Alphabet for Gourmets* (1949), *With Bold Knife and Fork* (1969), *The Art of Eating* (1976), and the autobiographical *A Considerable Town* (1978) and *As They Were* (1982).

JOAN DIDION's first collection of essays, *Slouching Towards Bethlehem* (1968), was immediately acclaimed as one of the most perceptive and original works from and about the decade of the 1960s; her subsequent collection, *The White Album* (1979), and her extended journalistic essay, *Salvador* (1982), further established her reputation as a uniquely acerbic observer of American cultural and political folly. A native of California, she is also the author of the novels *Run River* (1963), *Play It As It Lays* (1971), *A Book of Common Prayer* (1977), and *Democracy: A Novel* (1984).

HOWARD MOSS was born in New York City in 1922. He is the author of ten collections of poetry, including *The Wound and the Weather* (1946), *The Toy Fair* (1954), *A Swimmer in the Air* (1957), *A Winter Comes, A Summer Gone* (1960), *Finding Them Lost* (1965), *Second Nature* (1968), and *Selected Poems* (1971), for which he won a National Book Award; two books of criticism, *The Magic Lantern of Marcel Proust* (1962) and *Writing Against Time* (1969); and a collection of pieces, *Whatever Is Moving* (1981). Moss is at present the poetry editor of *The New Yorker*, whose staff he joined in 1948.

The John De Witt Professor of English Literature at Rutgers University, PAUL FUSSELL has combined a serious career as an academic scholar of English and American literature with a wide-ranging interest in the manners and morals of modern experience of both war and peace. His study of the literature of World War I, *The Great War and Modern Memory* (1976), won the National Book Award in Arts and Letters, and was followed by *Abroad: British Literary Traveling Between the Wars* (1980), *The Boy Scout Handbook and Other Observations* (1981), and *Class* (1983).

ELIZABETH HARDWICK is the author of three collections of literary essays, *A View of My Own* (1962), *Seduction and Betrayal* (1974), and *Bartleby in Manhattan* (1983). Her novels are *The Ghostly Lover* (1945), *The Simple Truth* (1955), and *Sleepless Nights* (1979). She has received, among other honors, the George Jean Nathan Award for dramatic criticism, and is a member of the American Academy and Institute. A professor at Barnard College and an editor for the *New York Review of Books*, she lives in New York City.

KATHERINE ANNE PORTER enjoyed one of the most distinguished American literary careers of this century. A native of Texas, she wrote for newspapers, acted, and studied art in Mexico before writing her first story at age thirty. She is best remembered today for her short fiction collections *Flowering Judas* (1930), *Noon Wine* (1937), and *Collected Stories* (1964), which won the National Book Award and a Pulitzer Prize, and her best-selling novel, *Ship of Fools* (1962). Her nonfiction books include *The Days Before* (1952), *Collected Essays* (1970), and *The Never-Ending Wrong* (1977). She died in 1980.